PRAISE FOR

M000167554

A wish–it-were-true revolutionary sci-fi thriller that would make Nikola Tesla smile and send the rest of us on a transformational journey back to a world worth living in!

—*Roger Herried, Clean-energy expert,
co-founder of the US Green Party*

This is the book to change entire generations. From a dystopian world where faceless connections have replaced human interaction, *The Parents* transports us into a future of limitless potential. With this impeccably crafted text, gifted writer Olga Sheean keeps the reader spellbound till the final chapter, delighting hearts, igniting minds and inspiring profound transformations.

—*Denise Rowland, author, educator and EMR activist*

Triggering tears and smiles, *The Parents* is an intriguing, educational, inspirational rollercoaster. An empowering must-read from one of the best.

—*Mirjam Schouten, BASc, PR/HR consultant*

Publisher's Cataloging-in-Publication Data

Names: Sheean, Olga, author.
Title: The parents : how far would you go to save your world? / Olga Sheean.
Description: Horsefly, BC : InsideOut Media, 2020.
Identifiers: LCCN 2020915598 (print) | ISBN 978-1-928103-14-1 (paperback)
    | ISBN 978-1-928103-15-8 (Kindle ebook)
Subjects: LCSH: Quantum theory--Fiction. | Time travel--Fiction.
    | Families--Fiction. | Science fiction. | Canadian fiction.
    | Suspense fiction. | BISAC: FICTION / Science Fiction / Time Travel.
    | FICTION / Thrillers / General. | GSAFD: Science fiction.
    | Suspense fiction.
Classification: LCC PR9199.3.S54 P37 2020 (print)
    | LCC PR9199.3.S54 (ebook) | DDC 813/.6--dc23.

THE PARENTS

How far would you go to save your world?

by

Olga Sheean

InsideOut Media

AUTHOR'S NOTE

In mid-December 2019, with a new day unfolding its fresh clean page towards me, I began to write a new story. I had no choice. The characters came to me, not letting me rest, demanding their say. Then a bigger say, and a starring role in my life. And then a whole new story unfolded, starting out in a world that is all too familiar, and ending up in a reality of unimaginable rewards that few believe possible.

All the bad, scary bits in this book are based on real life; all the advanced planet/people-friendly technologies are already possible; the characters and their story exist only in some other reality; and all the other bits are fiction... unless you decide otherwise.

The Parents renewed my hope in humanity. I was the willing scribe along for the ride, but the story is everyone's, and we are all writing our next chapters—pre-writing the history of our future.

In the quantum world, we can get there in no time.

—Olga Sheean
August 2020, somewhere in the south of France

With love and gratitude to
Evelyn and Gerald Sheean
…the parents, of course.

Prologue

It is a perfect night for it. The storm rages outside, trees thrashing, rain sheeting down, thrumming against the windowpane—loud, now that all the furniture is gone. The world outside seems impossibly angry, he thinks, seeing himself in the glass. A sad reflection.

He turns back towards the fire. And the embodiment of his life's magic. Hugging her knees, she is staring at the flames, numb with loss and despair.

"They are going to hate us," she says softly. "They won't understand and they will never forgive us. We will have deserted them and they will never know why."

He squats down behind her, legs on either side, bathing her in the river of love that he is.

"What are you thinking?"

"That we should have done more of this," she says, her arms overlapping his and gripping fiercely—their Morse code of touch.

"This feels perfect, just like always," he says, his chin on her shoulder. He hugs her tightly, trying to infuse her with some of the certainty she shared with him when he'd had his doubts.

"Lie with me," she says, smiling at the irony. He eases back and they roll onto their sides, spooning on the hardwood floor. Their final coupling.

As the fire softens to glowing embers and their bodies cool, he knows it is time.

"You first," he whispers into her hair.

She squeezes his hand and sits up. Reaches for her glass of water and pile of pills. Knocks them back in a few loud swallows. Lies back down.

He hugs her from behind, waits for her breathing to slow. Then he sits up and takes his own small pile of pills. Makes sure they all go down properly and then lies back down beside her. Pulls her close.

"We did it," he says.

She gives a final gentle sigh—a happy one, he hopes. After all they have been through. Thirty-five years is a long time. Another 30 would be nice.

He closes his eyes, holding on to her as she softens and relaxes against him. He feels himself sinking, breathes in the last of her familiar scent, and finally lets go.

PART 1

1

10 October 2019

They are sitting in the waiting room, 15 minutes early for their appointment. Matt sits rigidly upright, staring straight ahead. Lucy is still sniffling, dabbing a tissue at her red eyes. Marnie, as usual, is trying to be strong for them both.

The secretary is absent. *She can't face us*, Marnie thinks. *What to say? People must think we did something awful to our parents, to make them do this.*

"Why did they do it?" Lucy says. "I don't understand. They loved us, didn't they?" She looks imploringly at Marnie, her dark hair framing her fierce green eyes, so achingly like their mother that Marnie has to breathe herself through the pain that grips her chest.

"Yes, of course," Marnie says.

"And we loved them! So why?!"

"I don't know, Luce. We've been over this a thousand times and I don't have the answers."

"But—"

The door opens and Mr Williams emerges from his office. He looks distraught. Not his usual unruffled demeanour.

"I'm sorry to have kept you waiting," he says. "Please come in."

He stands back as they file mutely into his office and sit stiffly in the chairs in front of his large old walnut desk.

Mr Williams sits down opposite them, removes his round glasses and presses the bridge of his nose, briefly closing his eyes.

"I'm very sorry for your loss," he says. "As you know, your father and I go back a long way."

"Why did they do it?" Lucy blurts out, tears flowing again.

"I can't tell you, Lucy. I'm sorry."

"But Dad must have told you something," Matt insists. "You're his lawyer. You knew him."

"I thought I did." Mr Williams lifts his hands and lets them drop back into his lap. "I'm at a loss…"

He puts his glasses back on. "Let's get this out of the way," he says, opening the folder on the desk in front of him.

"The will," Marnie says.

"Yes," he says, looking down at the document, not meeting their eyes. "I'm afraid... it's rather disturbing."

"What do you mean?" Marnie leans forward in her chair. "It's just us. They had no siblings, no other relatives. It should be straightforward."

"They changed their will," he says.

"What?" All three exclaim at once, looking at each other. A wave of panic ripples through the room.

"Three months ago," he says.

"Why?" says Matt.

Marnie feels the first stirrings of anger. "What is going on?" she says. "None of this makes any sense."

"They sold the house," Mr Williams says.

"*What?* When?" Matt is up, out of his seat, reaching for the file.

Mr Williams slides it out of his reach.

"This is not easy," he says. "Please sit down." He clears his throat, takes a sip of water from a glass on his desk.

"The will is very simple and very short. Your parents left you... nothing."

The silence in the room is so thick with shock that no one speaks for almost a full minute.

Lucy stares numbly at her lap. Matt has gone pale. Marnie feels a cold steeliness seep through her, freezing out the searing heat of this impossible news.

"This... this can't be right," she finally says. "There's been a mistake. We'll come back later, when you've figured this out." She starts to stand up but Mr Williams waves her back into her seat.

"There is no mistake," he says. "Your parents sold the house and the money is gone."

"But what happened to it?" Matt shouts. "It can't just have disappeared. Did they gamble it away, did they have debts, were they ill and didn't tell us. *What?*"

"I have asked myself all the same questions," says Mr Williams. "But the money is gone and there seems to be no trace of it."

"Who bought the house?" Matt demands. "There must be some trace of the sale. It was worth millions."

"A shell company—untraceable, it seems," says Mr Williams. "The owner clearly doesn't want to be known."

"There's nothing left…" Marnie says, incredulous. "What about… their funeral, your fees…?"

"Both paid for, in advance, six months ago," says Mr Williams. "I don't know why or how. I'm as much in the dark as you are."

Lucy is rocking back and forth in her seat, her head bowed, moaning to herself. Still a baby in so many ways, Marnie thinks, even at 18. No parents, no money, no warning. She can't take it in.

"What about my… How will I…?" Lucy can't bring herself to say it.

"Your college fund, you mean?" Mr Williams gives her a compassionate look. "That's gone, too, I'm afraid."

"But how will I manage?" Lucy wails. Approaching meltdown, Marnie can see.

"It's certainly an… *arresting* development," Mr Williams says, without a trace of irony.

"No note? No letter with the will?" Lucy looks at him beseechingly.

"I'm afraid not. No."

Marnie cannot find the words she needs to say or ask the questions she knows must be asked. She feels as if she's been kicked in the stomach, blind-sided, betrayed.

Matt is gripping the sides of his chair, knuckles white, jaw grinding from side to side.

"What about their savings, their bank accounts? There must be some…" He shifts uncomfortably, but outrage outweighs impropriety. "There must be some money for us. They must have left us *something*."

Mr Williams looks at him. "The bank accounts have been closed," he says, "no trace of any money."

More stunned silence, minds churning in turmoil.

"You were their lawyer," Matt says accusingly. "You were supposed to advise them about… the right thing to do."

"I was obliged to execute their wishes, within the limits of the law— and to advise them, in some respects, to protect their best interests, but I had no hand in their estate planning."

"Did you not advise them to… to…?"

"Serve *your* best interests, Matthew?" Mr Williams helps him out. "I can assure you I gave them the best possible advice, but my role was to serve them, not to tell them what to do with their money."

"But they chose to end their lives. What about *us*? Why did they leave us high and dry like this?"

"I have no idea why your parents chose to take this course of action," Mr Williams says, choosing his words carefully.

"Of course not, Mr Williams," Marnie says, seeing his distress. "We're not blaming you."

Mr Williams nods, clearly relieved to know that the eldest, at least, does not hold him responsible for what has happened.

"What about the contents of the house?" Matt says suddenly. "There will be clues there."

"All gone," says Mr Williams. "Cleared out a week ago."

"How could we not have known?" asks Matt. His hand is shaking as he runs his fingers through his hair.

"We have our own lives," Marnie says, more to herself than to Matt. "Lucy away at college, you and me in our jobs an hour away…"

"I think you need some time to absorb this," Mr Williams says. "Then come back and see me."

"Why?" says Matt. "Can you fix this? Can you find out what happened? Will there be an investigation?"

"No crime has been committed," Mr Williams says, "as far as I know. But we can make some other enquiries—see if we can somehow trace the funds…" He trails off, gesturing vaguely, then looks down at the document again. "Legally, I am obliged to read the will," he says.

"Go ahead, please," Marnie says, and it's as if the whole room holds its breath.

My Williams clears his throat and begins reading in a monotone:

"We, Dr Daniel Dalton and Dr Francesca Dalton, née Francesca Sincera, of Providence, Massachusetts, being of sound mind and over the age of 18, do hereby declare this to be our last will and testament, replacing any and all previous wills and codicils, dated the ninth day of June 2019—"

"That's Dad's birthday!" Lucy exclaims.

Mr Williams continues, unperturbed, reading a full page of legalese before confirming what he has already told them. He turns the page but Matt raises a hand and stops him.

"Is there anything else in there that we need to hear," he says, "apart from all this legal stuff?"

Mr Williams shakes his head. "I'm afraid not," he says. "But it is my legal duty—"

"Please take it as read, Mr Williams," Marnie says. "Thank you for your time." She stands up. "Matt, Lucy, let's go. We need to… think about this."

Her mind is whirling. There must be some information somewhere, something to make sense of this nightmare.

My Williams stands too, nods, says nothing more as he watches them leave. It's the hardest thing he has ever had to do.

2

---

12 October 2019

It was raining when Lucy came out of Wholefoods with her groceries—two of Marnie's eco-friendly, unbleached, reusable, cruelty-free bags digging into her shoulders. She debated catching a cab but she couldn't afford it. It was a ten-minute walk back to Marnie's place and she didn't have an umbrella, but she had no choice. Anyway, who cared if she got wet? *Who cared if she got hit by a truck?* Not her parents. *Obviously.* Had they cared at all or had they just been playing Happy Families? Maybe they got Mad Cow Disease and no one detected it.

She could kill her mother for what she'd done. *Ha.* She laughed sardonically, and an elderly woman gave her an anxious look as she walked quickly past.

She would never see her mum grow old, and her mum would never see her graduate, get married, have kids… Not that she'd be doing any of those things now, and she didn't think she would ever trust anyone ever again.

Mum, she wailed. *Why?* How was it possible to so intensely hate someone you loved? And to hate loving them?

She had always liked calling her *mum,* the way her dad referred to her, instead of *Mom.* It somehow made her special, like no one else's mom—which she wasn't anyway, whatever Lucy called her. Lucy had been in awe of her mother, and maybe a little afraid of her, but calling her *mum* had somehow softened her edges and brought her closer.

She missed her dad, too, but in a different way that she couldn't quite define.

She remembered them all having dinner one night, when she was about 14, and she had challenged her parents about her middle name.

"How could you have called me *Sedona*?" she said. "What were you thinking?"

"But it's a beautiful name," her father said.

"That's not the *point*," Lucy said, frowning loudly at him. "It gives me the initials LSD!"

"Ah, yes, it does, doesn't it." Her father smiled.

"Didn't you realize that?"

"We did, but we just so loved those two names for you, Luce," her father said. "Maybe we should have changed our last name and taken your mother's maiden name instead."

"Lucy Sedona Sincera," her mother said. "Ohhh, I like that. I'm tempted to change my first name and use Sedona myself."

Lucy secretly loved her name, and the words from that old Beatles song always filled her with a wistful dreaminess. *Lucy in the sky with diamonds...*

But she rolled her eyes, because that's what rebellious teenagers did.

Parents were so *transparent*, she had thought, back then. Except, of course, when they weren't...

Beneath it all, Lucy was vaguely aware that her teenage petulance served to affirm her parents' parenthood, and that growing up would make them less her parents, although it was hard to see how they could be less of anything than they were right now.

Anyway, they were gone and she was *still* a teenager... Crap.

Back in the present, Lucy stopped and turned around. She had walked right past Marnie's place without realizing it. She was really losing it. She pushed open the main door, crossed the lobby and headed for the stairs. No elevator in this *character* building. Thank God Marnie's apartment was only one floor up.

She stomped up the stairs, cursing Marnie's two dozen organic eggs, her sulfite-free wine, kilo of coffee beans, a loaf of sprouted spelt bread the size and texture of a cinder block, a side of pasture-raised beef, a massive lump of goat's cheese, and two bottles of mineral water—*yes, Marnie, in glass bottles*. She immediately felt guilty. She'd be eating this stuff too, and she'd be out on the street if it weren't for Marnie.

That almost got her sobbing again. What did she have to live for, anyway? She'd quit college, given up her rooms on campus, and now she'd have to find some kind of job, with zero qualifications. She had visions of having to rent some dirt-cheap room and work as a waitress in some dingy diner. The thought almost made her retch.

She'd cut off all her friends. They had been there for her as soon as she got the news, and they kept phoning to make sure she was okay. But she couldn't stand their pity, feeling their awkwardness around her when they talked about their fabulous lives continuing without her—college, plans for the future, guys they were dating. And they all had parents who loved them, although Melissa's were divorced. But at least they were all still on planet *Earth*, interested in seeing how their children got on in life.

She stopped halfway up, feeling faint. Breathless. Was she friggin' unfit or just full-body fucked?

When had she last eaten? Two days ago? Three? Not since they'd had that awful meeting with Mr Williams, which felt like an eternity ago but had only been Thursday, and today was… Saturday?

She reached for the banister and hauled herself up the last ten steps. She needed to sit down, lie down, check out… She didn't care if she died; she just didn't want to be in pain all the time. It was like being on an emotional rollercoaster. Self-pity, rage, grief, blame, guilt and back to self-pity again. She was going to crack up if she didn't get her act together.

She fumbled for her key. Maybe she should get a prescription for sleeping pills and take them all at once—like *they* did. She'd have a lot to say to them both when they met up in hell. She was storing it all up, just in case.

She finally found her key and let herself in.

"Hey, Luce, thanks." Marnie met her at the door, taking one of the bags and heading for the kitchen. "Let's unpack this stuff and have lunch."

Lucy followed her into the kitchen and put the other bag down on the countertop. She pulled out a chair, collapsed into it and laid her head on the table.

"Luce, you must—"

"Please, Marn, don't say anything," she said, not looking up. "Just… for a few minutes."

She heard the fridge opening, things being unwrapped, cupboards opening and closing, a pan being placed on the stove, chopping, eggs being cracked, oil sizzling… She remembered her mother working in the kitchen, although she was a lot noisier and treated every meal like a lab experiment. The results weren't always edible. She could pretend it was her mum, here in the kitchen, just for a few minutes. Just a few moments of normality, *please*, because she couldn't imagine her life ever feeling normal again.

"Here you go, Luce." Marnie placed a plateful of omelette in front of her, handed her a knife and fork, and sat down beside her to eat. The smell of fried onions and melted cheese almost knocked her off the chair and she was suddenly ravenous.

She nodded gratefully at Marnie and picked up her fork, wolfing down huge mouthfuls, not caring that she was still in her wet jacket or that, for the moment at least, filling her stomach was more important than feeding the drama of her wretched life.

"Why don't you lie down for half an hour," Marnie said after lunch. "Matt's coming over at 3pm to discuss what we should do next."

"Great, since we seem to have got precisely nowhere," Lucy said, scraping back her chair. "But, yeah, we need to come up with a plan."

She paused at the door. Marnie was looking wearier than Lucy had ever seen her. She had their mother's slender build but was not as tall. Her blue eyes and blond hair came from their dad, and she kept her hair short and tidy. Whereas their mother had been a stunner, totally oblivious to her raw beauty, Marnie had a quiet beauty and gentle nature that wasn't asking to be noticed.

Right now, she looked despondent, which made Lucy's heart lurch. Her sister was always so positive and rarely let things get her down. Lucy felt bad for being such a selfish cow; she never even thought of Marnie being affected by things.

"Thanks for the omelette, Marn. It was a life-saver," Lucy said. "Leave the washing-up and I'll do it later. Maybe you should have a nap, too."

"I might," Marnie said, not very convincingly.

After hanging her wet jacket on the back of her bedroom door, Lucy lay down fully clothed and conked out as soon as her head hit the pillow. When she woke up, three hours later, it was dark. She padded sleepily into the living room, hearing voices.

Marnie was sitting curled up at one end of the sofa, holding a mug of tea.

"Good timing," she said. "Matt just got here."

"Hey, sis." Matt was sitting at the other end of the sofa with his stockinged feet up on the coffee table.

"You're looking a bit rough," Lucy said, rubbing her jaw to indicate his three-day stubble. "Not the usual natty Matty."

Matt shrugged but said nothing.

"Well, you look about 100% better," Marnie said, as Lucy curled up in the armchair beside her.

"Yeah, but my life is still about 500% fucked," Lucy said.

Marnie flinched and Matt raised an eyebrow.

"Our baby sis is changing before our eyes—5lbs lighter but armed with a whole new tough-kid lingo, ready to take on the world."

"If you feel so bad, you can leave," Marnie said stiffly, not looking at her.

Lucy grimaced, suddenly realizing what she had said. "Marn, that was shitty and unforgiveable, but will you please, *please* forgive me anyway?" She looked imploringly at Marnie. "I'm not dealing with this very well, but taking it out on one of the nicest people I know, in the whole wide world…" She could feel tears building up again.

"Yeah, okay, okay," Marnie said, looking into her mug. "But you still haven't done the dishes."

"Shit. I forgot. I'll do them after this, Marn, I promise."

Lucy suddenly remembered what Marnie had told her when she came to stay, two weeks ago. Lucy wasn't to create any clutter, leave anything lying around, her bed unmade, the shower full of hairs. *No mess.* Marnie liked things clean and tidy. She hated any kind of messiness. Lucy needed to smarten up if she wanted to stay here till she got sorted out.

"Sorry, Marn," she said. "I've been such a thoughtless bitch."

"Finally!" said Matt. "I've been telling you that since you were 12."

"I don't remember *you* being so hot when *you* were that age, *Fatso-Mattso.*"

Marnie laughed. She remembered that. Matt had still had some puppy fat when he was 12, but then he'd joined the squash club and he became one of the top players in the region. He'd been fit and wiry ever since.

"Watch it, *Lucille*," Matt warned.

"I should call you Laundro-Matt." Lucy grinned wickedly. "Have you been sleeping in those clothes all week?" Not that *she* could talk.

She'd been sleeping in hers for the past three days.

"Enough with the name-calling. What's wrong with *Matt*, anyway?"

"You tell *me*," said Lucy.

"Stop it, you two." Marnie sighed and put down her mug. "We need to focus and decide how to move forward."

But her brother did look stressed.

"How's work going, Matt?" she asked.

"Work is… not really working," Matt said.

"I thought you were going to take some time off."

"Yeah, but I thought it was better to keep working," Matt said, rubbing his stubble and running his fingers through his hair. His dark-brown mop looked as if it hadn't seen a shower or a barber for a while.

"Well, I think you should take the time off. We have to figure out what happened with Mum and Dad, and we need your help," Marnie said, tapping her notepad with her pencil.

"I thought I'd be able to do more from the office—you know, access the newspaper's databases and other stuff I might not be able to do at home."

"What about that friend of yours… the computer guy in your office," Marnie said. "Wouldn't he help you out?"

"Jed? Yeah. Probably."

"So take the time off. You need to get your head straight. And get back to the squash court. Work off some of that anger and stress."

Marnie looked at him sternly. "I mean it, Matt. You're not looking good and you need to take care of yourself."

"Yeah. Right. No point in digging myself an early grave just because *they* did."

"All this self-pity is wearing a bit thin," Marnie said. "Can we focus here and decide what to do?"

"You're right, Marn, you're right," said Lucy. "What's the plan?"

"The plan is for *you* two to come up with some ideas, for a change," Marnie snapped, picking up her notepad and flicking to the page where she'd made a list of things they—*she*—had done so far. Had another meeting with Mr Williams to see if he could offer some leads, and tried to track down some of her parents' former college friends. So far, nothing.

"I'm sick of you both expecting me to fix things, and I can't take care of you all the time, Luce."

That's exactly what she *had* done, though—for years, when their real mother was too busy doing important scientific experiments to take care of her own children, including her, Marnie. At least these two had *had* a mother, thanks to her. *She'd* never had one, though…

"You're right. We need to help," Lucy nodded. "Matt, got any ideas?"

"Lucy!" said Marnie, exasperated.

"Oh, yeah, okay. Let me think… I need some time to think, Marn. I'll come up with something over the weekend. Promise."

"Maybe we need to look at this whole thing differently," Marnie said, tapping her pencil against her chin. "Maybe they didn't do this to make us suffer. What if there's some other reason for all this?"

"What," said Matt, "like some silver lining to this fucked-up mess?"

"I don't *know*, Matt" she said, giving him another hard stare, "but I don't see the point in being victims. How's that helping, exactly?"

Matt said nothing, and Marnie put her notepad and pencil down on the coffee table.

"I don't think we're in the right frame of mind to do this now," she said. "Let's give ourselves a break and get some rest and then maybe come up with some ideas. It's not as if there's a rush. What's done is done, and it could take us months to figure this out, if we ever do."

Matt seemed relieved, although Marnie sensed that there was something else on his mind.

"How are things with Celle?" Matt's girlfriend Celle was his colleague Jed's younger sister and they had been dating for the past year and a half.

"Not great," Matt said, looking down at his hands. "She suggested taking some time out while I, you know, wrap my head around this mess."

"You're not talking to her about this, in other words," Marnie said, knowing how hard it was for Matt to talk about emotional stuff. "I'm sure she wants to be there for you, but she can't be if you keep shutting her out."

Matt shrugged.

"That's what relationships are all about, Matt—sharing the bad times as well as the good, and growing together as you process the tough stuff," Marnie said. "If you don't let her in, you're going to lose her." Not that *she* was any expert on relationships, although she knew what *not* to do.

"Yeah, I know." Matt ran his hands through his hair and stood up, tucking his shirt back into his jeans. He's lost weight, too, Marnie thought. This was taking a heavy toll on them all.

"I'll head out," Matt said, getting up.

"There is one thing you could do, Matt, that could help us," Marnie said. "I called Mr Williams and asked him for the name of the shell company that sold Westfield. I don't know why he didn't mention it when we saw him, or why we didn't think to ask. Maybe he didn't want us to get our hopes up."

"And?"

"It's called MLM Holdings. Mr Williams couldn't find any address or contact info but he implied that we might be able to do more than him, in some '*less-than-strictly-legal way*', he said."

"Marnie, Lucy, Matt!" Lucy said, excitedly. "Our initials!"

"Sorry to burst your bubble, Luce," Matt said, "but it also stands for *multi-level marketing*."

"And *making lots of money*," Marnie added ruefully.

"*Our* money." Lucy said.

"And *Miserable Lousy Mother*—"

"Enough," Marnie said. "See what you can find, Matt."

"I'll ask Jed to look into it," Matt said, taking his jacket from the coat stand. "But it will have to wait till after the 18th, when we've got this edition of the paper out. I don't want him getting distracted when we're working on some hot issues."

He shrugged on his jacket. "Later, sisters."

He opened the front door and was gone.

Marnie and Lucy sat in silence for a moment, processing the possibilities.

"I'm going to soak in a nice hot bath and forget about all this for a while," Marnie said, getting up.

"I'll do the dishes, Marn," said Lucy, "and make dinner."

Marnie smiled. Lucy being thoughtful and proactive, eager to redeem herself. She wondered how long it would last.

3

Friday was Marnie's favourite day of the week because she had the day off work. The elementary school where she worked was running a special trainee program for student teachers, and one of them taught her class every Friday, with the school manager supervising. It was just for this school year and she was relishing the extra time off—without a cut in her salary.

And this was her favourite time of day. First thing, when the world was still quiet, she sat at the table by the window overlooking the park, sipping her tea. Notepad beside her, she was making her usual lists. What to do next about The Situation, groceries she needed for the weekend, what lessons to have ready for Monday.

She was also jotting down ideas for the children's book she was writing (about a snake called Lester). She hadn't told anyone about it yet. She liked the idea and it felt like a good fit for 4–6-year-olds, but she'd never considered herself a writer, so she wasn't sure how far she'd get.

Her mind kept going back to her parents and what they had done. She still couldn't wrap her brain around it, although she seemed to be coping with it all okay. Maybe she was just numb—or distracting herself with logistics so she didn't have to feel her own emotions. Matt wasn't the only one. Taking action had always been her antidote to a crisis.

Matt and Lucy would hopefully come up with some ideas over the weekend. In the meantime, she was going to talk to her parents' neighbours next door to Westfield, the family home—the home that *was*—to see if they had any idea what their parents had been up to. They might offer a few leads that she could follow up.

Her siblings were going to have to sort themselves out soon. It was less than a month since they'd got the shocking news, but they'd have to get it together if they were ever going to figure out what had happened. It was hard for Marnie to believe that Matt ran a successful online political newspaper, managing a team of four people. He was pretty smart intellectually, but not terribly mature emotionally. Marnie was only three years older than him but she felt a lot older—*ancient*, the last few weeks. And Lucy was just plain spoilt and still too much of a baby to make smart choices, even though she was only three years younger than Matt.

Funny how their parents had had three children three years apart. What age would they have been when they had kids? They were both 21 when they met and had married shortly afterwards. It was 2019 now and she was 24, so they'd had their first child when they were… 33, the second one when they were 36 and the third one at 39.

Weird how there were so many of those numbers—3, 6, 9. Not that numbers meant anything to her, but some people claimed they were at the root of everything—like Steve, the mathematician she'd dated. But that had ended in January, 9 months ago, and had only lasted 9 months. She paused. Nine…

Of course, her parents had always worked with numbers—equations, fractions and who knew what else. *She* didn't. She just didn't have that kind of brain. She was just a teacher, teaching 9-year-olds. Blimey. There it was again. Nine.

What had Steve told her about numerology? She wasn't sure what use it was, but she remembered him saying that various numbers meant various things and that you could learn a lot about yourself if you added up all the numbers of your birthday—day, month and year—and reduced them down to a single digit. And the number 9 always got cancelled out, for some reason. But then what?

She started jotting down numbers on her notepad. Her parents were born in 1962, and her mum's birthday was 18 March 1962. So… March = 3; 18 = 1+8 = 9; 1962 = 1+9+6+2 = 18 = 1+8 = 9. Then she added them all up: 3+9+9 = 21 = 2+1 = 3.

Her dad's birthday was 9 June 1962. So, 9+6+9 = 24 = 2+4 = 6. Together, her mum and dad made up a 9, whatever that meant, if anything. They got married on 30 May 1984, which came to… she did the maths again: 3+5+1+9+8+4 = 21 = 2+1 = 3.

She was intrigued now. What about her own birthday? Hers was 3 March 1995, which came to… she worked it out: 3. Matt's was 18 June 1998, which came to a 6. Lucy's was 6 September 2001, which came to a 9. Blimey. Those three numbers again.

She was 24 now, which added up to 6. Matt was 21, which added up to 3, and Lucy was 18, which added up to 9. And the months of their birthdays—March, June and September—reflected the same 3–6–9 numbers and were three months apart.

She was getting more and more intrigued. But maybe everyone got these numbers, at some point in their lives, since the numbers were everywhere. She tried some random dates—10 November 2015, which came to… 10 +11+8 = 29, which came to 11, which came to 2. No 3, 6 or 9 totals there.

What about 4 January 1958? She added 4+1+1+9+5+8, which came to 19; then 9+1 made 10, which reduced down to 1. So, not everyone had those numbers.

She suddenly had another thought that sent a shiver down her spine. When had her parents… *checked out*? (She couldn't bring herself to say the D word.) It was on 24 September 2019, which came to what? She quickly did the numbers. 2+4 = 6; September = 9; and 2019 = 9. So 6+9+3 = 9. There it was again. *Nine*. She sat back, her brain buzzing.

"Marn?" Lucy stuck her head around the kitchen door. "Where's the jam?"

Jam. They were definitely in the middle of some kind of jam. "Busy, Luce." She waved her away, still contemplating the numbers.

"No probs. I'll find it." Lucy disappeared back into the kitchen, quietly closing the door.

Marnie didn't know what to think. Did any of this mean anything? Was it just random? What were the chances of all their birthdates adding up the way they did? And the years…?

She wondered… when might they add up again, if they ever did? Next year? She tried her own birthday: 3 March 2020 = 3+3+4 = 10 = 1. That didn't work. What about in three years' time? That would be 3 March 2022, which was 3+3+6 = 3. That worked. What about Matt and Lucy? She quickly did the numbers on her notepad. Matt's came to 3, as well. So did Lucy's. All of them came to 3! But what did that mean?

Then another thought. What about the third anniversary of her parents'… exit? That would be 24 September 2022. She quickly did the calculation: 2+4+9+2+2+2 came to 12, which reduced down to 3. Another one!

Her parents were 57 when they… died; adding 5+7 made 12, which reduced down to 3 as well!

This was too much. Her head was starting to hurt. Something very weird was going on. But what? And so what if these same numbers kept repeating in their birthdays etc? How did that help anyone?

She needed to research those three numbers. She reached behind her for her laptop, which she kept on the middle shelf of her bookcase. The router was on the floor beside it and she pulled the laptop over to the table, careful not to snag the cable on the back of her chair. She was the only young person she knew who did not have a cellphone and who hard-wired her laptop rather than using WiFi. *Wired is weird*, her friends at school used to say.

When your parents were physicists who knew all about electromagnetic fields—human and manmade—it was a no-brainer, although Lucy and Matt didn't seem to have got that message. They were both passionately in love with their cellphones, although they never turned them on in her apartment.

She was lucky; her upstairs neighbours were elderly and never used a computer or cellphone, so there was no radiation coming down from their place. Lots outside, of course, but she was far enough away from cell towers and other buildings—and her own building had lots of thick old marble flooring—that the levels stayed fairly low.

She turned on her computer and waited for it too boot up. *What time was it?* She'd completely lost track. She glanced at the clock above the fireplace. It was only 9am. Seemed much later. She paused. There it was again. *Nine.* Would she start seeing these numbers *everywhere* now? This was going to drive her nuts.

Maybe she should give Steve a call and see if he could shed some light on what all this meant. In the meantime, she was going to do a search for sites referring to 3, 6, 9 and see what she could find.

Lester the snake would just have to wait.

4

March 1983

When Francesca had her first *episode*, she thought nothing of it. Just the usual family psychosis. Nothing to worry about—certainly nothing to *tell* anyone about. She was consumed by her research and she had no time for distractions. Anyway, she detested doctors. Far too trigger-happy with their little pills, eager to find a pharmaceutical fix for every wayward hair follicle. Worse than lawyers, working so many *pillable* hours.

After four more episodes within a month, though, she decided to go for a check-up. Not that they'd find anything. She already knew that. And they didn't. Everything was normal—*excellent*, in fact, the preppy young female doctor said, although Francesca didn't tell her the real reason for her visit. Just said she'd had some dizzy spells and wanted to make sure she didn't have a brain tumour or some virulent cancer rampaging through her bones. The doctor did some blood tests and ordered a CAT scan, but the results a week later showed nothing abnormal.

But her kind of *abnormal* was unlikely to show up on any map. It wasn't something that could be found lurking in her cells, even with a high-powered microscope. She often had visions of sinister subatomic characters messing with her photons and protons, playing Snakes & Ladders on her DNA, and generally acting like delinquents let loose for the day without supervision. It kept her entertained, which was just as well, as most people were brain-numbingly boring. But it wasn't very helpful. In fact, it was her wild imagination that ultimately created so many problems, years after her first *episode*.

When it happened, it created a strange sensation—like being in the cool-down phase of a tumble dryer after a high-heat cycle. It left her feeling legless, floating, disorientated, as if some centrifugal force had moved her centre of gravity to the top of her head. Her lips refused to obey her brain so she was unable to talk for a few minutes—or walk, until her legs reclaimed her body. And she crackled with static electricity, her hair on end and her hands shooting sparks when she washed them.

It wasn't until she met Daniel that she began to make sense of things. Or was that when things really started to go sickeningly wrong? Would none of this have happened if she hadn't met him? Yes. No. Didn't matter. She couldn't imagine life without Daniel anyway, and they had achieved so much—most of it good. Was the fallout the price you paid for greatness? Or was greatness its own destiny, determined by how far you dared to go?

She had her college roommate Debs to thank for introducing them. *Thanks, Debs …I think.*

She and Debs were in their third year of physics. One more year to go and they would be free to do research, work as lab technicians, get a teaching diploma or sell their souls to some vast corporation with lots of funding and zero humanity.

Debs was determined to work for the military—*lots* of funding there, she said, and no shortage of gorgeous manly hunks, either. She'd probably marry some ruggedly handsome guy, have five army brats and live militantly happily ever after. Debs was never happier than when fighting some kind of injustice, and Francesca could never figure out why she'd wanted to become a physicist. Why didn't she become a human rights lawyer, an environmentalist or a social worker?

Francesca wanted to do research. There was something she needed to figure out; she didn't know what, and maybe it didn't matter what. Maybe it was just the *figuring out* that she needed. In any case, it wouldn't be some wonder drug that eradicated stupidity and made millions on the pill-popping market; that much she knew for sure. Something else—something people didn't even realize they wanted or could ever imagine having. Something shattering that defied all the laws of physics and human decency. Not that she didn't like people. It was just that most of them failed to activate more than about 0.1% of their brains.

She might be able to tap into some funding contacts via her father, who was a physics lecturer, but she'd get funding on her own, somehow. *Thanks, anyway, Dad.* Not that he would mind—or even notice. He was on another planet, most of the time, more engaged with his students than his own daughter. But his absence had made her self-sufficient and street-smart. Her mother hadn't contributed much to the family genepool either, but at least she had been there …until she wasn't.

"We've been invited to a party this weekend," Debs told her, one Friday night, a week before Spring break.

"Have fun, then." Francesca, not looking up from her computer.

"Come on, Fran. You need to get out."

"You know how I feel about parties," Francesca said firmly.

"Yeah, and people," said Debs. "But you're becoming a disgruntled, anti-social eccentric. You need to mix with normal people and have some fun."

"Wrong. I was *always* a disgruntled, anti-social eccentric. And normal people are exactly what I *don't* need," Francesca said, her hands flying over the keyboard as she typed.

"There's this quantum physics guy in fourth year who throws the most incredible parties," Debs said. "He calls them *particles*. You and your friend are invited to my *particle*, he told me yesterday."

"Another quantum nerd."

"Actually, he's a nice guy," Debs insisted. "He's a friend of Joe's and he's quite a hunk. Tall, blond handsome and a real brainiac. Could be perfect for you, Frannie."

Joe was Debs's current boyfriend who, for the moment, seemed to be keeping her fairly monogamous, despite her track record of playing the field—and making a big deal out of it. *"Hey, if men can do it, so can we."*

"A complete waste of time," Francesca said. "I've got this paper to hand in on Monday and I have a ton of work to do. I'll be working all weekend."

"God, you're so *boring*." Debs rolled her eyes.

"Go away and let me concentrate."

"You'll have all day Saturday and Sunday," Debs said. "If you don't come, I'll just sit here and bug you all evening anyway, so you wouldn't get *any* work done."

"Then you'd miss the party," Francesca said, still typing.

"Yeah, but it would be worth it, just to generate some kind of human reaction from you, assuming there's actually a human being *in* there."

"You are such a pest!" Francesca stopped typing and looked up at Debs. "What's his name? If I already know him, then he's not worth my giving up my Saturday night."

"The one you spend hunched over your desk, eating cold pizza and going to bed with a headache—*that* Saturday night, you mean?" Debs looked at her knowingly. "His name's Daniel and you don't know him. But I think you'd find him an awful lot more interesting than that paper you're working on. You might actually *enjoy* yourself."

So she went, and she could never decide if it was the worst or best decision of her life. Not just because of what happened afterwards, but because she had another *episode.*

The place was packed. It was a large loft apartment on the outskirts of campus—more professorial in style than *starving student,* with shelves of books lining the walls, an expensive sound system, solid, comfy furniture and real art hanging on the walls. There must have been over a hundred people there. Loud music, jostling bodies, good food, lots of liquids, and the buzz of great minds discussing great things. She felt a prickling portent of things to come, as if her subconscious mind knew something about the future that her conscious mind hadn't yet begun to grasp.

She had mingled a bit, feeling awkward and annoyed at the same time. *Why did everyone feel they had to be sociable and say all the right things?* This is why she hated parties—all that posing and inane conversation.

She felt a little scruffy—her long dark hair tumbling down her shoulders, badly in need of a haircut, her jeans well ventilated with several burn holes from some caustic chemical in the lab, and her runners looking very jaded from continuous wear. *Most people work hard to achieve that chic disheveled look,* Debs had told her earlier, but she hadn't tried to achieve anything, except finish her paper.

She and Debs couldn't have looked more different, with Debs being almost a foot shorter than Francesca's slender six-foot frame, and much more diligent about her wardrobe. With her short blond bob, sharp brown eyes, freckles and pixie face, she was cute in a way that most men found very alluring.

Right now, Debs was slow-dancing in the corner of the living room with Joe, her arms around his neck, her head on his chest and his large hands on her back. They looked good together. Maybe this guy would be the one to finally—

"Would you like something to drink?" A man had appeared beside her—Daniel, she realized. He *was* tall and relatively handsome, but it was hard to tell just how nerdy. Sharp blue eyes, laugh lines, a generous mouth and perfect teeth. *Had he been genetically engineered? Was he out of a test-tube? How soon could she leave and get back to her paper?*

He was holding up a glass of fizzing crimson-coloured liquid.

"Depends," she said. "What is it?"

"It's one of my quantum foamies," he said, smiling.

"And what is *that*?" She steadied herself against a bookcase. She was starting to feel her own quantum fizziness happening. Another *episode…*

"It's a totally benign but delicious concoction of sparkling mineral water and cherry juice."

"No vodka or other potent social lubricant lurking in there?"

"And no Rohypnol, either," he said, smiling again. *Was he always so inanely nice to people he didn't know?*

"Here. Try it."

She took the glass and knocked the whole lot back in three huge gulps. Maybe it would pull her out of the tumble dryer.

"Thanks," she said, handing him back the empty glass. "Could you get me another one?" That might give her enough time to recover before he noticed how weird she was.

He laughed and suggested she sit… somewhere.

"I'm Daniel, by the way. And you are…?"

"Francesca," she said. "Francesca *Sincera*." She pronounced it carefully, the proper Italian way—*seen-chair-ah*. She liked her name and hated it when Americans mangled it, calling her *sin sarah*.

"Ah. So nothing fake about you, then."

She was impressed. Very few people knew what the name meant, or where the word *sincere* came from.

Daniel noticed her surprise. "My parents were Irish but they travelled a lot around Europe—especially Italy—and my mum started out as a linguist. She was always telling us stories about the origin of words and phrases."

He shrugged. "So I just happen to know that *sincere* comes from the Latin words *sin*, meaning *without*, and *cera*, meaning *wax*. Right? And that unscrupulous sculptors or artists in the Renaissance often tried to hide flaws in their work or raw materials by covering them in wax."

He grinned at her. "Good to know you're not hiding anything, Francesca," he said.

Francesca just smiled. If she hadn't been feeling so woozy, she would have laughed out loud. Right now, she needed him to go away so she could hide her *episode* and try to recover.

He seemed to sense her impatience. "I'll get you that drink. Back in a sec."

She perched on the arm of a sofa as he made his way through the crowd to the kitchen, stopping to talk to a serious-looking bearded guy, and then a leggy blond wearing some kind of beige body stocking. Or maybe she was just plain naked. Francesca couldn't tell as her vision was going funny and the paintings on the walls were starting to look like Salvador Dalì knock-offs.

She took a few deep breaths and started doing some complicated equations in her head. Maybe that would help, although it never had before. Nothing had, apart from a shot of her own concoction …if she took it soon enough. She reached into the pocket of her jacket (she detested handbags) and pulled out a tiny bottle of clear liquid. A quick look to make sure Daniel wasn't already on his way back, then she took a swig. It burned her throat and seared her insides, making her eyes water. She'd pay for it later. Right now, though, it was saving her from ending up in a heap on the floor. Never her most dignified pose. She could feel herself slowly coming back down to earth, in the general vicinity of normal. Things were almost back in focus when Daniel returned with another glass of crimson fizzy stuff.

She took a few token sips and asked him to tell her his life story. Not that she was terribly interested, but it would keep him talking while the last of the *episode* passed.

He talked about graduating in June the next year and how he planned to do pure research. She discovered he was an only child, like her, and that his father was a lawyer and his mother had started out as a translator who often did contract work for the UN, but then became a lawyer too when they moved to the States.

"Don't hold that against me," he said.

"What?" She was momentarily confused. She had been focusing on his belt buckle, trying to dispel the last few fuzzy edges of her vision. *Hold what against him?* She was actually feeling quite swoony and benevolent towards him, thanks to her concoction. *What* wouldn't *she hold against him…*

"The fact that they're lawyers," he said, laughing at her expression.

"I'll try not to," she said. "They're obviously pretty smart, if their son is anything to go by." *Ugh.* Her episodes always made her so *gushy* afterwards, as if her brain hadn't quite resumed its normal faculties of discernment.

"In some ways, not at all," he said. "I took them to court once."

"*Your parents?* Why? What for?"

"They were neglecting me," he said. "Never home, no time for me. Court was always more important. I was farmed out to one nanny after the other. They were failing me as parents."

How come *she'd* never thought of doing that? Maybe he wasn't such a nerd after all. "What age were you?"

"Twelve," he said.

"Did you win?"

"In a way," he laughed. "I got their attention, and the judge was not impressed by their behaviour, even though he ended up ruling in their favour, with certain conditions."

"What conditions?"

"That they each spend at least an hour with me every day."

"Sounds like a win to me," she said. "Did they resent you for that? Did they counter-sue?"

"No." He laughed again. "I think they got to quite like me, once they actually got to know me."

"So, you must know lots of awful lawyer jokes," she said.

"I avoid them like the plague," he said. "I prefer jokes about scientists. We need to laugh at ourselves. We spend far too much time in serious research and heady debates."

"I've been surrounded by physicists for the past three years," she reminded him. "I'm sure I've heard them all."

"Well, here's one you might not have heard: *What do you get when you throw a party for astronomers, particle physicists and quantum physicists?*"

"Bored sick?" she said. "Hoarse, trying to make yourself heard over all the other experts?"

"The astronomers want to stay up all night, the particle physicists keep going energetically till at least 2am, and the quantum physicists try to be in two places at once to get the most out of the event."

"That's truly bad," she said, rolling her eyes—and instantly regretting it. *Never a good idea right after an episode, when her eyes felt tender and all her senses heightened.* "Time for me to go." Her legs felt as if they belonged to her again and she could see Debs heading her way.

"Well, thanks for coming to my particle," he said.

"Perhaps your particle could come to me sometime," her mouth shot back. Obviously, her brain still hadn't fully regained control of her faculties.

"I think I could persuade quite a few of my particles to go to you," he said. "Where and when might my particles find you?"

"Given the nature of nonlocality in our quantum field, I am nowhere and everywhere," she said, realizing that flirting with this very distracting male was *not* a good idea. "And since all time is happening at once, according to quantum physics, it could be tricky to fix a time and place."

She got up, brushed some quiche crumbs from her jeans. "But I'm sure you'll figure out a way, given your super-smart legal brain and precocious powers of persuasion."

He did, of course, and time and space took on a whole new dimension.

Love for Francesca had always been more like a distant relative she barely knew, than a sibling she tussled with every single day. She had been an only child raised within a loveless parental model, and she simply wasn't used to it. Her head had always been her safe place.

So she was confused by the tingling nervous energy she felt in her chest after meeting this man. Was it attraction—*something-like-love*—for Daniel? Or was it fear? Sometimes it was hard to tell, with one cancelling out the other, but which one was stronger? And how could you tell who had won if love was such a rare insurgent? Did love + fear leave you idling in neutral? Or was love always the greater force? It was a shaky equation requiring more in-depth research… ideally by someone else.

She was fearless in exploring the physics of the universe, while Daniel seemed fearless in the physics of the heart.

He's besotted with you, Debs had told her. *He's the coolest guy in college. He has money and he knows how to cook. How can you act so blasé?*

He wasn't exactly hard on the eyes, but it was his *brain* that Francesca found sexy. All those dextrous dendrites… She could see herself doing some fancy dendritic branching with this man.

Perhaps he had enough love for them both… *if* things evolved.

Daniel became a permanent fixture in her life and they spent so much time together that people started to see them as a single entity, fused in mind and name.

Have you seen Dancesca? they would say. Or: *Are you going to Dancesca's this weekend?*

But it wasn't their love for each other that kept them so close, except at the beginning, although that was more lust than love—for her, at least. Not that she didn't love him *in her own way*, although he loved her properly, much better than she ever could.

No. It wasn't love, lust or their intellectual compatibility that kept them so tightly bound. It was the secrets they shared.

5

19 October 2019

It felt very strange driving past their old home. Marnie slowed as she approached the large metal gates, looking down the long driveway towards the house. The ivy was already taking over the old stonework, but it had left the windows clear, letting the house see out. Everything was still. The gates were locked and there was no sign of life. The trees lining the driveway stood like sentries guarding some untold story. What had happened here? How had their parents managed to keep so many secrets from them? And why had they been so determined to eliminate all trace of their life and work?

Marnie felt a lump in her throat. She wasn't sure if she was going to throw up or burst out crying, but all these emotions were making her stomach churn. *Action*, she reminded herself. *Keep moving.* She drove on, skirting the fenced perimeter of the property towards the neighbour's place, almost a kilometre away. Westfield was on a large plot of three acres, surrounded by thick hedges and old trees, and they'd never had to worry about prying neighbours. *Had that been intentional?* Privacy wasn't necessarily secrecy, although they amounted to the same thing. Didn't they?

Slowing at the entrance to the Carpenters' place, Marnie turned her brand-new red Mazda 6 down the curving driveway. The car had been a present from her parents on her birthday in March and was now a constant source of inner conflict; she couldn't decide if she loved it or hated it.

Doug and Maisie never seemed to close their gates, even though they had two dogs. Their place had always been open to them when Marnie was growing up. Maisie seemed to realize that Francesca was not *mommy* material and she'd tried to make up for it, giving them cookies and hot chocolate whenever they came over after school.

Sometimes they stayed for dinner, if Maisie phoned the basement lab where Daniel and Francesca were working. Real food, a real meal. Dinner at the Carpenters' had always felt like a luxury, given her mother's unpredictable cooking, although Marnie sometimes felt disloyal. But when Maisie produced her famous chicken curry with steamed vegetables, roasted cashews and coconut rice, the feeling quickly passed. And when she got chocolate ice cream over homemade apricot crumble, Marnie sometimes even forgot that Maisie wasn't her real mother.

As Marnie pulled up in front of the house, the front door opened and Maisie came striding out to greet her, short curly silver hair framing her round, smiling face. Although they were about 15 years older than her parents, Maisie and Doug were fit and active, always gardening, playing tennis or going on walking holidays.

They had attended the memorial service for her parents, but they had all been too shell-shocked from grief to ask sequential questions.

Now, almost three weeks later, Marnie was hoping they could shed some light on what had happened and why.

Her legs felt shaky as she got out of the car. She closed the door and placed her hands on the roof of the car to steady herself. When she turned around, Maisie was there, enfolding her in a heartfelt hug.

"Wonderful to see you, darling girl," she said. "How *are* you?" With an impatient wave of her hand, she brushed aside her question before Marnie had a chance to answer. "Silly of me to ask. You're still devastated, of course. We all are."

She took Marnie firmly by the arm. "Come on inside and have lunch with us. Doug will be thrilled you're here. The dogs, too. We've all missed you."

Grateful for the reassuring grip on her arm, Marnie kissed Maisie on the cheek and they walked up the steps into the house.

The kitchen door opened and the two dogs rushed out to greet her. Tails spinning madly, tongues lolling, eyes bright, Baxter and Jen were the nicest dogs she'd ever known—nicer than many humans. Both Border Collies, they were highly intelligent and alert, seemingly aware of whatever was going on and listening intently to whatever was being discussed. She'd walked them many times, over the fields around both properties, and it had always helped her deal with things. They were getting on, now— surely 12 or 13 years old—but were still as lively as ever.

The dogs were followed by Doug, who reached out his arms for one of his famous bear hugs. A large, solid man of over six feet, with an unruly thatch of grey hair and a rugged, suntanned face with deep-blue eyes, he was kind, wise and unfailingly supportive.

Her dad had been like that too, Marnie realized, but he had been so devoted to her mother and their research that she rarely got to experience it.

They sat at the kitchen table as Maisie served up homemade soup. Pungent aromas of turmeric, ginger and coriander filled the air, soothing Marnie right down to her core. With a steaming bowl of soup in front of her, she just wanted to eat and soak up the healing warmth of this home from home. The questions could wait.

Maisie sliced some crunchy homemade bread and Marnie ladled on tahini and cherry jam—her favourite combo.

Doug talked about his plans to build a new deck off the living room, his work as a volunteer firefighter for the county, and their walking holiday in Scotland next year.

Maisie asked about Matt and Lucy, and talked about maybe getting a puppy. Her beloved dogs were nearing the end of their lives and she wanted to bring some new life into her heart and home.

"Come and help me choose one, Marnie," she said. "Mrs Maitland has a new litter of Collies that will be ready for weaning in another few weeks."

"I'd love to," Marnie said, and meant it.

The conversation was soothingly normal and Marnie felt herself relaxing for the first time in ages. This is what it meant to have a family, she realized—somewhere warm and safe and loving.

After Maisie cleared away the dishes and Marnie had her hands wrapped around a mug of thyme tea, Maisie sat down beside her and put a hand on her arm.

"Marnie…" She paused. "Your mother left something for you. She asked me to give it to you when you came to see us."

"What?" Some of her tea spilled onto the table as Marnie sat bolt upright, her head suddenly a traffic jam of questions. *What had her mother left for her? A letter explaining everything? Finally, some answers!*

"What is it? Is it…? Does it…?"

Maisie looked uncomfortable. "Nothing… significant, I'm afraid, sweetheart," she said, clearly disapproving of the whole situation. "It's just a small memento. I'll get it for you."

She left the room and Marnie felt her heart pounding.

"Don't let this turn you inside out, Marnie," Doug said gently. "This whole thing is enough to mess anyone up but I really hope it won't do that to you. God knows why they did this, leaving the three of you in the lurch. You all deserved better."

Marnie nodded, barely hearing him, her whole being following the sound of Maisie's footsteps up the stairs and across the landing, the sound of a drawer opening and closing, then her footsteps on the stairs again and the kitchen door opening behind her. Maisie was carrying a small object wrapped in white tissue paper. She placed it on the table in front of Marnie.

"As I said, just a small keepsake." Maisie sounded apologetic, as if it was her fault—or maybe it was regret, since she and Doug had never been able to have children of their own. They'd have done it *properly*, if they had, Marnie had always thought.

"Don't ask me why your mother did this, but I said I'd give it to you—before I knew what they planned to do…" She trailed off, at a loss for how to soften the blow.

Marnie stared at the object, not wanting to know what it was if it didn't provide some answers, yet compelled to find out. She picked it up and slowly unwrapped it.

She gasped. It was her mother's white ceramic travel alarm clock— something Marnie had always secretly coveted for its quirkiness and its closeness to her mum. Her dad had bought it for her mother shortly after they got married, and her mother had taken it with her whenever she travelled to a conference or on the rare family holiday. The clock had to be more than 35 years old, but it seemed to have defied the test of time, still looking almost new.

It was shaped like a globe, with a slice off the front for the flat face of the clock (with old-fashioned hour and minute hands in shiny gold against a white background) and another slice off the back for all the dials. Around the rim, five small digital displays protruded like the squared petals of a flower. Two on each side showed different time zones—Vancouver and Washington, DC on the left, London and Sydney on the right. The fifth one, on the top, showed the date and year. Marnie looked closer. The date read 24 SEPT 2019—the day her parents had… passed on. The main clock, which required winding up, seemed to have stopped. At 3 o'clock.

Enough, thought Marnie. I'm sick of this game, or whatever it is. She felt her anger surging. Why leave her this and not something useful—like a million dollars—which they could easily have done? Why destroy everything else and just give her this stupid clock, as if she should be grateful for her mother remembering she liked it? Well, she liked *life*, too—or used to, until they turned everything upside down. She was shaking with rage and loss and grief, on the verge of a massive meltdown, but she didn't want to lose it here or she'd never be able to drive home.

Maisie put her arms around her shoulders and hugged her from behind.

"Marnie," she said, "I don't know what possessed them to do this terrible thing—to leave three wonderful children in the most horrible way any parent could ever leave. But, for what it's worth, I know they both loved you very much."

She turned around, bending down beside Marnie and looking her in the eyes. "Don't let this spoil your life. They chose to end theirs, for whatever ungodly reason, but don't let it destroy yours."

Marnie nodded and squeezed Maisie's hand, unable to speak. "You will have to dig deep down inside to find the strength to pull out of this and get on with your life, and to live it on *your* terms," Maisie said. "But I want you to know that we are here for you and always will be."

Maisie's eyes were spilling over. Doug was looking down at his knees. The dogs whined softly but didn't move. Marnie could see now how much Doug and Maisie loved her—and Matt and Lucy—treating them as their own. She thought of all the dinners she'd had in this warm, lived-in, homey kitchen, with its scuffed wooden table, wild flowers on the wooden dresser, spice racks lining the countertop beside the stove, and always the smells of cooking or baked bread, with the radio playing in the background and the dogs happily curled up in their basket, panting after their daily patrols of the property. A real home.

She nodded at Maisie, managed a small smile for them both, and stood up.

"I need to go," she said. "But I will come back soon to visit, if that's okay with you both." She knew it was but she wanted them to know she needed and loved them as much as they seemed to need and love her.

She put the clock in her bag, rubbing her eyes as she bent down to pat the dogs. Doug stood up and they went into the hall. He put his arm around Maisie and they both reached out to her. Marnie hugged them both fiercely, then went out the front door and down the steps.

She could barely see where she was going but she headed for the red blur of her Mazda and got in. She grabbed a tissue from the box on the dashboard and dabbed at her eyes as she fastened her seat belt.

She started the car, put it in gear and waved to them both, standing together on the steps, as she drove slowly down the driveway. It was only when she was back on the road that she realized she had completely forgotten to ask them all the questions she had prepared.

6

The apartment was quiet when Marnie got home. Lucy must have gone out to do some shopping, or maybe she went out to give her sister some space. Marnie was grateful. She needed it. Dropping her bag on the floor beside the coat stand, she headed for her bedroom. She stopped at the bathroom on the way, splashing some cold water on her face and brushing her hair, which made her feel slightly better.

Then she saw Lucy's pink cashmere sweater on the laundry basket. Always the fashion queen, thought Marnie, although she probably wouldn't be buying any more designer clothes for a while. She picked it up and carried it to the guest room. The door was ajar but she knocked anyway, just in case.

"Luce? You in there?"

No answer. She went in and was about to put the sweater on the bed when she saw the notepad lying open on top of the duvet. Lucy's handwriting filled the page. Thinking it might be a note that Lucy had left for her, Marnie picked it up and started to read.

Dearest parents, you have cost me dearly in all the ways a parent never should.

Not a note for her, then, Marnie realized. Her body sat itself down on the bed, while her head told her to *stop reading now*; she was violating Lucy's privacy—not something she would normally do. But *normal* was dead and buried, never to be seen again.

Marnie continued reading.

I hate loving you but I refuse to love hating. I won't do that to myself. I refuse to be a reaction to what you did. You chose how to end your life, but why should that screw up mine?

How can your absence generate such a throbbing presence, when in life you seemed so tangibly absent?

Not that you were such a crucial presence in my life. But at least while you were there you had parenting potential. Dead, you have none. I can't even hold on to the illusion of you.

Dying so dramatically was perverse. Was it some grand statement guaranteed to shock us all? Did you intend to disrupt the natural order of things?

Is this some kind of experiment for the betterment of mankind? Did you sacrifice yourselves and us for some greater cause?

You deprived us of a normal life. Hey, why not normal mourning, too? We get to do all the mourning at once—every raw emotion in one sick lump, with no chance to move from one to the other, processing and integrating along the way to eventual acceptance.

Acceptance comes from understanding, but how can I understand or accept what you did? Why should I waste precious time and energy trying to, when you made zero effort to explain? If you were at peace with what you did, then I should be, too. Otherwise, a part of me dies with you, and I won't give you that. You've taken enough already, in taking yourselves. The rest of me is for me.

So you can fuck off out of my head and let me live.

Marnie felt a wave of despair sweep through her. Lucy's words stoked the emotions she had only just managed to suppress at the Carpenters'. *Oh, Lucy. So much pain. Will any of us ever heal from this?* Reading her sister's words again, she felt Lucy's grief magnify her own, and she didn't have the energy to keep dialing it back.

Sobs erupted from her gut and lunch threatened to come with

them. She lay down, curled up and let the grief, anger, frustration and resentment course through her till she felt drained and gouged, with nothing left inside.

Lucy found her there, two hours later, fast asleep, clutching the pillow and looking for the first time as if she has found some kind of peace.

***

When Marnie woke up, it was almost dark outside and she heard soft music coming from the living room. She got up slowly, feeling as if she'd just undergone major surgery, and walked shakily down the hallway.

Lucy was sitting cross-legged in front of the fireplace, holding a mug of tea.

"I hope you don't mind that I lit the fire," she said, looking almost angelic—her skin glowing, her long dark hair burnished by the firelight and her vivid green eyes sparkling with reflections. She was like a softer, miniature version of their mother, with the same edgy feistiness but less of her confidence.

"No, not at all," Marnie said, sitting down on the rug beside her. "It's very cozy. I should light it more often." She paused. "Luce, I'm very sorry for reading—"

"It's okay, Marn. It was just a rant. Sometimes it helps me to write stuff down, get it off my chest. I'm working through things, you know? In my own way."

Marnie nodded. "You're a good writer. I think you could do something with that."

Lucy said nothing, staring into the flames.

"If you're not going to pursue your degree in fashion design, what about doing some creative writing?"

"I can't think about it now," Lucy said. "It all seems kind of pointless."

"It will come back. It will, Luce. Give it time." She turned towards her sister. "You have lots of passion and I admire that. I may not always like the way it comes out…"

Lucy laughed.

"…but there is power there. If you learn how to channel it, I think you could be a really good writer. I really do."

She put an arm around her sister and hugged her close. Moved by her own tenderness, she felt tears welling up again, and she wondered if she was becoming emotionally unstable. But it would be unhealthy *not* to be upset, wouldn't it? Given what had happened? She just had to ride it out.

Lucy seemed softer than her usual prickly self, turning her head onto Marnie's shoulder with a big shuddering breath and holding on tight.

When had they last done this, Marnie wondered—her and Lucy sitting by the fire talking about tender things? Never, she realized. They needed to do it more often. Family was precious, and Lucy and Matt were all the family she had left.

"I went to visit Doug and Maisie today," she said.

"I love those two," Lucy said. "Did they know anything about Mum and Dad?"

"I don't think they had a clue, and they both seemed very upset about it—angry, even. But I'll go back next weekend and have a longer chat." *Maybe.*

She was beginning to wonder if she was just creating a whole load of stress and grief for herself. They might never work this out. Their parents would have left them some kind of explanation if they'd wanted them to know why they'd taken their own lives. And if they *did* discover some weird reason for it, how would that help? They would still be gone. They would still have got rid of the family home, photo albums, jewellery, furniture—all the landmarks of the life they had shared.

Maybe Lucy was right; she should get them out of her head and move on with her life. But she couldn't seem to do it. She wasn't ready to give up yet. She needed to work on this more, see if she could find some kind of closure. She might never find it, but if she didn't do everything she could to try to figure this out, she'd spend the rest of her life with a big fat *why* echoing around in her head, corroding all her experiences.

She'd give it till the end of the year—find out more about those numbers, see if Matt came up with anything on the shell company, ask Maisie and Doug if they knew anything—then she'd move on.

Lester the snake, the kids at school, maybe a holiday somewhere warm... She needed to fill the void her parents had left behind. And maybe she'd sell her car and get something else that didn't constantly remind her of them.

7

"Here you go. Your favourite fuel." Matt dropped a packet of fig rolls on Jed's desk.

"Yo," Jed said, not looking up from his manic hunt-and-peck typing on his laptop.

A true computer nerd, Jed had all the brainpower but looked nothing like a geek. He was tanned, fit and street-smart, with a steady stream of girlfriends but no desire to settle down. *Keeping all his options open,* he said. *What was the rush?*

With a large nose, spiky brown hair and a chin that just about did the job, he wasn't exactly handsome, but he had large brown eyes with the longest eyelashes Matt had ever seen on a man—not that he usually noticed that kind if thing, but Jed could look almost angelic if he looked at you right. He always said his brains plus his charm made him an irresistible chick-magnet, but Matt was fairly sure it was those eyelashes.

Jed was obsessed with code, databases and anything bearing a *no entry* sign online. That stuff was for ordinary mortals. He had a knack for accessing secret trap doors and finding seemingly non-existent information, providing many of the newspaper's 'inside scoops'. He was the go-to guy in the office—for fixing computer problems, obtaining insider information, or creating the occasional untraceable internet 'mishap' for a nasty neighbour.

"Coffee?"

"Yeah… What?" Jed stopped typing and swivelled his chair around to look at Matt. "What do you want? You never come bearing gifts or offer to get my coffee. What is it this time?"

"Just a small favour," Matt said, "when you've finished working on that Belgian corruption exposé."

"What kind of favour?" Jed looked at him skeptically, but the gleam in his eyes made it less than convincing. "I doubt it's *small*, whatever it is. Otherwise you'd do it yourself." No harm in reminding the *boss* of his superior skills.

Matt leaned over and spoke quietly, not wanting the rest of the staff in the office to hear. His assistant Jenny sat in the far corner of their open-plan space, talking to someone on the phone, and two of the other researchers—Harry Quinn and Laura Sterling—were typing on their laptops, preparing for the end-of-month deadline.

"See if you can trace this shell company, MLM Holdings—find an address or some way of getting in touch with them."

"Something going down, boss?"

Apart from me, you mean? "No, I just need some background information."

"Same old, same old, then. Us against the bad guys." Jed looked disappointed.

"Except this is personal."

"A personal vendetta, you mean?" The gleam was back.

"Cool your Jedi jets. It's a personal matter—nothing to do with work," Matt said. "So you can say no and I won't fire you."

"If I say no, do I get to keep the figs?" Jed tapped the packet of fig rolls.

"Yeah, you get to keep the bribe."

"What about the coffee?"

"Nah. That's pushing it."

"Okay, so who are these guys, MLM Holdings? What have you got on them?"

"Zilch, using conventional methods. But I need to trace them, find out who they are, using your more *unconventional* approach..."

"Hack into some secure databases, you mean," Jed said. "Why?"

Jed liked to know what he was getting into, especially if it involved something sinister. Not because he had any scruples about doing something slightly irregular. He *lived* for this stuff. But he liked to know the backstory, unless it was better for him *not* to know. He usually wanted just enough information to cover his ass but not so much that he couldn't potentially claim he hadn't known what he was getting into—*if* he got caught.

"It relates to my parents' inheritance," Matt said, shifting uncomfortably from one foot to the other. "Money gone... *astray*, you might say. Do you need to know more?"

"Nah, that's okay, man." Jed studied him. "How's it going, with all that family stuff? You okay?"

"Yeah, I'm dealing with it," Matt said. "I might take tomorrow off.

Work from home till the weekend."

Jed nodded. "I'll see what I can find."

"Thanks, bud." Matt clapped him on the shoulder and headed for his desk.

"Hey!" Jed called after him. "What about my coffee?"

After getting Jed's coffee and one for himself, Matt sat down at his desk and scanned his messages. Not as many as he'd anticipated. Jenny and Jed were looking out for him, doing as much as they could to reduce his load while he got to grips with his *situation*.

They were like his second family and he couldn't imagine life without them. Thank God for their sponsor. They'd never have got past GO if it hadn't been for that funding. They were too young to be reporting on complex political issues, but they weren't interested in political debate; their forte was exposés—dishing up the dirt on shady politicians and exposing the dark underbellies of government and corporate corruption. They were all in it together—a web of deceit, double-dealing, data manipulation, digital surveillance and self-serving spin, with no shortage of cover-ups to uncover.

He'd never met their sponsor but he'd talked to him on the phone. Travis Chamberlain. Seemed like a solid guy. He was based in California and had contacted Matt and Jed after reading one of their college newspapers. He said he liked their style—telling it like it was (*really* was), the truth and nothing but the truth, without judgement or commentary, letting the readers make up their own minds.

Matt had felt uneasy accepting money from a third party, convinced they'd have to publish whatever this guy wanted them to write, but they were given free rein to write whatever they wanted, provided they didn't report what mainstream media called *news* and they called *pure fiction*.

Jed's skills were indispensable, and he knew it. He fancied being another Julian Assange and called himself The Redeemer—bringing politicians, judges, corporations and even evangelists to their knees when his sleuthing revealed the hideous truths beneath their silken lies.

He worried sometimes about Jed getting caught and going to prison. He felt a twinge of uneasiness for asking him to find out about MLM Holdings. But Jed never did anything he didn't want to do, Matt reminded himself. Plus, those big innocent eyes of his seemed to throw people completely off track. Matt had visions of police officers arriving at their door, taking one look at Jed and saying, *Nah, we're wasting our time. That can't be him.*

But they often exposed corrupt cops, too, so he had no illusions about …well, anything.

8

Saturday, 26 October 2019

It was a shock to see himself in the bathroom mirror. He looked haunted, like some hopeless, homeless guy, living on the street. Bloodshot eyes, greasy hair sticking up in spikes, and skin like a used teabag left out in the sun. *Shit. I went into the office looking like this.* When had he become so ugly? Since *it* happened? He used to be an okay-looking guy. Now he looked haggard and ancient at the age of 21, *thank you very fuckily much.*

Everything was fucked. Up was down, down was up, the future in reverse, his whole life going sideways, parents giving birth then choosing death. Was he drunk? Probably. He felt shitty. Maybe he should lay off the wine in the evening, stick to sleeping pills till he got his head straight.

He stared at the face staring back. What the hell happened? If he could just turn back the clock… But what could he have done differently? Had he missed some crucial signs that his parents were mentally ill? Was their research getting to them? Had they lost touch with the real world and not been able to deal with normal everyday living? Ha! He was beginning to get a taste of that himself.

He thought back to when he'd last seen them. It was on Lucy's birthday, 6 September, when his parents had insisted on coming into town to take them all to dinner at Lucy's restaurant of choice. She'd chosen Sorellina, a fancy Italian place on Huntingdon in downtown Boston. Well, she wasn't going to suggest *McDonald's,* was she—not when they were paying.

He remembered Lucy getting a kick out of the name. "You know what it means, right, guys?" It meant *little sister* in Italian, she said gleefully, as if the whole place existed just for her. But it was her night—

an evening of family banter and normality. Or so he had thought, at the time.

What had they talked about? Had he missed something that could have alerted him to what happened just over two weeks later? But all he could remember was Lucy talking excitedly about her BFA in fashion design at MassArt, which she had started that week. She was chattering on about the annual fashion show hosted by the MassArt Fashion Department every May, already dreaming about the designs she could create.

What else? Marnie had talked about the kids in her class and how one of the parents had brought her a thank-you gift voucher from Harvard Book Store—for "*taking such good care of Sebastian*". Marnie had had to explain that teachers couldn't accept gifts from parents. Matt shook his head at the irony. Their own parents hadn't left any gifts for any of them, teachers or not.

What had their *parents* talked about? Had they seemed different, that night? He remembered his mother being a bit teary-eyed, but she was always like that on birthdays—the only times he ever saw her expressing much emotion. She and his dad had given Lucy an envelope containing a thick wad of cash from the college account they had set up for her years ago. You could practically see the dollar signs lighting up her eyes. She had it all.

His mother hadn't talked much… just asked Lucy about her course work and commented on the delicious artichoke carpaccio and arugula salad. But their mother had never given a damn about food, so this seemed odd, now that he thought about it. Not a reason to kill yourself, though. His mother had lived for her research and eating was just a necessary means to an end.

She had prepared some very dubious meals for them when they were growing up (UFOs, Matt used to call them—*unidentified foodlike objects*), and they often had to ask her what they were eating. He remembered one particular dinner that had made them all laugh, when Lucy had asked what was on her plate.

"It's lasagna!" their mother exclaimed. "What is *wrong* with you children?"

Their dad gave them a stern look, then winked at them when their mother wasn't looking.

"It's really good, Mum," Marnie said dutifully.

"No, it's *awful*," Lucy said, not very tactful at eight years old. She hadn't changed much.

Everyone froze. Then their mother burst out laughing. That set them all off. His dad was laughing so hard he had to wipe tears from his eyes.

"It's Cooking 101," their mother said, still laughing. "What do you expect?"

"I thought it was Science 101," Matt had replied, and that set them all off again.

"Well," his mother said, "the best experiments are based on direct experience, so let's eat this and see what happens."

They all groaned.

"Ice cream for whoever finishes theirs," she said challengingly.

They bent their heads to the task.

But Lucy wasn't sure about the deal. "Is it *real* ice cream, Mummy? Not homemade stuff, right?"

Matt smiled at the memory. They'd had their moments.

Later, they'd had Clara—a part-time housekeeper who'd cooked for them—and things got a whole lot more digestible at dinner time.

His mind returned to Lucy's birthday dinner. Had his mother been trying to distract them that night at the restaurant, talking about the food... or distract herself from whatever was on her mind?

His dad... had he said anything significant that evening? He had seemed happy—relieved, even—and Matt had the impression that his parents had made some kind of breakthrough in their research. But they often made breakthroughs so he didn't pay much attention.

He felt a twinge of guilt at not having taken more of an interest in their work. But he remembered his dad saying that their work was not for public consumption—or *family* consumption, either, obviously. The stuff they did was way beyond him, anyway—quantum mechanical phenomena, subatomic particles, scattering processes, muons, superposition and entanglement and other terms he'd heard them talking about but were meaningless to him. All he knew was that they worked on supercomputers that could do things normal computers couldn't do.

He needed to sit down. He hadn't slept in almost a week and he couldn't prop himself up on the bathroom sink any longer. He was going to knock himself out with some sleeping pills this evening.

Maybe then he'd be able to get his ass back in gear.

He shuffled into the living room and flopped down on the couch, reaching for the yellow legal pad he kept on the coffee table for his work notes. He flipped over to a clean page and wrote LEADS at the top.

He suddenly had a flood of questions about his parents' work. Where had they got their funding? He had always assumed they got research grants, although they seemed very well off for researchers. Who had provided the funding? Was there some way he could find out? How come he'd never thought to ask these questions before?

He vaguely remembered his dad talking about inventing something—some kind of measuring device used in labs, but that was before he or Marnie had been born and he didn't know what it was for or if other labs used it. Had that made them some money?

He wrote down: FUNDING SOURCES = ?

And what about their equipment? It was all gone now, but could there be some way to trace their purchases and find out what they had been working on?

He wrote: FIND OUT ABOUT LAB/COMPUTER PURCHASES

He wasn't sure where he'd start on that. His parents' personal computers were gone, so he had no way of looking at their browsing history, and he had never known their e-mail account details.

Another thought struck him. What about the people at the memorial service? Mr Williams had arranged for an obituary to go in the newspaper, shortly after their parents' death, but only ten people had shown up at the service. He hadn't known any of them, apart from the Carpenters. And he'd been too shell-shocked to think about asking for their names and phone numbers so he could contact them later.

He remembered an elderly, grey-haired, bearded guy shaking his hand at the door, muttering something about being his mother's professor back in her early college days, but he couldn't remember his name.

He made a note in his pad: COLLEGE PROF, MIT WEBSITE?

Maybe he could contact MIT and find out who he was, although Marnie might have done this already. She'd mentioned trying to track down some of the people who'd come to the service. He'd try MIT's faculty webpage first, to see if he could find a photo of this guy, but he looked old enough to have retired some time ago, so it was unlikely he'd still be lecturing.

His parents *had* gone to MIT, hadn't they? He was starting to doubt everything they'd said, but that was where they claimed to have met, so he'd start there.

There was also a *Deborah somebody* who came to the service with a tall military-looking guy—her husband? She had given all three of them a warm hug when she was leaving, telling them she'd been their mother's college roommate for a year, and that their mother had been special, one of a kind. And then she was gone, with no address or other info given. Matt had no idea where she lived—in Massachusetts or abroad.

He wrote: DEBORAH-SOMEBODY—CHECK WITH MIT CAMPUS FOR RECORDS OF MUM AND ROOMS, 1980–1983.

Had his mother worked somewhere to pay for her college tuition? Or had her father paid for it? His grandfather had died when Matt was 4, so he'd never really known him, and his maternal grandmother had died of some strange illness years before he was born.

Had his dad worked while he was at college? He had the impression that his dad had always had lots of money—maybe from *his* father? Some family inheritance? Could that have been the source of funding for his parents' research later on? Their paternal grandparents had died within six months of each other, when Matt was in his late teens. He had hazy memories of them, as they had retired in Europe and had only come to visit twice.

He knew so little about his parents, and Marnie didn't seem to know much more. *What had they all been thinking?* They hadn't been thinking at all. And they'd taken things for granted when their parents were alive, never asking how they earned their money—but why would they?—or why they had almost no friends and what was so top-secret about their work.

He vaguely remembered some old guy coming to the house once—four, five years ago, before he'd left home and got his own place. Was he an old college friend? Fellow researcher? Fund-raiser? He had no clue and no way of finding out.

What else? He drummed his fingers on his pad. His mind had gone blank. He needed some coffee to keep his brain alert.

He got up and headed for the kitchen, a compact space off the living room with gleaming stainless steel appliances. His apartment was more recent than Marnie's but had the same spacious rooms, big windows and high ceilings. It had come partially furnished when he signed the rental agreement four years ago.

The owner had flair, furnishing it tastefully, with charcoal-grey couch and armchairs, a russet-toned woollen rug that almost filled the open-plan living space, one wall lined with bookshelves, matching wooden dining and coffee tables, and a huge king-sized bed in the main bedroom. He used the second bedroom as an office, although he usually ended up working on his laptop in the living-room, often with the flat-screen TV on in the background, tuned to a news channel.

He ground some coffee beans, loaded up the espresso machine and made himself a double, nice and creamy on top, just the way he liked it. It was amazing how plain coffee and water came out looking like a mini-cappuccino.

Back to the couch. He was starting to feel better. Taking action, that was the key. Marnie was right. Maybe he'd even go to the gym tomorrow if he managed to get some sleep tonight.

He couldn't think of any other leads for his list, so he opened up his laptop and sat back, sipping his coffee while the computer booted up. He would browse the MIT faculty page and see what he could find.

He could do this. He was determined to find out what happened. And Jed was working on that other thing, so they might have some answers soon.

He was just about to pull up the MIT website when his phone rang.

9

February 1989

I'm going to go mad if I'm in here much longer, Francesca thought. Being stuck in a lead-lined $3m^3$ box for three whole days was sheer hell. The very idea of her being in a box made her laugh. Could there be anyone on the planet *less* conventional than her? She knew it was for her own good and a necessary part of their experiments. But that didn't make it any easier, and it felt like a waste of precious time.

The first day was always the worst, getting her mind to calm down and adjust to the stillness. Her brain was always working, calculating, calibrating, exploring all the angles, testing theories and equations. That was okay. It was extrapolating with her imagination that she had to avoid. That was when stuff happened that she hadn't yet managed to control. If this equalled that, which led to something else, *then* what might be possible? So she had to restrict herself to calculations and theories without allowing herself to imagine where they might lead.

She sometimes did some push-ups and a few yoga movements, but her heart wasn't in it and she usually found herself seated again, having barely broken a sweat and not even remembering having stopped, her mind already working out some other permutation of whatever experiment she had been doing. She often spent the whole day working out a complex equation in her head.

She got excited about testing her ideas in the lab, and then had to calm herself down all over again, flatten out her brainwaves and create a more peaceful, theta state of mind. She could make notes in her pad, but the light from her flashlight fired neural signals in her brain that got her more animated again. So she learned how to write things down in the dark and could usually manage to read her overlapping scrawl when she came out. She often forgot to eat, even though Daniel made sure she had enough food in there to feed a small African nation for a month.

Mental calisthenics were much more interesting than any physical workout, although Daniel kept telling her she needed to get out more, go for a walk, take some deep breaths, defuse some of that mental energy, spend time in nature—*act like a normal human being*, in other words.

By Day 2, she had calmed down a bit and was able to still her mind for as much as ten minutes at a time …before another brainwave hit. The problem with being in The Cube was that it was pitch black. No light at all, although she could switch on her little battery-powered flashlight when she wanted to eat. The absence of distractions provided her brain with an excellent blank canvas on which to project its ideas. So it was difficult to switch off completely, although that was one of the main reasons for doing this. And it was hard to sleep, since it was effectively nighttime for three days straight. She did still need to sleep—*to give your brain a rest,* Daniel insisted—but that was when she got her most inspired ideas.

By Day 3, she felt almost serene. She could keep her brain in a state of relative peace and stillness for an hour at a time, sometimes even two, minimizing the mental workout. There was just the soft hiss of air coming in via the ventilation system, and a faint earthy smell from her composting toilet. Couldn't manage without *that*.

This was when she could allow herself to daydream again. She knew Daniel would be monitoring the effects through the sensors feeding into The Cube, charting the electromagnetic fields that she generated.

She remembered the first time she stayed in The Cube, and how claustrophobic she felt—like being buried alive. That was shortly after she began having The Splits, which opened up a whole new set of parameters in their research. She'd had to learn to meditate and quieten her over-active mind in order to retain her sanity. Ha. As if.

You need to take this seriously, Frannie, Daniel had told her. *If you don't calm down your brain, you're going to do some permanent damage and we won't be able to continue.*

With their research, he meant. Or had he meant their marriage? Didn't matter. It was essentially the same thing. She'd grudgingly conceded and told him she'd be good. He snorted, not believing her, of course.

But he knew that dangling the research *hook* always got her cooperation and brought her back from the brink. Their research was everything. Without that… well, nothing could ever jeopardise it.

The work they were doing was beyond the pale and could take years to complete. Almost certainly would. But it didn't matter how long it took. They had to do it. *Had to.*

This will be the last time, Daniel had reassured her as she was preparing to enter The Cube. After this, he said, they would have enough data to proceed with the next phase. It would be worth it.

He did a silly ritual before she went inside, despite all her protests, arm-folding, frowns and exaggerated sighs. He ran his hand down her spine (*to down-regulate your nervous system*, he said), tapped her skull with his fingertips (*to calm down that phenomenal brain*), then kissed her passionately. Opening the door to The Cube, he bent low in an exaggerated bow, sweeping the floor with his hand. "My gorgeous, sexy, brilliant, stubborn, feisty, can-do, fierce-warrior woman, go forth and incubate!"

She rolled her eyes. "No way, in Cube *eight*," she said. "Only in Cube *three*."

He laughed and in she went. The kiss lingered, distracting her for a while. Not that she needed it. The kiss. Or him. Or anyone. Ever. But still.

10

Saturday, 26 October 2019

Marnie wasn't making much progress. She'd spent all day Friday trying to track down her mother's former college roommate, Deborah, calling MIT to find out how to access their records for alumni renting rooms in the early 1980s. She'd given her mother's name and was hopeful she could find the roommate's full name, but no joy so far.

But she came to my mother's funeral, she told the archives assistant. Surely that would penetrate the woman's administrative armour. Nope. She'd have to come into the office in person and provide some ID to prove she was her mother's daughter.

Fine. Okay. She'd find some way to get in there next week after school. She couldn't understand how she represented a security threat to the college. What on earth could be the harm in giving out that kind of information? *Some people didn't want to be contacted,* the assistant had told her, *and we must respect their privacy.*

Now, at 10am on Saturday, she was going to call her ex-boyfriend Steve to see if he knew what those numbers meant. She flicked through her address book and found his number.

She dialed, took a deep breath and sat back on the couch, her notepad on her lap.

He answered on the third ring. "Is this the elusive Ms Marnie?"

Ah. Call display.

"Hi, Steve. Yes, it's me." She remembered too late that she had dodged his calls for weeks before they actually broke up. And here she was asking for a favour…

"How are you?"

"Excellent. And you? Don't tell me you're calling to accept my marriage proposal after all this time."

She laughed. He had always been a funny guy, full of confidence and never one to hold a grudge. She admired that about him.

"I don't remember you asking me to marry you," she said, a smile in her voice.

"Girl, you just weren't listening. I must have asked you a hundred different ways." He laughed. "But if that's not why you're calling, then what on earth can it be?"

"I wanted to pick your phenomenal mathematical brain," Marnie said.

"Flattery will get you everywhere, girl, although it never worked with you." He paused. "What do you want to know?"

"It's to do with some numbers. I'd like to know if they have some kind of special significance. I remember you being very knowledgeable about numerology."

There was silence for a moment as Steve digested this.

"I get the feeling this is important to you," he said finally. "Am I right?"

"Yes. Maybe. I'm not sure," Marnie said. Would it feel awkward meeting up? Was this a good idea? She didn't want to get back into old stuff with Steve… and he seemed to be reading her mind, like he used to, which had always unnerved her.

"Look, Marnie, I know we're just friends, so you don't need to worry. But I'm happy to help if I can."

"My parents died a month ago," Marnie blurted out, realizing it was the first time she had actually said those words out loud. Her two closest friends, Millie Giordano and DeeDee Melina, had been away when her parents had died in September, but DeeDee had read the death notice in the paper and told Millie, and both of them had called Marnie straight away. So she hadn't actually had to say those words…

She hadn't even told the school principal or the other teachers at her school, although they must have seen the notice in the paper, too. If they had, they were respecting her privacy, allowing her to tell them in her own time.

"Marnie, I'm so sorry. I had no idea." She could hear some movement in the background, a chair being pulled out as Steve sat down. "What happened? Were they ill? Was it an accident?"

"No… nothing like that." Marnie didn't know what to say. How on earth did you explain something that you didn't understand yourself?

"Steve, they… they took their own lives and we have no idea why."

Marnie's heart lurched. She could feel it jumping around in her chest, pumping the tears uphill to her eyes, determined to make its feelings felt.

"My God, Marnie. You must be in bits." Steve was quiet for a moment. "Look, we should meet up, then you can tell me how I can help. Yes?"

"Yes." It was all she could manage.

"See you in the Mirror at 4pm?" That had been his standard joke when they were a couple. Café Mirror had been one of their favourite haunts, and it was only a short walk from where Marnie lived in Boston's Brighton neighbourhood. He was making things easy for her.

"That work for you, Ms Marnie?"

"Yes."

She needed to hang up and get rid of the lump in her throat, and she couldn't see a thing, even if she'd wanted to take notes.

"Thank you, Steve. I appreciate... you." His warmth and concern were melting her defences and reconnecting her with the pain. So much still in there.

"No worries, girl. I'm glad you reached out. I know how hard it is for you to ask for help. Hang in there and I'll see you this afternoon."

Marnie headed straight for the bathroom after she hung up. She was going to soak in a hot bath for the next hour, at least. She needed to soothe her nerves and relax her body. She felt jumpy and jerky, anxiety and grief doing a jig in her gut. And just a tiny tremor of excitement at the thought of seeing Steve again.

She poured some jasmine oil into the hot water, peeled off her clothes and sank into the heavenly warmth. She was going to lie here till her skin went pruney, then she was going to go to bed and read a book until it was time to meet Steve.

11

Steve had got there before her and he waved to her from a table at the back, by the window. Café Mirror was an unpretentious place with all-day breakfasts and very basic fare, but they did good coffees and teas.

Steve stood up as she approached, looking even better than she remembered him. Tall, rangy and ruggedly good-looking, with dark-brown hair and amber eyes, Steve Romero was a southern boy, raised in Georgia in a large family where hugs and get-togethers were a common occurrence. She had always envied him that close family connectedness.

"Marnie." He reached out his arms for a hug and she accepted gratefully.

"You look tired but lovely. What a hell of a time you must be having."

She smiled and sat down opposite him, shrugging off her coat.

"Tea, right?"

"Yes, but I can—"

He held up a hand. "No. Sit. I'll go."

She nodded, smiling, and he went to get it for her.

She pulled out her notes with all the numbers. Was she wasting her time—and rekindling something that was best left in the past? There had been good reasons for ending their relationship, after all. Right now, she couldn't remember what they were but she knew they had both tried hard to make things work.

"Here you go." Steve placed a mug of tea in front of her, a coffee for himself, and slid back into his seat.

"Marnie, I'm so sorry. I can't imagine what the three of you must be going through."

"Thanks. It's been…" She didn't have the words for it.

"Listen…" Steve reached for her hand and covered it with his. *Please don't,* Marnie thought. *Let's not go there.*

"I want you to know that you have my support, no strings attached, okay? I need you to know that so you can relax."

He looked at her, gauging her reaction. "I've changed, Marnie—and that's *not* a hook to get you back." He paused. "You remember my sister, Josie?"

She did. Josie was ten years older than Steve and very much his older sister. She was also very wise and big-hearted and Marnie had liked her a lot.

"Well, Josie made me promise to tell you this if you and I ever talked again," Steve said, looking a little uncomfortable. "I learned a lot about myself, thanks to our short time together. That may sound like a corny come-on, but it's the simple truth. So, I'm happy to be your friend."

He smiled at her. "So you can relax, girl. Okay?"

She smiled and nodded gratefully, taking a sip of tea. Steve called all females *girl*—even his 92-year-old grandmother—although Josie didn't always let him get away with it. "Don't you *girl* me," she used to say. "I'm your older, super-smart sister, and don't you ever forget it." But you could tell she loved him to bits.

Steve gestured at her notes. "Why don't you show me what you've got."

Marnie slid her notes across the table and Steve sat back, reading without comment for almost five minutes.

"Fascinating," he said, handing her back her notes. "I can see why you might have questions." He took a swig of coffee. "How much do you remember from our conversations about this?"

"Not much," Marnie admitted, "although I browsed some sites online about those three numbers."

She thought for a minute about what she'd read.

"My birth number is 3, which relates to creativity, although that's more Lucy's style than mine. Matt's is 6, which is about harmony, balance and security within the home. But *I'm* the responsible, care-taking one."

She laughed. "And Lucy's is 9, which is about wisdom, responsibility and serving humanity, although that doesn't seem to apply to her—not yet, anyway. So, the numbers don't seem accurate at all... although, between us, we seem to have many of those qualities."

Steve nodded, waiting for her to finish.

"Certain numbers are supposed to mean certain things about our individual personalities and even the particular path or career we might take in life. And numbers seem to relate to astrology and other esoteric sciences. But I can't see how they help me in my own life, in practical terms. I mean, how does it help me to know that my birthdate adds up to a number that is supposed to give me certain personality traits or qualities? How does knowing that change me or my life?"

"I hear you," Steve said. "Let's back up a bit and zoom out for a sec. Remember, though, I'm not an expert in numerology *per se*, although some say that mathematicians *are* numerologists, since we deal in numbers all the time. Here, though"—he pointed to her notes—"we're talking about a more existential or cosmic interpretation of numbers."

He paused to reflect. "Numerology is the study of numbers and they say you can discover things about yourself and the world by identifying your personal or life numbers and working with them—the way some people read their horoscope and see it as significant if it relates to their life. With me so far?"

"Yes, of course. I get the theory."

"Well, that's the simple part." He smiled. "The whole universe is governed by numbers. Think of sacred geometry, the patterns in nature, the Phi ratio, the Fibonacci spiral. It's all based on numbers. So you could say that the universe came into being as a result of numbers—or sound, as some would say, but that's based on numbers, too, so it all comes down to the fundamental elements, which are made up numbers."

He looked at Marnie. "Still with me?"

"Yes," Marnie said, smiling. "I think my brain can just about keep up."

"Everything in the universe has an energy vibration, including numbers. So, in numerology, every number and every letter has its own unique vibration that has an influence on the story of your life."

"But how?" Marnie said. "That's the part I don't get."

"Well, if everything is energy and if different numbers and letters have different vibrations, then they are bound to have different effects—just as certain vibrations have a healing effect or can even shatter glass, for example, if used in the right way."

He took another sip of coffee. Marnie could see that he was warming to his subject and enjoying himself.

"Think about music, for example," he said. "Music has been used for eons to heal, transport, uplift and unite people, or to generate aggression. It has a profound effect on the mind, the psyche and our brainwaves."

"Yes, of course," said Marnie, thinking about how playing certain kinds of music had often changed her mood or triggered powerful emotions.

Steve was on a roll. "Tuning forks, which were previously used to tune musical instruments, are now being used to heal and create certain physical and emotional effects on people. So the vibrational effect is very real."

"That makes sense," Marnie said, suddenly thinking of her friend Millie Giordano. Millie was a therapist who worked with tuning forks and crystal bowls, and she was currently in California doing some additional training in sound therapy. In her e-mails to Marnie, she'd said she was getting amazing results with her clients, and Marnie was looking forward to having a session with her when Millie got back in January.

"Think about some of the vibrational frequencies in music, sound and chanting," Steve was saying. "Some of those frequencies were considered to be sacred, capable of causing raptures, ecstasy and even miracles. You've heard of Gregorian chants?"

Marnie nodded again.

"Well, in earlier times, chants with certain frequencies were used in religious ceremonies, to powerful effect, but then the Church suppressed much of the ancient wisdom around those frequencies because it didn't want its followers to have that kind power. It wanted to control them and keep them subservient."

He took a sip of coffee.

"But the knowledge survived and those same frequencies are now used in tuning forks, chanting, crystal bowls, steel-tongue drums, metal xylophones and other instruments capable of generating the same kind of powerful resonance."

Steve pointed to Marnie's notes on the table between them.

"There's a set of nine tuning forks based on the numbers 3–6–9, reproducing those supposedly sacred frequencies, based on what was called the sacred Solfeggio scale. The frequencies all add up to 3, 6 or 9, using that ancient Pythagorean method of reducing the numbers down to their single digit integers—as you did with all those birth dates."

Steve tapped her notes.

"The frequencies of those nine tuning forks range from 174Hz to 963Hz, each of them creating different effects, but all of them adding up to a 3, 6 or 9."

He looked at Marnie again.

"Still with me?"

She nodded, still not sure where this was going.

"The frequency 396Hz, for example, is supposed to release feelings of guilt, which often gets in the way of people realizing their full potential. It can also be used as a means of grounding the body, awakening the self and connecting self to reality."

He looked at her. "Here's one that might interest you, given your awareness of wireless radiation," he said. "Using the tuning fork with the frequency 741Hz, which adds up to a 3, is supposed to help remove different kinds of electromagnetic radiation from the body's cells. It also clears out other toxins and can help fight viral, bacterial and fungal infections."

He paused. "Is this too much? Am I boring you?"

"No! It's fascinating." Marnie gestured for him to continue. She was wondering if Millie used these same forks or something else.

"Then there's the 639Hz frequency, which promotes harmonious community and relationships, and can also be used to encourage our body's cells to communicate with its environment. So, it enhances communication, understanding, tolerance and love. The 639Hz frequency can also be used for communicating with parallel worlds or spiritual spheres." He shrugged. "Esoteric stuff, but nonetheless very real."

He gestured at her tea. "Another one?"

"No. Thanks."

"Okay, then, I'll make this the last one in case I push you over the edge," he said, smiling. "The 963Hz frequency is supposed to take the body's system back to its original perfect state. It facilitates direct experience of oneness and the unified energy field that makes up the cosmos and connects us all. It's what some spiritual teachers call *unity consciousness*."

He paused to let Marnie digest this. It was not at all what she had expected Steve to talk about and she still couldn't see how this could possibly relate to her current situation.

"What does all this have to do with what my parents did, if anything?" she asked.

"Well, there could be any number—sorry, no pun intended—any number of possibilities," Steve said. "But think about who they were …both physicists, right?" Steve was looking off into the distance, pondering. "If we take the three numbers together—369—that creates a mix of energies of the individual numbers. As a blend, the number 369 symbolizes care and providing for others, especially family members. It also symbolizes philanthropy and love for humanity."

He paused to let that sink in.

"So maybe your parents were working on something that had significance for humanity, or maybe the three of you or one of you will do something that helps humanity. Whatever it is, you're all in this together, somehow."

Marnie nodded, digesting this.

"Could it mean nothing at all? Could all those 3, 6, 9s of our birthdates and other dates be pure coincidence?" She wasn't sure that numbers could really influence her life.

"Well, given how those three numbers occur in all of your birthdates and other key dates, I'd say that's more than coincidence," said Steve. "And I'm guessing you think so too, or we wouldn't be having this conversation."

He leaned back in his chair, spreading his hands. "But whether they explain what happened with your parents…? I can't say how exactly they might be connected. I do trust the numbers, though, and I get the sense that there's more going on than you or I may ever know."

Marnie sat quietly for a moment, thinking.

"Do you know what they were working on before they died?" Steve asked.

"I know they worked with electromagnetism or electromagnetic fields…" She paused, suddenly remembering something. At home, when she was in her early teens, she had sometimes heard a hum or felt strong vibrations coming from the lab in the basement, beneath the kitchen. She had always thought it was some machinery running in the lab, or maybe some music her parents were playing on the radio while they worked. Now she wondered if it somehow related to certain frequencies or sounds they were working with…

She shook her head. She would never know.

"Other than that, though, I have no idea," Marnie said. "I wish I did. It's driving me mad not knowing, and I keep imagining all kinds of horrible scenarios that would have caused them to do what they did."

"Do you feel guilty or somehow responsible?"

"No. Yes. Maybe a little." Marnie was surprised to realize that this might be the case. *Damn. Did he know her better than she knew herself?*

"It's normal, Marnie. You're a survivor, in a sense, and you're bound to feel guilty for not having seen what was going on for them or for not having helped them or somehow saved them from such desperate measures."

"I know. You're right. I keep thinking I should have seen the signs, though. I should have known something was wrong, you know?" Marnie felt tears threatening again. "How could I not have *known*, Steve?"

"Maybe you weren't meant to know, Marnie," he said gently, leaning towards her. "Has it occurred to you that they might have had a very good reason for doing what they did but you just don't know yet what it is—and may never know?"

"I've thought about that," Marnie said, "but every trace of them seems to have been intentionally erased, to stop us from finding out what they were working on or why they did this."

Steve nodded, looking thoughtful. "Have you heard of the multiverse theory?"

"What? No, I don't think so." Steve was trying to distract her, take her mind off her grief.

"The multiverse theory has been put forward by certain scientists who claim there's an infinite number of parallel universes, all existing at the same time."

"O-kaaay," Marnie said, not sure where this was going. She was feeling skeptical again.

"Some numerologists agree, seeing our world as part of an infinite cosmos in which the magical power of numbers could have impacts throughout those parallel universes."

Steve smiled at her puzzled expression. "Bear with me," he said. "Some believe that the power of numbers expresses itself by influencing the environments people are in and the decisions they make, which lead them to exist in one zone of the multiverse rather than another."

Marnie was starting to get exasperated.

"So," Steve said, "what I'm getting at is that we don't really know what's possible, although the more we discover, through quantum physics and other emerging sciences, the more we realize that really *anything* is possible. We just haven't yet figured out what *is* possible. And maybe our brains are only able to grasp so much at any one time, Marnie, and we have to discover things in small chunks so as not to blow our circuits."

Marnie nodded. Now she understood what he was getting at. There might be more for her to discover about herself, her family or the universe, but she had to let things unfold naturally, without forcing them, and wait for more insights to come, if they ever did. *But wasn't that how life worked anyway? How the heck did this help?*

"You know, Nikola Tesla is famous for saying that the numbers 3–6–9 held the keys to the universe. I don't know if he was right or what exactly he meant, but he did lots of experiments with vibration, which is sound, which is also numbers, and he claimed that vibration could do anything, provided you knew the required frequency to create a certain effect. If you wanted to understand the universe, he said, think in terms of energy, frequency and vibration."

Marnie realized she had been holding herself rigid, waiting for some kind of revelation that would make sense of things. But there was no big *aha*. What had she expected? That Steve would figure this out for her?

She forced herself to relax and felt her shoulders finally coming down from around her ears. Steve's words were seeping into her psyche, providing some context, if not some answers. She needed to stay open and not be so skeptical about everything just because it didn't initially make sense. She now had a better understanding of the power of those numbers, which made the issue a bit more interesting than before, when they had talked about it in the abstract. But she still wasn't convinced. She needed to go home and process all this information.

"We are bathed in multiple frequencies all the time," Steve said, gesturing around the café. "WiFi, cellphones, light, sound, electricity, the Earth's frequency, our own body's frequencies—they all have numbers attached to them, depending on where they are on the electromagnetic spectrum. And they all affect us, on some level, whether we feel them physically or not."

Marnie nodded again.

Steve was watching her absorb the information, and she felt a wave of tenderness and gratitude for his concern and support.

"Steve," she said, reaching for his hand. "You are a good man and I'm grateful to still have you as a friend." Touched by her own sincerity, she felt the tears welling up again.

"Come here, girl," Steve said, getting out of his chair and reaching out to her for another hug.

She got up and allowed herself to sink into his embrace, feeling the strength in his arms around her, the solid wall of his chest and the steady thumping of his heart. Reassuring signs of life.

He stepped back, holding her at arm's length. "We can meet up again in a week or so, if that would help," he said. "Think about what we've discussed and see if anything else comes to mind about your parents' work. Knowing you, girl, I'm guessing you'll have more questions."

"Thank you, Steve. Let's see how things… go."

He helped her into her coat and she turned and walked quickly through the café and out onto the street.

12

Sunday, 27 October 2019

Marnie was dreaming. She was on a beach in Mexico, walking along the hot white sand with her mother. It was just the two of them. No one else for miles. Her mother was wearing a floppy white sunhat and a flowing white linen shirt, but she was carrying her white alarm clock— or was it a compass? Marnie kept trying to talk to her but her mother just looked at her clock/compass, then looked at the sky, nodding to herself and then walking on.

Thunder clapped in the distance. But Marnie saw no clouds in the sky, just endless blue. *How could there be thunder?*

Slowly, she emerged from the dream and realized someone was hammering on her front door. She looked at her clock: 8am. Who on earth could it be, so early on a Sunday morning? Lucy had gone to spend the night with the Carpenters, so it couldn't be her. Anyway, she had her own key.

She eased herself out of bed, miffed at being disturbed during her one lie-in of the week. Pulling on her robe, she padded to the front door. She was just about to look through the peephole, when she heard Matt's voice through the door.

"Marnie! Let me in. Please!"

She slid back the deadbolt and opened the door. Her brother staggered through the doorway and clutched her arm, his eyes wild and bloodshot.

"Marn, he's dead and it's all my fault!"

"What? Dad, you mean?" *Was their father's death only hitting him now?*

"Matt, it's not your fault. It's—"

"Jed! He's dead! Jed! A hit and run. Because of me!" Matt dissolved into shuddering sobs, sliding down the doorframe and doubling over on the floor.

"What?" Marnie was too stunned to think. She had never seen her brother fall apart like this. She felt her knees go weak and the blood drain from her head. She knelt down and gripped Matt's arms.

"Come and sit down and tell me what happened."

He sat there, shaking his head, fat tears making dark polka dots on his denim jeans.

"Come on." She pulled him up and they stumbled to the couch where Matt curled into a ball again and sobbed like a baby.

Marnie hurried into the kitchen and took out the bottle of brandy she kept in her cupboard for medicinal purposes. Matt used to tease her about it. Yeah, yeah. We all know that one—*medicinal purposes.* With Marnie, though, it really was for medicinal purposes and it was exactly what was needed right now.

She got a glass and poured Matt a good two inches.

"Here, drink this." She held it to his lips and he took a gulp, then another one.

"Breathe," she said, rubbing his back and holding him against her. He took another noisy gulp of brandy and passed her the empty glass.

She leaned forward to put it on the coffee table.

"Now," she said, "tell me what happened."

In fits and starts, punctuated by sobs and ragged breaths, Matt told her.

Jed had called him yesterday to tell him he'd found some information about MLM Holdings—the shell company. Matt had been excited and asked him to explain, but Jed said he'd prefer to do it in person. He had sounded very agitated and said he'd bike over to Matt's place with his laptop to show him what he'd found. He'd be there in 15 minutes.

An hour later, Jed still had not shown up and Matt was starting to get concerned. He called Jed several times on his cellphone but got no answer. Finally, after waiting another hour, he decided to bike to Jed's place, taking the route he knew his friend normally took. Halfway there, he came to what looked like the scene of an accident, with a crowd of people standing around talking, some looking shocked, some curious. A police car was parked on the kerb and an ambulance blocked the street. Matt arrived just as the paramedics were loading a body onto a gurney …in a closed body bag.

He ran up to them and asked them what had happened, grabbing one guy by the arm.

"Please," he said, "I'm looking for my friend! He was coming to see me on his bike and never showed…"

The paramedic looked at him sympathetically. A guy on a bike had been hit by a speeding car that hadn't stopped, he said. It was a hit-and-run, and the biker had been killed. A tall, young guy, short dark hair and…

With a sickening jolt, Matt knew it was Jed. His friend since high school—*dead, because of him.* He turned and saw Jed's mangled bike on the side of the road. There was no sign of the knapsack he used to carry his laptop. He turned back to the paramedic and asked him if he'd taken his friend's knapsack with him in the ambulance. He had nothing on him but his wallet, the guy told him. He suggested Matt talk to the police, pointing to two officers talking to witnesses on the sidewalk and taking down their names.

But Matt felt so sick he could hardly stand, and he staggered back to his bike and used it like a crutch as he walked home.

He'd taken three sleeping pills and gone to bed, unable to cope with what had happened.

"It's all my fault, Marnie." Matt started sobbing again. "If I hadn't asked Jed to look into that company for me, he'd still be alive."

Marnie did the only thing she could do. She held her brother in her arms and let him cry himself out. Slowly, his breathing steadied and she felt him slump against her, asleep. She lowered him down onto the couch, lifted up his legs and put a cushion under his head. She got a blanket from her bedroom closet and covered him tenderly.

There was no way she could go back to bed after this. She sat on the floor beside her brother, draping one arm over his shoulders, and let her head drop onto the couch.

Two hours later, the sound of Lucy's key in the lock roused her. She got up slowly, her legs aching and her buttocks almost numb from sitting on the floor for so long.

As she went to the door to greet Lucy, she put her fingers to her lips and pointed towards Matt on the couch. Lucy nodded, put down her overnight case and took off her coat.

"Put your stuff away," Marnie said quietly, "then come and have some tea with me in the kitchen."

When Lucy came back, closing the kitchen door quietly behind her, Marnie had the kettle boiling and a pot of chai tea ready to brew. She poured the water over the leaves and put the pot on the table. Lucy took two mugs from the mug tree on the countertop and they sat down.

"What happened?" she said.

Marnie told her and Lucy sat, stunned, not knowing what to say.

"Marn, what's *happening* to us? All these tragedies!"

"I don't know, Luce. Accidents happen. Jed was unlucky."

Lucy poured them both some tea and sat back, thinking.

"Do you really believe that? That it's just an accident?"

"What do you mean? What else could it be?" Marnie looked at her sister. "Some random car ran him down and the driver probably freaked out and took off."

"I don't know," Lucy said, shaking her head. "This doesn't feel right. It just seems very strange that Jed would be… killed when he was on his way to give Matt some insider information about that secretive company."

"I think you're reading too much into it," Marnie said. "How could those two things possibly be connected? No one else knew that Jed was looking into that company."

Lucy took a slurp of tea. "Look, I know what you're probably going to say, Marn, but could this have something to do with Mum and Dad? We still don't know why they did what they did, right?"

"True, but…"

"Well, maybe they were involved with gangsters and owed them money or something for their research. But they couldn't pay it back and wanted to protect us, so they checked out. Then the bad guys needed to stop us from finding out about them, so they killed Jed…"

She looked at Marnie hopefully.

"It's an interesting theory, Luce, but I just can't see it, can you? Mum and Dad getting involved with *gangsters*?"

"No, I guess not," Lucy admitted. "But it still doesn't feel right."

"We need to think about how we can support Matt through this. He was already a mess over Mum and Dad. I'm afraid this is going to push him over the edge."

Marnie felt drained. She needed to look after herself, too, and her apartment was starting to feel like a halfway house for wounded souls.

"We can't let him go back to his place," Lucy said. "He can take the guest room and I'll sleep on a mattress in your bedroom, Marn, or on the couch. I don't mind. Just for a few days, so we know he's okay and isn't going to, you know, do anything stupid."

"Good idea," Marnie said, getting up to put her mug in the sink. "We may need to take him to a doctor and get some medication to get him through this."

She looked at her sister. "I haven't even asked about your visit to Maisie and Doug's. How was it?"

"Good, thanks," Lucy said, smiling briefly. "They couldn't have been nicer. We walked the dogs, tried out some new recipes and talked about normal, everyday stuff. Oh, and Maisie gave me some of her chicken casserole for us to have this evening."

She sighed. "But now this. Do you think things will ever be normal for us again, Marn?"

"Probably not, Luce. We're just going to have to create our own new normal and do the best we can with that."

13

July 1994

Francesca's episodes had long since morphed into something else entirely, but it took her and Daniel a while to figure things out. She hadn't been able to hide them from him for long, given how much time they spent together. But it didn't seem to change the way he felt about her, as she had anticipated. In fact, he became intrigued by the syndrome and did all kinds of research to see if he could identify what it was. It wasn't epilepsy, some kind of psychotic break from reality or any of the other conditions he found in the medical literature.

For several years, she continued to have the same strange

disembodied feeling—sometimes stronger and lasting longer, sometimes not appearing for up to a month. There was no apparent pattern or frequency to it.

Then came The Splits—her *disappearances.* The first time, she was sitting at the kitchen table, drinking coffee, mulling over some phenomenon she was exploring downstairs in the lab. One minute she was there; the next, she was gone, leaving just her coffee mug lying sideways on the table, the remainder of her coffee dripping onto the floor.

Daniel freaked out. *Where did you go? I couldn't find you. Don't ever do that to me again, Frannie.*

He had been down in the lab when she'd *split,* so he thought she had left the house without telling him. She had apparently left this *dimension,* but he had no way of knowing that. The front door was still locked from the inside, her keys were still on the dresser in the hallway, her coats and boots were all there, so he was worried that something had happened to her somewhere in the house and she couldn't call for help. He had searched every inch of the place for almost two hours.

She hadn't done anything to make it happen, as far as she was aware. She re-appeared about three hours later, back in the kitchen, sitting on the chair, picking up where she'd left off …except her coffee was gone and Daniel had put the mug in the dishwasher.

She felt dazed and disoriented, unsure of who or where she was. It was as if she'd got stuck in limbo between two worlds, with no awareness or memory of where she had been, as if she had ceased to exist for an indefinable time out of time.

She finally figured out that it happened whenever she let her imagination run wild, envisioning how some aspect of quantum or particle physics might ultimately translate into physical changes in the material world.

Daniel did some tests to track which part of her brain fired up when she got creative, pondering possibilities. But it wasn't enough. He couldn't see what was happening when she was in that state or how her brainwaves might interact with her external environment. Even with a functional MRI scanner, they couldn't tell enough about what exactly was going on inside her brain.

So he developed a more sophisticated and sensitive version of an oscilloscope, for detecting body voltages, subtle vibrations and electromagnetic fields emanating from the body and brain. When Francesca had first used The Cube, it was merely to isolate her from external manmade electromagnetic fields, to see if her own human electromagnetic energy were somehow interacting with them.

It was only when they hooked up the sensors to the *Franwave,* as they called it, that they began to understand what was happening. Her neocortex and thalamus—the parts of the brain that controlled imagination, consciousness and abstract thought—were extremely sensitive, reacting to neurological stimuli in a way that lit up her whole brain and generated powerful electromagnetic waves and vibrations.

Somehow, this translated into her accessing an altered state in an alternative reality, transporting her to some other dimension and then spontaneously bringing her back.

Their research took yet another fascinating turn.

Then they got some test results that changed things all over again.

Daniel was cooking eggs in the kitchen when Francesca came in to tell him. "I'm getting a positive on a test I was running this morning," she said.

"Great! Which test?"

"This one," she said, holding up the plastic indicator for him to see. "I'm pregnant."

14

Friday, 1 November 2019

The kids seemed to be fractious today. Marnie wasn't sure if it was her mood influencing theirs or theirs influencing hers. Probably a bit of both.

It was Friday, normally Marnie's day off, but the student teacher had called the Principal's office at 8am to say her car had broken down and she couldn't make it to class in time. So Leslie, the Principal, had called Marnie and asked her to come in. She could hardly refuse, since she was being paid for the full week, but she treasured her Friday mornings and resented having to come in unexpectedly.

Plus, she had a lot on her mind. Matt still in a state of shock, Lucy fielding calls from his very irate girlfriend, Celle—soon to be *ex-girlfriend*, undoubtedly—and the pressure of all three of them living together in her small apartment.

When Marnie had arrived this morning, 15 minutes before school began, Leslie had popped her head around the staffroom door and asked Marnie to come to her office for a quick chat.

Leslie Vauxhall was in her mid-30s—a trim, energetic woman with jet-black hair cut in a pixie style that accentuated her penetrating eyes. Marnie always felt as if those eyes could see right through you, and she found them piercingly disconcerting. Such untainted sparkling sapphire spheres had no right to be shining so luminously from an adult head.

Leslie was known for her temper. But she was usually very fair and considerate towards the kids and teachers, and Marnie respected her decency. She was a welcome buffer between herself and the parents, who often had unreasonable expectations for their children. Some were downright rude and demanding, although Marnie usually managed to calm them down and get them to see reason, whenever they approached her directly.

The door to Leslie's office was ajar and Marnie knocked before entering.

"Marnie! Come in." Leslie waved to the chair opposite her desk and Marnie sat down.

"Good morning, Leslie," she said.

"I'm sorry you had to come in today, Marnie. I'd have stepped in myself but I have meetings all morning." She paused. "I heard about your parents. I'm very sorry for your loss, Marnie. If you had told me, I would have insisted you take some time off. It's difficult to find replacements at short notice, as you know, but this is an exceptional situation and I can't imagine how you are coping."

"Thank you, Leslie."

"I know you took a few days' sick leave last month, but you are entitled to compassionate leave, in a case like this." Leslie leaned towards her with a searching look. "How *are* you coping, Marnie, if I may ask?"

Marnie hesitated before answering. Those eyes were very disconcerting. *Could Leslie see that she was barely holding it together? Steve had kind eyes… she'd never really been aware of them before…*

"Marnie?"

Focus, Marnie. Get a grip. "I'm okay, Leslie, thanks. It's a challenging time, but…" She trailed off, not sure that she *was* coping.

"Look, I imagine having Fridays off helps a little, yes?"

"Yes, very much," Marnie said. "My younger siblings, you know…"

"Yes, of course. You need to help each other through this." Leslie nodded her understanding. "Anyway, Alison just called to say she's on the road and will be here shortly to take your class, so you'll be able to head home in an hour or so."

Marnie wasn't sure if she was better off staying in school and keeping herself occupied or going home to deal with Matt and Lucy. Maybe she'd go somewhere for a quiet lunch on her own, and then take a walk in the park…

"Does that help?" Leslie was waiting for her to respond.

"Yes, of course. Thank you, Leslie. I really appreciate it."

"Okay, then. Good." Leslie paused. "If I can help with anything, Marnie, I hope you will ask. You are a valued and popular member of staff and we like to take care of our people."

Marnie thanked her again and shut the door quietly behind her as she left the office.

She headed for her classroom, relieved to be distracted by 20 noisy Fourth Graders for a while as she tried to collect herself.

The bell went just as she reached her desk and the kids were getting settled in their seats.

"Okay, everyone, settle down," she said. "Let's do roll call, then we're going to do a writing exercise.

Marnie had managed to keep laptops out of her classroom, having discussed with Leslie how much better it was for the kids to write things by hand. They learned differently and used different parts of their brains. Plus, they needed to be able to write, even if they only ever signed their names and used their laptops or cellphones for everything else. Cellphones were forbidden throughout the school, which made things a lot easier. For assignments or homework that required a computer, they used the laptops in the library.

"Where's Miss Marsh?" Sasha Rollins wanted to know.

"She'll be here shortly," Marnie said. "But I'm teaching you till she gets here."

She pulled out her attendance sheet and began calling out names.

"Isabelle Carson?"

"Here, Miss Dalton."

"Sebastian Finkerton?"

"Here."

"Miss?" Sasha again, with her hand up.

"What is it, Sasha? I'm taking roll call and you know you're not meant to interrupt unless it's urgent."

"But it's *about* roll call," Sasha said, insistently.

"What about it?" Marnie sighed. Sasha was a precocious 9-year-old who really belonged in a more advanced class to challenge her active brain. She was constantly asking questions, often disrupting things for the other kids. She was going to have to talk to Leslie about her.

"Why do you have to call my name if you know I'm here?" Sasha said. "Then I have to pretend you don't know I'm here and tell you I *am*. It's stupid."

Marnie couldn't fault the logic but she didn't have the patience for Sasha's questions today.

"Sasha, it's a school rule that all the teachers must do roll call to check that everyone's here." *If in doubt, blame the system.*

"But—"

"Yes, I know. It may not make much sense to you, but that's the way it is. Now, please let me finish."

"Matthew Lewiston?"

Silence

"He's sick, Miss Dalton," Sasha said. "He wasn't feeling well yesterday and I told him he should stay at home today."

"That's for his mother to decide, Sasha, but it was nice of you to be concerned for him."

She had to be patient and not let her delicate state affect her professionalism. One wrong word or move and the parents would be all over her. Sometimes, Marnie thought, teaching was a like a minefield, with every child capable of exploding or having a meltdown, depending on what was going on at home, if they were getting good grades or whether they had friends or were happy at school. Being a teacher involved so much more than teaching. She had to be a counsellor, a diplomat, a negotiator, and an ambassador for the school itself. All in the name of education.

She finished working through the names and turned to face the class.

"Today, we're going to work more on writing skills," she said. "Please open your exercise books to a clean page and write RECIPES at the top." She turned and wrote the word on the blackboard behind her.

"Think about the kinds of recipes you learn at home or you watch your mom or dad making."

"My mom never cooks," Jocelyn said, with a weary sigh. "We eat TV dinners watching TV and I listen to music on my iPhone. Since dad left, mom just drinks wine, so I don't think she's really interested in cooking."

"I help mum in the kitchen," Isabelle said. "But my dad is a better cook than my mom, although they sometimes fight about it."

"So we all have different experiences around food, and sometimes we have to learn recipes ourselves from a book, or maybe from a grandparent or friend," Marnie said. "But what *is* a recipe?"

Several female hands shot up.

"Savannah?"

"It's instructions for making something in the kitchen."

"Yes, very good. What kind of *something*, usually?"

"Something to eat. Cookies or bread or something for dinner."

"Correct. Let's look at some examples. Does anyone know how to make an omelet?"

Sasha's hand shot up.

"Yes, Sasha?"

"You break eggs into a bowl, beat them up, add some milk or cream, some salt, put oil in the pan, heat it up, then pour in the eggs and wait till they're cooked."

"Excellent. Thank you. So we see that there are usually two parts to a recipe: the *ingredients*, which are the things we put into whatever we are making, and the *method*, which is how we make it."

She wrote INGREDIENTS and METHOD on the board and paused to let that sink in.

"What about chocolate cake? Does anyone know a recipe for that?"

Isabelle raised a hesitant hand and Marnie nodded at her to share.

"My mom uses flour, sugar, eggs, cocoa powder and… something to make it go up like a sponge or like Brownies."

"That sounds very good, Isabelle. Thank you." She looked around the classroom. "Anyone know what you call that—the ingredient you use to make something rise when you're baking a cake?"

Marnie was surprised to see Sebastian's hand go up.

"Sebastian?"

"A rising agent," he said. "Like a secret agent," he added, grinning, "'cause you can't tell it's in there. You just see the result, making things puff up."

"Very good." Marnie laughed. "That's almost right. We actually call it a *raising* agent. Or a leavening agent. And we can use yeast or baking powder for that. Eggs can also help to make cakes rise."

She turned back to the board and wrote RECIPE FOR HAPPINESS. "Okay, so the assignment for today is for you to write your recipe for happiness."

Facing the class again, she said, "Think of the *ingredients* that you need for your happiness recipe and then think of the *method*—how those ingredients might work together. So, for example, some of the ingredients might be two good friends, a mom and dad and a brother or sister, your school, chocolate, sunshine, playing football, going on holidays, having a pet—that kind of thing."

She walked to the back of the room. "Any questions?"

Several unhappy faces turned towards her. "What if we don't have anything that makes us happy?" Brian wanted to know.

Marnie's heart sank. "Can you think of something that might make you happy? A new bike or something else you might dream about?"

Brian frowned, uncertain. "Maybe."

Stuart Smith was not so hesitant. "My dad says *nobody* is really happy, and if they say they are, they're just pretending."

Stuart often referred to his dad to back up his arguments, and Marnie had to tread carefully. Mr Smith was an enormous, aggressive man who looked like a nightclub bouncer, and he had challenged her a few times about being *too soft* and not teaching with a firmer hand. Marnie had no doubt that Mr Smith used a *very* firm hand at home, probably belting his son if he wasn't being manly enough. She imagined him teaching Stuart to use a gun when he was barely out of diapers, and taking him hunting at weekends.

"Sometimes it helps to stop and think about what we are grateful for in our lives," Marnie said, "even if it's just a pet or a friend."

"Yeah, but that's not enough to make someone *happy*."

"Well, see if you can figure out what *would* make you happy, Stuart. That's the whole point of the exercise. See what you're grateful for and what else you might like to have to feel happier."

Before Stuart could object further, Marnie said, "If you prefer, Stuart, you could write a recipe for *unhappiness*. You can choose."

She turned back to the class. "Okay, please work on your assignment now and I'll tell you when to stop. You've got ten minutes."

She walked over to Brian and leaned down. "See what you can come up with, Brian. Think about things you might like to do, even if you don't get to do them very often. Can you work on that?"

Marnie went back to her desk and looked around the room. Isabelle was chewing her pencil, looking pensive. Isabelle was extremely shy but had a gentle, sensitive nature that Marnie found endearing. She worried about what would happen to her when she reached her teens and was picked on for being *too nice*.

Marnie walked over to Isabelle and gently took the girl's pencil out of her mouth. She checked the clock above the blackboard: just after 10am. Alison would be here soon and she could leave.

Three minutes later, Sasha's hand shot up again. Marnie walked to the back of the room and bent down to hear what she had to say.

"That was *easy*," Sasha said. "I'm done. Now I'm bored."

"Then write something else. You still have five minutes left. Lots of time as you're so fast, right?"

"I write stuff all the time," Sasha said, sighing wearily. "I write in my journal every night and I write short stories on the bus going home. I'm tired of writing."

"Well, tell me what you wrote for your happiness recipe," Marnie said patiently. "It sounds as if writing is something you enjoy."

Sasha suddenly looked very much like the little 9-year-old that she was. It was the first time Marnie had seen her appear shy, as if revealing what made her happy was a deeply private, personal thing. Maybe it was, Marnie realized. She hadn't stopped to consider what made *her* happy, although she probably wouldn't want to share those thoughts with just anyone, whatever they were. And she was beginning to wonder if this exercise only deepened whatever unhappiness the kids felt, causing them to acknowledge what was missing in their lives, rather than it making them feel better.

She hunkered down beside Sasha again. "Just between you and me, okay? You don't need to share this with the class."

"Okay..." Sasha opened up her exercise book and hovered over the page. "Um, for the ingredients, I'd have a puppy of my own, a mom who liked doing stuff with me and who reads me stories in bed, one best friend who could keep a secret, and a holiday on the beach with the whole family—not just me going away to summer camp."

"I understand," Marnie said. "Anything else?"

"I'd like to go see my grandma—maybe even *live* with her. I think she knows how to be a good mom."

Marnie took a breath. "What about the method? How would you combine all those things?"

"I'd put my puppy in the bowl first, then add my best friend, then my grandma, then a holiday with everyone and then some writing to make it into a nice story with a happy ending—like a cake that rises perfectly in the oven."

"That's a wonderful recipe, Sasha."

Sasha looked disheartened. "Yeah, but it's just a *dream* recipe, and it makes me sad thinking about it." She looked at Marnie challengingly. "I don't *like* this exercise," she said. Sasha seemed to have a deep need to score points and be right, and Marnie couldn't help wondering if there was a lot of conflict at home between the girl's parents.

"Having a dream can help us create the kind of life we want. If we don't have any dreams, how can we make them come true?"

Sasha was not convinced, arms folded tightly across her slender chest.

"You can make amazing things happen if you decide that they will, and I think your writing will help you." Marnie stood up, mindful of time slipping by. "Sasha, I want to ask a special favour. It slows everyone down if there are too many questions and disrupts the other kids. So could you write down some of your questions and show them to me afterwards? Then we can go over the answers together. You're a smart girl, so I'm sure you can understand this."

"I'm not a *child*," Sasha said, indignantly, firmly back in defensive-Sasha mode.

"Well, you can't drive a car, get married or run for presidency. So, legally speaking, you are still a child. Sorry." She shrugged, as if to say, *Hey, I know you're exceptional but I have to follow these silly rules.* "But... I think you are very smart and that you can do whatever you decide you'd like to do."

Coercion. Manipulation. Flattery. Other essential teaching tools. Teaching was as much about the parents as the children, Marnie thought, and how you related to a child often depended on what the parents were like. You had to manage and placate them at every turn— and you had to justify *everything*. It was worse than being a politician because there was no place to hide. Teachers weren't paid or appreciated half enough, considering all the *skills* required.

Marnie headed back to her desk, then paused and walked back to Sasha. "I bet you know what coercion means," she said, hunkering down beside her, a gentle hand on the girl's shoulder.

"Yes, of course. I learnt that at home."

The word or the behaviour? Marnie sighed at the irony. Surely Sasha was too young to be that cynical.

"Well, I wasn't trying to coerce you with my praise," she said. "I think you write very well." She realized she'd said the same thing recently to Lucy. The two weren't so dissimilar. "In fact, I think you could be an exceptional writer, and you know that teachers know everything and are always right, right?"

Sasha laughed, and the whole classroom seemed to light up. She was a beautiful girl, when she wasn't grimacing, criticizing, frowning or otherwise showing her weary disdain for the way adults were running the world.

Whatever was happening to her at home, it was leaching the loveliness out of her, Marnie thought. She was glad she'd said what she'd said. Kids needed to know that they were exceptional in their own unique way.

Validation. Okay with you, parents, Principal, School Board, Minister of Education, global economy?

Marnie returned to the front of the room and sat down at her desk. Just two minutes left and most of the kids were still scribbling, gripping their pens with fierce determination as they wrote, or looking into space, dreaming up some happiness.

Whenever her mind stopped for a breather, Steve stepped in. Why had she agreed to have coffee? She was feeling vulnerable and his support was soothing. But she was afraid of getting sucked back into a relationship when her emotions were all over the place. Not a good time to get involved.

His input about the numbers had surprised her. She hadn't seen that side of him before. As a data analyst, Steve was up to his eyeballs in numbers at work, but it didn't involve this kind of esoteric stuff.

They had talked about the meaning of numbers when they were a couple, and Steve had claimed their numbers indicated they were a good match. Either he had been completely wrong about that or the numbers just didn't have the significance he claimed they did. There was one other possibility, of course, which was that she—

A tap at the door interrupted her thoughts. Alison had arrived. Marnie motioned for her to come in and started tidying up her desk.

Alison Marsh was a very capable, dynamic 22-year-old, full of creative ideas for teaching her class, and Marnie was grateful for her competence. She knew the kids would be in good hands when she left. Alison knew how to manage the class with just the right amount of discipline, humour and encouragement. Marnie had supervised her for a while, at the start of the school year in August—*before her life had been turned upside down*—and she had been impressed by Alison's confidence and sensitivity.

She filled Alison in on the lesson plan for the day and the writing assignment the kids had just finished, showed her the attendance sheet and said she'd drop by the office on her way out to let the secretary know that Matthew hadn't shown up for class.

Taking her coat from the back of her chair and putting her notebook and water bottle in her bag, she thanked Alison and said goodbye to her class.

As she finally exited through the main doors, Marnie breathed a huge sigh of relief. She loved teaching and found it truly gratifying, particularly when a parent came in to personally thank her, rather than to complain about something. And the kids always made her laugh. It was usually unintentional, yet they were often funnier than adults trying to be. Today, though, she desperately needed time to herself to sort out her feelings.

She paused when she reached the street; she still hadn't been to MIT to check out the residence halls archives, but it would have to wait till next week. She turned right, deciding to go to the library, relax in one of their nice comfy armchairs, browse some new books and maybe find out a bit more about numerology so she wasn't totally clueless when— *if*—she spoke to Steve again.

After that, she was going to go for a leisurely lunch somewhere nice and then go for a walk. It was a beautiful sunny, crisp, clear October day and she was determined to make the most of it.

15

Lucy had decided she wasn't very good at forgiveness. Come to think of it—*and she had lots of friggin time to think*—she wasn't very good at happiness, kindness or tenderness either. Maybe she needed to work on those qualities ending in *ness*.

She was feeling restless, listless and aimless. No problem with *those* words. Now that she'd had to give up 'her' room for Matt, on top of having no space of her own (homeless!), no job (jobless!), no friends (that she wanted to talk to) (hopeless!), and no idea where she belonged, she was feeling kind of stateless. See? Her life was just wall-to-wall *less-ness*.

Less is *not* more, people. Got it?

She must be heartless, too, if she couldn't summon up a bit more compassion and help her brother without feeling resentful. She had felt a wave of compassion for him when she offered up her room (not that it was hers to offer and Marnie would have commandeered it, anyway). Well, maybe not a *wave*, more like a ripple.

So much prattling in her head! Maybe she *should* become a writer. At least then she could get some mileage out of all this mental drivel. She could use all kinds of unacceptable words and sick thoughts, and blame them on her characters.

She had spent the last four days taking care of Matt, although she hadn't helped him much, emotionally. But at least she'd made sure he hadn't slit his wrists or taken all his sleeping pills at once.

God, she was such a *bitch*. But she was exhausted from all the care-taking. *How did Marnie do it?*

And it was just too damn ironic, her forcing Matt to go through the motions of living, when she herself had felt like checking out just a few weeks ago. *Was this some kind of sick cosmic trick to get her motivated?*

It occurred to her that people didn't have the kind of freedom they thought they had—apart from having none, thanks to government surveillance, pilfering of personal data, social media infiltration and all that other sickeningly fake stuff that claimed to serve and protect you.

Her parents had chosen to end their lives, which they were technically free to do, but she had taken it as a personal insult—something they had *done* to her. She hadn't stopped to think about the impact of taking her *own* life (doing exactly what she resented her parents for doing), or how that would affect Marnie and Matt.

Clearly, Matt wasn't thinking about that, either. God, it felt like a race to the ultimate finishing line. *Which one of them would get there first?*

She had taken Matt to the nearest walk-in medical clinic over the weekend and explained their situation to the young female East Indian doctor—a Dr Moorjani. The doctor had agreed to prescribe a sedative for Matt, plus a week's supply of sleeping pills that she suggested Lucy *"keep track of"*. They both knew what she meant.

Lucy didn't see the need to tell the woman that she herself would have gladly knocked back all seven pills in one go, if she'd had access to them last month. Some days, she felt as if she still might, but the feelings were fleeting and she was more or less resigned to sticking around on planet Earth a bit longer, just to see how things panned out.

Dr Moorjani asked them both if they were getting any grief counselling or other support to help them cope. Lucy shook her head and Matt showed no sign of having heard or of being remotely interested.

Taking a business card from a drawer behind her, the doctor suggested they both consider joining this group—she tapped the card—in a week or so, when some of the initial shock had passed. Lucy would rather sleep naked on the street than join a support group, but she took the card anyway—for *Matt*.

How the hell would it help for a whole group of *victims* to share their misery? You sit there in a stupid self-pitying circle, telling everyone how shitty you feel. Then what? They tell *you* how shitty *they* feel. *And you suddenly feel better?* Everyone gets all group-hugged and healed and can go back to their unhappy lives and live normally ever after?

It was total crap and there was no way she was ever going to let a bunch of random strangers pretend they actually knew how she felt. I don't think so, peeps, but thanks, anyway. She would sort things out herself.

They might also share some solutions, Luce. That was Marnie's voice in her head—the one that often barged right in, uninvited, to *reason* with her. Sometimes, it worked. But this wasn't one of those times.

"My heart goes out to you both," the doctor said, which surprised

Lucy. She couldn't remember the last time a medical doctor had expressed genuine compassion towards a patient. Maybe Dr Moorjani was still young enough not to be worn down by all the crises, sickness and human tragedies most doctors had to deal with.

They left the clinic and headed for the pharmacy, Lucy all but dragging Matt along beside her. She didn't want to let him go home on his own while she picked up the prescription, so he was just going to have to tough it out.

She looked at Matt as they walked, his head down, shoulders slouching, and she suddenly felt a huge lump of sadness for him, herself and the whole sorry world. Maybe she was just too numb and emotionally battered to be a good care-taker, right now. Was it possible to *feel* numb or could you only *be* it?

It felt as if all her energies were going into logistics—doing laundry, preparing meals and taking care of Matt. She was also diligently cleaning the apartment so Marnie didn't crack up with all the mess the two of them inevitably created, with Lucy sleeping on the couch and Matt leaving stuff lying around because, well, he just didn't give a fuck about anything any more.

When your best friend gets killed *because of you*, you don't exactly care about putting your socks in the laundry basket, or wearing socks at all, or washing yourself or eating... Exactly how she had felt, just a few weeks ago.

But Marnie insisted that Matt shave and shower every day, and Matt was too depressed and lethargic to argue. The shave was definitely a patchy job but at least he was getting up for a few hours every day. The rest of the time, he slept, curled up on the bed with the curtains drawn, disconnected from the world.

Marnie usually managed to get him to join them for dinner, but Lucy had the feeling he only complied so he could get his sleeping pill for the night. Marnie had taken over 'control' of the pills, telling Lucy that she felt her older-sister status might carry a little more weight with their brother.

On Monday, Marnie had called Matt's office and broken the news about Jed to Jenny, Matt's assistant. Jenny had burst out crying but agreed, through her sobs, to tell the others what had happened.

Marnie told her that she didn't know when or if Matt would be back in the office and could Jenny take care of things? Jenny said she would talk it over with the others, call their sponsor and figure out how to handle things. They agreed to talk again at the end of the week to see how things stood.

When Marnie got home from work that evening, Lucy had lit the fire and the two of them sat huddled together, soaking up the warm glow while dinner simmered on the stove. Marnie had badgered Matt into taking a hot bath and Lucy had run it for him. He had submitted to their sisterly ministrations, knowing it was pointless resisting.

Marnie had removed the key from the bathroom door, so he couldn't lock himself in. Matt had shaken his head sadly at this, and they weren't sure if he was disappointed that he couldn't end his wretchedness by drowning himself in the bath or that they didn't trust him to stick around.

Either way, they weren't taking any chances.

16

Thursday, 7 November 2019

Marnie was at work and Matt was still sleeping, so Lucy decided she'd experiment with some creative writing. Sitting at the table by the window in the living room, she'd been thinking about what to write and how to use her current emotional state to produce something with some *feeling* to it.

Right now, jaded cynicism seemed to be a predominant emotion— maybe not the richest vein for her to tap into, but somewhere to start. She might as well use her veins for *something*, if she was going to stick around. Yup. Cynicism was definitely up there. Was satire similar? Maybe one led to the other. Worth exploring that. She liked the idea of being a satirical writer.

Rein it in there, Lucifer. You haven't even started yet. She had to stop calling herself that, although she often *felt* like a fallen angel...

Anyway, it felt good to finally get interested in something again, so she'd allow herself this rare spurt of enthusiasm.

She wanted to write without censuring or editing herself. Could she let it rip without judging it? She thought about all the things that had seemed important in her life, before *it* happened: staying in touch with her friends on social media, posting fashion photos on Pinterest, Tweeting about the latest scandals in the news, swapping stories about dishy guys in college... Now, it all seemed empty, fake, meaningless—just a load of endless posing and posturing, everyone clamouring to be seen, heard, shared and *liked*.

It all seemed so desperate. Such neediness, playing into the greedy hands of marketers plying quick fixes, a million supplements to make you feel better, drugs and make-up to hide the pain, solutions for everything that ailed you but would never heal you, an endless conveyor belt of cheap seduction and empty promises.

The digital world had felt like so much fun ...until she had her blinders ripped off by reality and began to see what really mattered. Her cellphone was lying in a drawer in the guest room and she never used it now. What was the point? Who would she call? And how the hell could anything in that vacuous virtual reality fix her messed-up life?

She thought about what Marnie used to say about wireless radiation—how it affected the brain and might even prevent her from having children. She had nagged Lucy to give up her cellphone and not get so sucked into social media. *Think for yourself,* Marnie had said. *You're too smart for this.* Although she didn't do that any more. Either she'd stopped caring so much about what Lucy did or she'd given up on Lucy ever caring enough to take care of herself properly. Maybe she could write about some of that stuff and see where it went.

She smoothed the clean blank page of her large notepad and took the cap off her pen. There was something ceremonial about writing by hand and using an old-fashioned pen. This was a nice thick green one of Marnie's that she'd found on the dresser. It had a real nib and a cartridge of blue ink.

No one was going to be allowed to read this stuff, though—not even Marnie. Not till she'd produced something she was proud of, if she produced anything at all. She took a deep breath and started to write.

Hands on, hearts off, words unwired and uninspired. From the shallow depths of digital darkness, a daily dump of grammatical garbage and re-recycled non-words. Comma-less, comatose wordage, cluelessly clauseless. Yet everyone's a writer, righting wrongs while wrongfully writing.

Satire is a subtle skill, a social service to the unthinking—words that transport, without fossil fuels or burdened mules required to take us there.

But what kind of wake-up wordage will pierce the deafening daily deluge—the digi-din of manic marketing that hijacks your heart and steals your soul, so you spend your daze on Facehook, trying to get them both back?

Everyone wears a limpet phone, even if wireless wonders fry your brain and make you digi-mental, shrinking your gonads until they're the size of a lentil. Not just fatty figments of your imagination; you really are losing it.

There were digi-debts that never ended. *I will like-love-share you, if you like-love-share me.* And online dramas that just pretended …to be a real life lived.

Meanwhile, lilting lipsticks pout on love-seeking selfies, disgorging a wordy web of me-mails. Who will win, in the tortured tangle of tipsy texting and soulless sexting, in a spin cycle that wrings you digi-rigidly dry?

Could we all just die a peaceful digi-death now—before WiFi irradiates the Moon, spilling the un-tide-y seas into the sky and pulling the plughole on humanity?

Could lovers of language bring back the language of love?

Oh, please, someone. Bring back the love.

Bloody hell. Where had *that* come from?

Lucy sat back, not sure what to make of what she'd written. She didn't believe all that stuff about the radiation, but she liked the way it had come out, with all that *digi* stuff. Marnie would probably like it, knowing she'd inspired it. Or she might just laugh.

But that wasn't fair to Marnie, Lucy thought. She needed to give her sister the chance to condemn it on her own terms.

Ha. She could certainly do *cynical*.

But the writing felt inspired, in some weird, twisted way—like a moment of exquisite madness. Was that what inspired writing was—moments of madness strung together as you wrote yourself outside the conventional story of existence? It was certainly a way to escape from her own friggin' story, which was more like a sick tragi-comedy than a thriller that ends with everyone going home *happy*. Lucy was pretty sure that madness was a lot more fun than sanity, although the line between the two was starting to blur… which could mean she was already on the mad side of the blurry bit. Maybe she *was* losing it, regardless of the radiation thing.

Whatever. Not much she could do about it, except allow the madness to proceed.

But this writing thing… how did you know if a piece of writing was good or just utter crap? When was it self-indulgent navel-gazing nonsense and when did it have merit? And who decided? Was it like art? If someone liked it, it had value. If not, you were wasting your time. Was that how it worked?

No. Not like art, really, since words had a structure with a limited number of ways you could juxtapose or use them. Art seemed less definable, even though it was an actual *thing*, whereas writing wasn't something you could *touch*. Interesting…

Where would the visual arts be without words? If no one said anything about a painting, would it still have value? Wasn't it all the commentary, assessment, marketing and opinions that told people whether something was any good or not? Told them whether they should *like* it or not? Art could be powerful and it could stand on its own—for the *individual*. But if you wanted *consensus*, which then created a perceived value, you needed words.

Was it the same thing with fashion? If models walked down the catwalk and no one said a word, no one took photos and the press made zero comment, would the designs be seen in the same way, or coveted, as some were, if the labels conferred a particular status or good taste? But only because someone *said* they did.

This stuff was really making her think. How could you use one word to adequately describe another word, a taste to describe another taste, a personality to describe another personality, or something other than love to describe love?

Words… Was there anything more powerful than words?

Lucy was tentatively pleased with what she'd done. She'd started something. She'd given herself permission to write rubbish, if that's what it was. Maybe she—

The doorbell rang. Damn. She was just starting to get into this.

She got up and was about to open the door when she remembered the building manager was installing a new lock on the main lobby door, with a buzzer system so each apartment-owner could talk to visitors through an intercom and buzz them in if they qualified for entry.

But the intercom hadn't been fitted yet, so she'd have to go down to the main door to see who it was. Double damn. She ran down the corridor and quietly opened Matt's door. Still zoned-out on the bed, so it should be okay to leave him for a few minutes.

She grabbed the door keys and jogged down the stairs. If it was a delivery for Marnie, she didn't want the guy to leave before she got there.

When she opened the door, there was a mid-20s dark-haired guy standing on the steps. Jeans, light-blue fleece jacket, navy shirt. The kind of clean-cut, good-looking guy you'd feel comfortable introducing to your parents—if you *had* parents. No packages, though. Not a delivery guy. Someone looking for directions, maybe, which meant she'd interrupted her writing and run downstairs for no good reason.

"Yes? Can I help you?"

"I'm looking for Lucy," he said, smiling.

"Who are you? Do I know you?" She really needed to brush up on her social skills, or maybe just her manners. But she was *busy*. She didn't have time to talk to some random guy on the doorstep.

"You'd probably know if you knew me," he said. "You look pretty smart."

"You selling something?" Hey, she could do cynical in person, too.

He laughed. "No. Actually, I'm here to offer you a job, if you're interested."

Lucy folded her arms across her chest. "A job? You don't even know me. What *is* this?"

He held up his hands to ward off further attack. "It's not some sinister plot to sell you life insurance," he said. "My nephew—my sister's little boy, Tate—goes to the school where your sister teaches. Our sisters know each other, and your sister—Marnie, right?—mentioned that you might be interested in doing some part-time work."

What the heck...? Marnie hadn't mentioned anything about this.

He started backing down the steps. "If you're not interested, no problem. Sorry to have bothered you."

"Hang on. Wait." She needed to find out a bit more, even if it was just so she could be fully informed when she told Marnie to mind her own business.

"What's your name?"

"Nate. Nate Cordalis." He held out his hand. "Pleased to meet—"

"Tate. Nate." Lucy looked at him skeptically, still not sure he was legit. "Listen, if you have a brother called *Fate*, I'd really like to talk to *him*."

He laughed. "Nate is for Nathaniel and Tate is for Tatum, plus he's 6 and I'm 26, so we really don't have a lot in common." He paused. "So, you're Lucy, right?"

"Yes, sorry. Hi." Lucy stuck out her hand and they shook. "I'm being rude. It's just that I was in the middle of something…"

"Well, I won't keep you." He turned to go.

"Hang on." Lucy took a step down towards him. "That job you mentioned… What kind of job is it?"

"I'm looking for a copy writer and your sister said you could write."

"Really?" Marnie said *that*? "I can write… I'm just not sure how *well* I can write."

She didn't want to scare him off and make Marnie look bad if this guy told his sister she was a pain in the neck.

"I wouldn't be able to pay you very much," he said, as if he hadn't heard her doubting her skills. "But it might get your foot in the door in the industry."

He saw her quizzical look. "I run a web-development company and I'm looking for someone to help with content for various websites. To do with health, art, fashion—that kind of thing. It's a small start-up and I've been doing the writing myself but we're getting busy, which is great, so…"

Lucy wasn't sure what to say. She could think of worse things to do with her highly sought-after time (laundry, brother-sitting…), but would she be a fraud if she took the job, having almost no experience in… anything? She'd written essays for her fashion-design course, but that was it.

"Look, I understand if you need to think about it before you decide."

He pulled a card from his pocket and handed it to her.

"Call me if you'd like to know more and you can come to the office to check things out. See if we're a good fit." He gestured down the street to his right. "It's only about 15 minutes from here."

"Okay."

The card had some nice swirly graphics in blues and greens, with the name *Cordalis Communications* in a strong, no-nonsense font. Underneath was a tagline: *Promoting your success, beyond words.*

It was turning into a downright wordy day.

17

Monday, 11 November 2019

It had been an interesting weekend. Lucy had done more writing and was starting to get excited about the possibility of working for Nate.

She'd told Marnie about him and thanked her for saying nice things about her to Nate's sister. Marnie had had no idea what she was talking about.

"What's his sister's name?" she asked.

"I didn't ask him," Lucy said, "but his nephew's called Tate—a 6-year-old, probably in Grade 1. Do you know him?"

"The name sounds vaguely familiar," Marnie said. "Maybe I met his mother at one of the parent–teacher meetings, but I don't remember ever talking about you to any of the parents."

"Weird." Lucy frowned, not sure what to make of this. "Well, Nate knew your name and said his sister knew you, so maybe you've just forgotten…?" That wasn't really Marnie's style, but what other explanation could there be?

"Maybe," Marnie said, clearly not convinced. "But this sounds like a great opportunity, Luce—and I *would* have said good things about your writing if I'd talked to anyone about you."

Lucy smiled, making a mental note to ask Nate about it.

"Marn, do you ever think that life is sometimes almost unbearable and then other times downright amazing?"

Marnie laughed. "All the time. Why do you ask?"

"Well, I was thinking about this job offer. I mean, what are the chances of a random stranger coming to the door to offer me a writing job, the very day that I start seriously thinking about writing?"

"About one in a million, I'd say."

"Exactly," Lucy said, shaking her head in wonder. "It boggles the mind."

"Well, you know what Dad used to say about all that stuff. If you show intention and take positive action, things tend to move in your favour. The universe starts to bring you new opportunities when you dare to move beyond your own limits."

"Yeah, I remember." Lucy smiled. "But what about Matt?"

"You mean, if you're not here?"

"Yes," Lucy said. "I'd only be gone for like a few hours during the day, I think. But I feel uneasy leaving him on his own when he's like this."

"We'll figure something out, Luce. You need to get on with your life and you can't pass up on this opportunity."

"I know. I don't want to. I'll call this guy Nate over the weekend and find out more."

Lucy paused, thinking. "Matt needs to come off those meds, Marn. He's a zombie and they're not helping."

"I know," Marnie said. "I've been thinking the same thing."

They both knew the drugs were a necessary buffer for a while, as Matt adjusted to this second crushing new reality, but they only put the pain on hold. They didn't address it.

"The memorial service for Jed is next week," Marnie said. "But I doubt Matt will be able to go."

"How can we help him come out of this, Marn?"

Marnie had obviously been giving this some thought too. "Would you take him to that support group, Luce," she said, "just to get him there? I know you don't feel the need for it yourself, but I think he needs some kind of lifeline and I don't know what else to suggest."

She looked at Lucy. "Unless you have some other ideas?"

Lucy didn't. Going to one of those group things would feel like acting in some tawdry amateur dramatics production where she only played a minor supporting role and kept forgetting her lines. But could she do it for Matt? She didn't really have a choice. And couldn't she afford to be generous, since she was being given a break?

"If Matt agrees to go, I'll do it," she said. She knew she couldn't suggest that Marnie go with him, since she had already done so much for both of them. So it was her or no one.

What the hell. Maybe she could just sit and listen and then write about it afterwards. She knew those things were supposed to be confidential but she wouldn't name names.

They agreed to talk to Matt about it on Wednesday, when Marnie got home from work. If they could persuade him to go to the group, it would be a major breakthrough. Lucy knew she couldn't *not* do this for her brother if it helped him get back on his feet.

On Sunday, Marnie had gone out shopping mid-morning and spent the afternoon at the library, so Lucy had the place to herself for most of the day. Matt was still holed up in his room, only emerging to use the bathroom.

Lucy had taken advantage of the solitude to explore more writing ideas. She had appropriated Marnie's pen (with permission from big sis) and was really enjoying the physical process of getting the words down on paper. She felt far more reflective and connected to her feelings than when she wrote stuff on her laptop.

Funny how writing dredged things from your brain that you didn't know you knew. It was as if her right hand was a special faucet that siphoned off knowledge and feelings lurking in otherwise unreachable places. She had been experimenting with different themes, and she could almost feel the words charging down her arm, sometimes causing a traffic jam in her fingers as they jostled for expression on the page.

What else might she discover about herself if she kept writing? And if she didn't write, would she ever really know herself? This writing thing had come out of nowhere, but now that she'd got a taste for it, she couldn't seem to stop.

What would the world be like without words? Would people still love …or hate? Would actions be more considered and heartfelt, without words getting in the way? People would have to *feel* things more if they didn't have words, wouldn't they? Would that make their actions more loving?

She thought about all the verbal messages parents gave their kids: *Eat your dinner or you won't get any ice cream.* Punishments, hooks, rewards. It gave kids a distorted view of things—and gave dinners a bad rap. What would happen if they turned things around? *Eat your ice cream or you won't get any broccoli?*

But maybe that was just as bad—still a *penance–reward* dynamic.

Considering what was actually *in* the stuff they were eating, according to health-encyclopedia Marnie, those kinds of parental messages were even more loaded with subtext. *Eat your antibiotic- and vaccine-riddled meat and your pesticide-laden, waxed, glyphosated vegetables or you won't get any high-fructose corn syrup, artificial flavours, preservatives and other yummy stuff also used to remove paint, clean leather and kill lice.*

See, Marn? I actually *do* sometimes listen to what you say… One thing Lucy knew she was good at was remembering things. She had always had a phenomenal memory, which had made high school a cinch. If she'd seen something written or heard something said, she'd remember it, even if she didn't necessarily agree with it.

She liked the idea of turning things upside down. Now that she'd lived with a health nut for a while, she was starting to be more discerning about food.

"Have you ever really *looked* at broccoli, Luce?" Marnie had asked her last week when she was cooking dinner.

Lucy had laughed. She'd been a little too busy trying to salvage her life to study the intricacies of cruciferous vegetables.

"Every little floret is like a tiny forest," Marnie said, passing her one. "Look. It's amazing. If you had a magnifying glass, you'd see the complexity of it and how incredible nature is."

It was true, now that she thought about it. Up close, broccoli was really quite something.

Maybe writing was her way of processing what had happened. She wasn't sure she believed in God, but she was starting to believe in her own potential …a little.

She'd been thinking about her two closest high-school friends— Sherry Merickson and Delsie Roman. She missed them both, when she allowed herself to… especially Delsie. They'd been friends since elementary school and she knew Delsie felt hurt when Lucy withdrew after *The Event.* Sherry probably did, too, but she had moved to Canada right after graduation and it had somehow been easier to justify not being in touch. Although it didn't. *Obviously.* With the internet, distance meant nothing. She just didn't feel ready to reconnect yet….

But should she call Delsie? Would it be awkward? Wouldn't she just be a burden, with no news to share other than another death close to home …and maybe a part-time job?

Delsie was studying law at Harvard, so they hadn't seen each other much since September, when college had started. Delsie had a boyfriend, new friends at law school and a whole new life that Lucy wasn't part of. But she had dropped everything to be there for Lucy when she'd got the news about Lucy's parents. She was a good friend, and Lucy had rejected her.

She would call her. First, though, she was going to write about this… see if she could sort through some deeper feelings about what had happened and how it had changed her.

18

What to wear? For the last two months, Lucy hadn't given a damn what she threw on in the morning. Today, though, she wanted to look good. She had arranged to be at Nate's office at 11am to find out more about the job.

She decided to play it safe; nothing too dressy. She wanted to look like a professional who wasn't *trying* to look like a professional. Nate looked like a casual kind of guy, so she chose her well-cut grey trousers and her favourite burnt-orange cashmere sweater with a diaphanous blue scarf wrapped nonchalantly around her neck. It was amazing how long it took to create the nonchalant look.

At 10.45am, she put on her black wool coat and her floppy cream wool hat. She'd decided to wear runners for the 15-minute walk over there and then change into her cream leather ballet flats before she went in.

The address Nate had given her was for a lovely three-storey walk-up redbrick townhouse on a corner lot, with large windows on both sides overlooking the street.

There was only one nameplate beside the door—for Cordalis Communications. It was only when Lucy rang the bell that she realized she hadn't changed her shoes. Damn. Did it matter? Was this a formal interview?

The door was opened a few seconds later by Nate, dressed in a light-blue shirt tucked into black jeans, nicely integrated with a tan leather belt. Lucy noticed such things.

"Lucy! Welcome. Come in."

Nate took her coat and hat as she entered and hung them on the stand beside the door.

He led her down a short hallway and through a doorway into the office. It was a large sunny room with big windows along one wall, overlooking the street. In the middle of the room, two comfy russet armchairs bracketed a low wooden coffee table. The small seating area was bordered on two sides by soft grey partitions, with a large potted plant in the corner, creating a semi-private space.

Along the wall under the windows, there was a computer station on a large pale-grey desk, occupied by a guy with his back to her. Along the wall on the right, another computer station was occupied by a young woman. Both were tapping busily on keyboards.

"Lucy, meet the team," Nate said, gesturing grandly. "This is Tracy Weston, who does a lot of the web design work with me. Trace, Lucy Dalton. Our new copy writer."

Tracy swivelled round in her chair and got up to shake Lucy's hand. "Welcome, Lucy. Great to have you on board."

Tracy was a petite brunette with a short spiky hairdo and sharp green eyes that looked as if they didn't miss much. Wearing a snug long-sleeved black cotton top and loose-fitting black yoga pants, she was the picture of cool–casual.

"And this," said Nate, turning to the other occupied desk, "is Marcus Fitzgerald, who handles all the SEO, data mapping, PSP, CMS and other technical stuff. We call him Fitz."

"Or Fritz, if something goes wrong," said Fitz, grinning as he got up and gave Lucy a firm, warm handshake.

They were all so friendly and relaxed, Lucy thought. And they seemed to assume she was actually a *writer*, before she'd even written a word.

Lucy suddenly felt something brush against her legs and looked down in alarm. A small tabby was rubbing itself against her lovely grey trousers. Damn. But at least the cat was mostly grey. Not that she could say anything.

"That's Victoria, Tracy's cat. Just visiting for the day," Nate explained. "She's not a regular part of the team."

The cat looked up at Lucy imploringly, making persistent *wah-wah-wah* noises.

She bent down to stroke it. "Could you be a bit more specific?" she asked the cat. "I didn't quite catch that."

Tracy laughed and came over to pick up her cat. "I'm taking her to the vet this afternoon," she said. "That's why she's with me this morning."

"I'm afraid I don't speak cat," Lucy said, straightening up. "I'm more of a dog person."

"Ah. You'll like Beemer, then."

"Sounds expensive," Lucy said, "and fast."

"Expensive, yes. He eats more than I do," said Nate, grinning. "Fast? Not really, unless it's time for dinner or his walk." He cocked his head. "Here he comes now, making his stately way from the kitchen about 20 feet away. He should be here in about ten minutes."

As he spoke, a Golden Retriever came sauntering around the corner, into the room. When he saw there was a visitor, he immediately picked up speed and raced towards Lucy, skidding to a halt on the hardwood floor, nails scrabbling for purchase.

"Doesn't the landlord object?"

"I do, sometimes."

"This is your place?"

"Yes. Well, technically speaking, it's my dad's. He's a realtor and he picked up this place about 30 years ago." He gestured towards the upper level. "I live upstairs."

"It's a lovely space," Lucy said. "Where do you work? And where would I be?"

"Ah, yes. My office is down the corridor there," he gestured to where Beemer had come from, "and the kitchen is behind that wall, by the way." He pointed to the wall on the right, where Tracy had her desk.

"And this is where you will be working." He gestured towards a smaller desk in the left-hand corner beneath the stairs, butting up against the windowed wall facing the street. There was a computer terminal on top, a keyboard and a small printer.

"Looks perfect," Lucy said. She turned to Nate. "About the work…"

"Yes, of course," Nate said, gesturing towards the armchairs. "Take a seat and I'll tell you what's involved."

Lucy sat down and Nate brought some pages from her—*her!*—desk and put them on the coffee table in front of her.

"Sorry. I forgot to ask if you'd like coffee, tea or something?"

"No, I'm fine, thanks." Lucy shook her head.

"Water?"

"Yes, okay. Please."

Nate went into the kitchen and she heard the sound of water running. He came back and placed a glass of water on the table. "Filtered," he said.

"Great. Thanks." Lucy took a few sips and sat back.

"Okay, so here's the scoop," Nate said, flopping down in the other armchair. "We're on retainer with three large corporations, which keeps us ticking over nicely. We also have a few smaller companies needing web work, marketing, SEO, that kind of thing. All of them require blogs and other content for their sites, and we provide that for them, which is where you come in."

Lucy had decided she was not going to bullshit this guy. Even if she'd wanted to, she didn't have enough experience. You needed to have been in the workforce for a few years before you could convincingly bullshit anyone. What was she going to say? *I left school when I was 12 and have been honing my craft ever since?*

No, she was going to be totally up-front and honest with this guy. He was placing his trust in her and she didn't want to let him down.

"Nate, you know this will be my first job, right?" Should she point out that she was only 18 …*and two months?* That almost made her laugh out loud. It was the kind of thing 6-year-olds said. She had skipped a year at school, and was a year younger than most of her classmates, which meant she was the equivalent of 19, really…

But Nate didn't seem at all concerned. "I realize you're young, Lucy, but I see your youth and enthusiasm as an asset." He smiled. "You have a quick mind, without too many preconceived ideas, and I sense you're a fast learner."

"Don't you want to see a sample of my writing or give me a test or something?"

"Let's just see how things go. If they don't work out in, say, a month, we'll part ways, no hard feelings." He smiled at her. "Okay with you?"

"Yes. Thank you. I appreciate your confidence in me."

Nate reached across the table, picked up the sheets of paper and handed them to Lucy.

"I printed out a few examples of blogs that we've done for our clients, so you can get an idea of what we need."

"That will really help. Thanks." Lucy took the sheets and had a quick glance. There was a blog about a natural sleeping aid, one about how social media was affecting young people and family dynamics, and a third one on how things were changing in the fashion world.

"I look forward to reading these," she said. "How many hours a day would you like me to work?"

"Well, it's only a part-time position, but we'd probably need you for about four hours, four days a week. How does that sound?"

"Perfect," Lucy said. "Would it be okay if I didn't start till next week? I have a few family issues to sort out first."

"No problem," Nate said. "Shall we say Monday next week, then? As long as I know in advance, you can choose which four days you work, so I'll leave that up to you."

Lucy suddenly realized there was a small basket of donuts on the coffee table. *How had she missed those? Her favourites, with chocolate on top...*

Nate saw her look.

"Please, help yourself. They're for our distinguished guests."

Why not? She had a new job and she was starting to feel almost human again. She felt like celebrating.

She helped herself and took a napkin to catch the inevitable sugar cascade. She took a mouthful of chocolate divinity and almost groaned in pleasure as her taste buds took delivery. It seemed so long since she had actually *tasted* food.

"Lucy, you're hungry!" Nate seemed delighted.

She froze, a wad of dough in her cheek. Here she was stuffing her face and he was laughing at her! She felt mortified at the indignity of it.

Seeing her expression, Nate suddenly looked stricken. "Ahhh, sorry. Big foot in big mouth. I didn't mean... what I meant was..." He leaned forward, his elbows on his knees, and looked at her earnestly. "I mean you're hungry for *life*, for new beginnings, for words, for writing," he gestured around him. "You're saying YES to things, daring to stretch yourself, and you're not afraid to admit you might not be perfect or even experienced. You're spunky. I admire that. Truly."

Lucy was having difficulty swallowing the lump but she finally got it down, chasing the dry boulder with a swig of water.

"Am I forgiven?" Nate looked at her searchingly.

"Mmm... not quite," Lucy said, arms folded across her chest, suddenly feeling vulnerable... "Maybe you could grovel just a tiny bit?" ...but also quite brazen, apparently. *Don't push your luck, Lucifer. He's going to be your boss, after all.*

Nate laughed. "I like the rebel in you, Lucy. It's an essential quality for a good writer. That and your humour. I hope you won't let the world turn you sad and cynical."

"Actually, I gave that up last week," Lucy said, sardonically. He didn't need to know she wasn't joking.

"How about I give you the rest of the week off, to make up for my *faux-pas?*" He was grinning now, already forgiving himself.

"And *pay* me, you mean? Since I won't be working till next week anyway..." Might as well call his bluff, see what he's made of.

"Yes! Deal." He paused. "Okay if I pay you in chocolate donuts?"

She laughed. "You don't have to make it up to me. I'll get over it." There was a lot to be said for having a young boss with a sense of humour.

"May I take you for a coffee or something, before you head back?"

"No. I need to get going. But thanks."

She felt brittle. She needed to go home to absorb all this—the good, the wonderful and the little iffy bit in the middle.

She got up and brushed the sugar granules, the cat hairs and the last of her mortification off her trousers. The everyday wounds of battle in the workplace. She'd have to toughen up. But if emotional indigestion was all she had to worry about, she'd be fine.

She waved to Fitz and Tracy. "Nice to meet you both. See you next week."

"Bye, Lucy," they chorused together.

She picked up the printouts and Nate escorted her out to the hallway.

"If you have any other questions in the meantime, just give me a call," Nate said, helping her into her coat.

"Yes, I will." Lucy nodded. She pulled on her hat and put the printouts in her bag.

Beemer came to see her off, tail wagging furiously.

"You can see what an excellent guard dog he is." Nate laughed, patting the dog's head. "We all feel a lot safer having Beemer around."

"I'll be happy to take him for walks," Lucy said, smiling.

"Oh, Lucy Dalton, we both love you already. I think this is going to work out beautifully."

19

Matt could hear his sisters preparing dinner in the kitchen and he steeled himself to join them. He felt thick, groggy and unbearably heavy, as if someone had placed a lead-lined coat on his shoulders.

He slowly sat up, swinging his legs over the side of the bed. Sat for a moment, trying to find himself. He was in there somewhere, whatever was left of the guy he used to know. Or maybe that guy was long gone, whoever he was.

Jed haunted his every waking moment and even his drug-induced sleep. There was nowhere to go to escape the crippling grief and guilt. Could there be a more potent way to mentally, physically and emotionally paralyse a man?

In his mind ran a relentlessly looping movie of Jed… laughing, joking, working, sleuthing, scheming, cursing, being his faithful friend and business partner, always pushing him to live more daringly, take more risks, go for the hot stories. What would Jed say now, if he could see him like this?

Don't go soft on me, Mattress. Suck it up!

That almost made him smile, which almost made him cry. But he had cried himself dry and had only a desert of despair and despondency. Would he ever be able to dig himself out of this? Or want to? He didn't deserve to have a life.

Was there anything on earth he could do for his friend? Whatever redemption he might ultimately get from Celle (not that he deserved any), it would never erase his self-loathing and regret. A selfish request, an ill-considered task, a chain of events that caused his friend to intersect with his own demise on his way to help Matt get *his* life back on track.

How could he ever face the team at work? He couldn't imagine ever working again. He'd have to tell Chamberlain that the show was over and they were shutting things down. Maybe Jenny had already taken care of that…

He was aware that Marnie had been tapering off his meds. Lucy had got another seven-day prescription from Dr Roomjami, or whatever her name was, for a lower dose. He knew he had to come off the meds altogether or he'd get stuck on them for the remainder of his pathetic, aimless, stuporous life. Killing himself with drugs and apathy wouldn't bring Jed back, although he'd probably do it if it weren't for Marnie and Lucy. He might have more fun hanging out in hell with his buddy than toughing it out here on Earth.

He heard the kitchen door open, then soft footfalls in the corridor. A light tap on the door, then Lucy's voice.

"Dinner's ready."

"Yeah."

Lucy's voice could be like sandpaper on his soul or an angel calling him home. How was it possible to feel so sensitized yet simultaneously numb? The world had blurred around its edges, yet some things came into shocking focus. The luminous throbbing-red numbers on the digital bedside clock could sometimes sear his brain, while birdsong outside the window could make his skull vibrate like a tuning fork.

He eased himself up, ran his fingers through his hair and yanked up his jeans around his receding waistline.

Just go through the motions, one foot in front of the other, don't think about it, just show up, eat dinner and then… What? He was sick of his own inertia. The Earth seemed to have stopped spinning, leaving him without a gravitational grounding in reality. Like being in outer space, where everything floated away unless attached to something.

He walked slowly down the corridor towards the inevitable sister showdown. It was time for The Talk, and he'd be no match for the double-barreled assault.

***

Most evenings, the three of them ate at the corner table in the kitchen—a small horseshoe of humanity, briefly insulated from the world. Lucy liked the intimate feel of the small space filled with the heat and smells of cooking. Here, she felt… comforted, cosseted, like being wrapped in a warm blankie. The rare times they ate at the large table in the living room, she felt exposed, like sitting on a cold leather sofa in her undies.

She wondered if Marnie and Matt felt that same need for comfort and family binding. How could they not, given the emotional battering they'd all undergone?

Lucy had cooked a fish stew with vegetables and red rice, easily served up and spooned down, so they could focus on what they wanted to discuss. She was dishing it into large white bowls as Matt came into the kitchen.

Marnie was sitting at the table, marking some essays for school. But she gathered up her papers, putting them into the shoulder bag at her feet, as Matt sat down at the table.

"Let's get this over with," Matt said, as Lucy placed the steaming bowls of stew on the table in front of them. "Then we can eat."

Marnie and Lucy looked at each other, knowing what he meant.

"It's time to come off the medication," Marnie said. "It's not helping. Is it?"

"Nothing helps, Marnie," he said.

"Not even us?" Lucy asked.

"You're great. It's just…" How could he convey the enormity of what he had done, the futility of trying to move past it, and the dread of forever living with it? How could anyone understand the agony of breathing it in and out every day, every cell of his body ringing with the resonance of that one careless, throwaway moment?

"Look, Matt," Marnie said, "you've gone through hell, on top of the first hell that hit home two months ago, so you're going to be reeling for a while." She paused. "It's a huge shock to the system and it's almost impossible to come out of it and move on without some external help or impetus."

"I need counselling, therapy, psychiatric help, you mean."

"Actually, we've come up with a better idea," Marnie said.

Lucy couldn't contain herself. "Marnie has come up with a *fabulous* idea!"

"A lobotomy to erase all memories of my crime…?"

"Oh, please. Nothing quite so dramatic," Marnie said, shaking her head, "and a lot more life-affirming, we think."

"Tell him, Marnie," Lucy said.

Marnie smiled at her sister's enthusiasm. "You're going on a month-long diving course in Mexico," she said. "It's all arranged."

Matt looked at her blankly, so she kept going. "Phil, one of the teachers at school, was talking about this diving place he went to, earlier this year, and that gave me the idea. He put me in touch with the owner and I called him last night. He needs help in his dive shop and agreed to train you in exchange for helping out, provided you stay for at least a month."

Still nothing from Matt.

"You'll have to work in the shop for a few hours every day to cover the training, but the flight, accommodation and the other bits we'll manage together."

So far, so good. He hadn't outright rejected the idea.

"It's in a village called Sayulita, on the Pacific Coast, with SCUBA diving, surfing, snorkelling, whale-watching, beautiful beaches…"

Lucy was grinning from ear to ear, practically jumping up and down in her seat.

"What are you so happy about?" Matt growled. His tone was gruff, but Lucy could see that they'd managed to prise open a small chink in his emotional armour.

"I just want my not-so-Fatso-Mattso brother back," Lucy said, leaning into him and poking his concave stomach.

Matt angrily swatted her away. A good sign, Lucy thought. A reaction.

"Did you not think of consulting me first?" He was playing for time, a glimmer of life in his eyes.

"To make sure you had room in your hectic social calendar, you mean?" Lucy rolled her eyes dramatically.

"Matt, get a grip," Marnie said. "You're going nowhere and doing nothing to pull yourself out of this. Unless you do something radical, you're fucked."

Lucy looked at her sister, impressed. *Marnie swearing! You rock, sis!* Excellent tactic, coming from her.

Matt raised his eyebrows.

"This will force you to get out of your head and into your body—to stop torturing yourself with regrets, blame and self-loathing," Marnie said firmly. "Something physically demanding in a completely new, foreign environment, miles from any of this." She gestured around the room. "And from us—from anything that makes you think of the hell you've been through."

Matt sat with arms folded, still not re-committing to the world.

"You know what, Marn? I think we read this all wrong," Lucy said. "I can see why Matt wouldn't want to do this."

Matt and Marnie looked at her in surprise.

"It's clear he'd prefer the counselling/therapy option. Right, Matt?" She looked at him challengingly. "You'd much rather sit through hours of painful emotional analysis every week for the next two years than go surfing in Mexico. Of course! Silly us. What were we *thinking*?"

She looked at Marnie. "Can you cancel that arrangement? Or maybe *you* could go instead?"

Matt twitched in his seat. "Look, I just need to think about it, okay?"

"Matt, do you realize that Lucy is willing to go with you to group counselling? You know she'd rather pull out her own nails than go there but she's willing to do it for you."

"Easy to say if she knows I'd refuse to go," Matt said.

"You wouldn't have a choice," Lucy said. "We'd bully you into it—and still might, if that's the *less awful* option for you." She wondered at the irony of bullying him into doing something that she didn't want him to do at all.

The fish stew she had spent two hours preparing was going cold and she was getting pissed off.

"You're being a selfish, petulant, ungrateful brat," she said angrily. "Can't you see we're throwing you a life-line?" She felt herself go hot from the intensity of her emotions, only just realizing how much she'd needed to say that to him …and maybe also to herself. *Might those have been Marnie's words to her, just a few weeks ago?*

"And you've ruined my fish stew," Lucy said, tears pricking her eyes.

"It was a genuine offer, Matt," Marnie said gently. "Lucy was willing to join the group with you, if it would help."

"Okay, okay!" Matt put his arms up in surrender. He took a deep breath and they both looked at him expectantly.

"Yes?" Lucy held her spoon in front of him—a fake microphone. "You have something to say to your fabulous sisters?"

That generated a small smile, a hesitant thawing of the frozen interior.

"I. Will. Go. Okay?

"Yes!" Lucy did a high-five to Marnie, who smiled as she slapped Lucy's palm.

"Anything else you'd like to say?" Lucy prompted, the 'microphone' poised for another earth-shaking sound bite.

Matt took another breath, searching for something to give back.

"Yes, actually," he said, his face serious. "Cold fish stew à la Luce is my favourite meal. I'll be thinking of this when I'm in Mexico, sitting on the beach eating plain old barbequed fish from the daily catch."

Silence spun as this epistle hit the airwaves. It was more words than he'd uttered in two weeks.

Then Marnie and Lucy burst out laughing. Lucy had tears running down her face and her throat throbbed as her laughter coursed through joy, sadness and relief.

Then Matt threw his head back and laughed too, and they almost fell off their chairs from shock and hysteria.

Lucy felt an aching tenderness—for her siblings and herself, for hearts broken and mending, for parents departed, for the mystery of Nate, for tragedies surmounted, for grief shared, for emotions overflowing, for the chance to begin again.

20

April 1996

She landed on the grass like a dead body thrown from a plane. He had been scanning the fields with his binoculars when he saw her, about 80 feet from the back of the house. He flung the binoculars aside, pulled open the patio doors, raced across the deck, vaulted over the railing, and ran across the grass, calling her name.

"Frannie, I'm coming!"

He fell to his knees beside her and scooped her into his arms, cradling her to his chest. She seemed lifeless but he could feel her trembling against him. Her face was drawn, her T-shirt soaked with sweat, plastered against her body.

"Frannie, talk to me."

Her eyelids fluttered. She was coming back. He rubbed her back and her arms to generate some warmth in her frozen clammy limbs.

She opened her eyes, taking a few seconds to focus and get her bearings.

"Daniel!" She grabbed his shirt and pulled him closer, her eyes fiercely urgent.

"*What happened?*" Daniel searched her face. "You were gone for 24 hours and I was going mad with worry. Are you okay? Are you hurt? *Tell me*, sweetheart."

She was so exhausted she could hardly speak, but she had to tell him. "It's… impossible…" Her eyes were closing again and he caressed her face, beaming as much of his love and energy into her as he could. She was close to collapsing but she forced herself back into consciousness, focusing on him with all her might.

"*Oh, Daniel,*" she said, her tired eyes filled with wonder. "*I've been to the future.*"

21

Friday, 17 January 2020

The silence was almost tangible—a subtle ringing in her ears as the emotional echoes of the past few months reverberated through her system. As Marnie sat at her usual Friday-morning spot beside the window, doodling in her notepad and finally getting back to thinking about *Lester the Snake*, she reflected on all that had happened.

She had started a journal on New Year's Day and was keeping track of all the emotions, conflicts, frustrations and breakthroughs they had experienced. It had been a rollercoaster of a ride but she felt closer to her siblings than she could ever have imagined, and she was proud of how they had supported each other through hell and back.

Matt had left for Mexico at the end of November and e-mailed them regularly with updates. He had finished his SCUBA training just before Christmas and was now helping Zack, the owner, with some of the dives, whale-watching expeditions and snorkelling. He seemed content and there was no mention of him coming home yet. Marnie had the feeling he might stay there for good. And that was okay. They would try to visit him in the spring, if he was still there, and catch up on his new life.

Lucy was loving her job at Cordalis Communications. She had started off working Tuesday to Friday, but was now working every weekday, often not getting home till mid-afternoon.

Which suited Marnie perfectly. She had her Fridays to herself again and her home was almost back to normal. Lucy would be moving out next month and would be sharing an apartment with someone Tracy at work had told her about.

For Christmas, she and Lucy had decided they couldn't bear to spend the holidays at home and had to get away. Thanks to Leslie Vauxhall, who seemed to have wealthy contacts all over the place, Marnie had been able to rent a small cottage in Nantucket, at a greatly discounted rate. She and Lucy had gone there for a week, going for bracing walks along the beach, enjoying the Christmas lights, drinking hot cider in cozy cafés and generally immersing themselves in comfort foods, warm duvets, good books, open fires and mindless activities.

Now that she was finally getting her life back, though, it felt less fulfilling than before. Matt and Lucy had both taken off in completely new directions, with new friends, challenges and horizons, while she, Marnie, was still teaching the same classes, with the same routine, without having moved on in any meaningful way. *And she was writing a story about a snake with a lisp, for heaven's sake.*

What was *she* going to do with her life, now that she had helped her siblings find a new direction?

She thought about Steve. They had spoken again briefly on the phone in November, when Steve had called to say he was going away for two months on assignment for his job. As a data analyst for a large company, Steve often went to work on location for a client in Chicago. He would be back in early February.

The issue of contacting him again had therefore been taken out of her hands. Marnie was relieved, although a little disappointed. She had initially been afraid that Steve would start pursuing her again, but he seemed to be respecting her decision to just be friends. Anyway, *she* had contacted *him*, she reminded herself, so she could hardly complain if he responded positively. *Wasn't that how friends behaved?*

Marnie wondered if she was getting jaded and cynical. Had taking care of her siblings changed her—left her carrying the things she had helped then shed?

Her phone rang, interrupting her thoughts.

"Hello?"

"Marn, turn on the news!" It was Lucy. "I'll be home for lunch. Gotta go!" She hung up.

What the…?

Marnie got up and turned on her TV. It was the top of the hour and the news was just starting. She sat on the couch to watch.

"...still our top story today, the attempted terrorist attack earlier this week in Boston," the news anchor, Rick Weston, intoned gravely. "We go live now to Donna Mauvezin, outside Boston PD, for the latest. Donna?"

A live feed opened on his right, revealing a dark-haired young woman, standing in front of the Boston PD building. Wearing a belted red wool coat and holding a large phallic-looking microphone, she looked earnestly at the camera.

"Yes, Rick. The alleged attack now appears to be more political than terrorist in nature, but let me do a quick recap on the story for our viewers." She glanced at her notes.

"Two days ago, at 9am on the fifteenth of January, a Boston PD SWAT team apprehended a 55-year-old white male who was allegedly planning to unleash a deadly airborne toxin into the environment. The arrest came after BPD received an anonymous call alerting them to the event. The suspect's name was not immediately released but he was believed to be a physicist with specialized expertise.

"It is still not known what kind of toxin is involved but a large sealed canister of an allegedly volatile substance was seized from the suspect's home on Wednesday and immediately airlifted to CDC in Atlanta.

"Our sources indicated that the supposedly deadly toxin was intended to be released into the atmosphere and instantaneously transmitted to the entire population of the Boston Metro area, potentially affecting the entire state and beyond.

"The toxin, initially sent to CDC for containment and investigation, was subsequently transferred to a lab here at MIT, where specialized technicians have been working around the clock to identify the precise nature of the substance and the intended mechanism for its dispersal.

"Yesterday, the 55-year-old white male suspect was identified as Dr Raynor Spence—a physicist specializing in electromagnetism."

A photo of Dr Spence appeared on the screen, showing a good-looking man with silver hair, kind hazel eyes and a steady gaze. He looked like a man of conviction, not seeking the approval or acceptance of others, Marnie thought, as she leaned forward to look at him more closely.

"According to official reports, Dr Spence claims that he developed a biological interface between pathogens and the frequencies currently used for wireless internet connectivity. He also claims to have created a deadly toxin that would, and I quote, *'be dispersed and potentiated by the pervasive manmade electromagnetic frequencies used for WiFi, mobile telephony and other wireless technologies'.*

Marnie was riveted to the screen. Her parents had also specialized in electromagnetism. *Had they known this other physicist?*

"In an official written statement to the police, Dr Spence claims that he has, for the past ten years, consistently warned governments, scientists and the wireless industry about the serious harm being caused by these toxic electromagnetic fields in our natural environment, but that no one would listen."

Donna glanced at her notes again.

"Dr Spence also claims that, while his intended actions might, and I quote, *'be construed as terrorism, the real terrorism is happening every day in our world, with the wireless industry, endorsed by world governments, irradiating the entire population and all forms of life on earth. With the launching of thousands of 5G satellites into space,'* says Dr Spence, *'there is no more potent or scientifically effective way of disrupting the natural order of things and jeopardizing the viability of the human species as well as all other planetary lifeforms'.*"

Rick Weston interjected as Donna paused for breath.

"What's the mood there on the street, Donna? How is the general public reacting?"

"The public outcry has been intense, as you can imagine, Rick, with the issue being hotly debated on all sides."

Donna consulted her notes again.

"Rick, as you know, people have been calling and writing into the station, and also coming out in person to express their support or outrage, depending on their perspective."

Donna gestured behind her, where a small crowd of people holding placards were pacing back and forth.

"As you can see, there are some protesters here on the street, demanding that the government take immediate action to address the wireless radiation issue."

Donna held up her notes and read off a list of the parties involved.

"Over the past two days, we've had some very vocal—and angry—

individuals and groups from several camps. EMF activists and health advocates have applauded Dr Spence's stand, saying that this kind of extreme action is the only way to force the government to act, while several independent scientists have spoken out about the dangers of wireless radiation, expressing their frustration at the scientific studies being consistently ignored by governments worldwide.

"Then there are representatives from the wireless industry itself, claiming that the frequencies used for wireless communications have never been conclusively shown to cause harm and that they could never be used to transmit viruses or bacteria. One industry representative claimed that, and I quote, '*It is downright irresponsible for anyone to claim that such a thing could be possible.*'

"Some other very irate individuals have aggressively debunked the claims of harm and referred to the activists as, and I quote, '*freaks, cranks and nutters who get in the way of economic progress and should go and live in a cave*', unquote."

Donna looked up from her notes with a shrug.

"So, as you can see, Rick, all sides are weighing in on the issue and we expect to get a lot more reaction in the coming days."

"Thank you, Donna," Rick said, closing the live feed to the reporter and turning back to the camera.

"We'll bring you more updates from Donna as the situation unfolds."

The camera panned out to show an older man sitting to the right of the anchor, whom Rick introduced as he turned sideways to face him.

"Joining me now in the studio is Dr Fintan Pemberton, a former faculty member of Northeastern University and a one-time colleague of Dr Raynor Spence."

The man appeared to be in his early 70s, with thinning grey hair, rimless glasses and a salt-and-pepper goatee. Dressed in a creased black suit, pale-blue shirt and purple tie, he looked uncomfortable on camera.

Marnie got up from the couch, grabbed her notepad from the table, and made a note of the two physicists' names. She sat back down, all thoughts of Lester, Steve and work gone from her mind.

"Dr Pemberton, you and Dr Spence were colleagues at one point, is that correct?"

"Yes, that's correct," Dr Pemberton said. "He and I overlapped as faculty members for about five years in the physics department."

"What is your take on what Dr Spence has done? Does this seem like something your former colleague would do?"

"Absolutely not," Dr Pemberton said emphatically, shaking his head. "I'm as shocked as everyone else by his actions."

He paused to consider his words. "Ray—Dr Spence—was a solid scientist, very committed to his work and someone I always considered to be of the utmost integrity."

"Why would he do something like this, in your opinion, Dr Pemberton?"

"I really cannot speculate." Dr Pemberton pursed his lips, reluctant to judge his former colleague.

Rick consulted his notes. "You have retired now, correct?"

"Yes. I retired five years ago."

"But you both worked in the same department, doing research into electromagnetism?"

"Yes, correct."

"Could you explain, in simple terms, what that research involves?"

Dr Pemberton sat up straighter in his seat. "Electromagnetism is a branch of physics involving the study of the electromagnetic force, which is one of the four fundamental forces of nature and is a type of physical interaction that occurs between electrically charged particles."

He looked at Rick as if to say, you want more? Rick gestured for him to continue.

"It's highly technical and I won't bore your viewers with the details, but it is essentially the study of forces between charged particles, electromagnetic fields, electric—or scalar—potentials, magnetic vector potentials and the behaviour of conductors, magnetism and electromagnetic waves."

Warming to his topic, he added, "The concepts taught in courses on electromagnetism provide a basis for more advanced aspects of physics, such as quantum field theory and general relativity."

Rick jumped in. "Dr Pemberton, in your scientific opinion, is it technically possible to intentionally disperse a toxic airborne substance via the electromagnetic waves used to wirelessly communicate and transmit data through the internet?"

Dr Pemberton cleared his throat and hesitated before responding.

"This is a very controversial area of science," he said. "There have actually been studies at Northeastern showing that simple organisms, such as viruses and bacteria, can generate and communicate by radio waves, and physicists now know how this occurs."

He paused again, carefully choosing his words. "The work of Nobel Prize-winner Luc Montagnier has shown that cells can send electromagnetic imprints of themselves to each other, and we know that bacterial and other types of cells use electromagnetic waves at higher frequencies to communicate as well as to send and store energy."

Rick glanced back at the camera with a mixture of confusion and gravitas. "So... are you saying that what Dr Spence had proposed to do is technically possible?"

"I'm saying it is... within the realm of possibility," Dr Pemberton said, very deliberately. "The frontiers of science are being consistently pushed beyond what we think is possible, and the seemingly improbable is routinely becoming entirely feasible."

"But not possible yet?"

"I can't confirm that," Dr Pemberton said, folding his arms across his chest. "Studies are ongoing and the Russians and other nations with advanced expertise in this area are also carrying out their own research."

"Could it have been a hoax?" Rick consulted his notes. "Some industry scientists are claiming that what Dr Spence did was a publicity stunt to get people's attention and that he never intended to actually release anything into the ambient electromagnetic fields, even if such a thing were possible. What would you say to that?"

"Anything is possible, as I said." Dr Pemberton removed his glasses, rubbed his eyes, and put his glasses back on. "It would seem to be entirely out of character for the man I knew, but I really cannot confirm anything either way."

He paused for effect. "All I can say for certain is that Dr Raynor Spence is—was—a physicist with superior knowledge and expertise in electromagnetism, and he may well have developed... something along these lines if he continued his research after leaving Northeastern."

Rick touched his earpiece and nodded. "We'll have to leave it there, Dr Pemberton," he said, gathering up his notes. "Thank you for joining us."

Dr Pemberton nodded and the camera zoomed in once again on the anchorman.

"We'll bring you more on this story in our 6pm news update," Rick said. "After the break, we'll have more on the severe storms sweeping across the States and the current warm weather, here in Boston, with reports from scientists that the increasing climatic—"

Marnie got up and switched off the TV. Her head was buzzing and her throat was dry. She went into the kitchen and poured herself a glass of water, knocking it back in one go.

What would her parents have made of all this? They would probably have found it fascinating and would have disappeared into the lab for days on end to explore the possibilities.

But it was also downright frightening, if this Dr Spence could actually do what he claimed he could—transmit deadly toxins via the wireless internet. What would have happened if he had gone ahead, if it *wasn't* a hoax?

Had her parents had this kind of expertise? Surely they would have made it public if they had, or found some positive use for it.

Marnie had no idea what aspects of electromagnetism they had been studying, but she had always assumed their work was to do with… what? Now that she stopped to think about it, she wasn't sure she knew, exactly. Something to do with measuring energy for scientific or medical applications, designing electrical transmitters…? She had always thought of them as being like modern-day Nikola Teslas, but she was starting to realize that she didn't know her parents at all—as parents, as people *or* as scientists.

She sighed and decided to go for a walk. She'd pick up some soup from Whole Foods and she and Lucy could have lunch together when she got home.

Then she'd see if she could contact Dr Pemberton and find out if he knew her parents.

22

Saturday, 18 January 2020

Marnie was surprised to find Dr Pemberton listed in the telephone directory, which also gave his address. He must have been pestered with calls from the media and others, she thought, following his TV interview.

For this reason, she decided not to call him. She would go to his home and see if he would talk to her.

She reckoned she'd have the best chance of catching him at home in the evening, and it was now 7pm. Late enough for him to have had dinner, hopefully, and be relaxing with a book or watching TV—unless he did lots of entertaining at home, which she doubted.

His house was about 20 blocks from her place so she decided to walk. It was cooling down again outside, but the sun had been shining all day and the roads were dry after heavy rainfall during the night.

She pulled on her boots, black wool coat, an orange scarf of Lucy's, leather gloves, and a woollen hat with an Aztec design and drop-down knitted triangles to cover her ears.

She had nothing from her parents to show Dr Pemberton, but she had her driver's licence showing her name and she hoped that would be enough to convince him of her identity.

With her bag over her shoulder and her head bent against the biting wind, she set off at a brisk pace in the direction of his house.

Walking had always been Marnie's way of processing things, and she pondered what to say to this man, once she got there. What might he know? If he hadn't known her parents, then how could he help her? Were there other questions about his work in electromagnetism that might indicate what her parents had been working on? Were there issues in this field of research that other physicists were seeking to understand?

It was all just conjecture, at this point. She would just have to wait and see what he said—if he agreed to say anything at all.

Her nose was cold and probably turning red, but Marnie could feel herself sweating inside her wool coat. Whether it was from the brisk walk or her nervousness at confronting this man about her parents, she wasn't sure. But she was starting to feel a little anxious.

She turned down Nottinghill Road and started looking for his house. It was a quiet tree-lined street of older, detached three-storey houses with heavy wooden front doors, sash windows and slate roofs. The tenth house on her right was Dr Pemberton's. It had a yellow front door and looked a little cheerier and slightly more inviting than the others, but that didn't help much.

Her stomach was churning and she was wondering how on earth to introduce herself—a stranger off the street with a weird story. But she was hardly a threat to anyone, even an academic in his 70s who had probably done nothing more physically challenging than hefting large tomes of scientific papers for his research. Her only weapon was her handbag and her questions. She couldn't do much harm with those.

She walked up the steps to his front door, paused, took a deep breath, and rang the bell. She could hear the faint sounds of a TV or someone talking on the phone but she wasn't sure if they were coming from his house or next door.

If he didn't answer shortly, she was going to—

The door opened suddenly, revealing Dr Pemberton looking less than happy at being disturbed. He was wearing a grey turtle-neck sweater under a baggy navy cardigan with leather buttons, and loose black pants over tartan slippers.

"Yes? Are you a reporter?" He eyed her suspiciously, one foot behind the door, ready to close it in her face.

"No, I'm…" Marnie was suddenly overcome with emotion. "I'm hoping you can help me, Dr Pemberton… It's about my parents, who were physicists, but they died and…"

To her dismay, she found she was crying. She was falling apart in front of a complete stranger and she couldn't seem to control herself.

He looked at her with concern. "What's your name, young lady?"

"Marnie Dalton." She wiped her cheeks with a gloved hand and sniffled as she tried to find a tissue in her handbag.

"Dalton? Dalton, did you say?"

Had he not heard her properly or did the name mean something?

"They were researchers, stu… studying electromag… netism, but they di… died and I'm trying to find out wh… why…" She was sobbing now, mortified at losing her composure but unable to stop the flood of emotion.

Dr Pemberton opened the door and gestured for her to enter.

"Come in, my dear, and you can tell me what this is about."

He led her down the hall and into a dimly lit room where a gas fire cast a warm glow on two black leather armchairs, a low coffee table bearing books and a half-empty mug of black tea, and several large bookshelves lining the walls. An angled reading lamp arched over one of the armchairs, creating a spotlight where he had obviously been sitting, reading and drinking his tea.

"Take a seat." He gestured to the other armchair and sat down opposite her.

Marnie lowered herself onto the squeaky leather, feeling wobbly and fragile yet also aware of a tingling prescience, as if an inner part of her sensed some kind of imminent revelation. The room itself felt like a warm womb where things might be birthed and shared. She could almost feel the years of deep thinking and reflection that had thickened the atmosphere, giving it weight.

"How can I help you, Ms Dalton?" He had softened as a result of her tears, the look in his eyes vacillating between curiosity, uncertainty and concern.

Marnie took another deep breath.

"I'm wondering if you knew my parents," she said. "They were both physicists—Daniel and Francesca Dalton—but they… died in, um, unusual circumstance, and we've been trying to figure out what happened, and what they had been working on."

She paused, unsure what to say next.

"Dalton," he said.

Why did he keep repeating the name?

"How did they die?"

"They…" *Why did she always feel ashamed when she told people they'd taken their own lives?* Fortified by a spurt of anger, she continued. "They killed themselves." Let someone else deal with the shocking reality for a change, without her always feeling as if she had to soften or explain it. Not that she could.

"My dear, I'm very sorry to hear that." Dr Pemberton sat back in his chair, his shoulders sagging. He took off his glasses and put them on the coffee table. Marnie got the distinct impression that he was not surprised by the news. Maybe he'd seen the notice in the newspaper…

"This must be terribly distressing for you, but I'm not sure how I can help."

"Did you know them, my parents?" She searched his face for some clues. "Did you ever meet them or hear about them in your research?"

"Well, I'm not sure what to tell you, Ms Dalton…" He folded his arms across his chest, something Marnie remembered him doing in the TV interview. He was feeling uncomfortable or defensive about something.

"Did you know them?" She leaned forward in her seat, looking him in the eye.

"Not… exactly," he said, avoiding her gaze.

"What do you mean? Did you know them or not?" Marnie was starting to feel annoyed. *Was he hiding something?*

He hesitated, shifting in his seat and looking uncomfortable. "I worked… indirectly with them, you might say."

"What do that mean? Dr Pemberton, please tell me. I really need to know." Marnie looked at him pleadingly. "How did you work with them? What kind of work?"

Dr Pemberton held up his hands, as if to slow her words while he pondered his response.

"Your parents used to do online trainings for other physicists," he said, his voice guarded. "A select group of scientists and researchers who wanted to learn about their work."

"What kind of work?" Marnie was on the edge of her seat, fighting the urge to grab this man by the shoulders to shake the information out of him. Maybe she wasn't so harmless after all.

"I can't tell you that." He held up his hands again as Marnie started to protest. "I can't tell you because I don't know," he said. "They trained us in the use and manufacture of some advanced electronic devices they developed, but it was nothing earth-shattering. Just some new technology for measuring and controlling certain quantum systems and other highly sophisticated devices." He waved away the details.

"But there was something else?" Marnie could see he was conflicted, trying to decide how much to tell her. "What else were they working on, Dr Pemberton?"

"We all signed a non-disclosure agreement," he said. "Not that we could disclose much, even if we'd wanted to." He sighed. "In exchange for the training we received in the new technology, we were each asked to work on a specific part of a larger project. But we all worked separately. We never got to meet each other or to know each other's names, although we had our suspicions, and we were never given enough information to understand the goal or the full scope of the project."

Marnie's head was reeling. *What the hell…?*

"Where did they get the funding for all this? Do you know?"

"I don't know the details." Dr Pemberton shrugged apologetically. "But it was either some large overseas corporation or a foreign government. Whoever they were, I got the impression they weren't too friendly with America or its policies."

Marnie sat back in her chair, feeling as if the air had been knocked out of her. What had her parents been doing, colluding with foreign governments? *Were they spies?*

"Do you have any idea what the project might have been about?" She leaned forward again. "Please, see if you can think of anything that might give me some clues."

"I've given this a lot of thought, Ms Dalton, as you can imagine, but I have only pure supposition, nothing concrete to go on, I can assure you."

"And...? What were your suppositions?"

"I could only imagine that it might have had something to do with a new kind of weapon, but I only started to have some concerns along those lines towards the end of our agreement. Then the training ended and I had no further contact."

"When was that? When did you finish working with them?" Marnie was trying to get a sense of the timeline.

Dr Pemberton paused to reflect. "That would have been about six or seven years ago, shortly before I retired," he said.

"And how long did the training go on?"

"The training only took a few weeks, but the research I was asked to do took longer—probably a year or two, interspersed with my own work."

"Dr Pemberton, is there anything else you can tell me about my parents that might shed some light on what they were doing?" She looked at him earnestly. "Anything at all?"

"Well, I do remember hearing through the academic grapevine that someone—and it might not have been them, mind you—was working on some kind of sophisticated interface between biological processes and environmental stimuli."

"I have no idea what that means," Marnie said, frustrated.

"I'm not sure what it means, in terms of its practical application," Dr Pemberton said, shrugging, "but it could possibly have had something to do with manipulating artificial electromagnetic fields for potentially nefarious purposes."

"You mean using them as a weapon?" Marnie shook her head, unable to imagine her parents involved in such things. "Like what Dr Spence tried to do? Those rumours were probably about him, then—right? If he was researching that kind of thing?"

"Very likely," Dr Pemberton agreed.

Did he mean that?

"My parents would never have been involved in something like that," she said. *Would they…?*

"I'm sure you're right," Dr Pemberton said. "What little I knew about your parents led me to believe that their research was for purely beneficial purposes. I very much doubt they were involved in something harmful or criminal."

He paused, seeming to reflect. "Although…"

"What?" Marnie was back on the edge of her seat.

"I got the feeling that Ray Spence might have been part of the research project, although I have absolutely no proof of that." He shook his head at her inevitable question. "You would have to ask him about it. I really can't tell you any more."

He slapped his knees and got up, indicating the end of the conversation.

Marnie had had enough anyway. She needed to go home to process all this.

"Dr Pemberton, would you mind calling a cab for me? I don't live far away but I don't think I can walk home after this."

He smiled. "I can do better than that, my dear." He looked her up and down, taking in her boots, scarf, hat, gloves. "Ever been on the back of a bike?"

What was he talking about? "You mean a motorbike?"

"Yes, one of those noisy two-wheeled vehicles that youngsters ride around the streets to impress the girls."

"Um, yes, once…"

"Right, then. Get your bag and let's go."

He suddenly seemed full of energy and she had to hurry after him as he went into the hall. He opened a closet under the stairs and pulled out an old-fashioned leather motorbike helmet, thrusting it into her hands.

"Follow me." He hustled into the kitchen at the end of the hall, opened a door to the basement and hurried down the steps, flicking on a light as he went.

What the hell…?

"It's okay," he called up to her from below. "I'll open up the garage door and you can meet me round the back, if you feel safer. Then you won't see all the dead bodies down here." This was followed by a cackle of laughter.

Marnie heard a metal door rattle upwards and the roar of a powerful motorbike coming to life.

What did she have to lose? Her parents were obviously spies or mad scientists who ended up dealing with gangsters—*Lucy was right, after all!*—or she herself had lost her marbles, so it didn't really matter if she did something utterly brainless and out of character when the whole world had gone crazy anyway.

She ran down the stairs and out through the garage door to where Dr Pemberton was waiting for her, perched on a huge neon-green Kawasaki Ninja, looking like something from outer space in a leather bomber jacket and futuristic helmet, revving the engine.

Bloody hell! Ten minutes ago, she'd wanted to whack the old geezer with her handbag; now he looked like some sinister alien, capable of zapping her to stardust with one look.

"Put on your helmet." He tapped his own.

She pulled on the helmet over her hat and tied the strap underneath. It had detachable goggles but they were too big for her face so she left them up on the rim of the helmet.

"Address?"

She told him.

"Hop on!"

And she did, her pulse pounding and her heart trying to leap out of her chest, wanting no part of this demented caper.

He gunned the engine and the bike roared down the back lane, paused at the main road, then turned right towards her place.

She hung on for dear life, gasping at the cold air in her face, her mind reeling at the sheer insanity of it all and the fact that she, Marnie Dalton—*elementary teacher and Ms Responsible*—was on the back of a Ninja, driven by an old codger in a ratty cardigan, flying down the streets, hugging the corners, her arms wrapped around Evel Knievel disguised as a nutty professor.

Her eyes were streaming but the icy air was whipping the moisture away so fast she couldn't figure out whether they were tears of grief, the shocking thrill of the ride or just the normal hysteria that came from losing your mind.

Lucy would not believe this story.

But the person she really wanted to talk to, she realized, as she leaned into another hairy corner at 45 degrees, was Steve.

23

Matt was still adjusting to the everyday chaos of Sayulita. He was living a simple life, renting a hut on the outskirts of town, with just a small kitchen, a living room with a single bed, an outhouse and an outdoor shower. From there, he walked through the streets every morning at 7am to the beach.

The din and activity were constant—mangy dogs skulking for scraps, cocks crowing, motorbikes with engines like lawnmowers scraping his nerves, radios blaring from the numerous cafés along the way, friends shouting greetings to each other, kids playing ball in the pot-holed street, raucous laughter, car horns honking, restaurant-owners sweeping the pavement, pungent smells from roadside barbeques serving food… The rawness of life was in your face and there was no escape.

He stopped at José's juice bar and ordered his usual blend of celery, spinach, chlorella, papaya and passion fruit. Some passersby slapped him on the back, calling out his name. Some divers from last week. He couldn't remember their names…

José placed his green concoction on the countertop. *"¿Todo bien, amigo mio?"*

"Sí, gracias," Matt said, handing him three dollar notes.

José rapped his knuckles on the wooden countertop, obviously not entirely convinced. *"Golpea esto y te sentirás mejor."* *Drink this and you'll feel better.*

And it did usually help, a little.

When he finally reached the beach, he took a deep breath of cleansing salty air and felt his whole body relax. The sea was usually calm at this time of day, although it got a lot rougher as the day wore on. He didn't have to start work at the dive shop till noon, so he had his mornings free.

When he had first arrived at this place, he used to just sit on a rock at one end of the beach for an hour or two, letting the sound of the sea, the fresh morning air and the rhythms of nature wash over him. He thought a lot about Celle. He knew he had lost her—probably even before Jed had been killed. He decided his heart hadn't been big enough to deal with all that he had lost—his parents, his best friend, then his girlfriend. He had let her down, and she had turned on him with a viciousness that had hurt him deeply.

Shortly before he left for Mexico, Jen had come to see him at his apartment as he was packing for his trip. She told him they had wound things down at work and that Travis Chamberlain had been very understanding about the situation, offering to help them find other jobs, if they needed one.

But they were okay, Jen told Matt, and they would find their own way forward. Harry had already found another job and Laura was thinking of going back to college to study political science. He wasn't to worry about them.

Then she had all but forced him to sit down to listen to what she had to say. She told him he needed to let go of the guilt and blame he was carrying about Jed's death. If he didn't, it would corrode his happiness, his health and his life. If things had been the other way around, she said, and he had been killed instead of Jed, would he want his friend to destroy himself with guilt and blame over his death?

You know he wouldn't have wanted that, she said emphatically, and he had a feeling she was right. It didn't erase the guilt, but he was slowly allowing himself to let some life in.

"*Live for him, Matt,*" Jen had urged him. "You know how he relished life, living on the edge and always pushing the envelope. Let some of his qualities live on through you. Let that be his gift to you as his best friend. Allow yourself to have a life, even though his was cut short."

She had taken both of his hands in hers, as if to funnel some feeling back up to his heart. "Be the best friend you can be to him by being your best self. That is what he would wish for you, and what you would wish for him, if things were the other way around."

They hugged and cried and he felt a little bit lighter.

Marnie had also given him a parting pep talk.

"Celle wanted you to fight for her," she said. "She must have felt you didn't care for her when you just gave up on yourself and her. You let your grief consume you, without fighting for a chance at happiness together. Or, at the very least, the opportunity to help each other heal."

But Matt knew that Celle had wanted to fight *with* him. She needed a target for her anger—someone to blame for what had happened—but she also needed to physically and emotionally vent her anger, attacking him with accusations that, to him, felt entirely justified. All too willing to passively assume the blame, he gave her anger no worthy opponent to battle with. Which made her even angrier.

He knew she despised him for not defending himself, for not doing everything in his power to be there for her and for not even trying to redeem himself. But he knew—and he knew she knew—that there would be no redemption, and that they could never be friends again, let alone a couple. The grief, loss and heartache had permanently ruptured whatever tenuous connection they had had.

Celle had dropped by to see him, just before he left, but he didn't want to think about that. She had been angry. Furious. Enraged. And a few other things... He had never been attacked like that by anyone. How could the loss of a loved one generate such viciousness, such venomous wrath against him—someone she had supposedly loved?

He couldn't handle her need for him to be there for her so that she could be there for him. It was her need to be needed that had made it impossible for him to reach out—*and* made him realize that she might never have really loved him at all.

If he was honest with himself, he was relieved the relationship was over. He hadn't realized how depleting it was until Celle had needed him to be there for her when he barely had enough life force left for himself. Their pain had stripped the shallow topsoil from their love, revealing deep fissures and fault lines underneath—the matrix of their shaky selves. He had weak boundaries to shore up and much wisdom to distil from his ragged self-exposure.

He imagined Celle would bounce back faster than he would. Her anger would keep her fired up enough to carry her through the various stages of grief and out the other side. She might never again be gentle or tender—*had she ever been?*—but she would eventually move on and find some pleasure in life.

Now, two months later, he jogged for half an hour as soon as he hit the beach each morning. After pounding the hard sand close to shore, he often took the steep trail along the cliff, which dipped and rose between the small coves dotted along the coast.

It was a workout he welcomed as he sweated the toxic emotions from his mind and body, strengthening his physical and emotional muscles, and stoking the faint embers of life still simmering inside.

Zack had been good to him, allowing him to work erratic hours, at first, as he adjusted to the demands of the job and slowly shed the inertia that had been weighing him down for weeks. The interaction with customers, the hot sun, the bracing salt water, the physical exertion, learning to dive, and the other new skills he had to quickly master… it had all forced him to come out of his semi-comatose state and show up in body if not yet in heart and mind.

Zack knew first-hand the toll that grief took, having lost his wife in a diving accident ten years previously, and then his business when he used alcohol to numb his pain. He had been helped back up by his friends, and he told Matt he was happy to "pay it forward".

What Matt could not understand was how Zack could have gone back into the same business after losing his wife that way. But Zack said he couldn't blame life or the sea for what had happened, and he needed to prove to himself that he could *get back on the horse*, so to speak. He also confided to Matt that he felt his wife's presence very strongly whenever he went on a dive, as if the sea held her soul and she was everywhere, all around him, in the water. It was all he had left of her.

His boss was a large, rough-hewn, unpolished kind of guy, but Matt was often touched and surprised by Zack's heartfelt wisdom and the genuine care he showed towards his friends and customers.

Matt felt lucky to have landed here, and he was starting to glimpse some kind of life and light at the end of the dark tunnel of pain.

24

Friday, 24 January 2020

Celle was sitting on a bench at the crest of the hill on her usual 5km circuit, her chest heaving. Beads of sweat trickled down her neck and her spine was tingling. She pulled her water bottle from her bum bag and drank half of it, staring vacantly at the everyday busyness below as her pulse slowed and her mind started filing all the feelings she'd dumped straight into her mental archives without even looking at them. Why bother? As far as she could see, her life was totally fucked. Forever.

She'd had to really push herself this morning to leave the apartment and go for a run. It was over a month since she'd last hit the track and her head felt as if it was going to explode. All that thinking and agonising without any action. Fatal. Toxic. For her and anyone close to her.

Including her parents, although they were so lost in their grief over their precious son that they barely registered anything else. She needed them for *her*, for God's sake. At least *she* was still breathing. Had they *ever* been there for her? She felt trapped by indelible family dysfunction.

Why did her parents chose to teach history? How the hell had history ever helped anyone? It bloody hadn't. Ever. It was pure spin and even if anybody ever believed all that crap written by the victors, no one ever learned from their mistakes or their sick victories. There was no glory in winning a few more years of empty existence in a world of such petty, twisted values.

Why couldn't people teach a healthy future instead of a sick past? That would be a hell of a lot more useful. She should make up her own happy-ending story and see if she could live it, instead of living the destructive illusion handed down to her about how unworthy she was and how tough life had to be. Everyone was deluded. She had witnessed plenty of that yesterday, with all those placard-waving sickos! So she might as well create her own fantasy, instead of living in this horror movie.

But who was she kidding? There was no glossing over this.

She needed to pound the pavement and sweat all her feelings to the surface, to try to *exorcise* them. Otherwise, she couldn't feel them or even *find* them. Well, yeah, who would *want* to? Her emotions had gone into lockdown and she had become nothing more than a heartless body transporting an analytical brain. No lights on, nobody home, no WELCOME mat—certainly no welcome *Matt*... Just the endless whirring mechanisms of her masochistic mental judgements.

Would she ever feel clean again? Would she ever be normal, emotionally stable, loving or capable of making rational decisions based on reliable feelings? Most people had that faculty of discernment... didn't they? They knew right from wrong, moral from immoral. Not her. She just had a *fuckulty*. In fact, all her faculties had turned into *fuckulties*.

She was sick. Obviously. Emotionally and now physically. She felt tainted, ugly, untouchable, vile and forever corrupted by what had happened. It didn't matter that personal tragedy might justify or explain it. Now she had *two* men to hate, not just one.

It wasn't that she hated Matt for what had happened. She *did*, though, fuck it. He hadn't turned to her in his grief. She hadn't been that special person he'd instinctively reached for when his world collapsed. Did he think she wasn't strong enough to handle his pain? Did he not trust her enough to be vulnerable with her? Or did he just not love her enough to fight for a way to survive this together?

If one partner couldn't stay committed through the tough bits, did that mean the relationship wasn't really a relationship at all? So many things would have been different, if he had only—

But she was making it all about *her* and not him. She could see *that*, at least. She had really messed up, hadn't been there for him in the way he had needed her to be—*not* making it all about *her* feelings. And she'd already slammed the door in his face when it was her turn, when her own tragedy had taken her to the brink and he hadn't been there to pull her back to safety. Not that he could have done anything, but he could have *tried*. Fuck. She was doing it again. Making it all about her.

What about *his* pain? What kind of hell was he going through, in his own private prison, condemning himself to a life of solitary confinement? Men tried so hard to be strong for their women, and they would do anything to hide their weaknesses—even shut women out if it stopped them from seeing their failings. Was *that* what he had done? Thinking about that hurt her chest.

Could Cristal help her transform all her *fuckulties* back into normal, healthy faculties? But even she was tainted…

Should she tell him the latest shocking news? It was a deadly double whammy. How would he react? How could they possibly deal with this after all they'd been through? It was like metal fatigue, when something broke from being bent back and forth so many times. Could you solder a splintered heart back together?

No new life could possibly replace the one taken. And surely nothing could ever repair her dismembered family and all the fractured fallout.

Maybe she should say nothing, take her secret with her and go somewhere on her own, live a totally new life where no one knew her.

Did she even still love him? Had she ever loved him?

Right now, the most powerful emotion she felt was hate. She hated him for not loving her the way she needed to be loved, for not sharing his pain with her, for not being allowed in, to comfort his quaking heart …and hers. But she hated him most for not protecting her. He should have been *there*.

She was *doing* it again, making it all about her.

She knew it made no sense to hate him for not letting her love him. Nothing had stopped her from loving him except her own messed-up head. And her upbringing. It was her own fault that she did what she did, and she couldn't blame him for what had happened.

Truth was, she hated the world. Not just him… or the two of them.

Now her own heart was empty and broken and there was no one to comfort her. Not on the outside, anyway. Her parents were no help, crippled by their own pain. History wouldn't help them now, and memories only gouged the wound. They themselves were almost history.

She knew she was being cruel but she couldn't seem to help herself. All the tragedies had bled her dry and now only liquid lead ran through her cold veins.

How come no one went out of their way to love *her*? How come everyone else's pain was more important than hers? But then hers was far more toxic and twisted than theirs, so they were all fucked.

She still didn't know what to do or who to turn to for help in deciding what to do. She couldn't tell her friends about this, and she certainly couldn't tell her parents. She felt too ashamed, and her friends couldn't begin to relate. They'd just fuel her anger, telling her how badly she had been treated.

But they didn't know what a bitch she had been… what she had done.

Who could possibly understand the torture of this, on top of all that had happened? Who knew all the pained parties and could see all the angles clearly enough and with enough wisdom and compassion to advise her properly? And who would ever *forgive* her? She had really screwed up, and she'd waited too long.

She could think of only one person who might, *just might*, be willing to listen to her shocking story, to not instantly condemn her, and to help her figure things out.

25

There was a frantic knocking at the door just as she was sitting down with her tea by the window. Marnie sighed. What was it about the magnetism of her mornings off that seemed to pull people in off the street and into her precious personal space?

She had a horrible feeling it was someone else needing help or support. What was she, *Mother Teresa*? Was she emanating some *let-me-help-you-I've-got-nothing-better-to-do* vibe?

Lucy was at work, and still had a key. Matt was in Mexico. Steve was still away. She'd spoken to her two closest friends last night and they were fine. And it definitely wasn't her parents...

Her neighbours must have let someone in through the main lobby door, since no one had rung the bell. Or maybe it was her upstairs neighbours, needing help with something.

She opened the door.

"Celle! What are you doing here?"

The girl looked a sweaty mess, her face streaked with tears, dark rings under her eyes, ribs showing through her Lycra top, her whole body trembling.

"Marnie, I don't know what to do, I've been such a bitch, everyone hates me, and I don't know who to turn to, and nobody will ever understand, except maybe you, but you probably hate me too, or you will if you don't already, and then you'll never forgive me, but could you please *help* me?"

Well, what was she going to say to *that*? Sorry, but I'm busy writing a story about a *snake*?

Celle looked at her beseechingly. "I'm *pregnant*."

Marnie felt as if a herd of thundering buffalos were charging through her brain, blocking her hearing and any kind of rational thought. Yet a tiny clinical corner of her mind, some evil part of her ego, said she really didn't need to worry about coming up with a nice story for a children's book; she could write a tear-jerking TV soap opera based purely on her own life. She didn't even need to figure out a plot. She just had to document what was happening, day to day...

Somehow, they both made it to the couch, and Celle curled up in a ball of *déjà-vu* despair. Matt had sat in that same spot, just a few months ago. Those cushions were in for another tearful dousing.

"Tell me," Marnie said, unable to think of the right questions. It would be quicker this way.

Celle was tiny, just a few inches over five feet, and she had the same large eyes and long lashes as Jed, only her eyes were blue. She looked like a little doll, fragile and innocent. Yet Marnie had only ever seen her angry.

She has a fiery nature, Matt used to say. But he'd got that wrong. And so had she. She had always thought that Celle used her anger to challenge the world, to get attention or maybe to compensate for her small size.

But it was more than that; it was armour, a protective shield. Beneath all that anger, Marnie could now see, was a deeply wounded little girl. And she seemed terrified. How easy it was to misjudge the walking wounded, Marnie thought.

"Please don't hate me, Marnie. Please don't. Please. I couldn't bear it. I already hate myself, so you don't need to hate me too."

Marnie got up from her end of the couch and sat down beside Celle. She took hold of her tiny hands and tried to reassure her.

"I won't judge you, Celle. We all make mistakes. We've all been through a terrible time and we need to be extremely gentle and compassionate with ourselves, and each other. Tell me what's going on."

Celle was gripping Marnie's hands so tightly that her fingers were starting to go numb, but she couldn't let go just yet.

'The baby…"

"Are you afraid to tell Matt?" Marnie kept her voice gentle. "Is that it? You're afraid he'll be angry or won't want to support you?"

"No, it's not that… It's not…"

"It's not his child?"

"I don't think so." Celle's body seemed to crumple, as if her bones were shrinking.

"You've been with another man, is that it?"

Celle was shaking her head, moaning.

"Celle, it's okay. Matt has moved on. He won't… this won't…" She didn't want to say he wouldn't *care*. "You don't even need to tell him, if you don't want to," she reassured her. "You have your own life to live now. You can make your own choices."

"No, no, no…" Celle was shaking her head—in denial or dread, Marnie couldn't tell.

Marnie suddenly had a terrible thought.

"Did your father…?"

"No," Celle wailed. "Not him…"

"Then, who…" Marnie's spine went cold, the hairs on her arms standing up, on red alert. "Whose baby is it, Celle? Who did this?"

Celle looked at her imploringly. *Don't make me say it.*

Marnie nodded, squeezing her hands, letting her know she was safe. She understood. But it needed to be said, so she said it.

"It was Jed."

The buffaloes were back and the blood was roaring in her ears, but Marnie pulled Celle to her and lowered herself down on the couch. She held her and rocked her till they both sank into unconsciousness, their bodies on strike while their minds tried to process the impossible.

Somewhere in her dreams—or whispered in her ear—she heard the words, *Please don't leave me.*

An hour later, Marnie came to. Celle was out cold beside her—sleeping deeply, probably for the first time in months, Marnie imagined.

She reached for the phone on the coffee table beside her and called Lucy. Talking as softly as she could, she explained that Celle urgently needed her parents—no, she wasn't injured and she hadn't been in an accident—but she needed Lucy to contact the Ryersons and bring them over to her place.

Celle woke as Marnie was putting the phone down.

Marnie got up and went into the kitchen to make some tea. Her mind was whirring as the kettle boiled and she knew she needed to find out exactly what had happened—and Celle needed to let it out.

She handed Celle a mug of camomile tea and sat down beside her.

They sipped in silence for a few moments and Marnie felt some of the tension ebb from Celle's taut body.

"Tell me what happened, Celle," she said, gently.

Celle told her, in fits and starts, how her brother had come to her apartment one night in November, very drunk. It was shortly after Matt had withdrawn over his parents' death, and the day before Jed was killed.

"He was ranting and raving about what your parents did," said Celle, "and about something Matt had asked him to investigate."

Marnie tensed, instantly alert, but this was not the moment to ask about that.

"He was crying, talking nonsense, cursing, ranting about some woman who had blackmailed him or had some kind of hold over him, but that he was going to make her pay. He's always had a… problem with alcohol, but I'd never seen him like that and it really scared me."

Celle shuddered at the memory.

"And he forced himself on you?" Marnie tried to imagine the scenario.

"Yes," Celle sobbed. "I tried to stop him but he was so strong, and I knew he didn't see me at all. He was out of his mind with rage and…" She gestured helplessly.

"Are you sure this baby is not Matt's?" Not that that could ever cancel out Jed's criminal behaviour, but it might help with Celle's recovery.

Celle shook her head sadly, holding up finger and thumb a centimetre apart. *A very slim chance*, it seemed …unless Celle was referring to Matt's anatomy. But this was not the time for such jokes, Marnie chastised herself, amazed that she could even think of such things at a time like this. Perhaps it was a kind of controlled mental hysteria that never quite made it to manic laughter…

"But if it *is* his, maybe the baby could save us, bring us back together?" Celle was desperate for some way through this, something good to come from it, some forgiveness and hope.

Marnie shook her head sadly. "That's probably the biggest mistake parents can make," she said, gently, although she could think of a bigger one…

"Your parents must be hurting terribly," she said, referring to the loss of Jed.

This prompted more tears.

"But they don't hate you, Celle, any more than you hate Matt. Pain can come out in terrible ways if we haven't been taught healthy ways of dealing with it."

She put her arm around Celle's slender shoulders. "The only person who hates Celle Ryerson is Celle Ryerson," she said. "But she deserves all the love and support you and I can give her, because she too is hurting terribly, right now, and she has done nothing wrong."

Celle nodded, her jogging pants now soaked from her tears.

Marnie gently turned Celle towards her so she could look in her eyes. "Can you accept that, Celle? Do you understand that you are *not* to blame for what happened, and that you must forgive yourself for ever thinking this was your fault?"

Celle nodded, absorbing the idea if not the reality. Marnie knew it would take a lot more than one caring conversation to heal these deep wounds.

"Why do I feel as if I am to blame, Marnie? And I feel so *ashamed.*"

"The blame *and* the shame belong with your brother, Celle, not with you," she said firmly. "You need to believe that. And you need to start loving yourself for having the courage to share your pain and for trusting in the goodness of others to give you the love and support you deserve."

She paused, not wanting to overwhelm Celle with words. She was feeling overwhelmed herself with all the emotions stirred up.

"I have a friend who does intuitive bodywork and a special form of sound therapy for releasing trauma, anxiety and grief. It's very gentle and you wouldn't have to talk to her about any of this," Marnie said gently. "She works with a lot of young women who have had traumatic experiences. I feel she could help you."

She paused. "Would you like her number?

Celle nodded gratefully, and Marnie reached for her shopping-list notebook on the coffee table.

"Her name is Millie Giordano, and I think you'll really like her."

She wrote Millie's name and number on a clean page and handed it to Celle, who put it in the zippered pocket of her top.

"Celle, have you thought about what you want to do with the baby?"

Celle shook her head. "No," she said. "I really don't know what to do." She hesitated. "Marnie, please don't tell my parents about the baby yet. About the… other, yes, but I'm not ready to talk to them about that."

"Of course," Marnie said. "I understand. But you need to see a doctor. And you'll have to decide if it's… wise to keep the baby." She paused, wondering whether to encourage Celle to tell her mother, but decided the girl needed a little more time to process what had happened.

They both turned at the sound of the front door buzzer. Marnie knew Lucy had her key and it was her way of letting Marnie know that they had arrived and were on their way up.

Marnie helped Celle up. "Go and lie down in my bedroom," she said, pointing down the hallway, "and Lucy will join you in a moment."

Celle nodded gratefully and hurried down the corridor, closing the bedroom door just as Lucy came in with Mr and Mrs Ryerson, who looked shaken and concerned.

"Where is she? Is she okay?" Mrs Ryerson said immediately.

"Yes, she's okay," Marnie reassured her. "But she's had a shock and she needs our help."

She turned to Lucy. "Luce, would you…?" She gestured towards her bedroom and Lucy understood, leaving them to talk.

"Come into the kitchen," Marnie said to the Ryersons, "and I'll explain."

She sat them down at the table and gave them both a shot of courage from her bottle of brandy. Mr Ryerson knocked his back in one go, but Mrs Ryerson drank half and then clutched the glass, knowing she'd need the rest very shortly.

They waited in silence for Marnie to explain. They were probably still so shell-shocked by Jed's death that they were afraid to ask any questions.

She had met them briefly at the memorial service for Jed, back in November. Matt had decided that he couldn't not go and Marnie had gone with him for support.

Marnie chose her words carefully, aware that she could only reveal so much. But she knew the devastating impact that family secrets could have, and some things needed to be said.

"Your daughter has been through a very traumatic experience and she is terrified that you won't believe her if she tells you what happened."

She paused to let that sink in.

"I know you are both still in shock from losing Jed," she said, "but your daughter urgently needs your love and support right now."

Mr Ryerson reached for his wife's hand across the table as they waited for Marnie to continue.

"Celle has suffered a terrible betrayal. Her brother… violated her trust in the most devastating way a man can, and Celle blames herself."

Mrs Ryerson gasped, and her husband stiffened beside her.

Marnie knew she had to keep going or she would lose her nerve.

"She is terrified that you will blame her too and, as I'm sure you know, the victims of abuse often end up feeling deeply ashamed, when it is the abuser..."

They both flinched and Marnie paused to let them absorb the awful truth.

"If you blame her, you will probably also blame yourselves, and the pain will never end. Jed is not here to answer for what he did, so it will be terribly hard for you to understand or forgive him. He was a wonderful young man, in many ways, and we may never know what prompted him to do what he did."

Her body was shaking and Marnie took a deep breath to steady herself. She should have taken a shot of courage, too.

"Sometimes, good people do terrible things," Marnie said. So many painful reversals, and another irony all too close to home.

She noticed Mrs Ryerson's eyes flick towards her husband and she wondered if there was some history there.

"Celle mentioned that Jed had an issue with alcohol, which might help explain what happened ...although not *excuse* it, of course." *Just in case they didn't get that last bit.* Alcohol abuse was all too often used as a legal defence for indefensible behaviour, as far as Marnie was concerned.

The Ryersons sat mutely, offering no comment on this issue, so Marnie continued.

"Right now, Celle needs your unconditional love and support. If you feel you cannot give her that, I need to know. She came to me in deep despair, trusting me with her pain, and I cannot abandon her. She is close to cracking and may not survive this if you reject her. She already hates herself for what happened, and she will need your support in erasing that toxic emotion from her life."

She paused again, searching their faces. "Can you do this for her?"

Rachel Ryerson began to sob, clutching her husband's hand.

Crying was good, Marnie knew. It was the heart finally letting itself hear the truth and respond.

"I have no idea how to handle this," Mrs Ryerson said. "It's so awful... Marnie, do you..."

Marnie smiled sadly. "I'm no expert on grief or loss, Mrs Ryerson, although I'm learning how to let it guide me to a deeper understanding of myself, with the support of friends and family."

She paused. What to suggest for such a tortuous set of circumstances?

"You're facing a profound conflict: support your daughter and believe what she tells you, and condemn your son, whose death you are still mourning. An agonising situation for any parent to face."

She was thinking out loud, articulating what they must be feeling, and trying to give their hearts the courage to move forward together.

"Crises like this call for a tremendous amount of love and forgiveness. If we can find it in ourselves to give that to others, it can heal us at the same time." Marnie could feel the truth of this seep through her, having so very recently lived it herself.

"We are all capable of love and compassion when faced with tragedy and loss," she said, gently. "All of us here have experienced a huge loss over the past few months, and what I've realized is that the only way to bring ourselves back to life is to love those close to us as tenderly and as fully as we possibly can. They are there for us as much as we are there for them. And the healing goes in both directions, just like love." She shrugged, smiling sadly. "Maybe they're the same thing."

"You are very wise, Marnie, for someone so young," George Ryerson said, looking at her with kind, sad eyes. "Thank you for being here for Celle when we failed to see… what was going on. But we're here for her now and we will not let her down …or you."

He lowered his eyes, overcome by emotion.

Encouraged by her husband's words, Rachel leaned towards Marnie and grasped her arm.

"Marnie, I know it's a lot to ask, but Celle trusts you, and I wonder if…"

She paused, looking at George. He nodded his agreement, and she continued.

"Would it be okay if Celle dropped by sometime for a chat? Even knowing she had that option might help her …if that would be okay with you?"

"I would do that for Celle, anyway," Marnie said. "Also, I've given her the number of a woman who does some very gentle trauma-release work, which I think will help her enormously."

Rachel nodded her thanks, squeezing Marnie's arm, and they all slowly stood up. It was time to stop talking and start healing.

In the living room, Celle and Lucy were sitting side by side on the couch, talking softly. Celle was wearing one of Marnie's old sweaters that Lucy must have given her, and she looked like a little waif—small and shaky beside a solid, confident Lucy.

Marnie marvelled at how her sister had matured by at least a decade in just a few short months, and Celle looked softer, her defences down—for now, at least—and hope lighting her big blue eyes.

They got up and Rachel hugged her daughter fiercely. The last of Celle's sharp edges fell away and she sobbed in her mother's arms.

"I'm so sorry, Mom," she said.

"This is not your fault, sweetheart," she said fiercely. "You did nothing wrong. I'm just so sorry I wasn't there for you." Her voice cracked but she knew she needed to convince her daughter of her support. "We have neglected you and let you down very badly but we are here for you now, and we will get through this together."

She held her daughter at arm's length, searching her face as her own tears flowed. "Okay, sweetie?"

"*Thank you*, Mom, *thank you*." Celle seemed to wilt in her arms, exhausted from two months of hiding the truth and trying to protect herself from more pain.

The whole room seemed to breathe in the sense of a new beginning and the forgiveness to come.

Celle turned to Marnie and hugged her hard. "Thank you," she whispered in her ear, "for believing me and being there for me."

"George?" Rachel knew her husband was barely holding himself together. He was standing by the window, pretending he had something in his eye, but he turned abruptly, head down, and led his wife and daughter out the door, one on each side, giving Marnie's shoulder a fierce squeeze as he passed.

Marnie closed the door and rested her head against it for a moment. Her whole body was vibrating with emotion and she would need to go and quietly process it on her own.

But it wasn't just the grief; it was the power of speaking the brave raw truth. We are all being pushed to deepen our humanity, she realized, rather than running from the pain of confronting it. Life was a symphony of sorrow and joy that required the whole orchestra of humanity to perform. And she was only just learning how to play the basic chords.

She turned and joined Lucy at the window as they watched the Ryerson trio slowly cross the road, Celle now protectively bracketed by her parents, their arms overlapping behind her. A little tripod of humbled humanity. It was hard to tell who was holding whom up, Marnie thought, but Celle was bringing them back together.

"You saved that girl, Marn," Lucy said, putting her arm around her sister's shoulders.

"I think she'll be okay," Marnie said. She hoped that Matt would be, too. Tomorrow or the next day, they would have to think about what to tell him. For now, though, she'd had all the emotional heroism she could handle.

"Thanks for being here with me, Luce."

You're very good at this," Lucy said, with feeling. "I'm humungously proud of you."

Marnie smiled gratefully at her sister. All Lucy's anger seemed to have gone, and her resentment towards Marnie for mothering her but not *being* her mother, was no longer there.

That made all those sacrifices worthwhile, Marnie thought. In fact, she could no longer remember what those sacrifices had been. That must be what mothers experienced when they forgot the pain of childbirth as soon as the baby was placed in their arms.

She smiled at the thought, realizing that she herself was in the process of building a *whole* new family.

26

November 1997

"You can't keep disappearing. We have a 2-year-old child, for God's sake. How can you jeopardize your safety when you're a mother? Are you so blinded by your work that no one else matters to you?"

"There's another one on the way," Frannie said. Might as well tell him now. It was going to come out sooner or later.

"What? *WHAT?* When were you going to tell me *that?* What the fuck, Frannie?"

She flinched. Daniel never swore. She swore lots but he never did.

"Don't you give a damn about our children?" He hesitated. "Or me?"

If he only knew…

She waited, forcing him to finally look at her properly. "I'm trying to *save* them, Daniel."

He saw such devastation in her eyes that he almost couldn't bear it. Taking a deep breath, he reined himself in. "What do you mean, *save them?*"

"I saw the future," she said, her face crumpling, "and they weren't in it." She fought back a sob and bowed her head, haunted by the images imprinted on her brain.

"Frannie." He knelt down beside her and took her hands in his. "We all die, you know. You can't control everything, sweetheart. You've got to let life happen."

"But they were so young, Daniel, all three of them. Their lives had barely—"

"Three? We have three children... *will* have...?"

She nodded. "We can save them, Daniel," she said forcefully, her steely reserve returning.

"No, Frannie, we can't do that."

"Yes, we can. We must."

"You know as well as I do that we can't mess with time. It's a cardinal rule. Everything gets screwed up if we do that, with consequences that you can't imagine and will never see."

"This time, we can," she said, looking him in the eye." It's not just about us, Daniel. There are others... many, many others."

"What do you mean? What are you saying?"

"I've been to... different versions of the future," she said, carefully. "There are options..."

"You're mad. I can't believe this." Daniel was up again, pacing back and forth, arms flailing, his mind in turmoil. Then he turned back to her, his face resolute.

"Listen to me, Frannie. Go and feed Marnie and put her to bed. I need to go out for a walk to clear my head. Then you and I are going to sit down and you are going to tell me everything, okay? *Everything.* No more hiding or scheming. This is our life you're messing with and I have a right to know what's going on."

She was tempted to say that he couldn't control everything either—especially her—but managed to bite her tongue.

"Okay," she said. "We'll talk and I'll tell you everything."

27

Marnie was early, so she got a camomile tea and sat at a table by the window to wait. She was back at the Mirror, but she wasn't meeting Steve, this time. He had e-mailed to say he had to stay on in Chicago for another few weeks for his work, but he was "looking forward to catching up when he got back".

Marnie had never understood what his work as a data analyst involved. It sounded very tedious and boring, but there was nothing boring about Steve Romero. When they were dating, she had thought he was a bit weird. He was a mathematician who kept tropical fish, played the saxophone and studied numerology, for heaven's sake.

Now, though, she didn't think he was so weird, but maybe she was just missing him, which meant she necessarily missed his weirdness. But that was ridiculous, since she'd only seen him that one time here in the café in November, and it was now over a year since *she* had *ended* the relationship. They'd only dated for nine months, so their relationship had been over now for longer than it had lasted.

Maybe she just hadn't been wired for weird, back then. Had she been more stable and normal, and was more wonky and weird now? And was she really missing him or just getting used to her life being unrelentingly weird?

DeeDee would soon set her straight and tell her how it was. If anyone personified bluntness, it was DeeDee Melina—queen of the unvarnished truth.

Marnie hadn't seen her two friends socially for almost seven months, although she'd had two life-saving bodywork sessions with Millie a few weeks ago, when Millie had returned to Boston.

Marnie felt as if something inside her had shifted. She felt lighter, less anxious, less tightly wound, more relaxed about things, and more able to think positively about her life. A lot of her grief and resentment about her parents seemed to have fallen away, and she was actually… she was almost afraid to admit this even to herself… but she was actually feeling very *warmly* towards Steve—or, at least, the *idea* of Steve. The *reality* of Steve might be quite different …*if* they got together again.

She was impressed with the power of Millie's work, and she knew it was also helping Celle. Millie had gone to California in September last year to do some advanced training in sound therapy, only returning to Boston in mid-January. And DeeDee had just got back from Japan, where she had been doing professional development training for a team of businessmen for the past six months.

Now, finally, with all three of them once again in the same city, they could resume their regular monthly get-togethers.

Marnie looked up as the door opened and DeeDee swept into the café. She didn't *enter* a room so much as *own* it, Marnie thought, smiling as her friend strode towards her. Half-Greek and half-Kenyan, she was an exotic hybrid, with some Jamaican Rastafarian influence on her father's side and some very shady Italian Mafioso on her grandmother's—or so she claimed.

At six feet tall, with thick black Afro curls, ebony skin, huge blue eyes and full red lips that always made Marnie think of a plush sofa, DeeDee must have seemed like a giant goddess to the Japanese. It was a mystery to her how any businessmen ever got a scrap of work done once DeeDee swept into the room. Business or not, it would never be a *bored* room…

"Girlfriend!" DeeDee boomed, arms outstretched.

"Did you terrify the Japanese?" Marnie asked, smiling as she hugged her friend.

"Of course!" said DeeDee, sitting down opposite Marnie. "I haven't had so much fun in ages."

DeeDee shrugged off her coat—a kind of coat-cape in a colour Marnie couldn't quite define. Lucy would probably call it *metallic banana with a dollop of sunshine*, she mused, then smiled to herself. She, *Marnie*, had just called it that. Perhaps she had potential as a 'creative #3' after all, if there was anything to this numerology stuff.

The united colours of DeeDee left Benetton in the shade, Marnie always thought. With her exotic ebony skin and flamboyant fashion flair, she was like a tropical bird of paradise, whereas Marnie felt more like a sparrow or a starling. But that was okay, she had long ago decided. Everyone liked sparrows.

Today, DeeDee was wearing a sheer white chemise over a turquoise *bustier*, and flowing terra-cotta-coloured pantaloons with flat leather slip-ons.

She leaned towards Marnie, her arm bangles jangling on the wooden table like a tuneful drumroll for her grand entrance.

"So, when's Steve due back?" DeeDee never beat around the bush.

"Oh, the end of the month, I think," Marnie said offhandedly.

"Girl, you need to drop the martyr act," DeeDee said, folding her arms and regarding Marnie with one of her bullshit-stripping stares.

"What do you mean?" Marnie said.

"Don't you think you've done enough mothering and care-taking, what with your siblings and all the kids at school? It's time for *you*, now, unless you want to sacrifice even more of your rapidly aging celibate self."

Marnie laughed. "Remind me why I missed you so much while you were away," she said.

"Because I tell you exactly what you need to hear, daft woman. You'd be lost without my brutal honesty to bring you face to face with yourself."

Marnie was about to respond when Millie arrived and made her way to the table to join them.

"Sorry I'm late," she said. "A client needed a little extra time…"

She leaned forward and gave each of them a hug. Sitting down beside Marnie, she shook off her coat onto the back of the chair and put her bag on the floor by her feet.

"Here we are," she said, smiling her radiant smile. "Finally!"

Marnie always marvelled at how different they all were. DeeDee was like some extreme weather front—a force of nature that could bowl you over unless you were appropriately weatherproofed—whereas Millie was more of a warm gentle breeze that soothed your soul.

"I was just telling Marnie that it was time for her to get back with Steve," DeeDee said.

"What?" Marnie laughed.

"What did you *think* I was talking about?" DeeDee looked at her with mock astonishment.

"Of course it's time," Millie said. "But then you already knew that, didn't you Marn."

28

Raynor Spence had a fierce love of the earth, and he found it tragic that most scientists and researchers had forgotten what science was all about—knowledge, understanding the complexity of life in the cosmos and finding our place within it. Much of his own research had revolved around the electromagnetism of the earth, of life forms, including the human body, and of the universe itself. People all too readily dismissed cosmology as something *fringe* or irrelevant to everyday life, when it was all about the nature of reality and how everything worked and interconnected.

He had a special reverence for women, and he could never understand why men were not eternally in awe of what women were capable of doing—not just the obvious miracle birthing of life, but the way they could open their hearts, riding the sine waves of pain and compassion, while seeing and understanding men's blustering egos, masochism and desperate need to succeed.

Women were treated as secondary citizens, when they were the primary life-givers without whom no man would exist. Of course, man played a role in the procreation process, but it wasn't exactly a *hardship*. Ray was convinced that *men* were the ones trying to prove themselves, with women often being oppressed *because* they were so powerful. They had been before, and they would be again, if things worked out the way he hoped.

In college, in the early 1980s, he had developed a software program called Femail, which sent out encrypted electronic messages to all the females on campus—students and faculty—alerting them to men known or suspected to have been abusive or disrespectful to women in the workplace, in government, within the university or elsewhere in the state of Massachusetts. The program used a virtual spider to locate likely cases, even hacking into secure websites that were designed to protect the offenders, as well as porn sites and criminal behaviour that otherwise stayed largely beneath the radar.

He loved inventing things that served humanity or made people think for themselves. In high school, he'd become known as *Raynor*

Shine, which he rather liked. He could think of worse nicknames. He used to sell some of his inventions to his classmates—such as the nifty little camera that could zoom in on a neighbouring desk, which was great for cheating during exams.

He'd felt bad about the camera, though. He'd been caught, of course, and pulled into the Principal's office.

"You developed a camera to be used for cheating," she challenged him.

"I developed a camera," he said, "but I had no control over what people decided to use it for."

"Clearly, it was intended for cheating," she said.

He argued that there were lots of things in life that were supposedly meant to be used for one thing but were used for another. Such as this school, he said, which was meant to educate, enrich, expand and challenge young minds for the good of humanity when, in reality… He'd looked around the office, letting the thought hang between them, doing the job that thoughts were meant to do, until he was dismissed, as he knew he would be.

He understood the education system, even if it didn't understand him.

Raynor Shine. He *was* pretty reliable. He had always thought it would be a great name for a business: *Raynor Shine—he delivers.*

Not this time, though, although he'd still delivered quite a blow. He had been nervous about setting himself up for the fall—the fall he had been told would never come. But a lot could go haywire with a project like this, and that tip-off phone call had certainly caused a public outcry. It was his cue to stop the rollout and await further instructions. From whom, he had no idea, but all he could do was wait and ride the tidal wave of outrage at what he had supposedly planned to do.

Thank God his lawyer had got him off, proving that he never intended to unleash anything harmful, since there was, *of course*, no way to do that via manmade electromagnetic frequencies. Well, there *was*, but he wasn't going to tell them that, and the top researchers at MIT hadn't been able to find a way, so…

He'd felt pretty confident that they wouldn't be able to figure things out, and they hadn't been able to clearly identify the toxic substance, either, although they came close. He'd always thought MIT stood for *Mired In Theory*, with not enough focus on finding solutions to real-life issues, although there were some excellent minds there. He had been one of them, for a while.

He'd had to pay a hefty fine, for what his lawyer had called his *"well-intentioned scare tactics"*, but he had expected that and he'd already received enough support from various parties to more than cover the cost.

Now, here he was preparing to go on Misha Goldberg's new TV chat show, about to have his say…

He'd already been pestered by all the major networks but he didn't trust any of them. CNN was owned by Warner Media, which was owned by AT&T, the second-largest provider of cellphone networks. And Ray knew darn well that Warner Media wasn't *warning anyone* of anything they should be warned about.

The only reason he had agreed to go on Misha's show was because he trusted her to give him a fair hearing. Misha was young, sharp as a whip, and supremely confident, having worked for three years as a producer for RT America—a global TV news network based in Moscow and funded by the Russian government.

RT was one of the very few networks *not* influenced by government or the wireless industry—unlike CNN, FOX and the other usual suspects. It was gutsy, telling things the way they were, its reporting usually causing mayhem in the mainstream media (*NYT, Washington Post…*), which accused it of skewing the truth (as *Putin's mouthpiece*) and *frightening* hapless viewers with its *dangerous rhetoric*. He'd probably be accused of being a Russian spy.

Ray had done his research, and he knew the Russians were way ahead of the US in their expertise and coverage regarding wireless radiation—and had been, for decades. RT America claimed to take a very different perspective from mainstream American TV, reporting on the other side of the story and exploring unanswered and unasked questions.

That worked for him. Ray had seen Misha reporting on wireless radiation several times and he liked her style. She was well informed and clearly not taken in by government or industry spin.

She'd been offered her own chat show in March and hadn't missed a beat, lining up a slew of guests and doing her first show only a month later.

Now, as of early May, she had already done seven shows, and had covered several angles of what had become known as the Spence Debate.

He had a pretty good idea of the kinds of questions she was going to ask him, since she had already interviewed someone from the wireless industry, a human rights advocate, a lawyer specializing in environmental issues, a group of EMF activists, and two researchers who weighed in on the viability of Spence's claims. She had wisely chosen not to feature them all on the same show, and there were few surprises, with each camp trotting out the expected arguments and irate objections, all attacking each other and pretty much cancelling each other out.

Misha was known for being fair, willing to look at all sides of a story, yet perceptive enough not to allow those with political agendas to get away with too much bullshit or grandstanding on her airtime. And she never backed down, no matter how intimidating or aggressive her guests.

As the make-up girl put the finishing touches to his face, he took a deep breath, pondering yet again just how much he should reveal to the public.

Off set, he stood waiting as Misha introduced him, adjusting his tie and smoothing the front of his jacket. She usually spoke to the live audience before coming on the air with her guests, getting their take on things and the kinds of questions they wanted her to ask.

There was a smattering of hesitant applause from the audience, and Spence understood their ambivalence. Should they applaud a man who had possibly planned to kill them all? Or was he some kind of avenging angel for the good guys?

Maybe he was a vigilante with a personal grievance against those who didn't take his research seriously, or maybe even a plant from the wireless industry, designed to create a platform for debunking all the panic about wireless radiation.

Some even speculated that he had lost his mind *because* of the wireless radiation, given all the mental and neurological diseases it was supposedly causing.

The fact that people were considering these possibilities spoke volumes about the state of the world, Spence thought, regardless of what he did.

He had simply fuelled their concerns, giving them a context for expressing their fears and paranoia, although it wasn't paranoia if someone really *was* after you. *And they were, people, they were.*

If paranoia meant believing wrongly that others were out to harm you, what did you call believing wrongly that others were taking care of you and serving your best interests?

Paranoia only had meaning when measured against a benchmark for a healthy state of mind, and he'd seen nothing but an *un*healthy state of *mindlessness* for decades. Maybe paranoia was the new normal... para*noimal*.

He was pondering this sad reality when a young woman with a clipboard touched his shoulder, gesturing for him to go on set.

He nodded, pausing for a count of three before walking onto the small raised platform, and seating himself in one of the signature red armchairs diagonally opposite Misha. A small table nested between them, bearing a glass of water for each.

The choice of colour scheme was no accident. He was, metaphorically and literally, *in the hot seat.*

Having warmed up her audience, Misha jumped right in.

"Dr Spence, you caused quite a stir earlier this year," she said.

"Thank you, Misha." Dr Spence graciously inclined his head, smiling his charming smile. "It's very kind of you to say so."

Misha laughed. "So that *was* your intention..."

"As a scientist, I do most things intentionally, although my wife might argue otherwise."

A ripple of laughter wafted towards them from the live audience.

"Here's what everyone wants to know, Dr Spence," Misha said. "Is it technically possible to intentionally disperse pathogens into the population via the frequencies currently used for internet connectivity?"

Dr Spence paused, letting the suspense build as he considered his response.

"It's interesting that you used the word *intentionally*," he said, "as if that were a new phenomenon, when wireless radiation frequencies are, of course, already intentionally harming and controlling the population."

He paused again.

"But, yes, it is technically possible to do what you described."

Misha was about to speak but Dr Spence held up his hand. "Before I expand on that, I'd like to clarify something. What we're talking about here is not just the potential spread of a virus or even the dangers of wireless radiation. The key issue is fear—the best way to win any war or to start one, as governments know all too well. Fear inhibits our thinking and weakens our immune system far more than most common illnesses, and the statistics for deaths due to random viruses have been blown way out of proportion. Far more people die every day from malaria, TB, hepatitis and the plain old seasonal flu than the supposedly deadly virus that made the rounds a few months ago, yet governments generated massive panic, sounding the death knell and putting entire countries into lockdown."

"Some would argue that you're not qualified to speak on this, since you're not a medical doctor," Misha interjected.

"They could very justifiably argue a lot more than that," he said, with an indulgent smile to the camera. "I'm not a saint, a genius or a time traveller. But nor am I a politician, a spin doctor or a liar."

He paused for a breath, jumping in again before Misha could speak. "If governments took the same precautionary approach to the sickness and deaths caused by wireless radiation, we would almost certainly not be having this conversation." He looked at her pointedly. "Statistics can be very helpful, but we mustn't forget that we're talking about real people, here—young children dying of cancers from microwave radiation." He thumped his chest, his eyes moistening. "Does that not hit you *here*, Misha?"

"Yes, of course, it—"

But Dr Spence was on a roll. "The fallout from that virus was just a small taste of what's to come—not just in terms of the chaos caused by all the engendered panic but by the level of control that will result when people are not paying attention to what's really going on."

Misha leaned in. "And what *is* going on, Dr Spence?"

"Worldwide government fear-mongering about the virus very conveniently distracted people from the rollout of 5G, which is the latest and most harmful generation of wireless telecommunications. But what people don't realize is that all kinds of harmful bacteria and viruses can get transmitted via radio frequencies, including those used for wireless telecommunications, and 5G is actually the perfect delivery mechanism for countless other new viruses that will inevitably emerge and go viral."

"So you're saying it is *already* physically possible for bacteria and viruses to spread via the frequencies used for wireless networks?"

"Most definitely," said Dr Spence. "And here's the tragic irony: in our panic, despair, pain, illness or whatever crisis we face, we seek comfort in our digital devices—the purveyors of the problem. But if we get more viruses like this—and we will, no question—we will sorely regret having depended on our devices. Far from saving us in such a crisis, wireless technologies will be the very delivery mechanisms for such viruses to spread at the speed of light."

"That's quite a statement, Dr Spence," Misha said, sitting back and looking at him challengingly. "Could that, in itself, not cause widespread panic?"

"There is only one thing we should be concerned about," said Dr Spence, turning to the live audience. "Fear fed by ignorance— or ignorance fed by fear. Take your pick. We are living in a time of sanitized insanity, in a world where the natural order of things has been so profoundly disrupted that we can no longer see straight."

He faced the camera, his expression grave. "Make no mistake, my friends," he said. "This is *the Stockholm Syndrome of the digital age.*"

Misha was tapping out an urgent Morse code message with her fingernails on her armrest—*Eyes back on me, Mister*—but he feigned oblivion. If she challenged him on it afterwards, he would claim poor peripheral vision, an unfortunate condition specific to his gender. *Surely she was aware of this…?*

"Unless we disengage from our smart phones and re-engage our far smarter minds, we will keep getting sucked into the hype and drama that prevent us from thinking clearly, retaining healthy control over our own lives, or behaving like decent human beings. Most importantly, we will fail to make the connection between wireless connectivity and the wireless transmission of disease and dysfunction."

"That's a tough theory to sell—"

"It's not just a theory," said Dr Spence, emphatically shaking his head. "As some of your viewers will know from the news coverage of me being arrested for egregious civil disobedience in January, my esteemed colleagues at Northeastern have already shown that viruses and bacteria communicate via radio waves. So it's really not such a leap."

He turned to the live audience again. "The most powerful thing we can do is refuse to engage in the fear-feeding frenzy and start thinking for ourselves again, using our humanity and common sense. Getting caught up in panic and defensiveness is exactly what those stoking the fires of fear want us to do. But…" He paused for dramatic emphasis. "If you *really* love your wise, caring, fully informed government officials, then you should trust them completely and do whatever they tell you to do."

Exaggerated gagging sounds emanated from the audience and he allowed himself a modest smile.

Misha was not one to miss a memorable sound bite. "That was either the remnants of the flu virus," she said, nodding towards the audience, "or someone having difficulty swallowing the bitter pills doled out by government."

"One should help boost our immunity to the other," Dr Spence said, smiling. He reached for his glass of water and drank thirstily, a man of honest appetites, too busy for decorum.

"I don't like to be entirely negative about our governments, who may simply be incredibly uninformed and ill advised in their actions. *But…*" he spread his hands, "while people were diligently staying at home because of the virus, as instructed by our caring governments, IT personnel were out on the streets laying down cable and installing new systems in preparation for 5G …while no one was there to object. And, of course, all 5G conferences and demonstrations were cancelled."

He leaned towards her in confidence. "I don't know about you, Misha, but I'd call that downright sneaky, rather than caring… *if* I were a cynical man."

She was clearly getting antsy at all the radiation sidebars, and he smiled in capitulation. "We could talk about the weather—traditionally a nice, safe, neutral topic."

Misha laughed. "We could, but I have a feeling we'd end up in the same place."

"True." He smiled sheepishly. "But we'd have lots of dramatic things to talk about, with all the extreme weather events around the world—"

"*—due to the radiation,*" she finished for him. "Yes, I get it."

"That's because you're smarter than most and you know we can't blast high-frequency electromagnetic fields through the upper atmosphere without massively disrupting weather patterns around the globe."

"So you think CNN weatherman Chad Myers should give up his day job?"

"Well, he could get some training in disaster preparedness, then he could tell you when the hurricane is coming *and* be a first responder, when the disaster hits. Total job security."

Misha laughed, but she was clearly anxious to get back on track with the focus of her show. She cleared her throat, shifting in her seat to mark the end of frivolous banter. "Getting back to the issue of viruses spreading via the internet," she said. "Surely the higher frequencies used for wireless telecommunications would kill any viruses that were fed into them—*if* such a thing were possible."

"Many viruses communicate at quite high frequencies, and may even be potentiated by them," said Dr Spence. "If wireless radiation killed them, the virus in March would not have swept the globe the way it did." He allowed that thought to percolate on the airwaves for a second. "And the containment measures probably made very little difference, given that most viruses have a limited lifespan and usually run their course fairly quickly—like the flu virus. Although," he raised a hand for emphasis, "we should also bear in mind that microwave radiation is well known to weaken immune systems generally, making the very young and the elderly even more vulnerable."

He sighed, finding only one small bone to throw to the crowd. "The few remaining people living in areas with low wireless radiation levels have an advantage: they won't be exposed to viral hitch-hikers riding the internet airwaves and they're more likely to have a stronger immune system than those being constantly irradiated."

He grimaced gamely. "It brings a whole new meaning to the term *viral*, doesn't it? There will be online *sharing* like never before."

Misha regarded him wryly. "You think this is funny?"

"I think the irradiation of our planet is a deadly serious matter that is not being taken seriously," Dr Spence said, deadly serious. "Reason, logic and scientific facts are no longer getting through, but perhaps there's still hope for humour."

He leaned forward. "What do *you* think, Misha, as a reporter who documented this issue and now as a talk-show host?" He gestured towards the audience. "Does the truth still get a look-in or is sensationalism still running the show?"

"I think there's denial about the dangers, given the widespread dependence on wireless systems," she said carefully. "But people are also very stressed. They want distractions and some light relief, not more problems, so entertainment is always going to be in demand."

Dr Spence nodded. "Yes, the stress factor is huge. People no longer have the mental elasticity or emotional resilience to stretch their minds beyond what they have been told. And fear seems to be the only thing that can still get through to generate a reaction."

Misha leaned in. "Most people don't feel the radiation, so they see no reason to fear it. And many say it's not harming them at all."

Dr Spence sat back in his chair, arms draped on the armrests. "I remember a few years ago being in the basement of my house and noticing a smell of gas. I called my wife down but she couldn't smell a thing. Nor could my neighbour. But when the fire department showed up and did some tests with their meters, they confirmed that there was a small leak. So," he spread his arms, "some of our senses are more acute than others, and only a small percentage of people would have detected that gas leak. It's the same with wireless radiation. Some people can physically feel it. I can't, you can't, but many others can. And we must remember," he leaned forward again, "our senses are designed to keep us safe. They are also what make us human."

"Speaking of which…" Misha paused for effect. "Given what you've shared with us, Dr Spence, how can you expect people to believe that you were *not* intending to release a deadly toxin, as you originally claimed?"

She looked at him pointedly.

"Well, it would have killed me, too," Spence replied, shrugging and smiling his charming smile.

Misha looked at him skeptically… another pregnant pause. "You took desperate measures in creating the means to do this, risking imprisonment," she said. "Are we to believe that you were not willing to die for your cause?"

"What I would *like* to believe, Misha, is that the public and the media"—he looked at her pointedly—"will not continue to gullibly believe the lies being told by governments and the wireless industry."

He shook his head, taking a deep breath. "You want *me* to tell the truth? What about our governments? They are the ones to whom we are all paying taxes—and, it seems, *homage*—merely to fund our own destruction."

He shrugged benignly. "I was legally cleared of any wrongdoing, apart from causing mischief with my story," he said. "But even if I hadn't been, why should *I* have to justify my actions to *you*?"

"Because you broke the law, Dr Spence," Misha said, obviously not believing his story about his story.

Ray smiled his genuine, charming smile. "You know, as a scientist, I'm dedicated to understanding how the cosmos works, and I love life far too much to ever intentionally destroy it. I am genuinely baffled by leaders who knowingly, willfully harm people, the environment and the economy, when we are clearly all in this together."

"But *you* were planning to harm people. Even intentionally causing fear can have consequences. Don't you think you should be held accountable for that?"

Raynor Spence let out a raucous belt of laughter. "*Me?* An independent scientist trying to promote the truth? And you talk about *me* fear-mongering? That's priceless," he said, dissolving into more raucous laughter, slapping his thighs and wiping tears from his eyes.

Misha watched him for a few seconds, preserving her professional neutrality, and then leaned forward to challenge him with another question.

But Spence was intent on milking this for all he was worth, pointing at Misha, shaking his head and dissolving into more helpless hysterics that showed no signs of abating.

Misha seemed to be considering the motives behind these histrionics, and he could practically see her mind whirring through the possibilities: *Was he a man with nothing to lose, who didn't care what the millions of viewers would think because he already knew that this kind of debate changed nothing? Or that the world was in such crisis that nothing he or anyone else said would help? He was, after all, a man who had taken desperate action precisely because words and protests alone were not working...*

It wasn't that he'd lost the will to live, as some might believe. Spence knew that conventional approaches were not going to be enough to bring a devastated world back from the brink. And talk shows like this one certainly wouldn't.

It was unclear if Misha was getting embarrassed or trying to suppress a smile, but she had so far maintained her inscrutable expression.

She turned to the camera as it zoomed in on her. "We'll take a break here," she said calmly, finally allowing a wry smile to humour her face as Spence's guffaws continued in the background, "and we'll be back with more fun and games after these messages."

He'd been playing for time, conflicted over what he should say, but he had served her up a media gem, Spence knew. His hysterics would ignite another round of fierce debate among the various camps and everyone would be talking about it.

He's a madman! We told you! That would be the wireless industry.

What's it going to take for people to give up their hell phones? How insane do things have to get? The wireless industry is creating havoc... The EMF activists...

He's right! Politics in this country is a joke! The political pundits...

We will not give in to terrorists. Government spokesman...

Governments are terrorizing people with irradiation, surveillance, microwave crowd control, coercion and intimidation! Human rights activists...

Round and round it would go.

Off set, as the commercials pacified the nation, Misha confronted him with a hard stare.

"Well, that was interesting, Dr Spence," she said. "I imagine there was some method to your madness?"

"Actually, no," he said, quite sober now and feeling remorseful for having put her in such a spot. "It was an entirely spontaneous reaction to a ridiculous situation."

She studied him for a moment, squinting her eyes. "Any chance we could have a rational conversation," she said, sardonically, "and tell people why you did what you did... if I bring you back on air after the break?"

She raised her eyebrows but he just shrugged.

"That *is* why you're on my show, in case you've forgotten," she said pointedly. "We discussed this beforehand and you agreed to be honest about your *motivation*, at least, if not the exact details about what you allegedly planned to do."

Ray thought his laughter had been the most honest thing he'd shared in a long time, but there wasn't much point in telling her that. "I was entirely honest," he said. "What I said in there is all true."

"That may be so, but with all due respect, Dr Spence," she said, her tone implying some doubt about how much respect was due, "if you pull another stunt like that, you can take your circus act elsewhere. Clear?"

"Crystal," he said with a smile, admiring her spunk as she turned on her heel and walked smartly back on set. "Stella will tell you when to come back in," she shot back over her shoulder.

He waited in the wings while Misha explained to the audience that they would now further explore the real reasons Dr Spence had done what he did.

What else could he say, beyond what he'd already said? That he just wanted people to know disease could be spread via the internet, so they could protect themselves? But would he be resorting to the same nasty tactics used by the authorities? Or was instilling fear the only way to counter the government fear-mongering? He'd prefer to inspire and empower, rather than instilling more fear... Knowledge was power, after all.

PART 2

29

June 2000

Sometimes Daniel thought he might lose his mind from all the shifting timelines. What if Frannie went to the future and had sex with him there, then came back pregnant in the present, gave birth to that child, and then got pregnant again with him later, in the present, but in that previously future time… Would they end up with the same child born twice?

And what if she had sex with someone else, in the future, and came back pregnant and he was convinced it was his because she hadn't left the house for a month (not physically, anyway), but it could be anyone's, from any time, anywhere… Although Frannie would never do that …would she?

He remembered when they first met and he'd joked about her maiden name, *Sincera*. About her having nothing to hide and there being nothing fake about her. He shook his head. Could any woman on the planet have more to hide than her?

It wasn't that she was *fake*, she'd told him last week, when he challenged her about this. Was it her fault if she just naturally had the most devious, brilliant strategic mind that was light years ahead of anyone else's? Except *his*, of course, she added, smiling sweetly and meaning it, as only Frannie could.

He was certainly smart enough to know that she was far smarter than him. And it was almost impossible to be even one step ahead of her, since she got so much *advance* input about things. It was hard to surprise a woman who knew so much, ahead of time.

What if she travelled to a future time where she no longer existed? Would she come back dead? Would she come back at all?

What if she went to the exact moment when her death happened? Would she die then, in real future time? Or would she be there as her present and future self—one lying dead on a slab in the morgue, and the other standing there, beside herself?

He was beside himself with all this mind-bending madness. How did Frannie manage to stay sane? Maybe she didn't. Maybe she had lost it years ago and he hadn't noticed because he was so madly in love with her and she was so caught up in trying to save the world—*their* world. How could he not want that?

She had started telling him about their children in the future, but he stopped her.

"No," he said. "I want to be able to live their lives with them, in the present. I want to see their lives unfold in real time."

"Well, then," said Frannie, folding her arms and giving him her *fait accompli* look, "we have to do this. Otherwise, they won't be around to live those lives and you won't be around to enjoy them."

When she put it like that, what choice did he have? But isn't that what murderers said, when faced with some impossible choice between saving themselves and saving someone else?

On the other hand, they were doing phenomenal things for humankind. Did that justify the other things they had done …or might still do?

"Think of all the criminal behaviour that governments are responsible for, every single day, and no one does a damn thing about it," Frannie said. "All they do is rant and rave about all the crises and injustices. If activism or new policies achieve anything at all, it's just a *lessening* of the awfulness, like maybe stopping 5G—and I've already seen what *that* technology does in 2021—but nothing really *improves*. It's just not quite as *awful* as it might otherwise have been."

She was adamant. "Right now, politics is nothing more than palliative care."

Things definitely seemed to be getting steadily worse, Daniel conceded.

"At least we're *doing* something about it," Frannie said. "Saving lives, creating real change and forcing governments to actually do what they're meant to be doing."

She looked at him innocently. "How can that be wrong?"

She had knelt down beside him and looked at him with those all-seeing green eyes of hers. "And we can make it *right*," she said.

He knew she would be lost without all his precise computations. Temporally, geographically and physically lost—out there in some unknown time, unable to get back. Maybe he should just refuse to cooperate, since she couldn't do this without him.

But she'd just go ahead on her own, anyway, and probably get all the numbers, coordinates and frequencies wrong and end up permanently stuck in some other universe, and he'd be left holding the baby, figuratively and literally, and then he'd be accused of having killed her, since she had disappeared off the face of the earth, so they'd have sniffer dogs all over the property, looking for where he'd buried her body, and he'd be in prison trying to plead his case, which would be impossible, unless he pleaded insanity, because not even his lawyer would believe his insane story, so his children would end up in foster homes, he'd be a convicted murderer, forced to take anti-psychotic drugs in some looney bin because he kept ranting on about other dimensions and saving the world, and he'd die a tortured death, on his own, having actually gone raving mad in the process.

No. It wasn't worth the risk of her doing this on her own or of even arguing with her about it.

He knew it was only because of his grounding presence, meticulous planning and programming skills that she could be as brazen and reckless as she was. He was the safety net that allowed her to walk the tightrope of time, and she knew he would always be there to catch her if she fell.

He didn't rub her face in it, although she had no qualms about taunting him if he got cold feet about any collateral damage.

"*Denial*, Daniel," she'd say. "They spelled your name wrong on your birth certificate."

This kind of masterplan called for cosmic courage and unflinching determination, she reminded him, and they could not afford to have anyone upset the precisely calibrated equilibrium. It would cause absolute havoc if they didn't stop anyone who got in the way.

He knew this, but he still felt sick when he thought about it, and he still regularly told her he thought she was mad, even though she made so much sense.

She laughed. "Of course I am, darling man, but it's a sane madness," she said, "whereas most people are living a mad kind of sanity. Much sicker."

She was relentless in her logic. "What's the point of us all so dutifully obeying the laws when the lawmakers themselves are breaking them?"

"You want me to answer that question?"

"We *all* need to answer that question," she said. "How come we're not all *asking* it?"

How come there were no politicians like her in the world? That's what *he* wanted to know.

"You've done the projections, Daniel. You know where we're heading, and I've *seen* it. How can what we're doing *not* be a good thing?"

Did he have a choice, given how he felt about her, their children and the work they were doing?

He couldn't leave her—and she already knew from her time travels that he *wouldn't*. Even if he *could*, there would be no one to temper her madness, and she could end up anywhere, doing anything. She needed his calming presence and rational calculations if this was ever going to work.

It was just that she had this infuriating ability to back him into a corner, and then glare at him triumphantly with her folded-arms-*fait-accompli* pose. If she couldn't get him in the present, she'd get him in the future.

But he also found her downright sexy when she was like that, legs akimbo, looking at him defiantly.

"You think you know what I'm thinking," he said to her, the last time she did this.

"Of course I do," she said, grinning.

"Well, just because I had that thought the last time we had this conversation in the future, doesn't mean I'm thinking that same thought now, you know."

He folded his arms and leaned nonchalantly against the kitchen table—his own version of triumphant. "Going to the future changes everything, you said."

"Yeah, but some things never change," she said, grinning gleefully. "Race you to the bedroom!"

She won, as usual.

The damn woman was a witch. He couldn't even get one step ahead of her with *sex*. Although there were times when she *was* powerless to resist him.

He smiled, forcing his mind back to the present.

He had to admit that their Gengineering work was truly inspired, and very exciting. Combined with their latest adjustments to the Franwave, it was mind-blowing—way beyond anything else yet conceived, even in the Frannie-forseeable future.

Until recently, they'd only been able to measure and interpret certain electromagnetic frequencies from the body. Now, with Gengineering, they could *generate* very specific frequencies, program them into the

Franwave and, from there, broadcast them into the human energy field. That changed the electromagnetic signature in significant ways, modifying the potential DNA and creating particular anomalies, which then created an uplink to certain cosmic frequencies that enabled them to literally go where no man—or woman—had gone before.

They had almost perfected their Gengineering technology, and his conscience still pricked him occasionally, but it was no more than a temporary oscillation passing through his system and Frannie made sure it passed quickly.

"Would you rather be an accountant, *Dr Dalton*," she said, "with a nice safe *desk job*?"

He shuddered at the thought. Who was he kidding? There was no way he could tear himself away from this project—*or* the other one. He had no option but to stay the course and make sure he was ready.

It was going to be one hell of a ride.

30

Friday, 15 May 2020

Marnie was lying on the massage table, cocooned in a warm blanket, having another session of sound therapy with Millie. She always found Millie's treatment room profoundly soothing, with a large-leaved plant in each corner, the aroma of lavender, sage and geranium essential oils wafting through the air, soft cream carpeting, and nothing but muted sounds from the outside world.

"Before we start, tell me about Steve," Millie said. "I know he's been away a lot and you two have been trying to connect."

"I'm confused, Millie, and conflicted," Marnie said. "Back in January, I was nervous about seeing him, not wanting things to start up again. But then he had to go to Chicago for two months on business. At first, I felt relieved, but then he ended up having to stay several more months, and I found I was thinking about him more and more."

She took a deep breath, thinking of their last conversation on the phone, and their e-mail exchanges. Over the last two months, Steve had been back and forth to Boston but had been so busy that he hadn't had time to meet up in person. Now, finally, his work with the Chicago client was finished and he was back in Boston. He had called Marnie earlier in the week and suggested they catch up.

"We've agreed to get together tomorrow," Marnie said.

"And how do you feel about that?"

"Nervous, excited, unsure."

Instead of going to the café, they had agreed to meet at Marnie's place. The café had too many associations with their past and Marnie wanted to be able to relax with Steve and have a meaningful conversation, without interruptions.

But what would she say? What did she want? Did she want to get back into a relationship with Steve? Would all their old stuff come rushing back as soon as they re-engaged, and just cause more heartache?

Millie brought her back to the moment. "When I'm working on you today, think about all the caring, compassion, love and support you have given to others, Marnie—to Lucy, Matt and Celle. Think about giving that love to yourself and see how you have withheld it, all these years."

Millie put a hand on her shoulder. "It's time for you, now."

"Okay." Marnie was hesitantly hopeful. She had seen the progress Celle had made after seeing Millie several times, but she could not understand how such a profound transformation could have occurred in just a few months.

"How is it possible for Celle to have changed so much, so fast, Millie? She was in so much pain, but now she's like a completely different person." She took a deep breath. "I guess I'm wondering if that's possible for me, too, or if she was an exception."

"It's amazing what we can shed when we're ready," Millie said, "and most of what torments and saddens us is locked into our energy field, circling around and creating all kinds of emotional angst in our minds."

"But how can these sounds—these frequencies or vibrations or whatever these tuning forks produce—get rid of all that stuff?"

"Emotions have a frequency too, and the vibrational frequencies from the forks can break up those emotional patterns, which are discordant—like musical dissonance—and return the body to a more coherent, harmonious resonance."

"I like the sound of that," Marnie said, feeling her body relax as her mind got the mental reassurance it needed.

She heard Millie reach for one of her tuning forks, ring it and pass it close to her head and shoulders.

"We're meant to be in tune," Millie said, "with ourselves and with our environment, but that's rarely the case, given everything that's coming at us."

The sounds were resonating powerfully around her and Marnie felt herself being gently pummeled by the vibrations.

"Tuning forks are used in conventional medicine to break up kidney stones," Millie said. "The right frequencies can break down physical things too, which gives you an idea of the power of sound to create changes in the body and mind."

"Mmm…" Marnie was tuning out, eyes closed, happy to let Millie do her thing and not keep using her mind to try to figure things out.

Millie asked her to take some deep breaths and let go of all thoughts and concerns. She rang some high-pitched forks and Marnie could hear and feel the sounds moving through the air around her. It felt as if a magnetic force were being drawn across her body, flexing her energy field as if it were an elastic bubble.

Then Millie asked her to think about Steve. Marnie felt herself immediately stiffen, as if her body knew there was something to be afraid of, even if her mind didn't.

"It's okay," Millie said gently. "You're just so used to taking care of others who were vulnerable—your siblings and yourself—so the body remembers that need to protect, even if there's nothing you need to protect yourself from now.

Millie rang another tuning fork, sweeping through the body's energy field, she explained, to clear those old emotions from her system.

"I want you to think about being with Steve, but without worrying about a future together or whether he's right for you or anything like that. Just as friends. Okay?"

"Mmm…"

Marnie imagined sitting with Steve at her kitchen table, drinking tea. It felt warm, cozy and safe… *Why couldn't it always feel like that? Why did relationships have to be so complicated?*

"Good." Millie was sweeping a fork around Marnie's lower torso and down over her knees. "Now imagine being in a relationship with Steve. See yourselves together and just let yourself feel that, without judging it or worrying about it not working out."

Marnie took a deep breath and let her mind wander, seeing herself and Steve at the park, walking hand in hand through the trees, the sun warming their backs and a sense of peaceful partnership between them. That felt nice too, but she was just imagining it. That didn't mean it would *be* like that…

"Deep breath."

Marnie breathed in and let it go.

"Now I want you to think about the problems you had with Steve in the past. Conflicts, arguments or whatever wasn't working."

Marnie cast her mind back. She remembered a feeling of conflict but she couldn't remember what their conversations or arguments had been about. That was weird.

"I can't remember what the problems were."

"Good," Millie said. "Now think about whatever objections or concerns you have about being in a committed relationship with Steve now."

Marnie reflected, trying to remember the reasons they had broken up. Definitely her choice—*that* she could remember. But why, exactly, and why had she been so sure it would never work?

Her mind went blank. Was it because she was being put on the spot or because her mind was so relaxed it didn't want to think about anything, right now?

"I can't think of any objections, Millie," she said. "But maybe I'm just not focused or thinking clearly."

"Is it possible those objections are gone?" Millie asked gently. "Or are no longer valid?"

Marnie felt her breath catch.

"Keep breathing."

"Right now, I can't find them. Doesn't mean they're gone, though, does it?"

"Would you prefer to believe that?" Millie asked. "You could regenerate them, if you wanted to. But do you want to?"

"I'm not sure," Marnie said.

"Why might you want to do that?"

"Mmmm… To stay safe?"

"How would fear keep you safe?" Millie continued to ring her forks and pass them around Marnie's head, shoulders and down over her hips.

"Well, it wouldn't," Marnie said. "I suppose I'd just be alert to danger in case I got hurt."

"Well, I think we all learn that one, somewhere in our lives," Millie said. "I want you to feel where that fear might live—where in your body. Just point."

Marnie thought for a few moments, then pointed to her lower abdomen.

There was a pause as Millie chose another tuning fork, then a deeply resonant tone swept over Marnie's torso and Marnie imagined the fear being dissolved, like the pixels of a photo dissolving on a computer screen.

"Remember, every emotion has a frequency," Millie said. "I'm using the 417Hz fork, relating to the second energy centre, which is all about creativity, reproduction and sensual connection. This frequency helps to cleanse the body of traumatic experiences and the destructive influences of past events."

Marnie felt the tones wash over her, her whole body thrumming from the vibration.

"A tuning fork is like a musical instrument itself," Millie said, "but it's also like a conductor's baton, telling the body's orchestra of sounds how to play harmoniously together, and catching anything that's off key or out of tune."

She rang the fork a few more times and then let the vibrations die away into silence.

"How do you feel now?"

"Different, somehow," Marnie said. "I'm not sure how."

"Good," said Millie. "No need to try to figure it out. Just let things percolate through your system and see how you feel when you meet up with Steve."

"Okay. But…" Marnie paused. "How do you know when to trust your emotions? I mean, I seem to be full of good advice for other people, yet very unsure about my own stuff. How can you tell if your emotions are reliable?"

Millie chose another tuning fork, struck it and passed it over various parts of Marnie's body.

"It depends on the emotions," Millie said. "I look at it this way. Anger, resentment, self-doubt and other negative emotions are usually the result of negative beliefs, which are nothing to do with who we really are, although they're useful guides towards wholeness. Positive emotions such as gratitude, compassion and joy are a natural part of human nature, although they often get squashed by all the other stuff. Those are the ones to trust and cultivate. Does that make sense?"

"Yes," Marnie said, thinking how strange it was to be having this kind of conversation with a friend she'd known for decades. *Had they never talked about this kind of thing before?* "What about love?"

"I don't really see love as an emotion," Millie said. "I see it more as a way of being—the result of all the other positive emotions we cultivate, and the springboard for lots more. It's certainly the most reliable feeling and the one to feed more than anything else. Love brings the most rewards, whereas fear—its opposite—brings contraction, withholding, withdrawal, self-doubts and all kinds of self-rejection."

"Mmmm… I like that. It's the negative stuff that creates the confusion, too. I need to focus on the good stuff and trust that, right?"

"Yes. And you don't even need to ask yourself if you can trust it. That would be like asking if you should trust the air you breathe. It's the matrix of the universe, so having love in your heart and mind will bring you what you ultimately want."

Millie struck another fork and passed it over Marnie's right shoulder.

"Now, I'm going to use a few other forks to clean up the energy field, free up any other stuck energy, and bring it all back to its relevant centre," Millie said. "Just relax."

Marnie felt herself drifting off, her mind relaying a kaleidoscope of fleeting images—the kitchen at Westfield, her mum combing her long dark hair, memories of feeling shy and excluded at school, her dad bringing home a cat she called Felix then searching the fields for hours when Felix ran off, taking care of Lucy as a baby, her first day teaching in her classroom… So many memories, all with their own emotional charge.

She was startled when she felt Millie's gentle touch on her shoulder. "Take your time getting up. No rush."

"Is this like housekeeping?" Marnie asked, feeling far too woozy to get up yet. "Do you have to keep doing it or is it gone for good?"

Millie laughed. "Usually, it's gone, although there are layers of emotions in the various layers of your energy field, which relate to various phases of your life."

Marnie imagined her energy field littered with debris—barbed wire, tumbleweed, empty wrappers, KEEP OUT signs, boxes full of old junk, faded photos, broken toys…

"We carry the vibrational echoes of our past," Millie said, "and they can reverberate through our system unless we clear them out."

Marnie had felt she'd never be clear of the echoes from her parents' death and all the stuff from her childhood. But she felt lighter, now, as if she'd finally shed some of the excess baggage from her system.

"This work is like ripping out old carpets," Millie said, "tearing up the underlay, stripping off the dirt from the original floorboards underneath, sanding them down and then putting on a nice fresh coat of varnish."

Marnie liked the sound of that, and Celle certainly seemed like a shiny new person. If Celle could do it, after the hell she had been through, then Marnie could, too.

Her head was starting to clear and she could feel energy coming back to her limbs, as if they were being reconnected after going offline for a while.

She checked in with her heart to see how it felt now about seeing Steve tomorrow, and with her mind, to see if it still had all the same old fears and objections. Both seemed quite open to the idea—her mind pointing out how he had been there for her, after her parents died, and her heart reminding her how gentle and supportive he had been, with no pressure on her to give anything back. Just friends.

For a moment, Marnie felt her heart swell with love—for Steve, Lucy, Matt, Celle, her parents, her kids at school and maybe even the whole wide world.

Suddenly, she couldn't wait to get off the table.

31

Saturday, 16 May 2020

Marnie had cleaned the windows, vacuumed the whole apartment, wiped down all the kitchen surfaces, scrubbed the bathroom, tidied up the living room and plumped up all the sofa cushions. And it was still only 9.30am. Another hour before Steve got here. What else could she do? She couldn't sit still long enough to write in her journal and she didn't have time for a relaxing bath. She could bake some cookies, but that felt too domestic and might give him the wrong idea. But what was the *right* idea? What idea did she want to give him?

She had tossed and turned all night, trying to figure out what to say to Steve when he arrived. How to play it. Cool… just friends? *Sorry, could we try again? I don't know how I feel… what about you?* Maybe that was best… more honest.

Was she wearing the right outfit? She ran back into her bedroom and looked in the mirror. Her favourite blue jeans, bare feet, stretchy navy cotton V-neck top. Were the bare feet too bohemian? No way was she going to wear her slippers. Jewellery? She had decided against it. Keep things simple. Just the plain gold earrings that she normally wore. Steve was a simple guy, and he was just coming for a friendly chat. Right?

Should she wear the red top instead? No. Red was such a dangerous, passionate colour and she didn't want to wave any red flags in his face.

Leather slip-ons, maybe, to cover her feet? Yes. Better. That felt safer.

Maybe a thin gold necklace? Steve had given her one with a lovely amber pendant when they were together. But if she wore that, wouldn't that indicate… something?

Darn. Now her lips were dry so she ran back to the kitchen, gulped down a glass of water and then back to the bathroom to brush her teeth again and re-apply her natural lip gloss.

Maybe she could—

The doorbell rang and she gasped, looking at her watch. It was only 10am so it couldn't be Steve… Damn. She didn't want any random people interrupting her obsessive focus. Take it easy. See who it is.

She pressed the intercom buzzer. Yes?

"Morning, Marnie. I'm a little early."

It *was* Steve. "Okay! Come on up."

She buzzed him in then ran back to the bathroom to check the armpits. No sweat marks, although you couldn't really tell with navy, which was why she'd worn this top. Lips? The gloss still looked okay. Back to the hallway. Deep breath. *Calm down*, for goodness' sake!

She heard Steve outside the door and opened up before he had a chance to knock.

"Hi," he said, casual and laid back, in jeans, white cotton shirt and a blue Goretex jacket. He looked tanned and healthy, and a lot more relaxed than she was.

"I came early," he said, "because I know you, Marnie Dalton." He grinned. "You've been up since the crack of dawn, polishing the whole place from top to bottom, changing your outfit at least three times, fretting over what to say, and if I'd waited till 10.30, you'd be so exhausted that you'd have to go to bed—*on your own*—and we'd have to postpone our chat."

He looked at her, smiling. "Am I warm?"

"Scalding," she said, and burst out laughing. "Steve, it's so good to see you." She gave him a fierce hug, and it felt like the most natural thing in the world. He knew her better than she knew herself—perhaps he could save her *from* herself, if she could just *relax*.

"Well," said Steve, shrugging off his jacket and hanging it on the coat stand, "that was a lovely welcome. Definitely worth not waiting for."

She laughed again, her heart light.

"I didn't want to give you flowers because I wanted you to focus on me," he said. "Was that very selfish?"

"No, it was very smart," said Marnie, feeling only a tiny bit disappointed. "I would have had to go and put them in a vase straight away, which would have got in the way of the welcome hug."

"Exactly what I thought." He held up a finger. "Hang on, then." He opened the front door, leaned out and came back in with a huge bunch of two-toned orange-yellow tulips.

"For you, Ms Marnie, and my apologies for keeping you waiting all these months."

Marnie's heart did a little somersault of vindication. *See? I told you to trust this guy.* "Thank you, Steve. These are beautiful."

"Let's go into the kitchen and you can put them in water," Steve said, a warm hand at her back, guiding her kitchenward.

"I have fond memories of us sitting at this table and chatting over some very good coffee."

"Is that a hint?" Marnie laughed as she unwrapped the flowers and reached for a vase.

"Definitely." Steve smiled. "Want me to make it?"

"Yes, please. You remember where—"

"I surely do," Steve said, reaching around her to fill the kettle at the tap, then getting two mugs from the shelf above the toaster. Marnie couldn't help smiling as he took the bag of coffee from the fridge and then found the cafetière in the cupboard beside the stove.

"My work is almost done," he said, flopping into a chair at the table. "Come and sit, Marnie, while we wait for that to boil."

Marnie put the flowers in the centre of the table and sat down beside him.

"Beautiful," she said, looking at the flowers.

"Yes," he said, looking at her. "Although I can see that you've changed."

"Have I?" Marnie felt mildly alarmed.

But Steve was grinning. "Same gorgeousness, just more of it."

The kettle clicked off and Steve got up to make the coffee.

"Madam." With a small bow, he placed the cafetière on the table beside her and a mug for each of them.

"So, how are you, Marnie, after all that's happened?" He paused, reflecting. "Apart from e-mails, we haven't spoken since…"

"November," Marnie said. She depressed the plunger on the cafetière and poured coffee for them both.

"Nearly five months," he said. "Fill me in. What's changed? How are you feeling about your parents now? And how's work?" He leaned towards her. "Tell me, girl. I want to know what's going on inside that precious hermetically sealed heart of yours."

So she told him about working with Millie and the tuning forks, about Celle and how she had blossomed, about Matt starting a new life in Mexico, and about Lucy working for Nate and getting her own place. She told him about being on the back of the neon-green Ninja with the nutty professor, and he laughed, as she knew he would.

She had shared all of these things with Millie and DeeDee, but sharing them with Steve was different. Was her heart more engaged? Or was it because he loved her and wanted to live all her special moments with her, even if he could only do it retroactively?

"I'm sorry I wasn't here to help with any of that," Steve said.

"I'm glad you weren't," Marnie said, and a small cloud of hurt passed over his eyes. "What I mean is… it was perfect having that time to myself to think about things, to process all that happened, to think about our relationship and to realize that I… miss you."

"I've missed you too," Steve said. "And I know exactly what you mean. I needed that same time-out when we split up or I'd never have got my head straight."

"What *did* go wrong between us, Steve? I've been trying to remember but my mind is a blank."

"Ah. So you don't remember being a tiger in bed? The neighbours complaining about the noise? The bed breaking? None of that?"

"Ha. No." Marnie laughed. "I don't remember any of that, strangely." *Could he not be serious for one minute?*

"How come I can't remember the other stuff—why we split up, the things that annoyed us? Am I in denial or just emotionally numb or what?"

Steve undid his cuffs and was rolling up his sleeves as he reflected. *How was she supposed to concentrate or remember anything when he was exposing his gorgeous tanned hairy forearms?*

"I don't think you're emotionally numb," he said. "In fact, you've softened in some beautiful way and this whole place feels different." He gestured around her apartment. "Some devastating emotional tornadoes have swept through here, but they seem to have cleared the air and left behind a peaceful wisdom and some space for new things to come in."

"That's exactly how it feels," Marnie said, loving the way he made sense of her life. "But what about us? How come I can't remember what the issues were or what we used to argue about?"

"When you change, it's hard to remember who you were before." He paused, reflecting. "But I think I was trying too hard to please you, and maybe you found it hard to let love in, having always been the care-taker, so I guess our emotional baggage was clashing." He laughed. "That's what Josie tells me, anyway. And I think she's right."

Marnie nodded. "She is right. And I've been thinking about what I want to do with my own life, with everyone else moving on to new things."

"After taking care of everyone for so long, I think it's definitely time for you, now," Steve said.

"Yes, I know." Marnie sighed. "That's what DeeDee says."

"I always liked DeeDee," Steve said. "She knows you almost as well as I do." He reached for her hand. "Has the work with Millie helped you deal with the loss of your parents?"

"Yeah, and other stuff, too," Marnie said, feeling a lump in her throat. *Why did Steve's concern for her always make her feel weepy?*

"You're a lot more tender-hearted that you give yourself credit for," Steve said, gently.

Marnie looked at him in surprise. "I should give myself *credit* for that?"

"Of course. What could be more important than feeling things deeply and caring about other forms of life, including me?" He squeezed her hand.

Marnie suddenly remembered something from her childhood. It was her ninth birthday and she was sitting at the kitchen table with Matt, Lucy and her parents, eating chocolate peppermint ice cream— her favourite. Suddenly, a bird slammed against the windowpane and fell to the ground outside. Her dad opened the window, leaned out and picked up the little body of a sparrow, limp and lifeless in his hand.

"He's gone, poor little fella," he said, placing the bird gently on the ground. "I'll go out in a minute and make him a little grave."

Marnie shot up from the table and ran to her room. Slamming the door, she threw herself on her bed and sobbed. Her mother came and sat beside her. "Marnie, I know it's sad, but these things happen in nature, sweetie. You know that."

"But it's our *fault*," Marnie wailed. "Our window got in its way!"

"You're right. Birds can't see the glass. We could buy some birdie stickers and put them on the window to warn the other birds. Want to do that?"

'Yeah, but it won't save *that* bird," Marnie said. "It's my birthday but his *deathday*."

"You have a wonderful big heart, sweetie," her mother said, stroking her hair. "I really admire that in you. I hope you never lose it."

"Earth to Marnie? Is there anybody there?" Steve's voice brought her back to the present.

"Sorry. I was just… thinking."

"Look, I know you try to hide your feelings and be strong for everyone else, so I'm glad you're finally getting some support for yourself." He looked at her. "Is there anything *I* can do for you?"

"Um, I'm not sure. Like what?"

"Well, I could give you another hug, or massage your shoulders, or just listen while you talk." He paused to let her consider the options. "I was going to take you to lunch and then I thought we could go for a walk as it's such a lovely day. Then we could come back here for the hug and massage, or skip lunch and curl up on the couch while you tell me what you'd like to do with your life."

"Sounds good," Marnie said.

Steve grinned. "Which bit?"

"All of it, actually." Marnie laughed. "It's a while since anyone spoiled me like that."

"Mmm… let me guess. Not since that guy… what was his name? Romeo? No, Romero! Yeah. That pushy southern guy."

"You're assuming there was no one else after you," Marnie said, trying to look offended but unable to stop smiling.

"True. Arrogant, shameless male that I am." He drained his coffee and put his hands on the table. "So, girl, what's it to be?"

"All of the above," Marnie said, smiling, "but perhaps not in that order."

"Ah. Okay. Men always get the order wrong, don't they? Wanting to talk first, then eat, then walk, and then the cuddles—*if* there's time—whereas women always want it the other way around. Sex first, and then sex and more sex. Then maybe some food just so you have enough energy for more sex. Right?"

Marnie laughed. "Not this woman," she said.

"What?" Steve looked delighted. "You mean you already have enough energy and don't need to eat first?"

"I know what you're doing, you know."

"What?" Steve looked at her innocently.

"Getting me to laugh so I relax and stop worrying about… all this."

"Busted," he said. "Is it working?"

"Yes," Marnie said, standing up. "Let's migrate to the couch and mess up the cushions I spent hours arranging symmetrically, and we can talk about what you came here to talk about."

"You don't want me to talk about numbers again, do you?"

"No. I don't. In fact, I think I'd like you to stop talking altogether and just give me that massage–hug thing." She paused, looking at him pointedly. "Or was that why you were talking so much, so I'd eventually beg you to shut up, put me out of my misery and just kiss me?"

"Busted again." He grinned. "That first bust was just a warm-up." He grabbed her around the waist and carried her, laughing, into the living room. She kicked off her shoes on the way, deciding that she *liked* the bohemian look, especially with Steve around.

He laid her gently down on the couch, and leaned back to look into her eyes. "Marnie, we can talk more, if you want. I don't want you to think that I came over here just for the… coffee and pristine couch cushions."

"I can't think of a single thing I want to talk about, right now. We can talk more, later."

"Suits me. We can curl up and talk like an old married couple."

"No way!"

He looked at her in surprise.

"Not *old*," she said. "Why not a *young* married couple?"

"Girl, you *have* changed. I thought you'd wait for *me* to ask *you*— *again*. But you're right. We do not need to talk about that right this minute." He gently raised her head, sat down behind her, stretching out a leg on each side, put a cushion on his lap and lowered her head gently down.

Marnie laughed. "You know what I meant."

"I know exactly what you meant, girl," Steve said, kissing the top of her head. "Now, tell me where it hurts and I'll make it all better."

"Well, since you ask, *Romeo*," Marnie said, suddenly feeling joyfully reckless, "it hurts absolutely *everywhere*. There is not one inch of me that does not hurt."

"This could take a while, then," Steve said, seriously. "Good thing I had a four-course breakfast." He leaned down and whispered in her ear. "I had no idea you missed me so much, darlin' girl. But I'm here now, so you can relax and let yourself be loved."

32

---

16 May 2020

The air was quiet as Lucy walked through the park, doing her daily 'de-frag' to process her thoughts and reflect on her life. It seemed unusually silent among the trees today. *Did birds ever sulk? Did they ever go on strike?* She wondered.

That's it. I'm not doing any fucking singing today. I'm staying in my tree. You can just do your own sweet thing without me. See if I care that you don't care. Do you give a crap about us birds? Do you? Do we ever complain about not being noticed, liked, shared on social greedia? You think *you* invented twitter? *And* we gave you *aviation*. That came from us avians. You can fly around in your machines, thanks to us. You didn't come up with *that* little marvel on your own, you know. And the thanks? Did we even get some extra worms? Do you even stop to listen? A bird on the wire will always be smarter than you walking wireless birdbrains. Do you ever look up from your gadgets and listen to the splendour of us, singing our exquisite song every single day? Not that we need your approval, although a little more consideration would be nice, and a lot less pollution. But we don't do this for *you*. We do it for the sheer joy of singing, loving life, being birds, doing what only birds can do.

Blimey. Where did that come from? She was constantly getting these missives from nature or out of the ethers or somewhere beyond her physical self... stuff just arriving in her head, demanding to be downloaded. Did she have some kind of cosmic uplink or just a really twisted imagination?

Yet the messages always seemed timely and vaguely meaningful. How often *did* people look up? She was looking up now, at the green canopy against the blue sky, and she couldn't see any birds anywhere. Most people were so engrossed in their gadgets that nature might as well not exist... apart from the fact that humans wouldn't exist then, either. *Obviously.*

Birds made no judgements—unlike humans, who rarely missed a chance to condemn whatever they didn't like, including themselves. Especially themselves. Been there, done that, Lucy thought. Birds were perfect little parcels of pure symphonic resonance, attuned to the rhythms of the earth, transmitting their joyous frequencies into the air for all to receive. Another avian lesson for clueless humans: unconditional giving and living, just for the raw bliss of it.

When had she last sung? Had she ever sung her heart out? If she had, Lucy couldn't remember doing it. She could come up with lots of smart-assed remarks. But sing? That was much more personal and intimate, exposing—and liberating?—a much deeper part of the self. Probably why most people didn't go there, afraid of not hitting the right notes or of revealing something they didn't want others to see.

It felt eerie when birds didn't sing, as if there was something fundamentally wrong in the airwaves. Or they knew something humans didn't, and they were quietly tweeting in the trees, spreading the word.

Were *humans* being purely human, doing what only humans should do? Or were they trying to be something they were never meant to be—high-performing producers, mobile databases, conveyor belts of consumerism, soon to be just an accessory to some bigger satellite intelligence orbiting their abandoned bods?

Lucy did wonder. And she was aware of her brain not feeling quite the way it used to. As if it had been compartmentalized into separate bits that no longer liked each other very much or shared input on how best to proceed. Her mental faculties worked fine. She could still think, write, research, banter and come up with a quick retort—even faster than before, come to think of it... And she could still impress Nate, which she certainly wanted to do. So she could *function* really well, but she wasn't deeply *feeling* things.

Nate seemed to be a pretty well adjusted guy, although she hadn't seen much of his emotional side, with him being so professional towards her, keeping things *cool*. But she wouldn't mind seeing a bit more of that side of him... and maybe a few other bits.

Lucy sighed. This was what happened when she allowed her mind to wander. It usually ended up in some slutty fantasy scenario, lusting after her boss. No, her *lifeline*. This was the guy who had magically appeared on her doorstep and rescued her from her own wretchedness. She could not afford to blow it. Or him. *See?* Her mind was *such* a slut. The man had no idea.

But she could dream, couldn't she? No harm in that... She often wondered what went on in his mind. *Was* he emotionally present? Lucy knew he listened to a lot of music. She could hear it playing upstairs when she was working at her desk in the office. Sometimes he played his iPod in his office, too. Maybe that helped keep him... *balanced*, if that's what he was. She should bring some music into her life and see if that made her heart a little happier...

Had she shut down part of her heart when her parents checked out? Although she was pretty sure the heart didn't do things by halves.

Brains could compartmentalize, but not hearts. It was all or nothing. Shut down part, you shut down the whole heart. Ha. That was one thing humans seemed to be able to do *wholeheartedly*.

But she sensed that her feelings were somehow less connected to her core. She wasn't sure why or how that could be, but something subtle was definitely *off*.

She would have to let it come to her, the way all the weird stuff did… weirdly.

Which brought her back to the birds. They sure could teach humans a thing or two about how to stay tuned into their true selves. Lucy had never seen a bird head for a branch and then miss, crashing into the tree trunk. Birds never missed or did dumb stuff, cringing with embarrassment and skulking off to the nearest bush to hide themselves. Because they were so tuned in to what was around them? They were laser-sharp and sang flawlessly, never once off-key or croaky, even after staying up till 10pm during the long summer days, serenading everyone to sleep and then singing them awake again a few hours later.

Was there anything more pristine, constant or humbling than nature? Not that people ever compared themselves… or gave a shit about these tiny vibrant flutes. Even though they had no friggin' clue how to tune their own instrument—their own unique PA system for broadcasting themselves to the world. Most people just sounded brash, raucous and totally off-pitch, convinced that louder was better. Megaphones of megalomania.

But she was starting to sound strident, even in her unspoken thoughts. And she was walking faster, as if to escape herself. Was she sick of playing someone else's tune? Is that what she was doing, writing all this promotional stuff for someone else's success?

Just how attuned *was* she—to what she wanted or to the kind of success she might ever achieve? She wasn't sure she trusted her logic, her heart or her intuition, none of which had predicted the mighty life-stopping fuck-up of her parents' train-wreck ending.

She sighed at her own exhausting anger. *New song, new story*, she told herself. This martyr act wasn't the kind of music her heart needed to hear.

As she walked, Lucy came to a large bush with tightly woven leaves forming a perfect ball of impenetrable foliage. Impenetrable to humans, at least. Inside, a million voices chattered excitedly, and she felt her heart lift. They were having a tea break. A tea party! They hadn't left, got pissed off or gone on strike. Why was that so infinitely reassuring, as if things were precisely as they should be and she could just relax? The birds were still singing. It was all okay. Whatever it was.

Her breathing relaxed and her pace slowed.

Birds had really got their act together—and they knew *how* to act together, with no bickering, fluffed-up egos, hidden agendas or *me-first-me-first-me-first* mantras. They really knew how to fly—together, with a unified intelligence connecting all their soaring, swooping acrobatics, their elegance and majesty never changing. Birds were still as essentially, beautifully birdie as they had always been. Whereas humans, it seemed to Lucy, had no idea how to take off in their own lives, sometimes doing stuff that seemed downright *sub*human. They were having a hard time just staying physically planted on the ground, bumbling around with their feet barely—and rarely barefoot—on the earth, while their minds were always somewhere else, seeking something external, leaving their neglected physical bodies muddling through on their own.

It didn't seem right and she was pretty sure it would have to come to a head—or a heart—sometime soon.

33

Sunday, 17 May 2020

"Hello?"

"DeeDee, it's Marnie. Got a minute?"

"Yeah. Hang on… I just have to turn something off." Marnie heard muffled noises in the background, then DeeDee came back on the line.

"Tell me everything, girlfriend. How did it go with Steve yesterday?"

"Heartbreakingly wonderful and then heartbreakingly awful," Marnie said. "I can't believe I was so *stupid*, DeeDee. I got my hopes up for nothing. I should *never* have reconnected with him."

"Whoa, girl. Back up a bit. What happened? He came over in the morning and then…?"

"Then it was beautiful, funny, sexy and fabulous."

"And? Details! I can't do proper girlfriend duty if I don't get all the details and make sure you didn't miss anything."

"I definitely missed something." Marnie groaned.

"Explain."

"He brought me flowers, made me laugh, gave me a full-body massage …and then his cellphone rang and I suddenly remembered why we split up the first time." Marnie groaned again." DeeDee, how could I have *forgotten* that? I'm doubting my own sanity. I can understand forgetting some of our petty arguments about… whatever, but how could I forget *that*?"

"Probably because you wanted to get back together so badly," DeeDee said.

"I'm pretty sure *he* remembered why we split up, but he avoided the issue, probably hoping I'd got over my little stint of *humanitarianism* and joined the real world."

"Possibly."

"Did *you* remember us breaking up over the cellphone thing?"

"Well, yes, but I thought you might be able to work it out, this time around."

"No way. He's as addicted as everyone else. He *needs it for his work.* He *can't operate without it.* He wants to be able to *protect me if he ever needs to call for help.* All the usual justifications."

"I'm not sure it matters," DeeDee said, pragmatically. "You've changed, Marnie, and so has our world. Look at what's happening with wireless networks—how much more invasive things have got in the past year. Even if you remembered his cellphone being an issue and tried to convince yourself you could handle it, for the sake of the relationship, I don't think you could. Not with the way things are heading now."

DeeDee paused to let Marnie digest this.

"Yeah. You're right, DeeDee. Somewhere in my subconscious, I *must* have remembered, though. It's too big an issue for me to have forgotten." She took a noisy inhale. "Maybe I'm still traumatized by my parents dying like that, and I'm not thinking clearly. Is that possible?"

"Of course it is. I'd be surprised if it hadn't affected you profoundly, in all kinds of ways. Especially you, as you tend to contain your emotions. Most people would be incapable of working after suffering a tragic loss like that, and you barely took any time off at all. But trauma affects memory, focus, everything. Don't be so hard on yourself."

"Yeah, but look where it got me. Even more traumatized than before!"

"But that's how trauma works, Marnie," said DeeDee gently. "It throws us off and we sometimes end up in other upsetting situations—or in situations where we can't handle the emotional overwhelm because we haven't yet fully processed the first one—so another layer gets added."

Marnie sighed. "I suppose that makes sense…"

"You know it does. You need time to process all that's happened, including this recent encounter with Steve, which may have helped, in a way—stirring up some of those old contained emotions so you can really work through them this time."

Marnie felt herself softening. DeeDee's words were helping her make sense of the turmoil she was feeling.

"But I think you probably *did* suppress the memory of why you split up," DeeDee said. "You desperately wanted this to work *because* of losing your parents. You needed the love and comfort only Steve could give you. Who wouldn't want that? Especially those of us choosing to stay human."

"Yeah. There is that…" The truth of this made Marnie want to sob again. She had *ached* from wanting the comfort that only Steve seemed able to offer. But she was slowly letting herself off the hook for being so clueless.

"Take a breath and tell me what happened after the passion-killing cellphone call."

"Nothing. I told him I couldn't live with him having a cellphone, not with everything I knew about the radiation, and he left. End of story."

"That's a sad short story. Are you sure there's no chance of a sequel?"

"No. It's done, and I'm *finished* with men. They're all addicted to their cellphones and seem to think it's essential to their manhood, like an extension of their pleasure-seeking periscopes."

DeeDee laughed. "You can't give up on procreation so soon, girl. You're only 24."

"I don't care. If I ever want to have a child, I'll do it via a sperm bank." She laughed sardonically. "Or maybe not, if the cretins donating their sperm are on their cellphone while they ejaculate into the cup." She sighed. "All those Wi-fried gonads out there are already producing deformed babies. No, it's hopeless, DeeDee. I've completely lost interest in relationships. Honestly."

"Well, for someone so disinterested in men, you seem very passionate about him."

"I'm *not* passionate about him," Marnie said, passionately. "In fact, I think I might actually *hate* him for this."

"There's a lot of passion in hatred, you know. Couldn't you put that energy to good use?"

"What? How? I'm not wasting any more energy on him, DeeDee. Really."

"Let me think about it and see if I can come up with something."

"Forget it! But thanks for listening to my drama rant."

"If you'd called me to give me your latest chocolate-chip cookie recipe, I'd have hung up on you."

"That could happen yet," Marnie said, laughing. "I'm just going to live my quiet life, enjoy the few intelligent friends I have, and stay away from men."

DeeDee paused while Marnie took a breath.

"Marnie? Why don't you tell me what you're *really* feeling. You're holding back a flood, girl. Give it to me."

"I'm just so *sad*," Marnie wailed. "I look at him, his hands, his arms, his gorgeous face, his strong body, and he is so *beautiful*. The human body is so *beautiful*, DeeDee. Why would anyone want to irradiate it? Why do we all walk around oblivious to our beauty and our courageous hearts, all trying to love and be loved? Steve is such a loving man and all he wants to do is please me, do things for me and make me happy. I can't explain how beauty can be so *painful*…"

"I hear you, sister," DeeDee said quietly. "There is an aching beauty in our miraculous anatomy—in a splayed hand, a narrow wrist, a body raised on tiptoes, the pivot of a slender ankle, and the curve of joyful lips. Perhaps that's what we cannot bear, all this beauty. We don't think we deserve it so we destroy it, ignore it or deny it."

"That's exactly how it seems to be." Marnie sighed. "But it doesn't change things, DeeDee. It's just not going to work, and I'm sick of trying to convince people to behave like decent human beings, when they all think I'm just a cranky old school teacher."

"You're hardly old and only very rarely cranky," DeeDee said, "and you need to stop thinking of yourself as some kind of nut."

"But people think I *am*. They don't get it because they don't feel the radiation or—"

"You don't feel it either, nor do I or the hundreds of scientists who understand what it does."

"Well, I'm sick of explaining things to people and feeling as if I have to apologize for trying to protect my health and the kids at school…"

"It's only because the insanity has been so normalized," DeeDee said, "that sane people end up sounding abnormal. Why do you think your parents worked in isolation?"

"I never thought of them as not being accepted."

"By their peers, they were, in the same field, but certainly not by the main stream," DeeDee said. "Brilliance is always in the minority, Marnie. You know that."

"When I see what's happening to the kids at school, DeeDee, it almost breaks my heart. It's not just the harm from all the wireless stuff, but the neglect, with parents glued to their cellphones. The phones are the main event and their children are becoming *accessories*."

"I hear you," DeeDee said. "Just keep doing what you do, girl. You've already helped a lot of those kids."

"Yeah, for all the good it does," Marnie said, sighing. "I wish I could talk to my parents about all this. My mum was obsessed with this stuff. I know she would have done something to fix this, if she'd stuck around… I really miss them, DeeDee."

"I know you do, sweetie. I wish I could help more." She paused. "Why don't you go for another session with Millie, to help you process all this stuff. We'll chat more on Wednesday, if you're still on for our girls' night out?"

"Yeah, I might do that. Thanks, DeeDee. See you Wednesday."

34

"He has the anatomy of a fruitcake and the mentality of a runaway train," DeeDee said.

"With no passengers, presumably," Marnie said.

"Zee-ro," DeeDee affirmed.

"What are you two talking about?" Millie breezed up to their table, cast off her jacket, flopped into a chair and exhaled the last of her workday.

"A certain presidential pretender, who will not be getting another molecule of our attention," DeeDee said.

"I'm surprised you gave him any airtime at all," Millie said.

"He was merely a dumbbell with which to flex our laughter muscles," DeeDee said.

"And not a reflection of our loss of sanity or the will to live," Marnie said, laughing.

"Glad to hear it," Millie said, although she didn't look very happy, Marnie thought.

"Let me go and get our bevs," Marnie said. "Dee, coffee for you?"

"My usual unadulterated black, please," DeeDee said.

"Millie?"

"A cappuccino, please, Marn. Thanks."

Marnie grabbed her purse and headed for the counter.

As soon as Marnie left, Millie leaned over the table towards DeeDee. "I don't know if I should tell her," she said in an urgent whisper.

"Tell her what?"

"I swear I just saw her mother in the street," she said.

DeeDee's eyebrows rose in disbelief. "Her parents died almost a year ago, Millie. It had to be someone else."

Millie shook her head emphatically. "You know how striking her mother was—and tall, like you. She didn't exactly blend into the crowd. As soon as she saw me, she turned and then disappeared…"

"You mean she disappeared into the crowd…"

"No, I mean she *disappeared*, DeeDee. One minute she was there, then she was gone. She—"

"Here you go, Millie." Marnie had returned with Millie's cappuccino and DeeDee's coffee.

They both stopped talking and looked up.

"Okay, now it's *my* turn to ask," Marnie said, observing their expressions—DeeDee, brazenly benign; Millie, sheepishly guilty. "What were *you two* talking about?"

"Oh, nothing important," Millie said, taking a sip of her cappuccino.

"Millie fancies a married man," DeeDee said.

Millie sputtered mid-swallow and started coughing. "Sorry," she said, hoarsely. "Went down… wrong way…"

"Is it true?"

"Is what true?" Millie looked alarmed and started coughing again.

"That you've fallen for a married man."

"No!"

DeeDee shot her a look. "Well, DeeDee's exaggerating a bit," Millie said. "I was just saying one of my clients was, um, cute, that's all."

"I don't know what's going on with you two, but let me get my tea. Back in a sec." Marnie went back to the counter, returning with a tea for herself.

She sat down opposite DeeDee. "Okay, so tell me what's going on."

"Millie has fallen for this hunk of a client but he's married with two kids, so it's really a non-starter," DeeDee said. "Right, Millie?"

"Mmm…" Millie looked cornered.

"Millie, you know you deserve better than that," Marnie said. "After all you've told me about healthy relationships."

"Yes, of course. I do, Marn." She shrugged in embarrassment. "It was just a momentary thing that I foolishly shared with the drama queen, here, who made *a big thing out of nothing*." Millie glared at DeeDee.

"Speaking of men," Marnie said, "you've been very quiet lately, DeeDee. We need an update to entertain us, since Mille doesn't want to talk about the non-starter married man and I don't want to talk about the non-starter Steve. What have you got for us?"

"Yeah," Millie said. What's going on with that Japanese businessman you were so keen on?"

"Lots, probably, but it's all happening in Japan, without me," DeeDee said. She seemed unusually reserved, one hand clasped demurely over the other on the table.

"Come on. You've got to give us more than that," Marnie said.

"Make it up, if you have to. Can't you see we're desperate?"

"Well, okay, then," DeeDee said, lifting her right hand to reveal a massive diamond on her ring finger.

"A ring!" Millie said, so gobsmacked that she was perfectly entitled to stupidly state the obvious.

"That's not a ring," Marnie said. "That's the GDP of Bhutan!"

"Happiest country in the world," DeeDee said, grinning. "Apparently."

"What's Bhutan got to do with this?" Millie was confused.

"Nothing. Sorry. Forget about Bhutan." Marnie swept the entire country aside with a wave of her hand. "Spill," she said to DeeDee. "All the details, please. Now."

"Yes," Millie said. "Colour, career, age, looks, height, weight, net worth, geographical location, intentions, values, sense of humour, whether he wears boxers or briefs, and anything else we need to know before we give our approval."

"Don't you want to know his name?"

"Yes! Plus a damn good reason for you holding out on us and not sharing this monumental piece of girlfriend news before it actually happened."

"If you insist," DeeDee said, taking her sweet time and having a sip of coffee before continuing. "His name is Jordanis, he's 6ft3, 36 years old, black but certainly not unadulterated, a stock broker, wealthy, lives in Boston or the Bahamas or on his yacht, is not married, has no kids, has a wicked sense of humour, honourable intentions—I think—and wears boxers. Oh, and he's… rather handsome."

"Blimey." Marnie sat back, amazed. Had she been so caught up in her issues with Steve that she hadn't even noticed DeeDee falling in love?

"How did we miss this? Has our man radar failed us utterly or have you been very, very good at hiding this? Please tell me it's the latter."

"I've been very, very good at hiding it—from you two and from myself, for a while."

"How long a while?" Millie wanted to know the extent of their oblivion. "How long have you known this guy?"

"About a year," DeeDee said. "But I'd been deflecting his advances, not sure if I liked him or not."

And now," Marnie said, "now you're sure?"

"Not 100%," DeeDee said, smiling, "but I'm certainly *interested*."

"Looks like 100 carats of interest," Millie said. "I don't know how you can wear such a whopper." She took DeeDee's hand to get a closer look. "Wow. This is weight-lifting, not jewellery," she said. DeeDee laughed. "You'll need to wear this on your right hand every other week so you don't get overdeveloped biceps on your left arm."

Marnie suddenly realized why DeeDee hadn't told them sooner. She was shy! DeeDee was comfortable with big, grand, colourful gestures and sweeping statements, but the delicate tenderness of love was foreign territory that she was only just beginning to explore.

She put her hand on DeeDee's, avoiding the door-knocker. "DeeDee, I'm so happy for you. You deserve all the love in the world and Jordanis is a very, very lucky man. When did he pop the question?"

"About a month ago," DeeDee said, smiling happily.

"A month!" Millie turned to Marnie. "We've been cheated out of a whole month of drama, speculation, wonder, covert surveillance, online research and daily updates on this guy," she said, sighing.

"But I only said yes this morning," DeeDee said, laughing, "so you are the first to know."

Despite being friends with DeeDee since high school, Marnie had a hard time reading a black person's more subtle emotions. She could tell when DeeDee was happy, angry or very sad. But how did you know when a black person was blushing or going pale from shock or anxiety?

White people were so much more transparent and overt, she thought, wearing emotions on the open white canvas of their faces, whereas black people were more dignified and enigmatic. Marnie felt an aching reverence for black people's beauty—especially women's, which seemed to emanate a primal power and a spiritual earthiness, as if black people had emerged from the earth itself and were its inherent owners, with white people looking half-baked beside their black counterparts' ebony splendour.

She realized that DeeDee had probably not wanted to gloat about her new man, given how upset Marnie had been about Steve.

"DeeDee, it was sweet of you to not rub this in, given the Steve thing, but let's agree not to ever keep love small for someone else's sake. Please don't dim your love lights. Let them shine on us so we can bask in this with you."

For once, DeeDee seemed at a loss for words. She got up and came around to Marnie's side of the table. "Here," she said, opening her arms, and Marnie obliged. DeeDee hugged her fiercely and Millie joined in. All three stood in a tight nugget that squeezed tears from all six faucets.

Love belonged to everyone, Marnie thought. It didn't matter if one person felt it first and then shared it. It was like a relay race. Everyone would eventually be touched by it and transformed. For her, it might not come in the form of Steve, but she had to believe it would come around again, somehow, sometime.

35

Thursday, 28 May 2020

DeeDee swept into the lobby like a mini-tornado, the leaves of a large rubber plant nodding enthusiastically in her wake. She strode up to the reception desk, where a young woman—*or was she a teenager playing dress-up?*—was engrossed in some crucial manoeuvre on her cellphone.

DeeDee slapped the desk with her hand, making the girl jump in her chair and drop her phone.

"Mr Romero, please," she said.

"Is he expecting you?"

"Possibly, if he's smart."

"May I have your name, please?"

"I don't think my name would suit you," DeeDee said sweetly. "Best to keep using your own, assuming you have one." *Or I could come up with one for you…* But she knew she was being uncharitable. She'd been young and innocent herself, once—until that Japanese businessman had corrupted her so deliciously last year.

The girl looked at her blankly.

DeeDee sighed. It was pointless trying to resuscitate dead brain cells.

"Please tell him the Greek Ambassador, Mz Melina, is here to see him."

The girl took a moment to engage her brain and remember why she was there, then dialed a number on her desk phone. She spoke meekly into the mouthpiece, informing Mr Romero of the ambassador's arrival.

"Mr Romero will be right with you," she said. "Please take a seat." She gestured to some chairs along the far wall, but DeeDee preferred to remain standing. Being 6ft tall sometimes came in handy on the intimidation front.

She knew she wouldn't have to wait long. Three minutes later, the door to the stairwell opened and Steve strode over to greet her.

"DeeDee," he said, smiling. "What a nice surprise… I think."

"Is there somewhere we could talk?"

"There's a meeting room, over here." He led her to a door beside the chairs, opened it and gestured for her to go in. It was a small room, with four armchairs arranged around a coffee table.

"Take a seat, DeeDee, and tell me what's on your mind."

DeeDee sat, crossing one long, slender leg over the other and smoothing the front of her cream silk skirt.

"I know you and Marnie have reconnected and tried to make a go of things again."

"Yes." Steve nodded. "Not that it's any of your business."

"Marnie doesn't know I'm here, and I doubt it will help your cause to tell her, but I thought I'd act as ambassador for you both as I don't like to see her suffer needlessly."

"Nor do I," Steve said. "But I'm not sure I like you interfering, either."

"Well, you may not like her suffering or me interfering, but that's not enough to resolve things." She looked at him pointedly. "I'll just say my piece and then I'll go. It's up to you whether you act on it or not."

"Yes, it is," Steve said, folding his arms and looking at her quizzically.

"Here's the thing, Steve, and it's pretty simple. I know you adore Marnie and I know she loves you—probably more than she herself realizes. But it's never going to work out unless you give up your cellphone."

"Listen, Dee—"

DeeDee held up her hand. "I know all the arguments and I'm not here to discuss them. I just wanted to let you know that this is a deal-breaker. Lots of people manage without a cellphone, and I'm one of them. There are always ways to make things work if you're smart and really want them to."

Steve smiled at her. "I think I know that," he said. "I'm not the cloddish southern oaf you seem to think I am."

"How did you know I thought that?" DeeDee looked at him innocently.

"Look, I know how protective you are of Marnie. I am, too—"

"Then we have different definitions of *protective*. I don't irradiate my friends—or anyone, in fact—knowing the harm it causes."

Steve looked annoyed. "I don't turn it on when she's around."

"Please, don't feed me that feeble line. You know as well as I do that cell towers transmit 24/7. They don't stop transmitting just because you so kindly refrain from using your cellphone for a few hours. We're all being irradiated just so you can make your precious calls, Romeo."

Steve shrugged. "I need it for my work. It's the way the world works, DeeDee."

"Same old, same old. Find yourself another woman or give up your cellphone. It's that simple."

"I never took you for an activist."

"Is that intended as a compliment or an insult, Steve?" She looked at him, incisive eyebrows raised in mock enquiry. "I'm a realist, not an activist. Not that the two are mutually exclusive. In fact," she graced him with a wry smile, "I like to think of myself as an active realist, acting on real data." She cocked her head. "As a data analyst, you must understand that, surely."

She paused, debating whether to expend the additional oxygen required to further plead her case. "Did you know that Dr Dalton, Marnie's mother, used to go into elementary schools and do presentations about the dangers of WiFi? That's how Marnie got it removed in her school. I bet she didn't tell you that."

"No, she didn't." Steve shrugged. "What difference does it make?"

"It's just an example of an intelligent person taking a stand for what they believe in and making a difference," DeeDee said, examining her manicure. "She probably also didn't tell you about the seven kids in her school who got cancer over the past three years, five of them dying less than a year later. The school no longer allows WiFi or cellphones, but the parents use both—all diligent working people like you, *needing* their cellphone for their work."

"Thanks for the lecture, DeeDee. I appreciate you taking the time to do this for Marnie. Really, I do." Steve stood up. "But I must get back to work."

"Find yourself another woman, Romero—one who also *needs* her cellphone, then you can have a cozy little *ménage à quatre*, the two of you and your phones, justifying your mutual disregard for the environment and young lives."

DeeDee got vertical slowly, coming eye to eye with 6ft Steve. She sighed and softened, recognizing his need to be a manly assertive male and not surrender to her harangue.

"Look, obviously, Marnie's far more informed about the radiation than most people, given her parents' expertise and what she sees happening to the kids at school. She knows they're being harmed at home with wireless devices and she sees the effects every day. That's very hard for her—seeing the kids agitated, anxious, mentally confused, finding it hard to focus, getting headaches, exhausted because they can't sleep at night, and being given some kind of drug to control their symptoms. It's like being the concerned mother of 30 kids in distress and not being able to help them."

"I can understand that," Steve said.

"So for her to support the wireless industry, even if only indirectly, through you, would be like cutting off her arm. It's not just that she's against it in principle. She'd have to witness you using the technology every day, while she's doing all she can to protect herself and others. Marnie will not accept this—*cannot* accept this. She cares too much. It's one of the things you love about her."

DeeDee sighed again, feeling the love lost.

"She just can't do it, Steve. It would be a betrayal of all she stands for, to the kids and to her parents who knew better than anyone how this stuff worked. She knows this issue would keep getting in the way of your relationship and would make life hell for you both—again."

DeeDee headed for the door. "If you love Marnie, you'll give up your cellphone and find a way to operate without hurting people *or* your bottom line, which I believe amount to the same thing."

Steve said nothing, so she gave it one last shot. "That's what it comes down to—choosing between life with Marnie and life with your cellphone. I travel the world and I manage without one. And watching my favourite 12-year-old nephew die from a brain tumour certainly helped with my conversion."

She opened the door, shaking her head at him sadly, poor clueless sod that he was, and—

"Eíste mia megáli liparí ageláda."

She froze, turning slowly back towards him. "Did you just call me a *big fat cow?*"

"Well, if Google Translate got it right, I think I did," said Steve, grinning. "It was the best I could come up with, at short notice."

"Your Greek accent could do with a little work," she said, "but did you have a particular reason for insulting me?"

"Not really, except to get your attention and to mention that I'd already decided to give up my cellphone. I'm just working out the logistics, which could take another few days, and I don't know how the hell I'll manage when I travel. But I should be terminally cell-phone-less by the weekend."

"Well, why didn't you say so, *eísai megálos tsíchla.*" She smiled at him sweetly.

Steve laughed.

DeeDee was surprised. "You know what that means?" Maybe he wasn't such a red-neck southern oaf after all.

"Haven't a clue," he said, "but I'm pretty sure it was extremely colourful and profane, probably pertaining to certain parts of my lower anatomy, knowing you, DeeDee."

"Well, southern boy, there's hope for you yet." She smiled. "My ambassadorial duty is done, although it looks as if it wasn't needed after all." She leaned towards him and kissed him on the cheek. "I'll leave you to share the good news with Marnie."

She hesitated. "One more thing, if I may."

"As if I could stop you." Steve sighed, folding his arms.

"Make sure you're fully committed to doing this before you tell Marnie. A promise like this can get undone over time, as complacency sets in, and you know how much pressure there is in the business world to use cellphones." She looked at him appraisingly. "But if you stick with it, I think you'll be glad you did. There are some big changes coming."

"Do you know something I don't, DeeDee?"

DeeDee laughed her full-bodied throaty laugh. "If I were to stay here and answer that question, we'd both end up in hospital suffering from malnutrition and sleep deprivation."

Steve laughed. "Get outta here, woman. I have work to do."

"I'm gone," she said, smiling. "In fact," she tapped her nose, "*I was never here.*"

36

Somehow, having her Fridays off no longer held the same appeal as before, and Marnie found herself trudging around the apartment, unable to work up the enthusiasm for anything beyond the bare essentials. She knew why, of course. Steve, Steve, friggin' Steve. Or the absence of.

Well, she'd just have to get over it and move on. She'd find some other source of pleasure or distraction. No way was she going to let this—

The buzzer sounded.

Damn. She hadn't even brushed her hair and she was still wearing her comfies. She did not want to see or talk to anyone—not even DeeDee or Millie.

Maybe it was a delivery. She'd ordered a book about cosmology and was looking forward to reading it. It would certainly help distract her today, so this could be very good timing.

She pressed the intercom button. "Yes?"

"Marnie, it's Steve. May I come up for a minute?"

What the hell was Steve doing here? She did *not* want to see him. No point, just more pain. Damn. She hesitated, feeling conflicted, angry, frustrated...

"Okay," she finally said, buzzing him in, then standing immobile, frozen with indecision. Should she make herself more presentable? Or stay as she was and make it clear she no longer cared?

Too late now. Steve was already at the door.

She opened up and he stepped in.

"Hey, Marnie."

"Steve."

"Not quite the welcome I got last time."

"Well, considering how we left things…"

"But things have changed since then."

"The wireless industry has collapsed?"

"Not quite, but it does have slightly fewer customers."

Marnie stood, arms folded, unwilling to be drawn in.

"What does that mean?"

"It means they no longer have me as a customer. As of yesterday, I no longer own or use a cellphone." He grinned at her. "You don't look very pleased. Was I supposed to take down the industry single-handedly?"

"Steve, it won't work. If you give up your cellphone for me, you'll just end up resenting me. There will be times when you'll feel the need for it and will blame me for you not having it. If we went on a hike or something and you broke a leg, you'd immediately think of your phone and the need to call someone—and then curse the fact that you didn't have it. And I would always be anxious about that kind of thing happening, knowing how you'd probably react."

She kicked the edge of the mat in front of the door. She was wearing her really tacky furry slippers, *but she didn't care!*

"So there's no point in doing this for me."

"What the hell else would I do it for, if not for you, Marnie?"

"The planet, the environment, children, humans in general. That's the only way this will work—if you do it for yourself because you genuinely want to protect your health and the health of the planet."

Steve stood still, breathing heavily, saying nothing for a whole hour. It might have been a bit less, Marnie was willing to concede—possibly more like ten seconds, but still an eternity.

"I'll have to go away and think about this," Steve said, eventually, opening the door, stepping out and closing it quietly behind him.

Marnie stood still, listening to his heavy tread on the stairs. Then… silence.

Well, that was that…

Then she heard lighter steps, followed by a modest tap on her door.

What now? She really didn't want to talk to her neighbours. She was *not* in the mood. She wrenched open the door.

"Steve…"

"I thought about it and you're right. This will only work if I do it for me and not for the most cussedly stubborn, gorgeous, principled, compassionate, sexy, selfless woman I have ever met. Definitely not."

Marnie almost smiled. But this felt like a trap. "I don't trust this, Steve. It sounds good now, but I can't trust that it will last."

"You don't believe me, you mean?" Steve looked hurt and maybe a little pissed off.

"I believe you now, in this moment, but I don't trust that it will last. I know what it's like out there, with a cellphone required for all kinds of transactions, online verification codes, security measures."

"Well, how do *you* manage?"

"I've found other ways. I changed banks when my old one refused to let me do online banking without a cellphone. It's blatant discrimination, but I decided they didn't deserve my business. I can only imagine how devastated they were at not having my annual teacher's earnings going through their books." She almost smiled.

Steve was more daring and went for the full smile. "Well, if Marnie Dalton can do it, Steve Romero sure as hell can." He paused, looking at her critically.

"It's not a competition," Marnie said frostily.

"I didn't mean it like that. I admire you for living your values, Marnie. Very few people do that. And it's not even that I disagree with what you say. It's just that we're all in the habit of saying certain things that no longer match what we claim to believe. We've lost touch with our values, which should matter more in our hearts, to keep us happy with ourselves, than in some corporate boardroom impressing investors with mere words. For that reason, I can see why some people might see your high standards as lofty ideals that few can attain."

"They're not lofty standards. They're basic survival skills. It's Humanity 101."

"I know. I get it." Steve paused. "Anyway, how come I'd be the one to break a leg if we went hiking?"

"You wouldn't, necessarily, but if I broke one, you'd carry me back. I'm not sure I'd be able to return the favour if it were the other way around."

"Ah. Right. Good point." He looked at her. "Could we sit down for a minute?"

"I suppose…" Marnie eyed the couch warily. It had begun to take on a life of its own, with a chequered history of anguish and ecstasy that she didn't want to re-live by sitting on it.

"Let's sit at the table," Steve suggested.

Marnie pushed aside her journal, which had languished unloved since the Steve Seduction episode, and she couldn't see the point of continuing. It wasn't exactly bringing blasts of illuminating insight into the *film noir* of her life.

"I know it's hard for you to trust me, Marnie, particularly on this issue, but I get the feeling it's hard for you to trust me anyway." Steve paused, looking at her gently. "If we didn't have this radiation issue, would you trust me then? Or would other fears hold you back?"

Marnie glared at him. How dare he go rummaging in her sheltered spaces and ferret out her secrets.

"I have to trust you, too, you know," Steve said.

"What?" That took her by surprise. "Why would you have to trust me?"

"Because you might go running off again, leaving me high and dry, and then I'd have no phone to use for phone sex with some random social-media addict, and I wouldn't even be able to call for help if I suffered a total meltdown and was unable to get out of bed to call the neighbours." He grimaced. "Can you see the painful injustice of that?"

He paused, hoping for a thaw of the Marnie ice floe. "So we'd both be taking a huge risk, when we could be mercilessly crushed at any moment, and not just when you're being a tiger in bed."

"Could we please leave the tiger out of it?"

"But it's the best bit." Steve sighed. "Okay. For now, then." His look was full of mourning... and then mischief. "But what about tomorrow?"

Marnie smiled, suddenly feeling an aching sadness and fatigue.

Steve turned to her, sensing her mood. "How come you never mentioned the kids at school?"

God, it was uncanny how he read her. "I get too upset," Marnie said. "They're so *young*, Steve. They look up at me with their eager, innocent faces and all they want is to be loved and praised."

"But they are, aren't they? Isn't that what you do for them, Marnie?"

"Yes, but most of them aren't getting the attention they need at home. And they're all anxious and jumpy, tapping their feet and unable to sit still. Some of them have rings under their eyes from not getting enough sleep. *And they're only 8 or 9 years old*, Steve. It's not normal for kids that age."

"But maybe it is," Steve said gently. "You got the WiFi turned off in the school and there are no cellphones, so..."

"It's still coming at them from outside, and the minute they're out the door, they're hit with cellphones and then WiFi and iPads and wireless speakers and all kinds of other crap at home."

She turned to face him. "I'm not sure I can continue teaching for much longer. It's getting too hard to see this every day, and half the kids are on medication for ADHD or some other label to keep them quiet. Then I can't reach them. They look at me with their sad, heavy eyes and I feel they're pleading with me to rescue them. It's tragic." She swiped at her angry tears. "My mum told me that when she was growing up, there was no such thing as ADD or ADHD. Kids were naturally boisterous and energetic, but they burned it off in the playground and they slept like babies every night."

"But maybe there was less awareness about those conditions back then," Steve said.

"No," Marnie said, hotly. "Those conditions didn't exist, not like this. Why is everyone so intent on defending disease?" She shook her head. "It's okay. I know the answer." She looked at him sorrowfully. "They've won, Steve. They've already won."

"They…? Who, Marnie?"

"Governments, the wireless industry, everyone with wireless gadgets. I can't compete." She took his hand. "I love you for giving up your cellphone so we can be together. I can't tell you how much that means to me. But in the big picture…?" Her shoulders slumped.

"That sounds a bit defeatist—not like you at all, Marnie."

"I know. Sometimes it just… gets to me. Sorry."

She took a deep breath, shaking herself out of it. "You know what?"

Steve looked at her expectantly, ready for whatever the *what* was, and Marnie marvelled at how the whole world seemed to be paying attention when Steve was.

"I'm sick of the whole radiation issue. Could we *unhave* this conversation?"

"Maybe. Let me check…" Steve closed his eyes and seemed to be reflecting. "Yep. It's okay. It hasn't made it to the archives yet so we can unhave it." He held up a finger, closing his eyes again. "Just deleting it from the OUT tray… hang on." He smiled. "Okay. Gone."

Marnie smiled fully for the first time since… forever, surely. "What about going for a hike this weekend?"

"Excellent idea. I'll do my best not to break a leg," Steve said, grinning. "But, if I do, I'll just hobble heroically home with my woman, with no need of outside assistance, although I'll bring my walking stick, survival rations, sleeping bag, rope, maps and compass, just in case."

"And maybe some tiger balm," Marnie said, allowing a smile with a little more conviction.

Steve tapped his temples. "On the list," he said. "Just one more thing…" He leaned towards her to whisper in his husky, conspiratorial voice, "*Very. Sexy. Slippers.*"

37

June 2025

She had landed in some eerie place. There was a strange smell of singed hair and her clothes and hair were full of static electricity. The air seemed charged, as if she had to push solid molecules out of the way in order to move even a few inches.

She instinctively felt for her Franometer, strapped to her left arm. She pushed the green button and the screen lit up, showing the coordinates, relevant frequencies, time, date, location, cosmic numbers, and how much time she had left before she went back. They had finally figured out how to pre-program the return or re-program it to an earlier time, if necessary.

Then she hit the red button to record the ambient electromagnetic frequencies and other screen data for Daniel to work on when she got back.

Only then did she allow herself to take in her surroundings.

She was on a park bench in Boston Common, facing the Parkman Bandstand, but she barely recognized the place. It wasn't that the city itself had changed; the buildings bordering the park were still standing, the roads were intact. It was the vibe, the charged atmosphere and the people around her. And something was missing. She looked around and it hit her. There was no nature or greenery as far as the eye could see. It was as if she had been transported from a technicolour movie into an old black-and-white one—the very opposite of the shiny, futuristic reality anticipated by those who loved wireless technologies.

What about oxygen? With no trees or plant life, there had to be some other system in place to keep people breathing. She'd have to find out.

Above, the sky was roiling, dark clouds churning unbroken across the horizon. Crackles of lightning sparked in the distance—a steady discharge of electromagnetic energy. The air was warm, as you'd expect for Boston in mid-June, but it wasn't the kind of *warm* you got on a sunny day, tempting you to cast off a layer of clothing. It was a charged heat, like static energy from synthetic fabrics rubbing together or charged particles colliding.

Frannie stood up and walked slowly along the path, feeling the air push against her skin, her brain sizzling with electricity, her nerves buzzing. Her mouth was parched, the dry air sucking the moisture from her body.

Bordering the path, she could see the tiny skeletons of birds, strewn on the cracked earth like stick figures in some crude cartoon, legs pointing skyward in silent supplication. Some larger four-legged skeletons lay partially hidden under the carcasses of denuded bushes, bones and branches looking brittle enough to dissolve in a puff of wind.

No birds twittering in the trees. No *trees*. No piercing trills. No lilting song knitting the air with promise. Frannie had never realized just how reassuring birdsong was, how vitally life-affirming. Without it, the world felt truly sterile, with nothing left to sing about. And no one left to sing it.

People were walking robotically through the park, plodding along in a stupor, staring vacantly ahead and looking right through her as she passed. They seemed to be babbling to themselves, their lips moving but no words coming out. *They'd walk right over my body if I fell or lost consciousness*, Frannie thought, *not even seeing me*. They seemed devitalized and heartless, as if their soul had been unplugged. These trudging zombies were not about to break into song anytime soon—or ever again. They were more likely to break apart, crumbling to dust on the sidewalk.

The few children she could see were likewise robotic—and almost all bald! *Did they have cancer or was this the new normal?* Their faces were pale and blotchy, and they looked drugged, trudging beside their parents, expressionless, with none of the boisterous exuberance of normal young children. There was no joy, no sense of life happening, no sense of engagement. It was nothing like the lively park she remembered.

Frannie's heart was aching. She might not have gone out into nature much, due to her work, but she had a deep reverence for the intricate latticework of life. Where others saw rivers, lakes and oceans as the backdrop for leisure activities, or as commodities to be exploited, she saw the Fibonacci spiral, the phi ratio, sacred geometry, photons, the seamless web of quantum particles, the stellar stuff that made the cosmos and everything in it. For people to get sucked into an inanimate technology when there was such phenomenal majesty and mystery all around them boggled her mind and depressed her profoundly.

Why was cosmology not taught in schools? If it were, people would be walking around perpetually gobsmacked at the beauty and wonder of life, gazing at the galaxies, exploring the matrix of a cell, inventing amazing things, investigating their own photon-filled bodies, healing their own bodies, leveraging the unlimited power of their minds to create their ideal reality, marvelling at the multiverse, communicating telepathically, communing with the cosmos itself, working with their own frequencies to create astonishing effects, and generating the kind of sublime experiences that could never ever be produced by wireless gadgets.

They would not be at war, squabbling over resources, mired in emotional dysfunction, desperate for approval or acceptance, convinced they were innately sinful or unworthy, mentally and physically ill, sick with angst and self-loathing, depressed, suicidal, hopeless, in debt, in pain and completely oblivious to their astronomical greatness.

Not in a world where you could be and do anything—and didn't need money to do it, although the money automatically came with the mastery of mind and spirit. Manifesting money was easy when you knew how to operate your body, mind and spirit. She and Daniel had done it often enough.

Enlightenment elevated people, up to a place where they could truly see themselves. Electronic entrainment took them down—in ways that ensured they would never get up again. Forever lost to themselves. It was tragic that so many were already lost and disconnected from themselves, even before this, Frannie thought. They had to have been, for this kind of takeover to be possible.

Frannie could never understand why people marvelled at the Seven Wonders of the World, when humans were the first and greatest wonder of all, without whom none of the others would be possible. Yet people travelled great distances to take photos of those manmade wonders, oblivious to the endless wonders inside, where every cell had its own organizing intelligence and complex communication system.

She brought herself back to the moment, realizing that something else was missing in this scary new place, and it took her a moment to place it. No one was using a cellphone. Already, in 2019 and long before she left the planet, people were practically glued to their gadgets, talking or texting obsessively, as if their lives depended on it. Here, they all seemed collectively entrained by some invisible force, as if something in the air was now orchestrating things. They seemed to be communicating internally, hooked up to some system that no longer required an external handheld device.

She knew what was going on. Thank God she had known what to do before coming here, scrambling her signal via the Franometer, otherwise she'd end up like all the other zombies here and would not be able to go back. The system she and Daniel had created had been hijacked, and this was the insidious result. They had developed a way of interfacing the human biofield with global internet networks, to be used for a higher purpose—the very opposite of what it was being used for here.

One of the things they had figured out was that everyone had their own unique electromagnetic signature—what Frannie called an *EM-SIG*—and they had found a way to map and record them into their interfacing system. This was what governments were now using to track and control the population—far beyond what 5G was intended to do, tracking people via their wireless devices. Everyone alive in 2021 had been registered by the system and all their movements, purchases, bodily needs, work performance and activities were now monitored and adjusted as needed.

This was why she and Daniel had had to check out, in 2019—to remove their electromagnetic signatures from the biosphere. They also had to eliminate all physical and logistical traces of their existence— their assets, bank accounts, belongings—everything that could be used to confirm their physical existence or tie them emotionally (electromagnetically) to their children.

If they hadn't done that, they would have been registered in the system, and she would have been snagged as soon as she landed here, in 2025. She would be trapped. Right now, she was invisible to the system because she had been able to program the Franometer to block her frequency so she was undetectable. But the system would eventually detect her rogue EM-SIG and program it into the network, placing her under its control. She had to move fast if she wanted to get out of here before that happened.

Beyond the Common, she could see cars driving slowly along the streets, but the traffic was eerily quiet. No one was blowing their horn, making a noise, getting angry. There was no spectrum of emotion, just a dull, dampened-down monotonic hum of existence.

Then she realized why. Of course! Cars were now mostly driverless, so there was no need for humans to get all worked up about someone cutting them off or not going fast enough. No more road rage. *Such huge progress for humankind*, she thought, sardonically, remembering how eager people were in 2019 to usher in the fabulous new *smart* world. *Did people realize how doomed they were?* Of course not. They were too far gone to realize anything—or do anything about it.

She needed to go to a café to get some water. And she wanted to check out how things worked in this creepily controlled reality. Did people even *drink* coffee any more? Did they have any say in their choices or lives? Could real food still be grown in this barren environment? She had so many questions.

She walked to the edge of the park and observed the traffic. No one seemed to be sitting behind the wheel of any vehicle—or, if they were, they had their heads down and were clearly not driving. Everything moved as if in a seamlessly choreographed ballet, but there was nothing beautiful about it. She would have to time it carefully if she was going to get across unharmed. Since her EM-SIG was not in the system, she would not be detected by the moving cars and they would run her over if she got in the way.

An alternative system to traffic lights seemed to be in use, and it took her a few minutes to work it out. At junctions, a certain number of cars moved north and south, then they stopped and the same number of cars moved east and west. Sensors in the vehicles were obviously detecting when it was whose turn to move.

But Frannie was about 100m from a junction, so she braced herself to catch the brief lull between one stream of traffic stopping and the other starting, then darted across the street.

There was a café right opposite the exit to the Common. She paused outside, wondering if she was exposing herself to detection or if she still had time to check things out a bit more. While she was reflecting, the sliding doors opened. *Had the system detected her energy field or had the door just opened in response to her weight on the pavement?*

She could see some people inside, at the counter, and she was so thirsty she decided to risk it. She had an EMERGENCY EXIT function on her Franometer and she kept her finger poised over it, in case she needed to leave urgently.

Walking up to the counter, she could see that everything was automated. There was no one behind the counter, just customers in front of it. They were lining up with their mugs, waiting their turn at some machine that seemed to instantly recognize their EM-SIG and know what they wanted. Or maybe the system decided what to give them, based on whether it wanted them to be more alert, more performant or something else. She couldn't tell.

No money was required for the machine to operate, so the system must have been instantly debiting individuals' bank accounts, or whatever auto-payment system was being used.

She shuddered. Since she wasn't in the system, it wouldn't recognize her existence and she would not be able to get a drink. She turned and walked out of the café. Her brain felt fried and foggy and she was aware of a profound heaviness in her limbs. She had to leave quickly or she would get stuck here.

How could so much have changed in such a short time? And what was the next step in this soul-numbing progression? Were there others untouched by this phenomenon? Was it just the working class or everyone? Those in control of the system were presumably protecting themselves from being tracked, monitored and controlled.

Her stomach churning, Frannie felt a chill down her spine. Were Marnie, Matt and Lucy like this? Had *they* turned into zombies, devoid of human compassion, love and laughter? She didn't want to know. If they had already been taken over—and she couldn't see how they would not have been—she couldn't bear to witness it. It would be too awful to see her babies like that.

Ray had warned governments about this, although he was far from the only scientist who understood the issues. But, because of their work together, he knew better than most what manmade electromagnetic radiation was doing to people and how it would ultimately take over, running people like machines.

She would need to do a separate trip to 2026 to see what happened next... Or would she? She already knew what to do. Nothing good could come of this and there was no way this wasted world could transform into some kind of happy, healthy utopian wireless lifestyle in a few years' time. Or ever, given how far things had gone.

She had to get back. She had to find a way to fix this. She could feel her body weakening, as if the network were trying to hook her in, preparing to simultaneously disconnect her from herself and take over her mind and body.

She re-programmed the Franometer for an immediate return, keying in the frequencies and adjusting the time remaining. Taking one last look around her, she hit *Go*.

38

Sunday, 31 May 2020

Marnie was reading an extra-ordinary book, curled up on the sofa for some time out. After a five-hour hike yesterday, her body ached and the flop-n-read felt all the more delicious. Steve had gone home yesterday evening as she needed some space. Her head was still spinning from the turnarounds of the past few weeks and she needed time to steady herself.

The cosmology book she'd ordered hadn't arrived yet, but she had picked up a novel at the bookshop—a book DeeDee had recommended …and she could see why. The writing was devastatingly good, stirring an emptiness in the soul, reminding it that there was a much bigger untold story.

Set in the Congo, it was no complacent escapist's read. Reading it, Marnie felt achingly present, a guilty, silent witness to the defiant walking corpses of a nation despoiled. She could not put it down and pick up *Cosmopolitan* for distraction, abandoning these people to their white-man's torture. Had it been less richly endowed, the country would have been left in peace to own itself and prosper. *Like every human being*, Marnie realized, *left to their own devices, without any negative conditioning.*

The depth of the writing left her feeling challenged and chagrined, her whole world axis shifting towards a new perception of selfish self.

Had the writer been exhausted at the end of each exquisitely rendered page, Marnie wondered, *or did it all flow seamlessly from an uncensored core?*

There was something almost sensual about powerful writing. A well-crafted sentence, cleverly articulated with graceful grammar, was enough to make Marnie swoon. She didn't get much of that from the kids at school, so her quality-reading time was precious. When people spoke eloquently, their literary prowess powered by their hearts, it was a potent aphrodisiac. When they used fragmented sentences, on the other hand, churning out grammatical garbage and mangled punctuation, it was a complete turn-off. She sometimes despaired over the loss of linguistic loveliness—surely the most potent wordy weapon for winning hearts and waiving wars.

Marnie had given up on Lester the Snake, although she felt bad abandoning her pet project. She imagined Lester glaring at her from under the dresser, a tight coil of haughty rejection.

Now, instead of using her journal to regurgitate the details of her daily life, she'd decided to write what she would *like* her day to be like, which seemed like a much healthier endeavour. Instead of documenting each day after it had unfolded, she wrote about it beforehand, deciding how she wanted it to go.

If her day wasn't stellar, she didn't want to re-live it in the writing. If it *was* stellar, she would invest that happy fuel in the day to come—a pay-it-forward to herself.

She had the eerie feeling that the act of writing in this way was cuing her subconscious to upgrade her life. Not such a quantum leap, since affirming the positive while pre-living and pre-loving it compelled the universe to deliver a matching reality—or so her dad had always told her.

She had mentioned it to Steve.

"Why do I feel as if writing about my ideal future actually changes things, out there, wherever things materialize?"

"Because you sense, deep down, that that's how things work, on some level," Steve said. "Everything begins with a thought or an idea. If we feed it, it becomes something more. Right?"

"That's kind of what my parents used to say."

"No wiser folks."

Marnie smiled at him. "How do you know that, never having met them?"

"I know what they produced. They dreamed *you* up, didn't they? They left you with all the right questions to be asking… and answering."

"I have no idea where to find the answers—so many answers, Steve…"

"Marnie, darlin', you have all the answers you need. And you've given me all the answer I could wish for. Anyway, the questions never end and never should."

She certainly hadn't found the answer to the next chapter of her life—yet. She felt an inner gnawing for something new. Something different. She loved teaching and she couldn't imagine her days without the kids, but something inside her was beckoning, and she was having a hard time seeing the kids suffer so much.

She felt a yearning for something deeper, more gratifying. Was it for a baby of her own? With Steve? Was that it? She didn't feel ready to have children, although she could imagine it happening with Steve …if she allowed herself to think that far ahead. Maybe it was for some kind of deeper understanding of who she was, an exploration that would give her access to more of herself.

Since her parents had died eight months ago, she'd gone through an emotional wringer. Unfamiliar feelings had been wrung out of her and mirrored by others as they dumped their anguish—and their love—on her couch. But who *was* she, really? What kind of person did she *want* to be? Was she a teacher by nature …or nurture—the inevitable result of mothering her siblings and being the go-to, can-do, fix-it person?

She'd talked to Steve about this on their hike. "If I continue teaching much longer, I'm afraid I'll shut down emotionally to avoid feeling so concerned about the kids, and I don't want that."

"I hear you," Steve said, as he always did—what she said and what she didn't.

Marnie often felt as if he knew what she wanted before she herself had figured it out, if she ever did. Maybe she should ask him for some insights… There was definitely a yearning to grow beyond her current state, to learn or to know… something. Did her birth or life numbers hold any clues?

She remembered what Steve had said about her possibly doing something that helped humanity. She couldn't imagine what that could be, and she wasn't feeling terribly humanitarian, at the moment.

She had a sudden urge to look at the clock her mother had left her. She got up and hobbled down the corridor to her bedroom, her hamstrings objecting painfully and threatening to go on strike if she didn't get horizontal again fast.

She took the clock from the top drawer of her dresser and hobbled back to the couch. Turning the clock over in her hands, she tried to absorb its hidden messages, the things it had seen in her mother's hands, the places it had been, the things it had heard. What did it mean? Did it mean anything? Why had it stopped at 3pm on the day they died? Why had her mother left her *this*, rather than anything else? Was it just because it had sentimental value for Marnie? Well, lots of other things would have had that, too, including two live parents. Why did they take *themselves* away?

She had returned to the eternal unanswerable question, promising nothing but a frazzled brain and dizzying circular speculation.

She closed her eyes and leaned back on the couch cushions, the clock nestled close to her heart. If she let her mind drift, might her subconscious tell her something—sneak up on her sideways with some unguarded revelation plucked from the universal mind?

She was transported back to the beach of her dream, with her mother walking beside her, carrying her clock/compass and squinting at the sky. The sun was blinding, bleaching the world around them and making her mother look like an angel in her white shirt. Again, Marnie spoke to her.

Mum, why did you leave?

This time, her mother turned to look at her, as if only just realizing she was there. She reached out, the clock in her hand, urging Marnie to take it. In her dream, Marnie took the clock and examined it, just as she had a few moments before. When she looked up again to ask what it meant, her mother was gone.

Marnie sat up, miffed. That was about as helpful as being shoved down a crevasse when you'd asked for a hand up out of your chair.

She examined the clock again. Still just a clock. But the dream had given her an idea.

39

3 June 2020

Ray was watering the banana plant in his living room when she arrived.

"Ray, it's me," she said, gently. "Don't have a heart attack."

But he looked as if he might, his face frozen in shock and astonishment as he stared at her and the watering can clattered to the floor.

"Come and sit down," Frannie said, guiding him to the sofa.

He fell into the seat, like a man taken hostage at gunpoint.

"Holy fuck," he said, shaking his head in wonder. "You figured out a way."

She sat on the coffee table opposite him, placing her hands on his knees.

"Take a few deep breaths," she said. She needed him to get grounded so he could think clearly and take in what she needed to say.

"But you're... you're dead," he said, suddenly. "You died in September..." She had to be an apparition, the product of his sleep-deprived brain.

"Well, yes," she said, "and no,"

"Holy fuck," he said again.

"I'm dead now, in this particular reality, but I'm visiting you from my past, where I'm very much alive," she said.

"I can't believe it," he said. "But how... So precisely, here in my living room..." He was still in a daze of wonder.

"We've become very good at working out the coordinates, the frequencies and the other bits," she said.

"I want to know about all the bits," Ray said.

"I may not have much time," she said.

"I thought you could take as much time as you wanted," Ray said, grinning, "given what you can do."

"Let's just say I found a window of time that would work," Frannie said, smiling. "We've got about 90 minutes till your wife gets back from her yoga class. So don't be alarmed if we lose track of time and I disappear before your eyes."

"Ah. I see." Ray nodded, smiling, then pointed a shaky finger at her. "Don't you ever scare me like that again, Frannie," he said.

"Sorry," she said. "I'll try to make a slightly less dramatic entrance next time. Maybe ring your doorbell or something boring like that." But she could never do that, in case someone else saw her.

Ray smiled. That wasn't what he had meant and she knew it. He meant, *Don't come back from the dead without warning me in advance.*

Even for an open-minded scientist like Ray, having a dead woman show up in your living room was a little disconcerting.

He was shaking his head, still trying to take it in. "I wasn't sure what to think, what to do, with you both... gone. But I went ahead with what we'd planned anyway."

She leaned towards him to get him to focus.

"We need your help again, Ray," she said. "There's a problem with the original plan."

"Did I do something wrong?"

"No. You played things perfectly and threw everyone off track. No one even suspected what you were up to."

Ray snorted. "Fat chance of that, Frannie. You know how governments work. They only think in terms of defending themselves from attack—or attacking other nations. This is the last thing they'd ever think of."

"What did you use for your 'deadly airborne toxin'?"

"Ah, now, that was fun," Ray said, chortling. "It was a mixture of black shoe polish, dish detergent, nail polish and manure," he said. "A real stinker."

Frannie laughed. "Didn't the MIT guys figure out what it was?"

"Probably, but the mixture had hardened before it even got to CDC, so they couldn't be sure that some essential volatile compound hadn't been lost when it was exposed to the air." He laughed. "And they were so sure it was toxic that they kept looking for some deadly new viral strain hidden in the everyday stuff."

"Well, it was brilliant."

"Frannie, is there no way you could figure out a way to stick around. Couldn't you find a way to get around dying and come back?"

"We've tried for over five years to make that work," Frannie said, shaking her head sadly. "I don't want to leave, but we had to do this for our children, for everyone..." She took a deep breath and forced herself to focus on what she needed to do.

"I understand, but I miss you," Ray said, patting her on the arm and letting out a big sigh. "It's a masterful plan, Frannie. It boggles the mind what you and Daniel have done, and I'm honoured to be a part of it."

He covered her hands with his own and looked at her with his wise, warm eyes. "Let me get you some water," he said, getting up.

"Yes, please."

Ray went into the kitchen, got two glasses of water and brought them back to the coffee table.

"Thanks." Frannie drank all of hers in one go. "Time travel is very thirsty work." She smiled gratefully at Ray.

"Now, tell me what you want me to do."

"You averted a very real disaster by taking the fall the way you did, Ray. And we were able to... *take care* of the guy who somehow hacked into our system. But we didn't realize he had already sold our program to a government agency, and they were already starting to implement it. So our original plan would not have worked, once the program was already running, even though the government was using it for something else altogether."

She sighed. "The problem is that I can't change something that has already happened, and the system got hijacked in early 2019, before we realized what had happened. I can only go ahead in time and adjust something *before* it happens. And I wasn't able to travel ahead as often as I needed to, so I missed that crucial development, plus a few others."

She looked at Ray, checking that he was paying attention. "That's why we had the back-up plan, with the tip-off phone call being your cue to abort the EM-SIG roll-out and bring out the 'volatile toxic substance'. We had to divert attention away from what was happening by getting people all worked up about the wireless internet being used to create disease. Not that it isn't already, of course." She laughed sardonically. "Just as you were about to roll out the system, we discovered that our EM-SIG program was already being implemented to do the very opposite of what we had planned to do with it ...and I saw the consequences of that in 2025. It's not pretty, as you can imagine."

Ray nodded. "Turbulent weather, electrical storms, parched earth, no flora or small fauna, everyone wirelessly controlled, walking around like morons, children getting all kinds of cancers, no more laughter or compassion, people dropping dead on the street, hospitals no longer operational, food and vitamins produced artificially... that kind of thing?"

"That's exactly how it was," Frannie said, remembering the horror of seeing people so dehumanized. "I didn't see all of that, but I saw enough to know that the rest would be inevitable."

"Millennia of human evolution down the drain, just like that," Ray said, shaking his head. He got up suddenly and walked over to the window.

"Ray…?"

"I'm so fucking angry!" he said, his back to her. "It's bad enough that people are being killed and humanity is going to hell, but I can't see the *point* of what they're doing."

"I know—"

"What do governments hope to get from destroying life? How does that create a *win* for them? It just makes no sense." He shook his head, staring out the window at nothing.

"I don't think they're thinking beyond the money or the power they get through the wireless industry," Frannie said.

"They're not thinking at all," Ray said. "Maybe they've all been so affected by the radiation that their brains are literally unable to think logically about the consequences of what they're doing." He looked back at Frannie. "That's the only explanation I can think of."

He looked back at the window. "Sometimes, I get so angry I could *kill* someone…" He took a deep breath. "Given the way things are going, I'll do just about anything to stop what's happening, Frannie. Sign me up for whatever I can do to stop this insanity. As far as I'm concerned, this is war. Governments are using terrorism, manslaughter and a total disregard for the rule of law to serve their own interests."

He turned back to Frannie. "They're supposed to *support* the existence of civilized society, yet here they are demolishing it! Whatever happened to social justice, democracy and actually *serving* the people who elected them?"

Catching himself, he checked the clock on the wall and saw that they had less than an hour left. He took another deep breath and returned to the couch. "Sorry, Frannie. Sometimes it's just all too much." He looked at her. "I don't know how you and Daniel stay sane, doing what you've been doing for so many years—and seeing what's coming, unless you intervene. I'd have lost my mind long ago."

"It hasn't been easy," Frannie said. "But at least we were working towards a solution. Most people being harmed feel powerless, unable to protect themselves or get governments to listen. That must be much worse."

Ray nodded and reached for his glass of water. "Where were we…? Okay, let me see if I've got this straight." He took a long drink and then another deep breath to clear his head. "Because your EM-SIG program had been hijacked and was already being used by government, it would have overridden what we had planned to do with it, and you didn't know in time that it was being rolled out, so you weren't able to stop it?"

"Yes, exactly," Frannie said. "The program was hijacked while I was still alive, but by the time I'd figured out what had happened, it was already in the past, which I cannot change."

Ray nodded again, still processing the impossible.

"Anyway, we can only change so much, and every change generates unimaginable consequences that could take a lifetime to unfold, so this seemed to be the least disruptive way to go. And we had to move fast as it takes an eternity to reconfigure all the data, numbers, frequencies and timelines."

"Got it."

"We had to come up with a way of supplanting the government program with a revised program that would override it. It's highly complex because we have to ensure that no one else will be able to use the system for anything else, or override our new program, once we've got things rolling."

"Yes, okay. Makes sense," Ray said, mental cogs still churning.

"We've had to adjust things and insert all kinds of sensing mechanisms and other processes to take down the current government application, but I think it will work if we can implement it within the next few months."

She paused, considering. "We originally thought of generating a massive global crash that would bring the whole world to a standstill," she said, "and you know what that would be like, with all communications systems down."

"Total chaos," Ray said. "I used to think that crises brought out the best in us humans, but I have a horrible feeling things would go the other way, in this case, with so many people numbed out and dependent on their gadgets."

"I tend to agree," Frannie said, "although it would still be nothing like what will happen if we don't intervene, and we'd only have a few years before things went to pieces anyway."

"People won't even know they've been taken over, Frannie. Once they've lost their connection to self, they'll be nothing more than a commodity."

"I know. I've seen that," Frannie said, steeling herself against the images. "And I can't bear to think about that happening to my children. How could any parent bear such a thing?"

"It's hard to think of it happening to anyone," he said, "let alone your own children."

Frannie nodded and took a deep breath. "We're taking a different approach now, and I think you'll like it," she said. "Rather than providing a massive wake-up call, we've come up with something a bit more life-affirming and productive."

"Playing devil's advocate for a minute," Ray said, "here's an ethical question for you. How is this different from what governments have been doing—invading people's privacy and stealing their personal data? Some might argue that you have no right to take their electromagnetic signature and use it for anything."

"We grappled with this one ourselves," Frannie said. "But I think it's quite different. For one thing, all of our signatures are already out there, in the unified field. So we're not using some devious invasive mechanism to access them without people's permission—or harming them, in the process, as governments are currently doing. There *is* an ethical question around how we use the EM-SIGs, though. We can justify it and say we're using them for positive, life-affirming purposes—to save the species, in fact—but that's still a judgement call that we are making. Do we have that right?" Frannie shrugged. "What do you think?"

"I think I'd prefer your approach to the alternative," Ray said, "although I'd be unaware of either one being used. I'd be clueless about being taken over and equally clueless about getting myself back, until I *was* back, and then I'd realize what I'd been missing—hopefully— and be grateful for it. Although maybe not, if I'd never known the alternative."

"The thing is, we'll be giving people choices," Frannie said. "With the revised EM-SIG2 program, which will override what governments are doing with our original, we'll be reconnecting people with themselves, giving them back the autonomy they should always have had."

She sighed. "To be honest, Ray, I still feel morally conflicted, given the losses to come… but ethically resolved," she said. "Governments were using our system purely for control, to the detriment of the human spirit and all life on the planet. The EM-SIG2 will enhance emotional and spiritual connections and elevate human potential."

"Well, you don't need to convince me," Ray said. "In terms of what governments are doing, I don't think THE END justifies the meanness."

"To put it mildly." Frannie laughed. "The thing is, we can't make conscious choices unless we are conscious," she said. "Essentially, EM-SIG2 will enable people to regain consciousness so they can decide who and what they want to be." She smiled. "Changing human thinking and feeling is the only way to stop the destruction. And with all the global crises, with disease, toxicity, climate change and social fragmentation, we need to do this anyway, not just to stop the wireless radiation madness."

"I know," Ray said. "I can't listen to any more of the government spin. I just want to get this thing rolling."

"The *best* part," Frannie said, "is that we'll be giving people totally new tools to play with, and I doubt anyone will be complaining, when things get rolling. Of course, they won't have seen what would have happened otherwise, which is almost a shame." She shook her head. "Not that we want anyone to suffer," she added, "but you know how it is, Ray. Sometimes people only appreciate the good stuff if they've been through hell and are desperate to escape."

"Lots of people are already in that position, Frannie, being affected by the radiation, but I know what you mean. The majority are still clueless and may never appreciate what you're doing for them. And they won't ever know, will they?" He looked at her. "Will you want people to know about this, after the fact? Is that one of the things you want me to do when we roll this out?"

"I don't think so, Ray. We're not looking for glory. We just want our kids and everyone else to have a life. Anyway, people might think they'd been manipulated," she said sardonically, "even though they're already being manipulated to death. But I like to think of our EM-SIG2 as hitting the human *reset* button and restoring the natural order of things. It gives everyone a second chance, even though they may just see it as the natural evolution of things, given that the horror scenario will have been averted."

"I get the science," Ray said, sitting back and rubbing his temples, "but the crazy timeline is making me seasick."

Frannie laughed. "Tell me about it. We had to chart everything on a huge map in the lab, factoring in timelines, locations, events, frequencies, rogue governments and lots of other fun stuff. It makes my head spin, and I have to thoroughly ground myself in the present before I go to sleep every night, so I don't wake up in some other reality altogether."

"Please, my head hurts just thinking about it." Ray groaned. "Let's focus on the rollout. I think that's going to take whatever mental bandwidth I've got left. But…" he looked at her sternly, "I have to say I'm disappointed."

"Why?" Frannie sat back, surprised.

"I thought all time travellers arrived at their destination naked."

Frannie laughed. "We finally figured out how to get around that, although it was a long, chilly process of embarrassing trial and error." She pointed at her T-shirt. "I can only wear natural fibers and no belts, metal, jewellery or accessories. And I can't carry anything with me."

"Except for that thing on your arm," Ray said, pointing to her Franometer.

"Yes, but that transmits the same frequency as I do, so it stays with me."

"And the clothing?"

"Well, that was surprisingly simple," Frannie said. "I just have to cross my legs and have my ankles touching to make a closed circuit with my electrical field and the trousers stay on. Same for the top—I put my right hand on my left, and the top stays put. So I usually sit in the lotus position before I vamoose. Doesn't work for the shoes, though, as you may have noticed." She pointed to her bare feet. "And I don't know how many of my hats, boots and scarves are floating around in spacetime."

"What about the new program? How can I install it if you don't have it with you?"

"Well, I do have it with me." Frannie grinned and rolled up her sleeves. "I wrote all the frequencies and other data on my arms and legs, since I couldn't bring a hard drive with me or send you an e-mail into the future." She looked at Ray. "So you might get to see some skin after all, but you'll be too busy transcribing and trying to get to grips with the formula to get distracted by my body-blackboard."

"Don't count on it," Ray said, laughing, "but let's see what you've got."

"Actually, I've brought a back-up, to make things easier," she said, turning her back on him. "Although the skin-board is really the back-up, in case my clothes somehow got sucked into the ethers." The back of her T-shirt was covered in figures and formulas. "It's one of Daniel's T-shirts, in case Lily finds it and wonders… Hopefully she'd just think you'd bought a funky science-y T-shirt for fun."

"Well, this one won't be going in the wash," Ray said. "But you will have to remove it, Madam, and leave it with me in the interest of scientific advancement."

"Good thing I wore two, then," Frannie said, laughing as she pulled the T-shirt off over her head.

She spread the T-shirt out on the coffee table and started to explain to Ray what to do. For a nominal fee, she and Daniel had sold all their specialized equipment and software to Ray before they left, and he kept it in a small rented space, with internet access. "So, you will have to install this new program into the Gengineering system and then begin transmitting these various frequencies over certain time frames." She tapped the T-shirt on the table. "It's all here."

Ray was on the edge of his seat, looking at the data on the T-shirt and listening attentively.

"There will be three waves or phases to this," Frannie said. "The first one will be the most challenging and will create chaos. Phase 1 is to be rolled out in early September, continuing in a pre-programmed pattern over a period of four months." Frannie pointed to some figures on the T-shirt. "With EM-SIG2, we can track certain populations, although we don't do that unless it's necessary. But what's great about that is that we can also *target* certain populations or geographical areas. It's a bit like having an IP address for bodies, enabling us to hone in on a particular city or region while other areas remain unaffected."

She looked up to make sure Ray was getting all this. He nodded his understanding, totally rapt. "The second phase will begin in early 2021," Frannie said, "but I'll try to come back again for another visit before then, to make sure it's all going smoothly."

"Thank God for that," Ray said. "This is a huge responsibility, Frannie. I'm up for it, but I'm also aware of the enormity of it all."

Frannie looked at Ray intently. "No one must know about this, Ray, okay? You must not tell *anyone*. If you do, this whole thing will fall apart. You understand that, right?"

He sat up, pulling himself together.

"Of course, Frannie," he said. "I haven't said a thing to anyone, not even Lily, and you know how close we are."

"It can't be easy, keeping this from her," Frannie said.

"No, it's not, and I have no one else to talk to about this," Ray said. "But I won't let you down, Frannie. You know me. Raynor Shine—I always deliver."

She did, and he did. That was why she was here. She had already trusted Ray with her life. Now she needed to trust him again—with the lives of her children and a few billion others.

"If you can do this, Ray, it will change everything."

40

Friday, 5 June 2020

Having seen so much of life up quantum-close, Ray often paused to marvel at gross matter. After his usual bowl of Swiss muesli and yogurt, he turned his attention to his daily orange—a perfect orb of tangy-tart exhibitionism.

He had always thought that oranges demonstrated the most flagrant fragrant form of citrus activism. If they were going to get eaten, they made damn sure everyone within a radius of 30 feet knew about it, squirting their pungent particles into the air as each piece of skin got flayed.

He had just started peeling when the doorbell rang. He wasn't expecting anyone, and Lily was out visiting a friend. Maybe it was Frannie again, arriving in a slightly more conventional manner. But he knew better than that—partly because she couldn't risk being seen by anyone else but mostly because there was nothing conventional about Frannie. He smiled at the thought, wiping his juice-sticky hands on the tea towel, knowing he'd get flak for it later.

If it was Jehovah Witnesses, they could witness his resolutely unmoving door. Case closed. If it was gushy Gloria from next door, the dear woman would have to gush elsewhere. He had bigger things to do today than fix yet another of her 'leaky' pipes while she flirted away her boredom.

He walked softly to the front door and peered through the peephole. On his doorstep was a bulbous alien. But his superior scientific brain deduced that it was more likely a young woman distorted through the fisheye lens. And there was something vaguely familiar about her.

Please, God, let it not be an 'abandoned' daughter he had unknowingly fathered, pre-Lily. Although there was that one other time...

He squared his shoulders and opened up. "Yes? Can I help you?"

"Yes." The young woman had a fiery certainty in her blue eyes. "My name is Marnie Dalton, and I believe you worked with my parents, Daniel and Francesca Dalton."

Shit. Why hadn't Frannie warned him about this? What the hell was he supposed to do now?

"Um... possibly, at one time..."

"No point denying it," Marnie said, edging past him into the hallway. Every bit as brazen as her mother! "I already know you did."

How did she know? *Did* she know or was she bluffing?

She turned to face him. "I want answers," she said, lifting a defiant delicate chin. "And you're the man to give them to me." She pointed towards the living room. "Shall we?"

Not waiting for an answer, she strode ahead, leaving him to follow in uneasy trepidation, bemused by how quickly he had lost the upper hand in his own home. *Such fabulous audacity.* How could men not bow down in awe of women? Righteous men never had this kind of impact. They should take night courses in the art of being powerful like this. But you couldn't teach this kind of thing. It either came naturally or not at all. For him, right now, not at all.

"May I?" Marnie gestured towards an armchair, knees already bent in anticipation. There was no saying no to this woman.

"Please," he said, sitting down on the couch facing her.

"I want to know everything," Marnie said firmly.

"That would take lifetimes, dear woman," he said, his mouth smiling while his mind fired up a frenzy of neurons to urgently send down a strategy. But his brain had regressed to the logic of a 3-year-old,

instructing him to tell her what he could, and not what he couldn't…
if he could figure out which was which.

"About the work you did with my parents, I mean." Smiling but
undeterred.

"I'm not sure what I can tell you." That was true, but ahead lay
a minefield of unexploded answers. He'd never get through these 20
questions unscathed.

"I want to know what kind of work you were doing with them."

He paused to consider, prepare and carefully edit his answer.

She leaned forward, eyes intense. "Is there an encryption button on
you somewhere that I could switch off?"

He laughed. What the hell. Should he tell her everything? No, he
couldn't do that. Frannie would kill him, even though she was already
dead herself. But he knew what she could do from the past. If she could
remotely influence the lives of billions of people, dealing with him
would be a cinch.

He sighed, saddening at the thought of her so permanently gone,
apart from a few ephemeral visitations. On the other hand, he consoled
himself, she needed him more than anyone. Without him, her plan
would simply not happen… and they'd all be doomed. He had to keep
his promise.

"Could you please come back?" Marnie was getting impatient.

"Sorry?"

"Back from wherever you were, having a private conversation with
yourself, deciding what you could and couldn't tell me." She tilted her
head, looking achingly like Frannie. "Look, I've already been given the
runaround by your pal Dr Pemberton, although he at least admitted
that he *and* you worked with my parents."

"What do you want to know?"

"What were you working on with them?"

"Something…"

"Well, yes, I gathered *that*."

"Something that would help humanity," he said, a tentative step on
a tightrope that seemed to stretch into infinity. It made him think of
string theory. Maybe he could distract her with some of his dazzling
knowledge.

"To do what?"

Dodging her question, he volleyed one of his own. "Did you know that particles contain vibrating filaments of energy, like string, that can vibrate in different patterns, like a cosmic symphony, playing a magical music all their own? The music of life." He offered one of his charming smiles as an added bonus. Clearly, not enough. "And space is filled with tiny particles constantly popping in and out of existence, interacting, becoming entangled, then going their separate ways—which points to the existence of numerous parallel worlds."

She paused, considering the input, then shook her head. "What does that have to do with my parents?"

"Nothing... and maybe everything."

"Could you please explain, in simple English, minus the physics lesson, what they were doing to help humanity? With no more diversions or delaying tactics, okay?"

"Okay," he said, sitting back. "Your mother was an extremely gifted physicist. She figured out things that no one else on Earth had figured out, and she found a way to... steer humanity in a more... positive direction, you might say."

"How? Doing what, exactly?" Marnie leaned forward, hungry for details.

"She developed a system for..." *Please forgive me, Frannie...* "generating positive frequencies that helped people be... more themselves."

"More themselves how?" Marnie was hooked and no way was this woman going to let go. And she was reeling *him* in, not the other way around.

"More human, more natural, more connected to themselves, to nature and to their true nature than they are right now, in our toxic, frazzled world." *Keep it general.* "People are stressed, unhealthy and disconnected from themselves, and your mother found a way to help them return to a more balanced state."

He looked up, hopeful. But he could feel the persistent tug on the line.

"And where is it, this system? Do you have it? Can I have it?"

"I'm afraid I can't help you there. If they left anything behind, you'd know more about that than me."

"They left nothing," Marnie said, lips in a line. She took a breath. "What did they do with their system? Did they use it?"

"Your mother had only just finished developing it when she...

died." He had to get her off the hook. "I can't tell you any more than that," he said, firmly.

"I don't believe you," she said, eyes narrowing.

He shrugged. *What could she do, make him take a lie-detector test?*

"Tell you what," he said, leaning forward. "Come back in a month and I may be able to tell you more, after I've done a bit of... investigating." He paused, gauging the effect, which was not stellar. "I need to get permission from some other... parties involved, before I share any more details," he said.

Marnie considered the deal. "You're either dangling a carrot to string me along or throwing me a bone in the hope I'll get fed up and not come back."

He smiled. "Take your pick, depending on whether you're a vegetarian or a carnivore."

She laughed, conceding a temporary defeat.

"Okay, but I WILL be back in a month," she said. "You can count on it, Dr Raynor Spence."

"I have no doubt about it, Marnie Dalton," he said. He just hoped that Frannie paid him another visit in the meantime or he'd have to make up some story about... something.

As Marnie retreated down the path from his house, Ray closed the door behind her, leaning against its trusted solidity. Sadness washed through his bones—for the loss of his friend, for her daughter's loss of a mother, and for the general loss of humanity that left everyone trying to be someone they were not, oblivious to how phenomenal they really were.

Frannie, please come back to me, he whispered to the secret treasured love of his life. Maybe somewhere, out there in the ethers, she could hear him.

***

As Marnie walked homeward from Dr Spence's house, marvelling to herself at how brazen she had been, barging in like that, she replayed the conversation in her mind. That stuff about parallel worlds seemed to be significant, but she had no idea how or if it related to her parents. Raynor Spence most definitely knew more and she would be back to get it.

In the meantime, she felt fractured and in need of reconfiguring. Retail therapy might be the answer. She'd seen a lovely cream suede-leather shoulder bag that she knew Lucy would love and she wanted to buy it before it got snapped up, even though Lucy's birthday wasn't till September.

She walked her fast walk, her mind digesting what the physicist had said—about her mother developing something to make people more themselves. How come her mum hadn't shared that valuable process with *her*? Or at least left the system or whatever it was behind, so everyone could benefit from it. Instead, Marnie was feeling *less* like herself than ever before. Or did that mean she was becoming *more* of who she *really* was…?

Pondering all these imponderables was exhausting. She headed for the boutique where she'd seen the bag in the window, then paused as she came to her favourite bookshop. She went in. After finding the right sections, she selected a book on creative writing and one on fashion design. For Lucy's birthday goodie bag.

The suede bag was still in the window, so she got that too. They also had a little wooden display case of essential oils and she got a tiny bottle of pungent bergamot—*good for elevating mood, alleviating, stress, reducing inflammation and lowering cholesterol,* according to the little label below the tester bottle. She got two—one for Lucy, one for herself. That should do it for Lucy's birthday. *Okay, September, I'm ready.*

In mid-May, she had sent Matt a book on sailing, two weeks before his birthday, but it still hadn't arrived. It was probably on the slow mule to Sayulita, taking its own sweet time. It would get there when it got there. Marnie believed there was a book for every birthday—or should be. Birthdays just didn't seem right without some kind of new book—a doorway into another world for an expanding awareness. Mind mulch for growing ideas.

Next, Whole Foods for some dinner. She grabbed a cart at the entrance and did her usual circuit. It was early afternoon, and mothers were out in force, small children directing things from their carts, pointing to their preferred essentials in the candy aisle. Mothers chatted on corners, their carts blocking traffic, and Marnie caught the snippets of conversation as glimpses from her own mothering future. One cluster was talking animatedly about babies needing to sleep in the dark—*crucial* for their overall health and development.

Babies in the darkness. That pretty much summed up the state of fumbling, helpless humanity, as far as Marnie could see.

As she rounded the corner towards the deli counter, she almost collided with a man carrying a basket, although he looked as if he was carrying a globe of the world stuffed under his straining T-shirt. He had a massive, tightly pumped, close-to-bursting belly that must have prevented him from using a cart, since he probably couldn't get close enough to it to drop in his purchases. But, surely, by now, at his mature age, he had become quite a good shot? Her mind clearly needed something more worthwhile to work on.

But she was concerned for him. With a belly like that, he should be careful to avoid all sharp objects, Marnie thought, her mind conjuring up visions of him getting pronged by someone's pointy umbrella and zooming around the room, pinging off the walls, sputtering like a farting balloon.

Really, she needed to get a life.

41

July 2020

Matt had set up his own small business on the beach—a small open-fronted wooden shack where he served lunch every day, Monday to Saturday.

Zack had helped him get set up, sorting out the business licence, and Matt had bought an old Jeep from one of Zack's friends. It was little more than a noisy hammock on wheels with a flat canvas top, but it got him around, and the weather was always either warm, hot or boiling, so he didn't mind not having any windows.

One of the local fishermen brought him fresh fish every morning, straight off his boat, and he had two huge coolers full of ice that he kept under the counter, out of the sun.

He offered a set menu: barbequed fish, steamed fresh vegetables with lots of roasted onion, garlic and spices that he brought from his own kitchen in a huge cast iron pot, and big fat slices of juicy strawberry papaya with fresh lime juice to finish off. He sold chilled coconuts with the tops hacked off and a straw stuck in the opening, as well as bottled water, and that was it.

His lunches were hugely popular and he had usually sold out by 3pm. It wasn't what he wanted to be doing for the rest of his days but, for now, it was a good place to be while he waited for the next set of clues in this treasure hunt called life. He was starting to realize that life rose up to meet you if you believed in it enough to bravely live it without knowing how things might work out.

He felt like a new man—strong, fit, healthy, cleansed—and he could barely remember his former life. After almost a year of working with Zack, he knew he had to do something of his own, although he still helped out occasionally with some surfing lessons or other water sports.

He was under the counter when it happened, cleaning up some papaya seeds that he'd dropped on the floor when he was clearing up after lunch. If he didn't do it straight away, he'd have a whole army of ants on top of it in seconds.

Someone rapped loudly on the counter, making him jump and bang his head on the shelf above him.

"¿*Tienes algo de comer?*" It was a reasonable question, since he sold stuff to eat, but something about the voice made the hairs on the back of his neck stand on end.

He got up slowly, rubbing the back of his head with one hand, the plate of papaya seeds in the other, and almost dropped the plate on the floor.

There was a petite young woman standing at the counter—blue eyes, sun-bleached blond hair, pixie haircut, tanned, toned body, and a smile that could knock a man off his perch. Not the fish kind of perch, either... although that, too...

He stood gaping at her, like a complete moron, unable to speak, and for some reason he thought of Forrest Gump. *Life is like a box of chocolates...*

"Celle..." That was it. He might graduate to a full sentence in a few minutes but, for now, that was all he could manage.

She was luminous. Transformed. He couldn't believe it was the same person.

He wasn't, either, of course. He could barely remember who he had been. He had lost touch with his former buddies and he no longer had anything in common with any of the people in his life back there, including himself. Except his sisters…

She looked serene, confident and drop-dead gorgeous.

"Mateo," she said, smiling at him. He'd forgotten she spoke Spanish, although he'd never heard her speak it. Her accent was the sexiest thing he'd heard since… he couldn't remember when.

"I can't believe it's you," he said, shaking his head in wonder.

"You can't believe I'm here or you can't believe that the me you see is the me you used to know?"

"All of the above," he said, loving every syllable.

He remembered her request for food. "I have some papaya and some chilled coconuts…?"

"A coconut would be good," she said, smiling.

"Let me close up and we can sit over there in the shade and have a drink." He gestured to the white wooden chairs beside the shack, under a *palapa* that was whispering softly in the wind.

"Be with you in a sec."

He walked around to the front of the shack, pulled down the shutter and joined her under the *palapa* with two coconuts already beheaded and sporting pink straws.

"Celle, it's wonderful to see you, but I don't know what—"

She was shaking her head, so he stopped.

"I will not be the woman who was raped by her brother," she said firmly. "I am not that woman and I will not let someone else's actions define my life."

Wow. He hadn't expected that. She was strong—stronger than him. He had certainly let his parents' actions define *his* life… for a while.

"If you think of me as that damaged person, if you even give it airtime in your head, I will know and I will walk out of here and never speak to you again. Do you understand, Matt?"

He nodded, in awe of her strength and determination—her *self*-determination.

"If you hold that abusive image of me in your mind, you perpetuate the abuse," Celle said gently, loving them both with her words. "If I see pity or shame in your eyes, I will know that you see what *happened* to me but not who I really *am*."

She sipped some coconut juice. "My brother may have lost his mind, but that doesn't mean I have to lose my identity."

Matt felt something release inside him—the liberation of a space held hostage by fear, anger and frustration. Relief and understanding were seeping into his senses, washing away the shaky foundations on which his life had been built.

He swallowed hard, marveling at her strength and humbled by his own predictable knee-jerk reactions. This tiny woman was a bridge to understanding, not a place of pain for the projections of his pity. His whole life, he had unconsciously done this disservice to women.

"You know I lost the baby," she said calmly.

"Yes," he said. "I'm so s—"

"No," she said, holding up a hand. "I have no room for sorry. That kind of sorry just assumes that I'm a victim, which I am not."

She paused, looking at him with a clear, unwavering gaze.

"My body knew what it needed to do," she said. "My heart and mind dealt with the rest. And here I am."

She smiled and sipped more coconut juice.

Bloody hell. He felt a wave of emotion wash over him and had to fight hard to stop himself from crying. He didn't want her to think he was pitying her or regretting not having been there for her—

"It's okay," she said. "I know why you're crying."

How *could* she? *He* didn't know why.

"It's partly because I was hurt very badly," Celle said, "and you know from your own pain that it can bring you to your knees. It's partly because my words are bringing up all sorts of feelings that you thought you had already processed. And it's partly because you mourn for what has been lost—for the things we do to each other when we've lost our way."

He sat back, stunned.

This was not the needy girl from his former life. This was a young woman who had found herself—forged an entirely *new*, rock-solid self—who liked herself and who didn't need anyone else to make her feel good about who she chose to be.

Her aura of calm confidence was almost tangible—an emotional self-sufficiency that was powerfully magnetic. Matt could feel the freedom that came from that, and how peaceful and liberating it was to be around someone who was emotionally present, with no need to gain the acceptance or approval of others.

"We were both wounded, Matt." Celle was looking at him with

blameless love and understanding. "Tragedy cracked us open. But the pain was already there, inside, and those crises dropped us right down into it."

Matt had thought *he* was the one healing—coming here to shed the pain of what had happened, to get away from all the other wounded souls so he could find a way to function. Now, he realized, he could *function*, but had he really healed himself the way Celle had? Had he grown at all, gained any wisdom, or had he just isolated himself in a nice sunny holding pattern?

When Marnie had told him what Jed had done, Matt had raged at the betrayal by his friend. He wanted to rip things apart, to escape his skin, to bring Jed back to life so he could kill him with his bare hands. Instead, he had exhausted himself by repeatedly swimming from one side of the bay to the other, pounding the water as he tried to purge the awful images from his mind.

He had been unable to compute the sickening reality, and a part of him had dissociated from it, pushing it back into the life he had left behind.

He had understood then why Celle had been so angry with him, even though she hadn't known what he had asked Jed to investigate. But if Matt had not asked him to do that, Jed would not have been threatened by that woman, whoever she was, and might not have ended up in a rage, raping his sister and then getting killed the next day.

But no amount of rage could justify what Jed had done. Matt knew his friend had had problems with alcohol and he had seen him, twice before, lose control when he mixed certain alcoholic beverages. But never to the point where he forgot who he was or who his sister was.

Marnie had mentioned that Celle had been aware of Jed's problem with alcohol, and she had the feeling the Ryersons were hiding something. She wasn't sure if Mr Ryerson had a similar problem or if Jed had lost control in the past and they had covered it up.

Whatever the case, something must have pushed him over the edge. But Jed was an adult and none of them were responsible for what he had done, although they all felt tainted by it and somehow collectively to blame.

Except for Celle. The one person who had every justification for hating her brother and life itself had chosen to embrace it as an opportunity—to learn how to love herself unconditionally and to forgive everyone else for not being able to fully love themselves.

In the process, Matt could see, she was touching the lives of those around her. Her mere presence here had already affected him profoundly and he was in awe of what she had achieved, while he, in his stumbling macho maleness, was only just beginning to realize how little he knew himself.

He wanted so much to hold her—but not to comfort *her*. She no longer needed that. It was to comfort *himself*.

But he couldn't, not after everything she had said.

He would just stay here in the shade, focus on drinking his coconut juice and wait for the feeling to pass.

A cloud passed over the sun, but it was Celle standing in front of him, her arms reaching for a hug.

"I get it, Mateo," she said.

He got up, his knees buckling, his coconut dropping to the sand, and she held him—this tiny woman with a heart as vast and warm and beautiful as the Andaman Sea. She hugged him so completely that he wondered if it was possible to hug a person whole.

He sobbed for all he had lost, missed and misunderstood, for all he had yet to become, and for the realization that he'd never had a clue what it meant to really love someone. Not a friggin' clue.

"Celle," he said, his whole body aching. "I had no idea…"

"I know," she said gently. "Nor did I. But now I do. And so do you."

42

July 2020

The bulbous alien was back on his doorstep. "I know you're in there," it called out, "trying to decide if you're *home* or not."

Not an alien, a witch! But it made him smile. His charm could usually disarm most women, if he worked at it, but this particular Dalton female was having none of it.

To hell with it. He'd just have to wing it. He opened the door, all smiles.

"Marnie, you're back! Wonderful. Come on in."

She gaped in surprise, caught herself and stepped smartly in before he realized he'd actually said yes to the Spanish Inquisition.

She gave him a penetrating look, gauging his encryption level.

"Please." He gestured towards the living room. "You know the way." She'd fight her way through virgin jungle if she had to, he thought, smiling as he followed her speedy form into the interrogation room.

She headed straight for the armchair, sat, took off her coat, took a book out of her bag, placed it on the lectern of her tidy lap, and was tapping it, as if to get his attention, before he'd even sat down.

As soon as his rear end landed on the couch, she launched right in.

"I've been reading this book," she said. "About parallel universes, the multiverse and all kinds of weird quantum stuff."

"Good for you," he said. "Very mind-expanding."

"And I remembered what you said last time about parallel worlds."

"What did I say?" he asked innocently. He honestly couldn't remember.

"That it had something—maybe *everything*—to do with my parents," she said, looking at him intently, a lawyer ready to catch a dodgy witness in a lie.

"Well, that would be true of everyone," he said, spreading his hands in largesse. Let everyone have it.

"*What* would be?" She looked like a dog ready to growl. "Please stop talking in Raynor riddles. You said you'd tell me more when I came back, and I'm back. So, tell me."

He toyed with telling her he hadn't yet heard back from those other parties involved, which was true. But she was persistent, as he'd expect Frannie's progeny to be, and she wouldn't be fobbed off quite so easily this time. But Frannie still hadn't shown up, so he had no idea what he could safely tell her daughter.

Suddenly, he felt exhausted from it all—the loss of his friend, the massive responsibility, being baited on TV, the need for guarded explanations, the angry world. And emotional; a wave of hot grief stole his breath and toppled the sense of purpose that had been holding him upright. He leaned forward, head in his hands, wiping his eyes.

Marnie dropped the book on the floor and was suddenly beside him on the couch.

"Are you okay, Dr Spence?" She put a gentle hand on his back. "I'm… I'm sorry if I was pushy…"

He looked at her, his kind blue eyes filled with a whole universe of knowledge and awareness that seemed to throb for release.

"I have it," he said. "The device your parents created. I have it, and I'm working with it. Maybe you can help me."

43

Wednesday, 2 September 2020

Vicky Phelps was pretty sure what she was doing was illegal. Tough titty. They could blame her stupid doctor for not giving her what she needed. *Twice* she'd gone to him for help and he'd told her it was all in her head. *Get more sleep. Stop worrying so much. Talk to your parents.* He hadn't a friggin' clue! He didn't believe her when she told him she felt anxious all the time and *couldn't* sleep. He was a total moron and he never listened to a thing she said.

But now she felt a lot better. Jules had given her some of her Propysta to try and that stuff really worked! She'd ordered her own supply and was looking forward to feeling normal again. It was going to use up all her weekly allowance but she'd get more cheddar somewhere, if she had to. Half the girls in her class were on Propysta and *they* found a way. She'd ask Jules how she managed. Jules's family was not well off, so she must have worked out some kind of deal, although Vicky had a feeling Jules stole money from her mom's purse when she wasn't looking.

It was such a relief not to feel agitated. God, it was so *exhausting* being like that all the time. It really messed with her head and she had a hard time thinking straight in class. Not that anyone noticed.

Anxiety seemed to be a *thing*. They texted each other about it all the time. Jules said it was because they were so smart and their brains generated too much energy for their own good. Vicky wasn't sure she was *that* smart, or that smarts had any downside.

She'd have to make sure she got her stash before they went on the school trip next week. A whole week in London! She could hardly wait. She'd never gone anywhere, never even been on a plane, and this would be her first time away from home.

Her cellphone was, like, the *only* thing keeping her from going nuts.

If she didn't have her friends to talk to at night, she'd go mental. Her parents were just totally AWOL, and they didn't care what the hell she did as long as she kept out of their hair and did her homework.

God, a whole week away! It was going to be a blast. Kev was going, too. She shivered at the thought. She'd be a lot more cool with her Propysta. Way more sassy and Gucci. She had taken two of the five pills Jules gave her, just to see what happened, and she felt like flying!

Shit, she hardly needed the plane! She could fly there all on her own! She laughed out loud. But it would be more fun going with the gang, especially if she and Jules got to sit near Kev and Martin. Vicky couldn't see what Jules saw in Martin. He was such a geeky creeper—smart, yeah, but she couldn't imagine ever *kissing* him. But at least Jules wasn't interested in Kev. Vicky wouldn't stand a chance otherwise. Jules always looked so cool and sexy, making all the guys drool. No way was *she* that sexy, Vicky thought, but she knew how to keep her body as thin as a model's and what to wear to show it off. Plus she had a nice smile—at least, Kev seemed to think so.

She was counting the days and she had her suitcase all packed, ready to go. Everything would be totally *dope*, as long as her Propysta arrived in time. She didn't know how she'd cope if it didn't. She would do whatever it took to get a week's supply. She'd scrounge from Jules, Belle, maybe even Sari or whoever else she had to suck up to get her quota. YOLO! Although she preferred *YODO*—you only *die* once. She could live plenty, as long as she had her stuff.

44

Friday, 4 September 2020

Lucy was working on a blog about vaccines for one of her clients, discovering all kinds of disturbing things. It was downright scary to read about DNA damage, and babies suddenly becoming ill, lethargic or unresponsive after being given a vaccine that was supposed to protect their health. It seemed crazy to her that doctors were injecting all kinds of nasty stuff, including mercury, and expecting these fragile young organisms to be unaffected.

She was learning a lot about health, corporate greenwashing, creative marketing strategies and how businesses were cultivating their clients. She'd been working for Nate for nine months now, and he seemed pleased with her progress, giving her more and more responsibility. She'd been writing product summaries and web copy for clients, and had even hit the streets with her notepad to ask people what they thought about the city's environmental policies or whether they preferred allopathic, complementary, integrative or alternative medicine.

She had the office to herself today as Fitz and Tracy had taken the day off to get the most out of the Labor Day holiday weekend. Nate hadn't shown up yet and was probably still upstairs in his apartment. Recently, he'd been quieter than usual, Lucy thought, and a little cooler towards her, although she wasn't aware of having done anything wrong.

Beemer was lying at her feet, flaked out after his run in the park. She had her own office key and Beemer usually came charging out to greet her when she arrived in the morning. She'd got into the habit of taking him for a walk before she sat down to work. Beemer was devoted to Lucy ...until about 4pm, when he began to get hungry. Then his loyalties shifted back to Nate, the Man who Bought the Dog Food.

Lucy had been at her desk for nearly an hour when she heard Nate coming down the stairs to the office. A second set of lighter footsteps sounded behind his familiar tread.

She looked up.

"Morning, Lucy," Nate said. "This is my nephew Tate. He's 7-going-on-47 and he's staying with me over the weekend."

Lucy got up to say hello.

For a 7-year-old, Tate looked surprisingly well put-together, with a serious expression, a steady gaze, closely cropped fair hair, impeccable black pants, a funky geometric shirt and big black designer glasses framing large dark-brown eyes.

"Hi, Lucy," he said, extending his right hand.

Lucy shook. "Pleased to meet you, Tate."

"Uncle Nate says you're a good writer, and he's right about you being attractive, but I think you should avoid pastel shades."

He pointed at her pink T-shirt. "You'd look better in russet, olive green or a strong blue."

"Wow. Okay. Thanks for that fashion tip," Lucy said, laughing but then wondering if she shouldn't be.

"It's okay to laugh," Tate said. "Some people just don't know when not to laugh."

"When should they not laugh?" Lucy asked.

"When they think I don't know what I'm talking about," Tate said, looking at her seriously. "But kids are smart, unless someone tells them they're not." He paused. "And honest. I'm monitoring this to see when kids stop being honest and start saying the ingratiating things adults say to make themselves more acceptable."

"I'd really like to know the answer to that," Lucy said. "Honestly."

"I believe you," Tate said. "I'll let you know."

He turned to Nate. "You're right. She's nice."

Nate grinned at Lucy, shrugging. *What can I do?*

"My uncle often feels he has to apologize for me," Tate said. "He tells people I'm a precocious brain child with an IQ of 350 and the social skills of a Neanderthal."

"Is he being honest," Lucy said, "or just ingratiating?"

Tate grinned. "Nuncle, you forgot to say she's funny."

Nuncle?

"You can have my full bio, if you like," Lucy said. "Just let me know when you're taking over your uncle's company and I'll be happy to sit a more formal exam."

She folded her arms and looked at him seriously. "I should warn you, though. I only have an IQ of 12.5 and the social skills of a Nicaraguan tarantula."

Tate looked skeptical. "I'm not sure about that," he said.

"About my social skills?"

"About the tarantula. I'm not sure they have tarantulas in Nicaragua."

"See? That just proves my point. If they're no longer there, it's because they were so socially inept that they got wiped out. They used to practically *run* the place."

Tate giggled and Lucy glimpsed the little boy behind the amazing brain.

Nate mimed making a phone call and gestured towards his office. Tapping Tate on the shoulder, he said, "Ready in ten, then we'll head out, okay?"

"Yeah. It'll be more like 30, but that's okay," Tate said. "Lucy is pretty good company."

Nate laughed. "She is." He looked at Lucy. "Okay with you? We're not interrupting your work?"

"My pleasure," Lucy said. "I get the feeling Tate is pretty good company, too."

"You won't be bored," Nate said, heading down the corridor to his office and closing the door behind him.

Lucy sat down at her desk. "Pull up a chair," she said, pointing to Fitz's desk. Tate rolled the chair over beside hers and hauled himself up onto the seat.

"You call your uncle *Nuncle?*"

"Yeah. He thinks I'm too young to call him Nate but it gets old calling him Uncle Nate all the time, so I shortened it to Nuncle."

"I like it," Lucy said. She looked at him, so small in Fitz's large chair, swinging his short legs and looking mildly bored.

"What do you do for fun?"

Tate seemed to be reflecting. Maybe the list was long or he wasn't sure what fun was.

"You play championship chess, sky-dive, design cathedrals, paint masterpieces, fly kites, do hip-hop or what?"

"I make clothes."

"You make clothes? That's amazing. What kind of clothes?"

"Suits, shirts, pants, ties—and shoes, but I usually just design those as they're more difficult to make. Sometimes I sell stuff and sometimes I wear things myself, like this shirt." He pointed at his chest. "I have a machine at home that can make all kinds of stuff."

"Wow. I'm impressed. I was going to study fashion design but… ended up here instead."

"I can help you, if you want. I've got lots of ideas." He looked at her earnestly. "It's never too late to do what you love, Lucy. You have to follow your dreams."

"Is that what your mom tells you to do?"

"Nah. I've been telling *her* that since I was 5! But she's much better now and her business is going really well."

"*You* are something *else*," Lucy said, laughing. "You could be a comedian."

"But I wasn't making a joke," Tate said, perplexed.

"Sorry, right. Of course not. How can I explain this to you, Tatum… What's your last name?"

"Rothschild."

"Yeah, right."

"I am a child of Roth," Tate said, all innocence.

"Ah, okay, wiseguy. That *was* a joke, right?"

"Yeah." Tate grinned, swinging his legs and kicking his chair. His humour seemed to get funneled through his legs as well as his giggle, Lucy mused, smiling.

"So, Tatum Roth… Where do you get your ideas for your designs?" Lucy was fascinated. *How could a 7-year-old produce such amazing stuff?*

"I just watch people," he said. "Most people are very uncomfortable in their clothes and they don't dress the way their bodies want to be dressed."

"You're right. Fashion has very little to do with comfort, these days. It's all about show."

How come Nate had never mentioned this wunderkind and his fashion flair?

"It's not just about comfort, though," Tate said. "It's about who you are here." He thumped his chest. "If you wear the stuff that everyone else wears, how can you be yourself?"

"I hear you," Lucy said, shaking her head in wonder. "It's like covering up who you really are with anonymous clothes churned out for the masses." She shook her head again. "Who helps you with your designs—selling them, making things?"

"My dad. He's an architect and he taught me how to draw things to scale when I was very young."

Seven being *old*, Lucy thought wryly. Such humbling mastery in a kid who'd only learned to *walk* a few years ago.

"He helps me with some of the patterns and my mom helps with other stuff. She's an interior designer, so she gets lots of ideas, and I give her some of mine."

"Sounds like a fantastic team," Lucy said. "How come your uncle Nate hasn't interviewed you for a blog?" *Or had ME interview you?*

"My dad says I'm too young but I can do that kind of thing when I'm 10, so another three years to go." Big sigh of forbearance.

"Your time will come, kiddo," Lucy said. "You're amazing." She pointed at his shirt. "Tell me about this design you're wearing. Where did you get the idea for all these geometric shapes?"

"My mom gets lots of fabric samples and gives most of them to me. I cut them up into squares and triangles and stuff, and sew them together. Then I work on a pattern using some of my dad's building designs, so sometimes the collar is like an archway, like this mandarin one, or I use strips of ridged fabric that look like wooden beams, like these ones on the back."

He swivelled in his chair and Lucy leaned forward to study the vertical strips of burgundy-brown corduroy alternating with strips of smooth white, bright yellow and pale-blue fabric. The tail of the shirt tapered into a V that made Tate's small shoulders look larger than they were. *Great macho design,* Lucy thought.

"Tate, I'm blown away. This is gorgeous."

Tate swivelled front again.

Lucy leaned in close and whispered, "Don't tell Nuncle, but could we elope and set up our own fashion house somewhere exotic, far away from boring Boston?"

Tate grinned. "I've already had a few offers," he said.

"I bet you have. The girls must be falling all over you."

"Nah. It's more for the designs. I don't have time for girls. Too busy." Tate shifted in his chair, looking uncomfortable.

"It must be difficult to relate to kids your age when you're into all this creative stuff."

"Yeah…"

They both turned as Nate emerged from his office and joined them at Lucy's desk.

"Okay, Magoo, let's go."

Tate looked at his watch. "Twenty-nine minutes and 23 seconds," he said, pointing at Nate.

"I thought you said you wanted 30 minutes with Lucy," Nate said, in mock surprise. "I've been sitting in there, twiddling my thumbs, just waiting for you to finish yakking."

"Yeah, yeah." Tate snorted and hopped off the chair.

Beemer half-heartedly raised his head, but repeat walks rarely happened so soon after the morning one, so there was no point in getting up.

Lucy turned to Nate. "Who's Magoo?"

"He was a cartoon character popular in the 60s who was short-sighted and always getting into trouble," Nate said. "Long before our time. My dad kept all the old comics, which are collectors' items now."

He grinned at Tate. "This little character reminds me of him, with his big glasses and huge brain."

"I see," said Lucy, smiling. She couldn't help envying these two their lovely relationship.

"We're going to the Museum of Science," Tate said. "Want to come with us, Lucy?"

She noticed *Nate* didn't invite her… "Thanks, but I want to finish this blog," Lucy said. "You two have fun."

"Well, we'll be back at around 5pm," Nate said, "but you should finish up early, since it's the holiday weekend."

"Come for dinner, Lucy," Tate said. "I make a mean *goo-lash*."

"Sounds good," Lucy said, laughing. "Let me see how things go here." She looked at Tate. "I've also got to go out and buy a new top. Can't be seen wearing this dull thing a minute longer."

Lucy heard their laughter echo down the hallway as they made their way out.

This Nate–Tate thing was too much. She'd have to ask Nate if she could call him Nat, But maybe she should call him Mr Cordalis, since he seemed to want to keep things professional.

"Later, Lucy!" Tate called from the front door.

"Later, Tater…" But the front door had already closed, and Lucy's mind was elsewhere. Tate had inspired her, reminding her what she had loved about fashion design and how creative and uplifting it could be. Her fashion fantasies were emerging from lockdown, and she was itching to get out her sketch pad…

First, though, she had to finish this blog. She opened the vaccines document on her computer and re-read what she had written so far. She wondered if Tate had been vaccinated. Would humans be smarter if they weren't injected with toxic, DNA-damaging stuff, right into their tender little bloodstreams?

Lucy wasn't sure what vaccinations *she* had had as a child… Maybe Marnie would know.

She needed to browse some other sites and find out more. So far, her online research had revealed almost exclusively disturbing facts, with very little evidence that vaccines were a good thing.

But if there was an outbreak of a deadly virus in the US, how could you avoid being vaccinated? She was pretty sure people would be forced to… She did a search for *mandatory vaccination* and found that many states made it mandatory for schoolchildren. She checked Massachusetts... Ah. *If you didn't want to vaccinate your child, you had to get a letter of exemption from a doctor or a religious leader.*

So she *must* have been vaccinated... unless her parents had qualified as the kind of doctors who could write such a letter. She doubted it.

She was finding it hard to concentrate. Her mind kept coming back to Nate. *What had she done to cause him to be less friendly?*

Suddenly it hit her. Her fingers froze on the keyboard and Lucy felt her cheeks flare hotly with embarrassment. Ever since she'd started working for Nate, she'd been flirting, cracking jokes and being a smartass. It was obviously making him uncomfortable, so he had backed off.

How could she have been so stupid! So unprofessional! But she had no experience at this. She'd never had such a hot boss before—or any boss, ever. *How could she have known?*

It wasn't easy being around Nate when he was so sexy and charming, with her hormones raging all over the place. But that didn't give her the right to act like an infatuated teenager, even though she *was* still a teenager... Oh, God. Lucy groaned, her head in her hands. He was just being a decent guy and she had been totally unprofessional.

Now that she'd figured it out, she would cool things right down. Like he had. If he felt her backing off, he might feel more comfortable with her.

Should she say something? It would embarrass them both if she brought it up, so she would just try to act like a professional and see how things went.

Thank God the other two weren't here to witness her mortification. They must have noticed the way she was behaving and how uncomfortable it made Nate feel. They probably thought she was incredibly naïve and innocent. Well, she was. Obviously.

She really didn't want to be here when Nate got back, and no way was she going to have dinner with them, even if Tate wanted her to. She'd get this blog done and then knock off early. She would be long gone by the time they got back at 5pm.

Okay, focus, focus. She pulled up a site that explained how vaccines worked. The theory was that they gave the body a minimal dose of a harmful pathogen that was supposed to create immunity to that particular illness. But now lots of studies confirmed that the flu vaccine, for example, often made people sicker than if they'd never received the vaccine at all.

But why was that?

She scrolled down and found one possible explanation. Apparently, the particular viral strain that scientists used when creating a vaccine was almost always the wrong one, and viruses mutated so fast that it was almost impossible to keep up. There were many options to choose from and if they guessed the wrong one for whatever flu virus was making the rounds during the flu season, people who got vaccinated were basically getting injected with sickness, rather than being protected against it.

But hadn't vaccines wiped out polio, measles and other diseases? She read on. Many claimed that those diseases were on the decline anyway, before vaccines were introduced, so vaccines may have had nothing to do with their elimination. Mmm… a tough one to prove.

Next, she did a search for the ingredients used in making vaccines. She already knew about the mercury, which was supposed to act as a preservative to extend shelf life, but one site claimed that ten other toxic metals were used in vaccines. A whole slew of them claimed that mercury alone could cause autism, among other things. Was that why there had been such a rise in autism over the past two decades?

Lucy did a search for autism statistics… Some sites reported 1 in 59 children in the US being autistic. Blimey. Would they be counting the kids who were *not* autistic by the year 2025?

Marnie had told her that electromagnetic radiation could also cause autism, or make it worse. She did another DuckDuckGo search. Nate didn't like using Google and preferred to use this incognito browser. She found a paper by an expert in childhood autism, who confirmed the autism–vaccine correlation. But she also talked about microwave radiation pushing up the autism numbers.

So many factors and so many environmental toxins. It was not a clear-cut case, and she already had far too much content for her blog.

But what about ADHD—Attention Deficit Hyperactivity Disorder? She knew Marnie had several kids in her class with this disorder. She did another search and discovered a 2017 report that said 6.4 million children in America had been diagnosed with ADHD. *Could there be a link to early childhood vaccines?* More DuckDucking… and she found one: lead and aluminum! Had Marnie made the connection?

When had humans started injecting and feeding themselves such crap? Lucy couldn't figure it out. Did their ancestors wake up one day and think: *All this natural stuff is boring. Let's mix in some chemicals, spray pesticides all over our food to make it look nice without worrying about what's actually in it, then use drugs to fight disease since our food will no longer be doing the job for us, and we'll all be a whole lot better off.*

God. She was already jaded and cynical and she wasn't even 20 yet.

Her mind went back to Nate and she found herself squirming. She couldn't wait to leave the office, but then she'd probably agonize over this all weekend, till she was back at work on Tuesday. Maybe she'd send him an e-mail tomorrow, saying she understood how uncomfortable she must have made him feel, but now she got it and she would be nothing but professional from now on.

She sighed. She needed to get outside and get some exercise.

She'd trim the blog on Tuesday. For now, she made a quick note of some of the other ingredients. *Diploid cells—cells taken from aborted fetuses.* Ugh. Then macerated cancer cells. *Cancer cells?* Animal tissues taken from rabbits' brains or horse or pig blood. Last on the list was detergent—presumably, to keep it all nice and clean.

Bloody hell. Most parents were completely oblivious to all this stuff, blindly trusting their doctors to protect their children's health. And, according to several of the sites she had explored, most side effects and fatalities went unreported. Why did *that* not surprise her.

She needed to find out about healthy alternatives and clicked on a site offering healthy solutions. Her blog was for a client promoting immune-boosting supplements and protocols, versus conventional medical-drug-driven approaches. So the piece needed to flag the likely dangers and then offer healthier options, as well as ways of mitigating vaccines' harmful effects.

As she continued reading, she realized it all came down to the strength of a person's immune system. Vaccines were supposed to help the immune system fight off invaders but often ended up weakening it instead. Strengthening the immune system naturally seemed like a much healthier and more effective way to go.

It's what everyone should have been doing during that global virus panic in March, Lucy thought. Everyone had gone nuts and people seemed to think—or were *told*—that a vaccine could save them, when it was likely to do them far more harm than good. It was mind-boggling, all the factors involved...

She clicked to another page, offering several natural approaches. Top of the list was breastfeeding for boosting an infant's immune system. A bit late for that, at her age! Lucy smiled. She'd have to find some other way to boost her own system.

A mother passed on her immunity to her children through her breastmilk, protecting them from diseases in ways that infant formula never could. One study reported that mothers who naturally built up their own immunity had three times the antibodies against pathogens and were protected four times longer than those who had been vaccinated. The same study showed that a quarter of the mothers who had been vaccinated had no protective antibodies at all.

If her own mother was anything to go by, Lucy thought, most mothers were far too busy juggling work and child-rearing to breastfeed their babies for more than a month or two, if that.

Other sites said a mother's breastmilk was almost always contaminated with drugs, heavy metals and pesticides from our food and the environment.

It was a minefield! There were no clear answers and this blog was turning into a monster. She'd have to chop bits out if she wanted to keep it punchy.

What other immune-boosting stuff was there? She scanned the rest of the webpage. Probiotics—healthy flora to boost the system, vitamin D to protect against cancer, autoimmune diseases and infections, other vitamins… Marnie knew all this stuff, Lucy realized. She could probably write this blog without doing a scrap of research.

Then there were Reishi and Maitake mushrooms. She didn't like mushrooms, but these guys were supposed to *naturally restore overall healthy functioning of the body's organs.* Not a bad rap for something that grew in the shade and required hardly any cultivation.

Okay. Enough. Her brain couldn't handle any more of this stuff. She needed to get outside and clear her head. She checked the word count—1,300 words. She'd chop it on Tuesday, but that wouldn't take long. She saved and closed the document, happy to have accomplished so much in just a couple of hours. She was getting quite speedy at this blog-writing thing.

At the bottom, the client would put an ad for one of their immune-boosting products. She'd add some links to the sites she'd browsed and then—

Noises in the hallway. She looked at her watch. It was only ten minutes to noon. Far too early for them to be back…

Beemer seemed to think so too, lifting his head in surprise, then getting up and trotting to the door as Nate came in, followed by a very morose-looking 7-year-old.

Shit. She had wanted to be out of here before they got back. "You're back early," Lucy said. "Was the museum closed?"

"No." Nate looked uncomfortable, and Tate looked downright ill. "Go upstairs, buddy. Get your drink from the fridge. Then go and lie down and I'll be up in a few minutes."

Tate glared at him, his eyes red and watering, then made his way slowly up the stairs.

"Is he ill?" It was all Lucy could do not to run up the stairs after him to give him a hug and make sure he was okay.

"He's got a migraine," Nate said, looking distraught. "He gets them sometimes."

"Oh, I'm so sorry. Do you know what causes them?"

"He's… very sensitive. It's kind of hard to explain." Nate leaned down to pat Beemer and Lucy got the feeling he didn't want to talk about this with her.

"I should go," she said. "Leave you two in peace." He definitely didn't want her getting too close. She got it.

Nate straightened up. "It's just… he picks up on other people's emotions and he gets frustrated when people don't tell the truth, which is sometimes too much for him to handle and gives him a headache." He shrugged. "It's like being sensitive to barometric pressure, which can give some people pressure in the head, you know?"

"I understand," Lucy said, although she really didn't. "I was about to leave anyway. I'll finalize the vaccine blog on Tuesday, if that's okay."

"Yeah, sure," Nate said, looking as if he really didn't care. She probably could have said she'd finish the blog on childhood pornography and he wouldn't have noticed.

Lucy turned back to her desk and shut down her computer. "Please, go up and make sure he's okay," she said, looking up at Nate. "I'm concerned for him."

"Okay. Thanks, Lucy." Nate nodded gratefully and made his way upstairs. "Talk to you later," he said as he reached the top and disappeared out of sight.

"Call me if there's anything I can do to help, okay?" *Darn. Too personal. Keep it professional! Too late now. She'd said it.*

"Yeah. Thanks."

She tidied up her notes, grabbed her shoulder bag and left the office, closing the door softly behind her. Taking her coat from the stand in the hallway, she let herself out and paused on the street. She didn't feel like shopping now, after seeing them both so upset. But she really needed to get her head straight about this work thing.

It was a sunny day, so she decided to go home for lunch. It was only 20 minutes away and she always walked to and from work, unless it was pouring rain.

She was concerned about Tate. He seemed to be in a lot of pain. Was it normal for someone so young to get migraines like that? She had no idea. There was nothing normal about Tatum, so maybe this was completely normal for him, given his incredibly active brain.

She'd call Nate later to see how he was feeling. Or not. Maybe e-mail him about the work issue instead? Shit. She was clueless about all this stuff. Maybe Marnie could advise her …or Delsie.

In the meantime, maybe she could distract herself with some design ideas and see what emerged.

The apartment she shared with Kara Kinsley was a small two-bedroom corner unit on the top floor of a three-storey building. Kara was a nurse who often worked the night shift. This week, though, she was on day shift, so Lucy would have the place to herself till dinnertime.

She loved having her own space again, and Kara was a very easy roommate. An avid reader, she always had her head stuck in a book, and she was a super-fit yogi. Lucy always marvelled at how Kara could turn any activity—boiling an egg or vacuuming the living room—into a kind of fluid dance, her body gracefully bending and flowing to accomplish the most mundane manoeuvres.

The apartment was quiet when she got back, the other tenants still at work or away for the holiday weekend.

Lucy hung up her coat and went into her bedroom to change. Tate was right: pale pink was not her best colour. Rummaging in the bottom drawer of her dresser, she pulled out a forest-green V-neck and decided that would work fine over her jeans. The pink top would go the Sally Ann, if Kara didn't want it. With auburn hair and lots of freckles, she seemed to like pastel colours, although Lucy was pretty sure Tate would take one look at her wardrobe and roll his eyes in despair. She smiled, remembering his serious expression when he was telling her about his designs.

Back in the kitchen, she found some tuna fish, some leftover quinoa in the fridge and a not-too-wilted lettuce and mixed them all up in a bowl. A sprinkle of sea salt, and it was ready.

She grabbed a fork from the drawer and sat down to eat. Yum. It was amazing how good simple food tasted when you were hungry. She couldn't imagine eating McDonald's burgers now. Her tastes had really changed, thanks to Marnie.

She spent the next hour doodling on her pad, jotting down ideas as she munched her salad. She felt drawn to do something more creative, and talking to Tate had stirred something inside her.

Right now, though, she needed to go grocery shopping before everyone took off early for the long weekend, jamming up the shopping aisles and cleaning out the fresh produce. She checked the time. Just coming up to 2pm.

She put her bowl in the sink, knocked back a glass of water, and was just about to go and brush her teeth when her phone rang.

"Hello?"

"Lucy? It's Nate. Sorry to bother you."

"That's okay," Lucy said. "How's Tate?"

"He's much better, thanks."

She could hear him in the background. *"No thanks to you!"*

"He means me, not you," Nate explained.

"Yeah! Tell Lucy why you gave me a headache!"

"Wow. He does sound better, although a little... *annoyed* with you, uncle?"

"Yes. He is." Nate paused. "Listen, would you mind coming back to the office this afternoon for a quick chat? There's something I'd like to discuss. About us working together..."

"Nate, I feel I should apologize for—"

"No, no. It's not you, Lucy... I'm just having a hard time working, right now. I'll explain when you get here."

"Okay. Well, I could be there in about half an hour..."

"That's perfect. See you shortly." He hung up.

What the hell...? So it *wasn't* about her? Or not her personally, but maybe her *work*?

Lucy went into the bathroom to brush her teeth. What was going on with her boss? Was she going to lose her job? Did he want to hire someone else? Had he realized that she just wasn't experienced enough to do all the stuff he needed her to do?

She caught sight of her frowning face in the mirror. *Stop! Wait and see what he says before you get all worked up.* She took a deep breath, brushed her hair, grabbed her shoulder bag and a light jacket from the hanger in the hallway, and went back outside into the sun.

It was just coming up to 2.30pm when she arrived back at the office. She let herself in the front door and knocked gently on the office door before going in.

Nate was sitting in one of the armchairs, his feet up on the coffee table, his face tight with worry.

He got up. "Lucy. Thanks so much for coming back in."

"No problem."

Tate was playing with Beemer on the floor beside her desk and didn't look up.

"Tate, go upstairs, please. I need to talk to Lucy."

Tate got up, glared at his uncle, and then stomped up the stairs, every step a noisy recrimination.

"Take a seat, Lucy." Nate gestured towards the other armchair, and Lucy sat down. She didn't take off her jacket as she wasn't sure if she'd be staying and might need to make a quick exit.

"What's going on, Nate?"

Tate shouted down from upstairs. "He's a coward, Lucy. He's afraid to tell you the truth. That's what gave me a migraine."

"Tate, we talked about this, buddy. I need some privacy here. Please go to your room."

"Not till you tell her the truth!"

"Look, Lucy, this is very awkward, especially with all this heckling from Midget Magoo upstairs, who has zero manners and won't shut up—"

"Tell her why you can't work with her."

Lucy felt her heart sink. "Look, if it's about my work…"

"No, it's not that."

"Is there a problem with the business? Is that it?"

Her heart lurched again. He looked ill and totally miserable.

"Are you sick? Is that it?"

"No, I'm not sick."

"He *is* sick," Tate said, charging down the stairs, unable to contain himself any longer. "He's *lovesick*, Lucy. Don't you get it?

And, suddenly, she did.

***

Lucy was stunned, unable to process what she'd just heard. Nate, in *love* with her. *That* was his problem?

Then she started to laugh. She laughed so hard she doubled over in her chair and felt tears rolling down her cheeks. She didn't care if her mascara smudged or if she wet the front of her T-shirt. She didn't care if she wet her pants. She laughed with relief and a sense of wonder.

Nate was looking at her with an anxious half-smile, not sure what to think. *Was she laughing at the idea of him loving her or was she laughing because she was happy?*

She could see his confusion and tried to pull herself together. "Sorry, sorry," she said. "That was just such a surprise. The last thing I expected to hear."

Tate was grinning. "I think she's happy, Nuncle."

"I think so, but I'm not sure…"

"Tell me about these migraines." Lucy forced herself to sober up. "You get them if people don't tell the truth, right?"

"Yeah, and other stuff they try to hide. It creates pressure in my head when people hold stuff back. You could feel it, Lucy."

"You're right. It doesn't feel comfortable if we know something is wrong but don't say it," Lucy said. "But how come your migraine went away so quickly, before we had this conversation and your uncle told the truth?"

"He said he'd tell you. I made him *promise*. I told him if he didn't tell you, I wouldn't nephew him any more."

"That was a deal-breaker," Nate said, "as I'm sure you can appreciate."

"Yes, of course. I get it," Lucy said. "This kind of nephew is far too precious to give up."

"And *then*," Tate continued, "he felt better, so I felt better too."

"I see." Lucy was still completely flummoxed. "Nate, I think I love your nephew."

Tate groaned and rolled backwards onto the floor in a mock faint.

"He doesn't care if you love ME," he said. "It's *him* he wants you to love!" Beemer came over to investigate, suspecting a game of let's-all-roll-on-the-floor, and Tate sat up to pat him. "Beemer, why are adults so stupid?"

Beemer did not seem to have the answer, although he seemed to like being asked.

"Of course I care if she loves you. Everyone should love you, you crazy genius." Nate beckoned him over. "Listen, kiddo, go upstairs and read your book. Leave us alone for a bit."

"No way. I'm not leaving. You need me. I'm like a marriage counsellor. That's what my mom says."

"You could go and watch TV."

Tate frowned. "You know my mom doesn't allow you to use the TV bribe."

"True. But I'm desperate," Nate said, laughing. "Lucy, you can see why I didn't introduce you to this relentless little truth guru sooner. I knew you'd love the fashion-design connection, but I also knew he'd completely blow my cover."

"I had to blow your cover!"

"I get it," Lucy said, smiling, "although how would we have managed without him?"

"I would have found a way to tell you eventually," Nate said, sheepishly. "I just hadn't figured out how or when."

"I thought you wanted me to leave. I couldn't figure out why—"

"I didn't want you to leave. I just couldn't see how to keep working with you, given the way I felt. It was starting to get very uncomfortable."

"So, what's the plan?" Tate looked from one to the other. "How are you going to fix this, Nuncle?"

"That's none of your business, Magoo. Upstairs. Now. Go and start making the goo-lash and I'll see Lucy out."

"Okay, okay," Tate said, heading for the stairs.

Nate looked at Lucy. "I don't want you to feel any pressure to respond right now... if you don't, you know, feel..."

"I do need some time to absorb all this," Lucy said. Like a *month*, or maybe just long enough to go and get her hair done and find something sexy to wear, in a *non-pastel* colour...

"I'm sorry about how that unfolded," Nate said, as they went into the hallway. "It wasn't how I, eh, hadn't planned it."

"I know," Lucy said. "It's awkward, with you being my boss and everything."

"I'd like to have a proper talk, when the midget matchmaker isn't around. Would that be okay?"

"Of course. It would be good to talk before the others get back to the office on Tuesday."

"My sister will be picking Tate up on Sunday afternoon. Let's talk after that."

When they got to the front door, Lucy turned to face him. "In the meantime, two things."

"Just two?"

"First, may I call you Nat? This Nate–Tate thing is driving me nuts."

"Yes, please." Nate smiled, then turned serious again. "And the second thing?"

"Would you like a hug?"

He didn't answer, just drew her to him and hugged her tight, one arm wrapped around her waist, the other cradling her head in the scoop of his neck. Lucy felt his tension slowly ease in her arms, and her own. Her heart was still reconfiguring the new terms, from *hands-off behave-yourself boss material,* to *help-yourself boyfriend buffet.*

"You've no idea how much I've wanted to do this," Nate said.

"Just out of curiosity," Lucy said, "since when…?"

"Since the day I met you outside your sister's place, all gorgeously fiery and pissed off at being interrupted by this random stranger off the street."

"Nine months," she said. "No wonder you're a wreck." She paused. "It hasn't been quite that long for me."

"What?" He pulled back to look at her. "Why didn't you tell me?"

"Why didn't *you* tell me? I was hardly going to tell my boss I fancied him and risk losing my job and embarrassing us both. I'm not *that* clueless."

He shook his head, smiling, and pulled her close again.

"Well, I feel I'm on the way to recovery. And *you* feel amazing."

"I *do* feel quite amazing." Lucy laughed. Then she whispered in his ear, "I think we're being watched," as Tate poked his head around the office door, grinning gleefully. "Finally!" he said. "*Now* I can go and make the goo-lash." They heard him scamper off and thump his way upstairs.

"He's quite something, your little nephew," Lucy said.

"He can be exhausting and a real pain in the neck," Nate said, "but he's worth every minute. I'm not sure if he's going to be the next US president or if he'll revamp the United Nations before he reaches his teens, but I have the feeling he won't be an accountant *or* a marriage counsellor."

"He'll definitely be the best-dressed, whatever he decides to be," Lucy said.

"You know you're welcome to come back later for dinner, but you probably need to rest as much as I do." With a sigh, he eased out of the hug and looked at her. "I haven't slept properly for weeks, worrying about this. And I'd really prefer to have you all to myself the next time we talk."

He did still look tired, Lucy thought. She suddenly felt exhausted too. Now that she'd finally relaxed, she realized how tense she had been, worrying about her job and Nate not being happy with her work. If she'd only known…

"I'm going to go grocery shopping, make dinner and get an early night," Lucy said. "But I look forward to our chat on Sunday."

"Not as much as me," he said. "Although who wouldn't want another 48 hours with the goulash Ninja."

She laughed, her heart still giddy while her brain warned of the urgent need for a defrag.

Nate opened the front door, hesitated, then took her face in both hands and gently kissed her forehead. "See you Sunday."

She re-entered the world, which seemed to have radically shifted on its axis since she'd been swept up into some magical parallel universe. The sun was sparkling, the trees were happy, and did she even *need* to buy food when she felt this jazzed?

Ten months ago, she'd been scaring old ladies with her thunderous looks. Now, she wanted to hug the world.

45

On the clifftop overlooking the restless sea, Celle had a favourite rock where she sat, in the noon-time shade of a golden cottonwood, contemplating love and loss and everything in between. And there was very little in between, it seemed. Loss so often came from need, which was simply love forgotten.

Back in the misremembered world of her former life, her work as a massage therapist belonged to another being altogether. The hands that had worked so many bodies no longer felt the need to knead. The relief of pain was hers alone to savour for as long as her soul desired.

She felt not bereft of family but replete with self. Entire weeks flowed by without her being aware of having parents. Distance had further dissolved the dysfunction and allowed for unfettered evolution. Connected to the larger natural world, she was inside herself completely. Here, the two seemed to fuse in effortless communion, their borders blurred by the searing sun and relentless ocean wash.

She had brought herself back—back from a lonely crowded place where you didn't even know you were missing. Now, if her body got too busy or her mind too fraught, she found herself missing inaction.

Here in Sayulita, despite the clamour of lives more crudely lived, her spirit was lulled into a gentler rhythm of existence. Yet she could still have fun, be young and carefree. And *carefree* came easily when life revolved around sun, sea, sand, surf, sex, siestas and salsa.

When she finally retraced the earthen trail back down to the beach, if felt like coming down from the mount. Not with more wisdom to share, but an even lesser need for the spoken word.

Sometimes, she did her own blend of intuitive bodywork on the tourists who over-extended themselves surfing or diving. For the sensation-seekers, pulled muscles, twisted ankles and aching lumbars were the regular results. Rather than massaging taut muscles into submission, Celle had a way of lifting tired limbs in an arc of gentle undulation—an invitation to surrender and unwind.

As for what her future held, she had no idea. For now, she was where she wanted to be: dwelling deeply in the vivid present moment.

As Matt morphed from grown man to mature male, just as she had so recently stepped into her fully feminine self, her heart stood by in compassionate allowance, waiting to see what emerged.

46

Sunday, 6 September 2020

"Happy birthday, Luce." Delsie sounded flat and far away. They hadn't seen each other for months and Lucy missed her friend's cheery presence.

"Thanks," Lucy said. "I'm so sorry you couldn't get here, Delsie. How's your mom?"

Delsie had promised to come to Boston for Lucy's birthday but her mom had fallen ill and Delsie, being an *only* whose dad had died when she was very young, was all the family her mother had. So Delsie had gone to Washington, DC, to be with her.

"She's okay, thanks…" But Delsie Roman didn't sound okay at all. It sounded as if she was sobbing.

"Delsie, what's wrong?"

"It's… I don't know. I just feel so *sad*… Something's going on. Something's not right." More sobs. "I can't stay on my phone. I'll e-mail to explain. Bye."

What was *that* about? Lucy had never heard her friend sound so distressed. If it wasn't about her mother, what was it?

She turned on her laptop and waited for it to boot up. It seemed to take longer every day. Maybe she needed to free up some memory or file space or something. She hadn't a clue. Maybe Nate would know. Nat, Nat, Nat. She had to practise calling him that …in case things worked out. She was telling herself not to get too excited and was trying not to think about seeing him later in the day.

Finally, her laptop was ready and she opened up her e-mail.

Nothing yet from Delsie… One from Matt, wishing her a happy birthday.

Hey, sis! Have a happy one. Then get your butt down here for some fun in the sun with us. It's all happenin'. Your lean-mean Mattso-bro xx

Lucy smiled. She was happy for Matt. Things seemed to be working out for him and Celle, although they still had stuff to sort out. *Who didn't?* Maybe she'd fly down there in October for a visit. It was almost a year since she'd seen her brother and she missed him. She liked that— that she missed him. It meant there was something between them worth missing. They'd come a long way since their parents had died.

There was a message from Marnie, of course. Her wonderful, faithful sis.

Happy birthday, Luce! May drop by later, if you're home. Tell me if when. Heading out for a walk – back by lunchtime. I've got pressies for you, and we must celebrate!

Lots of love,

Marn xxxxx

Her e-mail pinged and up popped a message from Delsie.

Lucy, there's something going on here that I can't explain. People are out on the street, bawling their eyes out. Businessmen sitting on park benches, sobbing. Teenagers having hysterics and clutching each other in group crying jags. It's unreal. And if I'm on my cellphone for more than a few secs, I start feeling sick and sad, like I'm in mourning for something. So don't call me. I can't use my phone. There's something creepy going on. Email instead, okay? I'll let you know when I figure out what's going on.

But don't let this spoil your B-day, okay? And send me every scrap of your news, girl. Missing you like crazy. Mom sends her love too.

Later!! xoxoxoxoxo

PS: The Man is no more... but I'm not sad about THAT.

Lucy sat back, bewildered. *What was going on?* Was this some kind of new virus that originated in DC?

She and Kara didn't have a TV in the apartment, but she pulled up a news channel on her laptop and looked for a headline referring to DC... There it was!

Sinister Emotional Syndrome Brings Washington, DC to its Knees – another deadly virus about to go global?

Lucy scrolled down. There were reports of people collapsing in tears on the street, just as Delsie had said. People were banging their heads against lampposts, moaning in grief.

She clicked on video footage that showed men in suits, tears streaming down their faces. Women were dropping cellphones, handbags and shopping bags and turning to each other for comfort and hugs. A few young children looked on, bewildered and visibly distressed at seeing their parents fall apart in front of them.

Others on the street were frantically pulling their cellphones from their pockets or bags to call for help, then dissolving in tears themselves, chucking their phones on the pavement.

What the hell... Would Marnie know what was going on? Lucy reached for her cellphone, then stopped herself. Best not to use her phone till she figured out what was happening. And it was only 10.30am, so Marnie was out anyway. No point in calling yet.

Lucy went back to her e-mail to compose a quick message to Marnie.

Thanks for bday wishes, Marn! Seeing Nate at 4.30pm and may stay into the evening to chat. Could we meet up tomorrow, holiday Monday? And have you seen this? xxx

She added a link to the webpage she'd found and hit SEND.

Should she call Nate–Nat? She eyed her cellphone warily. Best to just go there at 4.30pm, as arranged. Then they could talk about it in person.

In the meantime, she felt completely discombobulated. Kara had gone away for the holiday weekend, so she had the place to herself. She had left Lucy a big bunch of meadow flowers in a vase on the kitchen table and a new yoga mat in a lovely multi-coloured satin shoulder bag. Both had made Lucy smile when she got up, lifting her heart after a night of anxious restlessness and the recurring pain of losing her parents.

Lucy went back to the news webpage on her laptop but there was nothing new, and no new 'outbreaks', or whatever they were, anywhere else... *yet*, the news reporters were saying.

This was turning into the weirdest birthday ever. Her best friend was miles away, traumatized. The whole of DC seemed to be in meltdown. She wondered about the White House. Was everyone in government bawling their eyes out, too? She tried to imagine the President crying like a baby and couldn't. Maybe it would teach him some humility, whatever IT was, although she doubted it.

An e-mail pinged in from Marnie.

Luce, if you're with Nate this evening, let's celebrate tomorrow. Dinner or lunch on me. You choose. E me! Marn xxxx

Lucy smiled, her jittery heart softly steadied by Marnie's persistent presence. She'd reply later. Right now, she needed to get outside and soak up some nature in the park. This was all too weird.

She had turned 19 today and couldn't help thinking of her last birthday with her family, all obliviously happy and joking over dinner at the Sorellina restaurant. The last time she'd seen her parents alive. What would they make of the madness that had unfolded since they left?

They had always seemed to have reassuring answers to any questions Lucy had ever asked. She missed them painfully today and wished they could be here to help her make sense of this.

With a heavy sigh, she grabbed her bag and jacket and headed out to the park.

47

It was pandemonium in the news studio, and anchorman Rick Weston was already sweating under his shirt collar. With the panic on the streets over the cellphone phenomenon, there had been a frenzy of activity in the control room as the news line-up got reshuffled and wireless devices were either switched off or hard-wired. He was going over his notes yet again for the noon broadcast, with less than ten minutes to go.

Everyone in the studio had already broken down at least once—himself included. It was like being inside a mental institution, dodging colleagues in the corridor as they sobbed in wretched abandon, clawing the walls, and the director barking orders even as he mopped tears from his eyes and shuddered with waves of unchecked emotion.

What the fuck? He had no idea what was going on or how to deal with it. He still felt shaky from his own breakdown this morning, when he had tried to call his wife, and it had left him feeling exhausted and disorientated. He had no idea if she was okay or not but he would call her on one of the studio landlines as soon as he got off the air. Thank God they still had some wired phones.

Val, the producer—a perky young woman with spiky black hair and a beanpole body—was prepping him on his pitch, eyes still raw from her own morning meltdown, but he was finding it hard to focus as more reports came in of mass meltdowns and human tragedies all over the city.

"You know you won't be able to wear your earpiece," she was telling him now, as if he didn't already know. He had no intention of turning into a blubbering idiot in front of millions of viewers.

"You're *sure* all other wireless devices have been removed?" He had to be certain, before going on air.

"Yes, all checked," she said. "Damon swept the news desk out to a radius of 30 feet, so you should be clear." Damon was the sound engineer—a good guy who knew his stuff—and Rick felt reassured.

"So," Val continued, "watch for my hand cues in case we need to cut to commercials. Word is, you're to give this 15 minutes, if necessary. Focus on the emotional aspect, not the cellphones. The Board want us to soothe the public and minimize the panic." She rolled her eyes at this mission impossible, and consulted her clipboard.

"We know the line Spence will take, so make sure he doesn't take over. He's going to slam the wireless industry, as usual, but you know what Sutter said this morning. Stick to the usual parameters, keep things neutral and, of course, take your usual *balanced view*." She gave him a look, eyebrows raised.

He knew damn well how the director, Ronald Sutter, wanted him to pitch things. It had been drummed into him often enough—the pressure on the station to avoid any overt condemnation of the wireless industry, allowing some of the naysayers to pitch in but then cancelling them out with industry rebuttal. As usual, it all came down to funding and the power of the industry to shut them down if they didn't toe the line.

But it might not work this time, he thought. Their usual go-to industry *experts* had no clue what was going on and didn't want to be drawn into a debate… yet. Although *that* wouldn't last long. They were working on their spin and would have plenty to say once they'd figured out a way to cover their asses. Another few hours, and he could expect a highly finessed spiel to land on his desk for dissemination to appease the panicking masses.

He was getting tired of being told what to say, not say and to disregard his instincts. He was nothing more than a malleable mouthpiece—a marionette, dancing to whatever twisted tune was politically expedient.

He remembered being a naïve young producer, busting his ass with crazy hours, urgent deadlines, constantly changing briefs, in the hope of reaching the elevated status of newscaster so he could bring people breaking news and human-interest stories that made some kind of meaningful difference.

Now, here he was at 38, feeling like 50—a jaded actor in a B movie, mouthing the words and trying to stay in character when he wanted to tell them all to go fuck themselves.

Rick took his place at the news desk, shuffling his papers and readying his smile as he got the final countdown.

Three, two, one... he was live.

48

When Lucy got back from her walk, she pulled up the same webpage as before to see what other news had come in.

There were reports of a school bus crashing on the outskirts of Washington, DC, killing four of the children on board and injuring several others. The driver had been on his cellphone when half the children on the bus started crying for their mothers and rushing to the front of the bus, trying to get off. Then he too fell apart with grief and lost control of the bus, which swerved across two lanes of traffic and crashed into the median, tipping over and coming to a halt, facing in the other direction.

Multiple crashes and pile-ups were being reported on streets and highways around the city, as drivers lost control of their vehicles due to using their phones while driving. Routes were completely blocked by mangled vehicles and incoherent drivers and passengers sobbing in their cars or on the pavement.

The White House had issued an emergency directive to all airlines to ground all flights out of Reagan, Dulles and Baltimore airports until this bizarre situation had been brought under control. Under no circumstances were pilots to fly any aircraft—commercial or private—until further notice.

It was a miracle that no planes had crashed, Lucy thought, given how suddenly this thing had erupted and caused instant chaos on the ground.

She clicked on a video newscast that had just been posted, giving an update on the situation, from downtown Washington.

On the street, the female news reporter looked red-eyed and distraught, the microphone in her hand shaking uncontrollably. In the background, people surged in a mad mêlée of flailing limbs and hysterical cries. Many were running blindly across the street behind the reporter, car horns blaring and brakes screeching around them, without looking or caring where they were going, seemingly intent on getting home to check on loved ones or to process their grief in private.

"We have all been deeply affected by this strange phenomenon sweeping across Washington, DC," the reporter said, raising her voice and edging away from the mayhem so she could be heard above the noise. "Back in the news studio, many of us have personally experienced the effects of being on a wireless device and having a kind of emotional breakdown. As you can see…"—she pointed to her microphone—"I am now using a wired microphone, as the wireless one was making it impossible for me to function normally."

She took a deep breath. "We just received the tragic news that our news helicopter has crashed over the Charles River, near Memorial Drive, killing all on board." She drew another deep breath and wiped her eyes, clearly having difficulty maintaining her composure.

"Our news team had gone out to… cover the initial incidences of this phenomenon, not realizing it was linked to cellphone use, and the pilot, cameraman and reporter… were all using their cellphones as they overflew the city. We have some… very disturbing audio feed from the pilot, just before he lost control of the chopper and broke contact."

The microphone was shaking like a metronome and the reporter seemed close to breaking down. "We will bring you more updates as the situation unfolds," she said, nodding wordlessly at the cameraman for him to cut the feed and abruptly walking off-camera.

Lucy was stunned. It felt as if the world was falling apart. She clicked on another video of an interview with a Dr Raynor Spence. That name rang a bell… Wasn't that the physicist Marnie had mentioned a few months ago—the one who seemed to have similar expertise to their parents?

She hit PLAY.

News anchor Rick Weston was speaking to camera. "Joining me now on Skype is Dr Raynor Spence, who made headlines earlier this year when he claimed to be able to release a deadly virus via the internet."

A screen opened up on his left, showing Dr Spence sitting in his home office.

"Thank you for joining us, Dr Spence."

Dr Spence nodded, allowing a sober smile.

"You were cleared of any wrongdoing, back in January, but you clearly have expertise in this area. Could you give us your take on what the wireless telecom industry is calling *a random fluke reaction to cellphones?*

"Yes, certainly. Let me start by translating that for you. It is industry-speak for: *We haven't a clue what this is, but please don't stop paying your cellphone bill."*

Rick smiled. "Are you saying they are not behind this?"

"I can't imagine why they would be," Dr Spence said. "They're not in the habit of shooting themselves in the foot."

He gave a somber smile and looked directly at the camera. "What we see happening here is merely a more graphic portrayal of the harm this technology can cause. And while I mourn the tragic loss of those small children on that bus, as well as all the other lives lost today, I must point out that the loss of life due to mobile telephony has been ongoing and exponential since long before 4G and 5G got rolled out, but people have simply not made that connection. Now, they are being forced to do so as the effects are immediate and devastating—right there for all to see and to experience first hand."

Rick jumped right in. "But our governments and the World Health Organization have repeatedly told us that—"

Dr Spence held up a hand. "I'm going to stop you right there, Rick. I will play no part in any conversation that perpetuates the denial of the proven dangers of this technology. If you choose to continue supporting the industry spin on your news channel, you will be actively promoting the loss of even more lives." He looked at Rick pointedly and waited.

Rick finally nodded his agreement, but he was clearly unhappy about his spiel getting spiked. "So what do you believe is causing this phenomenon? Is there some virus being transmitted via cellphones, as you suggested could possibly happen, back in January?"

"No. This is not a virus. It is clearly not being transmitted from person to person but directly from a cellphone to whichever individual happens to be using it. It is not selective and it is not targeting a particular age group or demographic. All cellphone users are equally affected, although the degree of their emotional collapse seems to vary depending on their particular emotional state—how much grief or suppressed emotion they are carrying."

He paused to take a breath. "What is also becoming clear is that the impact becomes stronger with repeated use. So if individuals regain some composure and pick up their phone again to make a call, they are even harder hit than the first time around."

"But what is causing this? If it's not a virus or some kind of pathogen, what is it?"

"Cellphones and all wireless devices work through particular radio frequencies," Dr Spence said. "Those frequencies are harmful to all forms of life, with multiple known biological effects on our blood, brain, nervous system, emotional state, cognition, immunity and every bodily function, but there are many other frequencies that cause other effects—frequencies that can be transmitted to cellphone users just as directly as the calls or texts they wish to send or receive on their devices." He paused to let this information sink in.

"But where is it coming from? If it's coming through their cellphones, doesn't that mean the wireless industry is doing this?"

"Well, I'm glad you're finally looking at the industry itself," Dr Spence said, smiling, "although this kind of thing hardly seems to be in their best interests, as I said."

"So you're saying it's definitely *not* the wireless industry doing this," Rick said.

"Who am I to say who is doing this?" Dr Spence shrugged. "But what you are suggesting doesn't make sense, commercially speaking, and commercial profit is the only thing the industry is interested in."

"Some people have wondered if *you* did this," Rick said, leaning towards him.

"Well, that seems to be a popular approach," Dr Spence said. "I'm flattered to be considered so powerful but I really don't have that kind of power."

"So who *could* have done this? And how could those frequencies, whatever they are, get into people's cellphones if the wireless industry didn't put them there?"

"That's a very good question," Dr Spence said, nodding thoughtfully. "Frequencies permeate the air, otherwise we couldn't have wireless connectivity the way we do. In fact, everything has a frequency— sound, light, colour, plants, bacteria and every living cell in every living organism. So, as I've said before, if it is possible to transmit certain kinds of pathogens via radio waves—and it is—then certain other frequencies on that spectrum can also be transmitted, and they can ride the existing waves produced by the wireless industry, just as our bodies produce their own electromagnetic waves and the Earth itself produces its own subtle resonance."

Rick looked puzzled. "But how... how do those frequencies get there. We can't see or touch them, right? So how are they manipulated or contained or whatever the term is for them to be directed to people's phones?"

"Frequencies can be generated," Dr Spence said, choosing his words carefully. "Just as the wireless industry generates them from cell towers all over the globe. So, in theory, you'd just need a device that generated certain frequencies in the same way."

"Could that be done using the industry's existing devices?"

"You mean, could these frequencies hitch-hike on the wireless telecom industry's networks? Yes, of course, as I explained before. That is entirely possible."

"Is there some way to determine this? People want to know what's going on," Rick pressed, suddenly a champion for the rights of the people.

"That's another strange phenomenon isn't it?

"What is?"

"For as long as they could use their gadgets, people didn't want to know. In fact, they wanted *not* to know of any downsides or negative effects from their cellphones. But now that their phones are causing havoc and they can't use them, they demand to know what's going on." He shook his head. "Yet another of the many tragic ironies around this issue."

"That may be so, Dr Spence, but cellphones are key to the functioning of the economy."

"And we mustn't upset the economy." Dr Spence smiled wryly. "Humans will contain themselves, hold back even their deepest, most precious feelings and do whatever it takes to support the economy because they believe it keeps them safe. But that model isn't working so well any more, it seems."

"People are losing their minds, Dr Spence. Don't you care about that?"

Dr Spence sat back. "That must surely be the biggest irony of all. This is the second time I've been asked on TV the very questions that should have been asked of governments and the wireless industry for the past three decades. Why are you so intent on blaming the scientists and whistleblowers? So the industry and the economy can be protected at all costs?"

He paused. "People are not losing their minds. They are simply getting in touch with their emotions."

"But they're collapsing on the street, having emotional breakdowns. You don't call that losing your mind?

"No. I don't."

"But surely this is an illness, what we see happening here…" Rick was clearly convinced the phenomenon was a sickness interfering with people's right to use their cellphone. "Something must be getting transmitted to them through their phone."

"Yes, I agree. Something is. But it's not a bacterium, a virus or a pathogen. It's a frequency, as I said, triggering an internal dynamic, not depositing some nasty bug in people's bodies. There is no external pathology here. There is simply the triggering of emotions that already exist inside the person being triggered."

He paused and looked at Rick appraisingly. "Earlier today, I spoke on the phone to some of those affected in Washington," he said. "I asked them what they felt or thought about when they were upset. One woman said she felt deep sorrow at not being there for her mother when she was dying. She had been so wracked with guilt that she had never allowed herself to grieve. She said she also felt huge sadness over her marriage and her relationship with her two daughters, who were distant, angry and didn't seem to care about her. In the same way that she hadn't cared about her own mother."

He gave Rick a meaningful glance. "A young man told me that he was cut up because he had become an accountant, which was what his father wanted him to do, rather than becoming the musician he wanted to be. And a teenage girl told me she felt suicidal because her parents never had time for her, she was being bullied at school and she felt totally alone and unloved."

He sighed, shaking his head at the sorrowful weight of people's pain. "So, you see, these emotions are not random. People are not just falling apart because they have been affected by some pathogen that has damaged them mentally and caused them to lose their minds." He paused before concluding. "If anything," he said, "they are *finding* their humanity."

"Thank you, Dr Spence. Stay with us, please." Rick turned front again to face the camera. "Since this is such an emotional issue, we have invited renowned psychotherapist Dr Vera Virstenberg to give us her expert opinion on what is happening."

Another screen opened up beside the one with Dr Spence, revealing a woman in her late 50s, with curly grey hair, kind blue eyes and a warm smile.

"Dr Virstenberg, thank you for joining us," Rick said.

"Please, call me Dr Vera. Virstenberg is such a long name and I'm not getting any younger." Her smile deepened the lines around tired, wise eyes that had seen a world of sadness and pain.

Rick nodded. "Dr Vera, you've heard what Dr Spence had to say on this issue. What do you, as a psychotherapist, make of it all?"

"Firstly, there are many devastating tragedies unfolding across our city," Dr Vera said, "and my heart goes out to all those affected. That in itself is having a huge impact on the collective psyche. I don't think we've ever witnessed such a thing before, and it is likely to change things significantly, in terms of how we relate to ourselves, to each other and to technology."

She paused. "I am lucky, in a sense, in that I am fairly old-school. I still have a landline at home and I rarely use a cellphone. While I cannot help everyone, I would like to offer what assistance I can, free of charge, to those who have suffered a personal loss and feel unable to cope with what is happening."

Rick nodded. "Thank you, Dr Vera. We'll post your contact information on our webpage." He gestured for her to continue.

"As for the phenomenon itself, it certainly raises many emotional and ethical issues and questions," she said. "Is the release of all these suppressed emotions a sickness to be contained with medication? Or is it a gift to be appreciated, since it frees up so much psychic space and enables individuals to process things they had denied or couldn't move beyond?"

She paused, reflecting. "Is the fallout the fault of the government, in allowing a harmful technology to be used, or the fault of whoever provoked the emotional breakdowns? This issue of responsibility is always very significant in therapy, where individuals tend to seek someone to blame, until they are ready to explore whatever role they may have played in their situation. No doubt this will be hotly debated among all the various stakeholders, but those individuals personally affected will inevitably end up either doing a great deal of soul-searching or venting their anger at governments or at an industry that they may feel has let them down terribly."

She sighed. "Are people losing their minds—or, as Dr Spence says, finding their humanity? On this last point, at least, I would have to agree with him. Much humanity has been lost through cellphone use. Now, with this provoked emoting, people are feeling their feelings and turning to each other since they can no longer turn to their cellphones."

She inclined her head, reflecting. "I find it very interesting that we are seeing the opposite of what happened with the virus earlier this year, which caused social distancing. With this new phenomenon, strangers on the street are reaching out for hugs and emotional support as they experience deep grief. And that grief, as Dr Spence pointed out, relates to whatever sadness, loss or heartache they have been carrying—many of them for their entire lives." She spread her hands. "How can that *not* be a good thing?"

She raised a hand before Rick could intervene. "Please, do not misunderstand me. I am deeply saddened by the loss of life today, and I am not saying that such loss is in any way justified. Simply that, in and of itself, emotional release is usually a good thing and a necessary part of healing and growth."

"If that is true," Rick said, "why are people panicking so much?"

"It's not really the emotions themselves that are causing people to panic," Dr Vera said. "It's the loss of control. That is what is so scary. We don't like to lose control—especially in public. It's hard enough for most people to let themselves get emotional in a therapist's office, but to be *forced* to lose control in a public or professional setting—to lose one's composure, one's dignity and physical control over everyday motions and activities… that is truly frightening when we are so socially conditioned to hide our emotions and behave *appropriately*."

"Yes, indeed," Rick said. "But people are unable to function properly when they are in such a state."

"But what does that mean, Rick—to *function properly*? Does it mean operating unemotionally, robotically, getting things done without allowing any messy emotions to get in the way? Or have we forgotten what it means to function properly, as human beings?"

She gave him a kind smile, as if addressing him personally. "As a psychotherapist, I regularly see people crippled by emotional angst, suppressed guilt, grief or sadness, and an inability to fully feel or process their emotions. That is not normal or healthy. It does not produce healthy, happy, productive individuals who love life and themselves. So I suppose it depends on what value you put on the human heart, with all its wondrous, spontaneous, delightful, touching, powerful qualities—qualities that define humanity itself and make us *human*."

She paused, reflecting. "Perhaps we are asking the wrong questions. Rather than asking how we can bypass, contain, control or get rid of this inconvenient phenomenon, perhaps we should instead ask what good can come of it. What are our hearts and our psyches trying to tell us that we haven't been able to hear? And why are we so much more emotionally connected when we are deprived of virtual connectivity, while the door to our hearts is thrown open for all to see and feel?"

She paused again. "I'd like to add something else that I think viewers will find interesting," she said. "And Dr Spence also, I imagine. I understand that some frequency is possibly being used to trigger this emotional release. If so, I see it as acting like a kind of truth serum. It is bringing people face to face with their own emotional denial—and, once they've processed that, with their deeper truth."

Rick Weston turned to Dr Spence on the other screen. "Dr Spence, do you have any thoughts on that?"

"I think what Dr Vera says makes perfect sense. This appears to be a process of exposing cover-ups of all kinds—personal, emotional, governmental and industry-related. We all hide things from ourselves if we don't want to face an inconvenient truth, but this phenomenon is pushing us past our usual restraints and forcing us to see beneath the façades that we ourselves have created."

Dr Spence nodded soberly to himself. "It's ironic, too, since most of society has regrettably become such a sham, with businesses using friendships and other emotionally charged strategies to hook customers and sell products or services. Now, with grief and sadness being so graphically associated with cellphones, and so viscerally *exorcised* by them, perhaps we will see just how powerful our emotions are and what it has cost us to keep them repressed."

On the other screen, Dr Vera was nodding in agreement, eager to jump back in.

Rick nodded in her direction. "Dr Vera?"

"Thank you, Rick—and I *love* what you said there, Dr Spence. It brings me back to those essential questions I mentioned earlier. People may be asking: *What can I do to not be affected? Will this cause me to lose control? Will it wreck my business, my relationship, my life? Is there any way to avoid it?*"

She spread her hands and shared a warm smile. "As Dr Spence so correctly pointed out, we cannot sustain our denial in the face of this cleansing, exorcising force. Avoidance is no longer an option."

"Will this put you out of a job, Dr Vera?" Rick asked.

She smiled sadly. "I would be only too happy if we no longer needed psychotherapy to deal with our tangled emotions," she said. "I would simply switch my focus to helping others—and myself—find a new direction, once reunited with the fullest expression of our emotional prowess. I see emotional honesty as one of our most powerful human qualities, and if we all allowed ourselves to express it in healthy ways, the world would be a very different place."

Dr Spence was nodding as she spoke. "I applaud your wisdom and generosity, Dr Vera," he said, "and I am reassured to know that humanity is still alive and well in so many good people."

Recognizing the perfect sound-bite sign-off, Rick turned back to the camera. "On that positive note… many thanks to Dr Vera Virstenberg and Dr Raynor Spence for joining us today."

49

May 2007

"Daniel, come *on*!" Frannie was yelling up the basement stairs, impatient to get back to the lab. "We've got to *work* on this."

"I'm going to play ball with Matt," Daniel said, coming halfway down the staircase. "He needs some time with his dad. They *all* need some time with us, Frannie." He trod heavily down the last few steps to join her. "This is killing us as a family."

"I know!" Frannie glared at him, stuck between saving them the only way she knew how, and caving in to the demands of motherhood, which felt like letting everyone down. "What's happening out there is going to kill us *all* if we don't crack this. If we do, at least we die winners, rather than dying losers."

"Brilliant," Daniel said sardonically. "How do I explain that to our 6-year-old little girl? Explain it to *me*, first, would you? How exactly do we *win* if we die trying to survive?"

"We take the bastards down. Won't you be happy knowing you've saved the kids, plus a few billion others?"

"The kids need saving *now*, if they're going to have any kind of life. And if I'm not around to enjoy it with them later, will any of this matter? In fact, if I'm not around to even know we've *won*, it could all be for nothing. Anything can happen when we change something. You know that, Frannie. And once we're gone, we won't be able to fix it." Daniel was bristling with frustration. *There was no one more stubborn or brilliant or right even when she was wrong than this woman...*

"Could you please *trust* me on this? I have a plan, okay?"

"I *do* trust you... on the science. But you need to trust me—and yourself—with some of the parenting. It's not that difficult, Frannie. You just have to show up, once in a while. It's Saturday afternoon, for God's sake. One of us, at least, has to be there for them."

She glared at him again, furious at being reminded.

"I need a break, too. You can work on your own for a few hours. I'll help this evening, when the kids are in bed." Daniel turned to go back upstairs.

"Daniel, we *need* to work on these gravitational waves. If we can get the energy converters working and hooked into the background gravitational field, we should be able to figure out the modulation process using the harmonizing oscillators. Then we'll know if it's viable."

She looked up at Daniel, her eyes on fire. "Imagine if we can get this to work! Communication without any of that crappy radiation! The Russians had that figured out long ago. I don't know why they stopped." She shook her head, already lost in another world. "But don't you *see*? It's not just about *communication*. We can use this system for all those *other* frequencies we want to put out there, without anyone knowing, and we don't even need a transmitter!"

She cocked her head, as if remembering he was still there. "Are you with me on this? If you can see an alternative to this alternative, I'll be happy to explore it."

"I know that kind of *happy*—you kicking and screaming all the way, saying nothing else but this will work."

"Hon, we're running out of time. If we don't crack this, we'll definitely die losing. I'm willing to die trying, but if you want to try dying without doing any of this stuff, I guess I'll have to find me another man. But where the hell I'm going to find another brain like yours, attached to a body like yours, with a heart like yours, and a decent wardrobe, I have no idea."

Daniel groaned. "Same old, same old *franipulation*."

Frannie grinned. "Yeah, I forgot that bit."

"Me being such a pushover?"

"More like Fran-friendly," she said.

"You need to get friendly with your kids," he said, turning to go back upstairs.

"Could you play with Matt later?"

"Okay, that does it. You're coming with me." He grabbed her round the waist and hauled her up the first few steps of the stairs. No mean feat, given her tall frame.

"Hey, kids! Mum's coming up to play with us. She insists!"

"You call *me* manipulative!" Frannie was pissed off, on principle, but trying not to laugh as it would spoil the effect.

"I learned from a master." He put her down and took her by the hand so she couldn't escape. "Frannie, pretend you actually *love* them, okay?"

"Of *course* I love them, you evil man."

"Well, don't keep it a secret. How are they supposed to know that if you never spend any time with them?"

Frannie flounced up the stairs, stopping dead at the top when she saw Lucy's excited face. Lucy took her breath away when she looked at her like that—a mirror image of herself but a bubbling fountain of joy. *Please, God, don't let me ruin her.* It was like getting another chance to be her sweet self, having this miniature replica of the now-flawed original.

Looking through to the kitchen, Frannie could see Marnie at the sink with a glass of water, and Matt bouncing his basketball around the kitchen floor.

Lucy was desperate for her attention. "Mummy, Daddy says you're a… um…"

She ran over to Daniel and he leaned down to whisper in her ear. She dashed back to Frannie, gleeful. "You're a… *fran-attic!*"

"That's not a real word," Matt said, coming into the hallway, still bouncing his ball.

"It nearly is," Marnie added behind him, ever the diplomat.

"What does it mean, Dad?" Lucy asked.

"Well, the real word is *fanatic*, which means someone who does far too much of something, but because we stuck a little bit of mum's name at the front, it means something nicer—someone who doesn't have enough fun."

Lucy turned back to her mother, pondering this. "Mum, you need more fun." She frowned, brain working furiously. "I think you should be a… *fun-attic!*" She jumped up and down, delighted with herself.

Daniel laughed and Frannie almost cried. This beautiful child was hers—*hers! How had this happened?*

"Mummy! You're coming out to play with us!"

"Course I am, sweetie. Daddy tried to keep me prisoner in the lab but I *insisted* on coming up."

Daniel rolled his eyes and Frannie smiled at him sweetly, mouthing a kiss.

He took it at face value, grinning back. That face still stole his heart.

Matt did not look convinced. Cynical at 9, he was not so easily won over. Just like she had been, Frannie thought. Not a great legacy. But sweet Marnie was beaming, always ready to believe in her mum and make allowances.

"Hey, I've got an idea," Daniel said, determined to unite them all. "Let's make Saturday afternoon the day kids rule."

"What does that *mean*, Daddy?" Lucy asked, unsure of her commitment. "A new rule for kids?"

"No, it means *you* get to make the rules. Every Saturday afternoon, one of you three gets to choose what activity we do."

"I'm going to shoot hoops with dad," Matt declared, basketball tucked under his arm as he headed for the door. "You can do girly stuff."

"Can I choose first, Mum?" Lucy looked at her beseechingly.

"Yes, Your Majesty. What would you like to do?" Frannie lifted her up and swung her round. Lucy squealed in delight, flinging out her arms for more momentum.

"Play badminton outside!"

Frannie looked at Marnie. "Okay with you, sweetie?"

"*I* decide," Lucy declared. "*I* rule today. You *said*, Mummy!"

"True. Sorry."

Marnie smiled indulgently, turning to the hallway cupboard for rackets and shuttlecocks. "It's okay, Mum. We can play."

It was sunny and hot outside, blue-sky perfect, and Frannie felt her sallow skin expand as it soaked up the sunlight.

They had a net strung across the grass in front of the deck, and Lucy ran to one end of their makeshift court, jumping up and swatting the air with her racket. Matt and Daniel were at the side of the house, where they had a hoop over the garage door.

"Marnie, you're about 100 times better at this than me, so I'll play with Lucy for a bit, okay? Then I'll collapse and watch you two girls play."

She wasn't joking. She knew how unfit she was. Long days of mouse work, with very little housework, was not ideal for staying in shape. Daniel teased her about not being very *domestic*, but she laughed it off, knowing how pointless it was trying to stay on top of things upstairs when she was so engrossed with cosmic stuff downstairs in the lab. "It's amazing how much dust can accumulate in just a year or two," she said, as he rolled his eyes. "Who can keep up?"

He had lamented the state of the place when they had been without a housekeeper for a while, although he did more than his fair share of cleaning-crisis management. "The cobwebs around those door jambs are as thick as hinges," he commented one morning. "Good back-up," Frannie had replied.

She definitely needed the exercise. Joining Lucy, she turned to face the net. "Okay, girls, let's go!"

Marnie lobbed the birdie over the net, looking fiercely serious. Lucy ran for it and flicked it up in the air, nowhere near the net. She grabbed it off the grass and tried again, finally getting it over.

Marnie sent her some gentle shots, but Lucy kept missing, shrieking with laughter. At least she was keeping herself amused, Frannie thought. *How easy it was to please them, really.*

"Hey, don't I get a shot?" She should at least *try* to have some fun.

"Yeah, Mum, you try!" Lucy handed her the birdie.

Frannie lobbed it over the net in the vague vicinity of Marnie, who nimbly tossed it back to her before Frannie had a chance to move. She swiped thin air, missing completely.

Lucy collapsed into giggles. "Mum, you're hopeless! You're supposed to run!"

"I know, I know. I fell like an ephelump."

Lucy giggled again. "An elephant!"

"Watch who you're calling an elephant!" Frannie swatted her gently on the bottom with her racket.

"Not *me*, Mummy. *You* did!"

"Ahem. Could we *play*, please?" Even Marnie sometimes got impatient.

They lopped the birdie back and forth for another 15 minutes, missing more often than not, and Frannie could see that Marnie was not exactly getting a run for her mummy.

"Girls, I'm exhausted!" Frannie said. "I've got to stop. You play and I'll watch for a while."

She sat on the grass beside the net and watched her two girls love each other. As the shuttlecock floated through the air, punctuated by Lucy's laughter, Frannie was reminded about standing gravitational waves and what the Russians had discovered. How those waves organized all particles into synchronous oscillations, so communication could be instant... Unlike electromagnetic waves, they did not cause electro-pollution because all life on Earth had adapted to them over millions of years and depended on them for healthy biological processes.

The Russians knew you could use the Earth's benign, naturally occurring electromagnetic fields as carrier waves for information transfer. But natural frequencies couldn't be sold, patented or monopolized, which was partly why they had never been used. The *main* reason, Frannie knew, was human stupidity—not even thinking to look to nature for healthy answers or knowing they were needed.

Ray would love this, she thought—that information could be transported by existing natural wave processes, without even needing a transmitter... *or* greedy governments.

It was so *simple*, when you realized how it worked. Just using nanocrystals, a resonator... She was already constructing it in her head. Once she got the basic set-up in place, she could then work with the other frequencies to—

"Mum! You're not listening!"

Lucy was suddenly beside her, hot and thirsty.

"Sorry, sweetie. Have you finished? You need a drink?"

"We want to make fizzy drinks then take Maisie's dogs for a walk in the fields."

"Okay," Frannie said, trying to hold onto her mental construction and still be present with her daughters.

Matt and Daniel came around the side of the house, male bonding done for the day.

"What's next, Your Majesty?" Daniel asked Lucy.

"We're going to get drinks, Daddy, then take the dogs for a walk. You have to come with us."

"Absolutely." Daniel lifted her up on his shoulders. "You rule, remember?" He looked at his watch. "We've got another hour before dinner, so get your drink then see if Maisie will let you take the dogs out."

"Okay!" Lucy scrambled down, ran up the steps to the deck and went inside, Marnie following more sedately.

Frannie was lost in thought, barely there.

"Earth to Frannie?"

"What? Just thinking… I might have to go in and make a few quick notes…"

Daniel shot her a *don't-you-dare* look. "You're coming with us, end of story."

Matt caught the vibe. "What's the *point* if she doesn't want to be with us, Dad?"

Lucy appeared on the deck, slurping from a huge glass of fizzing liquid.

"Matty, you're right," Frannie said. "I'm being a selfish cow."

Matt nodded in agreement, and Daniel gave him a warning look.

"She said it, Dad, not me."

He could hardly argue with that.

Lucy needed to set the record straight before things got any more complicated. "Mum, you're not a *cow*, you're a fun-attic now, remember?"

"Keep reminding me, Luce. I need to practise more and you're the best teacher ever."

Lucy grinned. "It's not hard to have fun, Mummy. It's much harder to *work*. Isn't it, Daddy?"

"Of course it is. We all need to have more fun and do less work." He smiled at Frannie, putting his arm around her shoulders as they headed inside.

Marnie was in the kitchen, drinking a tall glass of water from the tap.

Frannie stood beside her at the sink. "You played really well out there, sweetie. Thank you for being so patient with me." She kissed the top of Marnie's head. "Will you go next door with Lucy when you've finished your drink, and we'll be ready when you get back with the dogs?"

"Are you sure?" Marnie turned to face her. She kept her voice low, talking as a parent to a child, not wanting the others to hear.

"Of course I'm sure. I think it's a great idea."

"I mean are you sure you'll be here when we get back, and not down in your lab again?"

Frannie took a breath. The gravitational waves and the rest of the weighty world would have to wait. The gravity of her children's needs was tugging at her more fiercely than the urge to document her ideas. She needed to achieve greater resonance and a better connection with the aching hearts right here in front of her. And maybe save her own at the same time. Daniel was right. This togetherness was precious.

"Yes, sweetie. I promise. I'll be here."

"I don't want you to disappoint Lucy."

"I don't want to disappoint *you*, either."

"I'm used to it. Lucy isn't." *Yet...*

Marnie didn't say it, but she didn't need to. They both knew it was waiting to happen.

50

Sunday, 6 September 2020

It was just after 4.30pm when Lucy rang the bell at Nate's place. She could have used her own key but it didn't feel right to just walk right in when she was there for personal reasons.

She was nervous, still unravelling her feelings for her boss and unclear about how to move forward. How *did* you move forward with so much freaky stuff happening in the world? Was some sick terr—

The door opened and Nate was there in all his handsome Nateness. Her stomach tumbled and her heart danced, while her face smiled … and in she went.

"You could have used your own key," Nate said, giving her a quick sideways hug. "Come on up."

He led her through the office. She hadn't been upstairs before and she felt as if her status were changing with every step as she climbed the stairs to his personal space.

A door at the top opened into a spacious bright living area, with the same large windows as in the office. A navy sectional couch contoured a multi-coloured woollen rug in the centre of the room, a coffee table in the middle. There was a large plasma TV screen opposite, and a wooden dining table with wooden chairs under one window. Shelves lined the back wall, crammed with books.

The apartment had the same configuration as the floor below, with the kitchen on the other side of the partition wall and bedrooms down the corridor.

But what drew Lucy's attention was the huge photographs on the walls. Up-close images of wizened ethnic faces looked straight at her, piercing her with their unflinching gaze. The photos had a surreal quality to them and seemed to be mounted in resin or acrylic, giving the appearance of vivid three-dimensionality.

She turned to Nate. "Are these yours?"

"Yes," he said, smiling at her reaction.

"They're amazing. I had no idea you were a talented photographer, on top of being a savvy businessman."

"Thanks. I've travelled a bit in Latin America," he said. "I've always been fascinated by those cultures and their ancient wisdom."

"You've certainly captured their essence," Lucy said, still captivated by the images.

Nate nodded modestly as Lucy took off her jacket and placed it on the back of a chair.

"Please…" He gestured towards the couch. "Take a seat."

Only then did she notice Beemer lying on the rug, tail thumping, looking exhausted.

"We've just been for a run," Nate explained, "so please excuse him for not getting up to greet you."

Lucy laughed. "That's okay. We know each other well enough to make allowances for that kind of thing."

"Something to drink, Lucy? I've got sparkling mineral water, red wine, beer…"

"Just some water, thanks." She sat down on the couch and leaned forward to pat Beemer. "Have you seen what's happening in Washington?" she asked as Nate was getting the drinks from the kitchen.

"Yeah. Freaky. I watched a few news reports then had to get out for a walk. I can't wrap my brain around it, but I'm staying off my phone until we know what's going on." He came back to the living room, put her glass of water on the coffee table and sat down beside her.

"Oh. Hang on. Almost forgot." He got up, disappeared down the corridor and came back holding a gift-wrapped box.

"Happy birthday, Lucy," he said, handing her the box and sitting down beside her again.

"How did you know it was my birthday?" she said, surprised.

"All those tax forms you filled out six months ago, when you went full time. They have their uses."

He nodded towards the box. "It's a rather… *practical* gift, but I thought it might be a good idea."

"I think I love it already," she said, touched by his thoughtfulness… *or did she mean him?*

She peeled off the wrapping paper to reveal a box depicting a funky bright-yellow telephone—the old-fashioned wired kind with large buttons and a wired handset. She looked up at him, puzzled.

"With that stuff happening in Washington, with cellphones, I wanted you to be safe," he said, "just in case it spreads here." He paused. "And I wanted to be able to reach you."

His concern brought a lump to her throat, and she leaned forward to kiss him on the cheek. "Thank you, Nate. This is a really good idea. I didn't want to use my cellphone this morning after seeing the news, so having this will be a big relief."

"If you don't have a land line installed in your apartment, you can get a VOIP line and run it through your router," he said. "But you'll need to hard-wire your laptop too, and switch off the WiFi, just in case."

"WiFi too?"

"Yeah. They're saying that all wireless devices could be compromised, so I don't think we should take any chances," he said. "I heard on the news that the White House is hard-wiring all its devices to prevent any other kind of infiltration. Apparently, they're afraid that this could be some kind of *invasion* via the internet."

Since Lucy had started working for Nate, she had resumed her love affair with her cellphone. But these cellphone attacks were putting a serious damper on her passion. She put the box on the floor beside her feet and drank some water from her glass. "There's so much fear out there, Nate," she said. "How can fear itself be so scary?"

"It's contagious, I guess. People panic when they don't feel safe. We just have to stay mindful, Lucy, and focus on the good stuff." He sat back on the couch, turning sideways to face her.

"Such as us, you mean." She smiled.

"Yeah. We could start there," he said, grinning.

"Um, I don't know how to start," Lucy said, "or what to think or how we work together or anything."

"It's all a bit overwhelming and sudden, I know," he said. "Let's talk about work for a sec, to put your mind at ease, then we can talk about you and me—if there *is* a you and me."

"Okay. Great. Please go ahead, boss."

He grinned. "That's awkward, isn't it. The boss–employee thing. So I've been thinking…" He paused to find the right words. "Until we, eh, sort things out on the personal front, I'd like to give you your own office down the corridor and have you take over some of the client accounts to handle on your own." He looked at her to assess her reaction. "What do you think?"

"Wow." Lucy sat back, surprised, flattered and a few other things she couldn't quite identify. "That's quite a responsibility. I'm not sure I'm—"

He waved away her objections. "You said that when you started working here and you're more than competent, Lucy. I wouldn't suggest this if I didn't think so, and I am *not* doing this because of my personal feelings for you. I want you to know that before we go any further."

"Yes, I do need to be sure of that…" Lucy nodded slowly, absorbing the possibilities. "And thank you for the vote of confidence." She felt discombobulated, turned upside down, her heart inside out, her future uncertain, yet suddenly she had a whole new world before her.

"You deserve it, Lucy. You've worked hard these past few months and the clients like what you produce. So do I, of course." He smiled reassuringly. "Let's get your new office set up this coming week and see how things go. Okay?"

She nodded, still finding her new centre.

"As for you and me," he said, looking at her shyly, "why don't we take things slowly. I'd like to ask you out on a date, if you're interested."

"I think I'm interested." She laughed and Beemer thumped his tail, liking the sound of this.

"Phew. That's a relief. Well, I've made dinner… if you'd like to stay."

"Is it goulash?"

"No." He laughed. "It's not goulash, although the kid makes a pretty good one. I think that's it, though. Goulash and Gucci-style clothing—those are his key strengths."

Lucy did *not* want to talk about Tate, right now, and it didn't seem like the right moment to talk to him about her wanting to explore more creative stuff, either. That could wait. "What's *your* signature dish, to wow a girl on her first date?"

"Well, I've still got about a kilo of *achiote* from my trip to Peru early last year, so I've been on a bit of an *achiote*-chicken bender for a while. Could I tempt you to some of that?"

"I have no idea what that is," Lucy said, "but I'd love to try it."

"One of the many things I love about you, Lucy—your courage." She laughed.

"While I'm doing impressive things in the kitchen, you and Beemer can kick back and relax. Here…" He gave her a remote control and gestured to an iPod sitting in a Bose speaker base beside his bookshelves. "See if you can find some music you like and dinner will be ready in 20."

She scrolled through an eternity of playlists, artists and songs, finally selecting some new world music. Nate didn't seem like a new-world-music kinda guy but she'd give it a whirl. As long as it wasn't pan pipes. She hunkered down for a listen. Not bad. Resonant but not demanding. A poignant melody but not too drippy. A gentle massage for the mind. It might keep the mood mellow.

Dinner was smelling good and Lucy's tummy was rumbling. She headed for the kitchen. Before she reached the door, Nate said, "Scram. You don't know what risky experiments are being concocted in here."

"True," she said, laughing. "But you've already been very daring with a birthday present."

"Yeah, but I need to make up for the missed ones."

"In which direction?"

"Well, obviously the ones in the past. I don't plan on missing the future ones. You?"

Suddenly, he was at the doorway, leaning towards her, smelling of cinnamon, lemons and surprises.

"Well, a few more would be nice," Lucy said, nonchalant.

He frowned at her sternly. "Are you hungry?"

"Ravenous. I haven't eaten since Easter."

He took her by the shoulders, about to spin her back to the couch, but she must have changed his mind. His lips landed on hers with a tingling heat, and Lucy realized just how very hungry she was.

She sank into Nate—gifted lip-reader, lip-sinker and spinner of magic roundabouts. When he finally allowed her some oxygen, his eyes looked blurry… or was it hers?

"Wow. LSC." He was beatific, all possibilities wordlessly opened up by a mind-blowing kiss.

"LSC?" Lucy was doubly puzzled; how did he know her middle initial—those damn forms!—and what was the C for?

"Lucy in the sky with Cordalis. Obviously." His legs started reversing into the kitchen, although the rest of him was still right there, yearning for more. "Will that keep you going till dinner's ready?"

Who cares about the diamonds? "I think so," Lucy said, floating back to the couch, chanting natnatnatnatnat *sotto voce*, a sacred mantra of name-imprinting.

"Would you please stop? You make me sound like a machine gun. You can call me whatever you want, okay? As long as it's not Boss or Mr Cordalis."

Lucy pondered this, reaching down to stroke Beemer. He raised his head, beaming at her with his usual toothy grin. Maybe *that* was his name—*Beamer*, not Beemer. She'd never thought to ask.

"Tell me," she whispered, "in total canine confidence, what should I call this man?" Closing his eyes, Beemer flopped back down on the floor, clearly having grappled unsuccessfully with this weighty issue for years and now thoroughly worn out by the question.

She called out to Nate. "What's your middle name?"

Silence in the kitchen. A pungent pause.

"Not fair," she said. "You know mine."

A pot clanged on the stove. "Webster."

"Webster? Like the dictionary?"

More banging in the kitchen.

"Nathaniel Webster Cordalis. You poor man. You've been carrying that around since birth? I need to meet your parents," she said. "Urgently. Before they do any more damage."

Possibly a touchy point. She drifted back to the kitchen to soften the blow.

"You, again," he said.

She shrugged. "I couldn't stay away."

"I get that a lot," he said, "despite the deterrent of my didactic middle name."

"Nah." Lucy grinned without mercy. "I'm only here for the food. Was it just a cruel rumour or will there be sustenance soon?"

"Coming right up, madam. If you would just haul your ravenous ravishing body to the table and sit down, dinner will be served. But please put away the machine gun. And do not mention the dictionary again."

"That's a lot to expect in exchange for some plain old *achiote* chicken," Lucy said, sighing. But her stomach was concaving from hunger, so she surrendered.

51

8 September 2020

Vicky was having a blast. She'd been high all morning, thinking about the tour. Not that she gave a fuck about the sights of London. She just wanted to be with Kev. And she was! On the open top deck of the double-decker tour bus, hanging out at the back, snogging her face off with Mr lush-lips, her hair waving like a freedom flag in the wind and her heart thumping crazily, like castanets doing the Fandango.

Jules had gone with the other half of the group to the museum. Sucko. Vicky couldn't imagine anything more boring than looking at old paintings, traipsing from one dead room to another, trailed by decrepit security guards who crept around like slugs. Jules wouldn't be snogging with fartin Martin—not when she was surrounded by anal art buffs sniffing their snobby noses in disapproval.

But they'd been texting each other since lunchtime and now she was doing selfies with her and Kev. Thank *godness* she'd received her Propysta before she left. It had cost a stinkin minto but it was worth it. She'd taken another two this morning, before going on the tour, just to make sure she was Gucci with Kev. No worries there. She felt like flying again. She pitied the poor suckers who didn't have any Props to make life perfect.

Her right hand was throbbing from all the selfies and texts, and her cheek was burning. Her head was starting to hurt, too. Gotta be the sun. She'd had some filthy headaches before she starting taking her Props. The pain made her skull vibrate with dancing, piercing jabs, and lying down in a dark room was the only thing that helped.

She didn't want to have to go back to the hostel with a *headache*. That would be like totally *awks*. She'd ease up on the phone fingering and get a bit more of the Vicky–Kev lip sync. She stood up to take one last selfie of her and Kev as they passed Big Ben. It was booming out the hour—three bone-jarring bongs that made her head ring and blurred her vision.

Suddenly, she felt a jolt, a wrenching eruption of something deep in her belly, like lunch coming up, but not. She dropped her phone, clutching her heart, which was beating like a maniac in her chest. She felt a tidal wave of sickening, depressing emptiness, from her scalp to her toes, her eyes flooding with scalding tears, hazing the horizon—her very own Twilight Zone.

She could hear Kev moaning and felt him groping for her, but she couldn't see a thing. She had to get off—escape whatever awful thing this was. She needed to fly, to flee the searing sadness, eject out of her scalding skin. The bus was lurching all over the road, horns blaring like demented rappers, swelling her aching skull.

She stood up on her seat, stretched out her arms like Kate Winslet in *Titanic*, and lifted off.

***

It hit the capital at 3pm, when the Brits were still at work. Parliament was in session and tourists thronged the streets, boisterous on this bright, sunny afternoon after weeks of rain. By 3.05, it was mayhem in central London, with the first fatalities occurring almost straight away.

An American teenager from Ohio on an open-topped tour bus flung herself into the flow of traffic below, dying instantly from severe head injuries.

The British Prime Minister was at 10 Downing Street, in a meeting with the French President debating the merits of Brexit, when one of his aides, seated close to him, received a text on his cellphone. The pulse from the phone affected everyone present, triggering an instant reaction. They broke down and sobbed on the polished boardroom table, papers scattering, coffee cups crashing onto the hardwood floor, and cellphones being flung across the room.

The PM and President groped blindly for some firm footing and ended up weeping in each other's arms, the contentious political issues at hand immediately forgotten. Aides and secretaries wailed and moaned, the whole room heaving in a symphony of sobs.

The effect wore off after ten minutes and an embarrassed hiatus ensued, people picking themselves up and dusting themselves off, eyes averted.

When the PM finally composed himself, finger-combing his electric hair and straightening his tear-stained jacket in mortified humiliation as the President turned away and did the same, he took a few moments to regroup. As his aides rallied, they were quick to point out the obvious: this was the same phenomenon that hit Washington the week before. It had been rumoured that it had been a purely US attack, given America's general unpopularity among certain factions, but that was clearly not the case.

The phenomenon, which the Americans were calling CEBS—Cellphone Emotional Breakdown Syndrome—seemed to have shifted in its delivery mechanisms, now operating via texts and tablets as well as phone calls, although the impact of the text transmission seemed less forceful and more diffuse than if someone had made a call.

The PM called for his press officer and issued an immediate directive to the nation, dictated between hiccupping sobs, strictly prohibiting the use of mobile phones under any circumstances, save for true life-and-death situations.

The BBC interrupted its programming to broadcast the news, its reporters rushing to the streets to capture the unfolding panic. Despite the government warning not to use their mobile phones, they instinctively reached for their devices, many of them calling family, friends or contacts even as they rushed to cover the news, before being felled by grief themselves and joining the general scrum of bodies.

Hot on the heels of the government's directive, Lloyd's of London issued an official statement saying that anyone injured or otherwise harmed as a result of using their mobile phone would not be covered by their insurance. Back in 2015, they had already excluded any liability coverage for health-related claims arising out of or resulting from electromagnetic fields, electromagnetic radiation, electromagnetism, radio waves or noise.

"We flagged this issue back in 2015," an official spokesman said, "but nobody took it seriously. Now, we are seeing the effects of that denial, and the costs to the government will be astronomical."

In the House of Commons, amid boring long speeches and rallying cries for support of whatever bill was being debated, mobile phones were covertly consulted, held low on laps while their users scrolled through their messages, texts and other news. At 3pm, all sense of decorum and feigned interest in what the Honourable Member had to say instantly dissolved as all those assembled scrambled blindly towards the exits, shoving their fellow *learned gentlemen* aside as they choked up with emotion, with absolutely nothing honourable about any of them.

At Guy's Hospital, a nurse attending at an open-heart surgery on a middle-aged woman reached for an iPad to check something in the patient's medical history and turned it on. The pulse from the iPad was instant and intense, hitting the surgical team like an invisible blast and throwing the whole operating room into chaos. The other nurses dropped dressings and sterilized instrument trays, the anaesthetist tripped over the base of an IV pole and fell onto the operating table, and the surgeon's eyes blurred with tears, an involuntary sob jerking his hand so badly that he sliced an artery and blood erupted like a geyser from the patient's chest cavity.

The patient died from blood loss, and three of the surgical team suffered head wounds and scalpel lacerations. Dr Timothy Roddington, the senior cardiac surgeon performing the operation, stumbled out of the OR, catatonic from shock and trauma. He leaned against the wall, sobbing for the dead woman and others who had died in his care. *He should have done more... he hadn't paid attention... too many emergencies... crippling fatigue... too high a dose... non-stop suffering, complaints, misery... He'd never be enough, do enough...*

Thanks to the antennas on the roof, there was blanket cellphone coverage and the entire hospital was in upheaval, with iPads, cellphones, pagers and cordless phones strewn along the corridors, and orderlies in blue gowns collapsing in heaps on the floor. Patients keened in their beds, pulling out their IVs, falling out of bed and crawling, butt-naked, towards the exits, slapping the floor as tidal waves of emotion coursed through their shuddering bodies.

Bodies oozed from the wards into the corridors, each one a wailing wall of bitter regrets as suppressed emotions poured out. Words unspoken, lovers unloved, risks not taken, rifts unrepaired, sorrys unsaid, mistakes left festering, passions unfulfilled, dreams unlived—a litany of lost last chances.

An elderly man was slumped against the wall, tears coursing down the tributaries of his weathered cheeks. *"I never got the chance to say goodbye! Ellen, my darling... I'm so sorry..."*

Crawling jerkily down the corridor, a battered wife admitted for a broken arm and two cracked ribs, moaned in shame and self-recrimination. *"Why didn't I do something? Why didn't I walk away?"*

A young businessman visiting his dying father, hung his head and sobbed. *"I abandoned you, Dad. Always too busy... Please forgive me..."*

A 26-year-old woman getting chemotherapy sat curled over, bald head between skinny knees, hugging her shins to comfort her shrunken body. *"I poisoned you... didn't listen... I'm going to die... I'm going to die..."*

Nurses and doctors were no less affected, pouring out their anguish over broken hearts, infidelities, missed opportunities, and grief for the patients they hadn't been able to help.

***

In Wellington, New Zealand, the Prime Minister was on her couch watching the early morning news, a heaping plate of scrambled eggs and grilled tomatoes on her lap. She reached for her cellphone, hesitated, then speed-dialed a number. What the hell. It wouldn't be the first time she'd shed tears in public—usually from laughter—and it wasn't going to kill her. Her cat would be the only witness, but Petals was fiercely loyal and would never tell.

"Sondra? Have you seen the news?"

"Yes, Prime Minister."

Of course she had. Sondra Roscoe, smart woman that she was, would have been expecting this call. She probably already had her skates on, ready to bolt out the door.

"This thing, whatever it is, seems to be heading our way and I will not be caught out. We'll need to shut down the wireless networks and instigate emergency measures for things to be hard-wired. I want you to call an urgent meeting here at my residence," the Prime Minister said. "Everyone on the list."

"Yes, Prime Minister. For what time?"

"ASAP. I'll expect everyone here in an hour."

"Yes, Prime Minister."

"And get yourself here in ten, if you can."

"I'm on my way."

"Oh, and Sondra?"

"Yes?"

"Don't use your cellphone again till you get here, okay? And tell everyone else the same thing."

Sondra arrived just as the PM was polishing off her second slice of toast and draining her second cup of coffee. Running the country gave her an insatiable appetite and there never seemed to be enough time to consume the fuel she needed.

Sondra had her own key but she did her usual double-tap knock before she let herself in—code for *PA incoming*. She was a powerhouse of determined efficiency. A tidy package of lean limbs and quick manoeuvres, with a mop of crazy terra-cotta curls sheltering a freckled face and sparkling green eyes, she offered little wind resistance as she sped through her tasks.

The PM eased herself stiffly upright from the couch, her lower back still aching from two hours on the floor with a kindergarten class the day before, explaining how to build a great nation.

"I'd kill for a chiropractor right now," she said.

"You'd probably have to," Sondra said.

Perhaps she'd been a bit hasty clamping down on chiropractors, the

PM thought, massaging her lower spine.

She was watching the last of the news as Sondra headed for the adjoining office to get things set up for the meeting.

"You know what this reminds me of?"

"Probably not," Sondra said.

"On Christmas Day, when I was growing up, we had a family ritual of opening our presents one by one, everyone giving their full attention to whoever was opening their gift. The presents were pulled at random from under the tree so we never knew who was going to be next. That's what this is like—capital cities being hit at random, one at a time, while everyone else watches the drama unfolding, wondering who's next."

"Not quite as much fun, perhaps," Sondra said.

"Oh, I don't know… Well, apart from the deaths, of course. No fun, that. But seeing big bad men cry… that's pretty special."

52

9 September 2020

She yelled at the sky. "Someone's made a terrible mistake!" Seagulls circled above, spreading the word. "This is supposed to be the balmy Pacific, not the nipple-nixing Arctic." She danced on the sand, pirouetting and slapping her purpling thighs. "Fix this!" she commanded the heavens.

God, she was gorgeous. He'd fix the whole wide world for her, if he could, Matt thought. He felt he *owed* her the world, and surely the world owed her, too, for donating so much love and wisdom to the cosmic gene pool. They'd be listening, up there, if they had any sense at all.

"I know we said we'd go swimming every morning, no matter how cold it was, but this is COLD!" Celle jogged on the spot, trying to persuade her disbelieving body to submit to sub-human temperatures.

"It's rare," Matt said. "But sometimes the water does get really cold."

"So cold that even my goosebumps refuse to come out," Celle said.

"So cold that a normally inquisitive part of my anatomy has receded back to the northerly realms it inhabited before my voice broke," Matt said, an octave higher than usual.

"Do you think it's worth the risk, or should we play it safe and go back to bed?"

"I think wading in up to our knees and walking back and forth for about 30 seconds would be the equivalent of a swim in more body-friendly temperatures."

"Then we can scarper back to bed?"

"Yes. Definitely. For the sake of our health and our medical insurance, which doesn't cover extreme sports."

She ran, screeching, into the waves, running back and forth in a frigid fountain of spray. He followed her, roaring, the cold almost stopping his heart but Celle keeping it very much alive. He'd spend a night in a fridge-freezer if it made her happy… as long as he lived to enjoy the reward.

Teeth chattering, they darted back to the beach and grabbed their towels, rubbing themselves fiercely, and pulling on T-shirts and shorts.

They walked home, hand in hand, along the slowly awakening street. Shutters were opening, metal storefronts clattering upwards, brooms sweeping away the detritus of the night, dogs stretching out of their slumbers, motors wrenching the air as people headed for work.

"I can't understand the appeal of such a noisy bike," Celle said, as a fuming bike sputtered by. "That thing sounds as if it has a bad case of congestion and is constantly trying to clear its throat."

Matt didn't care. Everything was wonderful. They could be in the middle of a hurricane and it wouldn't bother him. Sometimes he felt that nothing would ever bother him again, as long as he had Celle by his side. *But would he?* They hadn't talked about the future. Celle refused to go there.

"I'm taking each day as it comes, Mateo," she said, and calling him that in her sexy Spanish accent was enough to win him over, right there. "The future will take care of itself as long as we keep feeling our way forward. My head's on permanent holiday." She pondered that notion, seeing how it felt. "Actually, it's on probation, just doing two hours a week, for the unforeseeable future. My heart will tell it if it needs more."

They had moved into a two-bedroom wooden cabin down a small rutted trail in the woods on the outskirts of town. It was peaceful, a hidden sanctum, away from the reminders of commerce and the need to earn a living.

The space was simple: a cozy living area with a large window overlooking the woods, one bedroom with their futon bed, a second bedroom with a desk and single bed, a tiny bathroom with shower, sink and shamelessly naked, lidless toilet, a surprisingly well-equipped kitchen with gas stove, fridge, stainless steel pots and pans, juicer, blender, coffee machine, kettle, toaster, colourful Mexican crockery, huge coffee mugs with Mayan symbols snaking around their bellies, and chunky cotton tablecloths in vibrant hues to cover the wooden dining table in the living room. There was an internet router on a corner table, linked up to a satellite dish on a nearby tree, a smooth white sunflower gazing at the stars.

Celle threw her towel on the sofa as she padded to the kitchen. Opening the fridge, she peered inside, exploring the tangle of fresh vegetables, tubs of green powders, papayas and bags of mixed nuts.

"Another smoothie like yesterday's?"

Matt called out a valiant *yes* from the bathroom, but she was already pulling out celery stalks, carrots, chlorella powder, ginger, mango, maca powder, hemp seeds and other blendables. She threw a bit of everything into the blender with some water and let it rip.

Matt came back into the living room and nuzzled her from behind, smelling of jasmine soap and skin-toasted salty air. She arched back for a kiss, then turned to hand him a large loving glassful of green sludge.

They moved to the table and sat down, looking out at the trees. Matt took a tentative sip. Her blends were more potent than the ones José made and took some getting used to. But then everything about Celle was more potent than in the world of ordinary mortals.

"It seems to taste less awful today," he said, "but I think it's because my taste buds have gone into hiding."

"Your taste buds are loving it," she said, smiling. "You just don't want to admit it."

"Why wouldn't I? I'm healthier and more virile than I've ever been. Right? What's not to love?"

"Very little," she said, draining the last of her green stuff. "But I should check things out, just to make sure I haven't missed any flaws. We *did* say we'd go straight back to bed to warm up…"

"Good point." Matt grinned. "I'm still freezing, but only on the inside. And no one can reach those parts like you do, Celle."

Now highly motivated, he drained the rest of his sludge and

stood up. He took his glass and hers over to the sink, glancing at his cellphone on the sofa. *Should he quickly check his messages?* He never watched the news but Marnie had e-mailed him about what happened in Washington and London. It was hard to wrap his brain around it all, in this little corner of paradise, but he was concerned for her and Lucy.

But what man in his right mind would check his messages rather than going to bed with this angel in his life? His messages would keep.

Celle rose from the table and he joined her mid-stream, two flows fusing, like a human zipper closing, returning to the source of it all.

53

---

9 September 2020

When Marnie switched on the news for an update on what was happening in the UK, BBC reporter Brenna Renfrew was interviewing British clinical psychologist Dr Gregory Staunton. They were discussing the issue of suppressed emotions, with a particular focus on the recent Cellphone Emotional Breakdown Syndrome (CEBS) phenomenon involving wireless devices connected to the internet.

"Those who had a lot of suppressed emotions or emotional dysfunction would be the hardest hit by the emotion-triggering frequencies coming through their devices," Dr Staunton claimed. "Moreover," he said, "those who had ill-intentioned agendas causing harm to their fellow men would have had to suppress a great deal of emotion—consciously or subconsciously—in order to fulfill that agenda."

"What would that mean, in the greater scheme of things?" Renfrew asked.

"What we are likely to see," Dr Staunton said, "is that certain government leaders will be deeply affected by this emotional triggering, and they are likely to take far longer to recover, if they recover at all." He paused. "It is highly unlikely that they will be able to go back to what they were doing before this phenomenon hit."

A lightbulb flashed on for Marnie. Was this why they were targeting capital cities and seats of government rather than the general population? If what this shrink said was true, what would it mean for the governments currently doing nefarious stuff? Which would be all of them, of course.

She'd have to ask Ray about this. He'd been giving her a physics lesson once a week at his home—quantum/particle physics 101— explaining how frequencies worked, the theory of the multiverse and the importance of numbers, sound and vibration in the creation of life itself. Marnie couldn't tell if it all sounded so impossibly cryptic because Ray made it sound that way or if quantum physics was inherently sneaky, with particles popping in and out of existence, furtive as ferrets.

She suspected he was building up to telling her what he knew about this whole CEBS thing. Was he involved? And what had her mother hoped to achieve with her human-enhancing system. Another week or so, he said, and he'd take her to his lab and tell her what was going on.

Marnie couldn't wait. In the meantime, she was tracking the fallout from the attacks, trying to figure out where it might land next and why.

On the news channel, the psychologist was saying that the issue of untraceable frequencies being delivered via wireless internet could, in itself, be enough to bring down the wireless industry, causing a complete loss of trust.

"Isn't that more of a political call than a psychological one?" Renfrew seemed to think he should stay in his therapist box.

"Not really, when you consider what drives the industry," Dr Staunton said. "Think about what the billions of mobile phones are largely used for—social media, emotional support, sales pitches, exploitation, staying in touch with loved ones, meeting unmet emotional needs—all very much serving as an emotional lifeline, and addictively so. So much so that taking those phones away can elicit violent reactions." He raised a finger towards his invisible point. "But, if those same emotional props suddenly turn against their users, causing people to feel emotionally stricken and overwhelmed rather than emotionally supported, distracted or unfulfilled…" He spread his hands, head tilted at the obvious. "Then the industry loses its very foundation."

"So, you're saying mobile phones are really more of an emotional crutch than a communication device?"

"Yes, you could say that," Dr Staunton conceded. "With this recent syndrome, it's as if the direction of data flow has been reversed, with whatever emotional dysfunction that typically went from the user to the rest of the world now turning around and getting dumped back at the source. Quite a psychological coup, in fact."

"Let's get back to the impact of this CEBS phenomenon on governments," Renfrew said. "How might that unfold?"

"We are already seeing the effects, with the US President said to be in seclusion since CEBS hit Washington, DC on 6 September."

Renfrew was nodding. "Sources at the White House have revealed that the president is in mourning, mostly for himself, but also for how he has treated his fellow Americans. They say it could take a very long time for him to recover."

"Indeed, and since the Vice President also seems to be in seclusion, it's not clear who is running the country. But," Dr Staunton concluded, "whoever steps in will need to take a good long look at their conscience before they do anything."

"Are you saying that the degree of emotional collapse is some kind of indicator of moral integrity?"

"Yes. That's exactly what I'm saying. And now that this connection is becoming increasingly clear to the public, any elected official will be acutely aware that he or she could be exposed to this Cellphone Emotional Breakdown Syndrome and come under intense public scrutiny." He paused. "If they are affected by the frequency, their level of breakdown will demonstrate their level of integrity, honesty and honourable intentions."

Renfrew smiled. "Finally, perhaps, a litmus test for the inscrutable unscrupulous."

She nodded her thanks to Dr Staunton and turned back to the camera to wrap up.

"Not surprisingly, government officials are incensed at not being able to take down whoever is behind this," she said, her face grave. "They're used to being in control of things, and they don't like it when it's the other way around. This frequency or whatever it is has left them feeling powerless because it appears to be untraceable and invisible."

Renfrew paused, considering the incendiary potential of her next statement. "They can't see it coming or do anything about it when it hits—which seems to be pretty much how those harmed by wireless radiation say they have been feeling."

Her eyes flicked to the mid-distance, clearly registering a visual cue from her controllers to zip it and move on.

She shuffled her papers. "Meanwhile, the London Stock Exchange, generally considered to be one of the most reliable exchanges in Europe—"

Marnie turned off the TV and reached for her laptop, internet cable trailing behind it, back to the modem mothership.

She wasn't a big fan of social media, which often seemed to be little more than a gripe fest—a venting of personal grievances, dressed up as moral, political or economic concerns. But it usually provided alternative perspectives, beyond the usual government or industry spin, as well as some scientific information not available via mainstream media. It gave you a sense of the general consensus on things—like a digital finger on the collective pulse. Not that there ever really was a consensus, but you could see pretty quickly what the various camps were saying.

She was aware that whatever showed up on social media was usually in *spite* of censorship by the mainstream media moguls—except for some really nutty stuff that didn't get blocked as most people wouldn't believe it anyway, or the fanatics were in such a small minority that their extreme views didn't matter. Most of the teachers at her school just watched the news on TV, so they only ever got the government spiel and never saw what was going on behind the scenes. They thought they were getting the facts, debating them endlessly in the staffroom, when they were only getting what governments, Big Tech and Big Pharma *wanted* them to get.

Marnie found it disheartening that she'd never been able to really engage with her colleagues, especially on the contentious stuff, like that whole virus thing. It was almost like a religion or a new form of racism, dividing people into separate factions. And the more the dark underbelly got revealed, the more stuff was getting censored. It was getting hard to know where to find the truth—or how to recognize it.

How had her parents been able to *stand* it—all the small-mindedness they must have encountered in their mind-blowing work, whatever the heck it was. Not a reason to kill yourself, though. Right? *Stop.* She shook the thought away. She would *not* go back to torturing herself with pointless speculation.

She returned her attention back to the screen. There had been a brief drop-off in social-media activity as some people sought ways to hard-wire their wireless devices. Many were disdainfully dismissive of the issue, convinced that their cellphone could do no harm and was the best thing since sugar-dusted donuts.

Sometimes, Marnie felt that social media was just one big bulletin board for unfulfilled livers, and that really needed to be addressed. Who decided that *liver* should be the body organ that fulfilled over 500 functions, rather than the body doing the living? If you could *love* and be a *lover*, why could you not *live* and be a *liver*? It made no sense to her. This kind of one-sided conversation was how her anxious mind kept her distracted from bigger issues as her fingers did the stalking.

She did a quick scroll through her timeline and some news pages, getting the gist of the online mood. People were demanding to know who was doing this.

Why haven't the telecom companies caught the maniacs?

How could this thing go through their networks and not be traced? WTF?!

How come no airline accidents??!! A fluke, miracle or wot??

Some sicko terrorist with a conscience????

Get a grip!! Even governments don't have a conscience. Industry doesn't give a shit about your health, which means that governments don't, either. In case you haven't noticed who's running things…

On all the social media platforms, speculation spanned the spectrum from enraged rants at the perpetrators and gleeful delight at governments being literally brought to their knees, to heated debates about hidden agendas and earnest insights into the implications for the wireless industry and the economy.

Since some countries had so far been untouched, there was much social sparring about a particular government being responsible for this. China, aiming to be the next superpower? Canada, sick of its presidentially uncouth neighbour? How come *they* hadn't been attacked?

China is taking over the world, guys!

Huawei is global leader in cellphone tech. You want Chinks spying on U? If they control the tech, they can do whatever hell they want if they don't like what's goin down…

Canada, a peaceful nation?? No way! It's just as bad as the other fuckers!

This Pandephonium crap is giving governments a taste of their own sick medicine!

Brilliant, Marnie thought. *Pandephonium* summed it up perfectly. Social media certainly made a creative contribution.

Endless jokes, banter, cartoons and fake stories parried on all the platforms, laced with irate invectives against those still using their cellphones and putting everyone near them at risk. A lovely irony, Marnie thought, considering how using cellphones had *always* put anyone near them at risk.

There was a scathing post from an American chemist—a passionate advocate for the dismantling of the entire wireless industry, citing the diseases caused and how cellphones had been a key factor in worsening the impact of the virus that had caused such panic and chaos earlier in the year.

"We're all so hell-bent on getting cellphones to do everything for us," he wrote, "all the things we used to do ourselves and are *meant* to do ourselves, and now our precious irradiating devices have taken over *this* human function also: transmitting viruses from one person to another or, at the very least, weakening immune systems, causing respiratory distress and making people much sicker than they would otherwise be. I guess we're all bored with doing things the *old-fashioned* way, transmitting from one person to another, at a normal rate. *Well, now we can use our fancy cellphones instead and do this properly, globally and far more efficiently than we could ever do as just mere mortals.*"

His sarcasm didn't win him any points, Marnie thought, although some of what he said had the annoying ring of truth. But people didn't seem to realize that going on a rant, badmouthing or condemning others diminished their credibility, even if what they said was valid. Marnie felt it often revealed as much about the attacker as those being attacked.

The chemist went on to quote the Russians who, he claimed, had carried out "some 20,000 experiments showing that viral and other infections in cell cultures could be transmitted by electromagnetic radiation via biophotons in the near ultraviolet range," whatever that meant.

"It's in the literature, folks! Use your friggin brains! This is not conspiracy theory stuff! The Ruskies are way ahead of us and have been doing this kind of research for decades. *They're* not afraid of the truth."

He included a link to a radiation-sciences researcher in Canada who had researched some similar effects. Marnie clicked on the link but the information seemed dauntingly technical for the average brain. The researcher referred to *radiation-induced bystander effects*, and she seemed to be saying that infected cells had ways of communicating with other cells and infecting them.

Approaching mental overload, Marnie skimmed quickly through the abstract, which concluded that certain kinds of communication could happen through certain kinds of radiation—both between cells and between *individuals*.

Blimey. She felt herself getting sucked down a rabbit hole and decided to reverse out, closing the researcher's page. But it made her think of what Ray had said in his TV interview, about it being possible to transmit viruses via the internet... She made a mental note to ask him more about that, too.

The disgruntled chemist summed up his post on a surprisingly positive note, saying that radiation from healthy cell cultures could help reverse an infection in affected cultures. Well, *that* sounded good, at least. The paradox, he concluded, was that it was bad for healthy cells to be near sick cells, but very good for sick cells to have the healthy cells around. And the same was true for healthy and sick individuals.

Marnie sat back, reflecting. This made sense to her. It might explain why a doctor's positive physical presence could have an influence on the health of his or her patients. She'd experienced the flip side of this herself, feeling very flat and uninspired if she consulted a doctor who was less than excited about the possibilities for true health. Come to think of it, she couldn't remember ever having a medical doctor who got excited about wellness and who wasn't focused more on disease than health.

She remembered reading about Austrian philosopher Rudolf Steiner, who said that living in dread of disease was one of the most powerful ways to ensure you got ill. Fear was the real enemy. Governments certainly knew how to stoke it up, Marnie thought. It boggled the mind that leaders would intentionally terrorize and weaken their own people rather than inspiring them to be all they could be.

Steiner had founded the Steiner school model, which Marnie had always liked because it focused on developing the imagination and the whole person. Maybe she should try to get a job teaching at a Waldorf school, which was based on the Steiner approach. There was at least one Waldorf school in the city and she had been slightly envious to learn that the curriculum included emotional and social education, which was exactly what the kids in her class needed—what *all* kids needed. How could any school *not* teach that stuff, she wondered. She needed to look into this again… see if there were any teaching positions open…

On the other hand, she was finding all the quantum physics stuff so fascinating that she wasn't sure what she wanted to do next—or who she would be, after a few more months working with Ray on the frequency project.

She did a final quick skim of the latest items on her timeline. Someone had posted a news update on the US President's condition, confirming that he was now *stable* and *no longer critical*. This was met with a creative smorgasbord of derision and snide remarks about him *never* having been stable, even on a very rare, relatively *good* hair day, and always being Kamikaze-critical, so this update clearly qualified as totally fake news. Same old, same old.

She had seen enough.

54

9 September 2020

Marnie was loving loving Steve. A manly man, big-framed and rugged, he had a gentle side that constantly took her heart by surprise, dissolving her defences and turning her to mush. And it was surprisingly delicious being mush in Steve's arms. She had never felt so safe, so loved or so completely at home in her skin.

But he was not prime bed-sharing material—at least, not with the current sleeping configuration in her bedroom. On the nights he slept over, the dynamic was not ideal, although still worth it, she thought, considering the *benefits*. When he rolled onto his side to sleep, his broad shoulders created a mountain of the duvet, with Marnie left in the foothills, her left flank exposed to the air as the duvet rose away from her towards the summit of his shoulder. Between them, a triangular wind tunnel sucked in a draught of cool air, making it impossible for Marnie to sleep. If she managed to cocoon herself in her own segment of duvet, sealing it firmly under her body, she was often woken by

Steve turning over in his sleep. With him weighing twice as much as her, it was a seismic event—at least a 7 on the Richter scale, Marnie reckoned—causing mattress shudders and aftershocks that jolted her awake.

Plus, she was a very light sleeper; a mote of dust landing on her nose was enough to startle her into consciousness. Steve was the opposite, conking out almost mid-sentence, while she often lay awake for hours, waiting for sleep to take her under.

She needed to go Swedish—get two separate single mattresses pushed together, and two single duvets. Not as much fun, where cuddles and other intimacies were concerned, but at least she would sleep. Having your own piece of bedding real estate was, she decided, fundamental to her sanity and a lasting relationship.

But the pre-sleep state was often her best time for reflection and insight. Right now, she was thinking about her work with Ray and the extraordinary turn her life had taken.

There was a rumble from the other side of the mountain. "Turn it down, darling girl."

"What?"

Steve rolled onto his back and Marnie nestled into his shoulder, his arm closing around her, instantly soothing her busy brain. "You're thinking too loudly. It's keeping me awake," he said.

"It is not," Marnie said, a smile in her voice. "You've been in a coma for the past hour."

"Well, now that I've regained consciousness, tell me what you were thinking so loudly about."

"Just… what I'm learning from Ray—all this fascinating stuff about the multiverse, frequencies, the power of numbers." She looked up at his solid profile. "I think you were right about the numbers being important," she said. "I'd never have imagined myself getting into all this stuff…"

She had to be careful. She couldn't tell Steve what Ray was working on—what little she knew, so far—as Ray had made her swear that she would tell *no one*, before he agreed to let her get involved.

So she had told Steve that Ray was teaching her about quantum physics and sharing some of the concepts that her parents had specialized in. This was true, but there was a lot more to it. She felt horribly disloyal not telling him the truth—almost as if she were secretly having an affair. But the love affair was for what she was learning about the cosmos, the true nature of reality, the stardust humans were made of, the frequencies of emotions, how sound and vibrations affected the human heart, and how delicate yet stubbornly resilient life was.

Ray was a bridge to understanding—not just some of the concepts her parents had been working on, but what they were passionate about. It made her feel close to them, somehow, as if she was discovering who they really were... yet sad, too, that she hadn't known this when they were alive.

Marnie was finding it hard to focus on her classes with the kids at school, her brain taking off on its own private forays, contemplating biophotons, wave forms and the paradoxes of time, while her salaried mind tried to concentrate on spelling and syntax.

"Tell me about some of the stuff you're learning," Steve said, his voice resonating like a megaphone in his chest.

"Well, he's been telling me about the poly exclusion principle," she said.

"Ah, yes, I remember Polly," Steve said.

Marnie lifted her head in surprise, checking for a teasing smile. "You know this stuff?"

"Some of it," he conceded. "Tell me more so I can see if I've got it right."

"Mmmm..." Steve always seemed to be one step ahead of her, always surprising her with the diversity of his knowledge and intuition, which was fine with her... as long as he didn't see right through her on this. "I think it's to do with certain kinds of particles not being able to exist in the same quantum state, which means they can't exist in the same place and have all the same qualities."

She checked in. "Have *I* got it right, so far?"

He grunted agreement and she continued. "So a future self, according to this principle, cannot come into contact with a past self. But if a *later* version of self is not in the same quantum state as the earlier one, you could shake hands with your earlier self."

"I don't think I've ever had such a sexy conversation in bed with a woman at 1am," Steve said.

"You're teasing me," Marnie said, slapping his chest—a gentle slap that told him she loved him for humouring her.

"I'm dead serious," he said. "What could be sexier than going back to your gorgeous 27-year-old self when you're 93, toothless, forgetting who you are and wondering if you even existed?"

"This stuff boggles my mind," Marnie said, shaking her head to jiggle loose a bit more space.

"Minds should not be boggled this late at night," Steve said, kissing the top of her head. "Bodies can be boggled, but not minds."

But Marnie was not quite ready to surrender. "So, in theory, you could travel to the past of a *parallel* universe, but not your own universe," she said, still trying to grasp the concept.

"True," Steve said. "If you prevented your parents from meeting, let's say, you just wouldn't be born in that parallel universe, but your origin in the other universe would remain unchanged. Luckily for me."

He pulled her close.

"You know what else boggles my mind?" She turned over onto his chest, one hand draped over his heart. "How I hooked up with you, thinking you were just a *software analyst*, when you actually know a lot of this weird stuff that my parents were working on that even *I* didn't know about."

"You mean like how I connected with *just* an elementary-school teacher who turned out to be quite a bit more than that?"

"Sorry." She patted his heart. "I didn't mean it like that. I'm just… gobsmacked, as my dad used to say, that you turned out to be so perfect for me."

"Happy to oblige, MD," he said. "My parents obviously knew what they were doing, prepping me for you."

She laughed, relaxing into him, her brain finally winding down after its end-of-day filing.

"Remind me of your middle name again…" He paused. "What was it… Aphrodite? Anastasia? Agamemnon?"

"You know what it is." Marnie giggled, aware he was distracting her from issues of cosmic significance so she might finally sleep.

"Ah, yes. *Astrid*. Meaning *godly strength*."

Marnie shuddered. "I think my parents must have been drunk when they filled out birth certificates for Lucy and me. She got LSD and I got MAD."

"Which you still do, sometimes—very sexily," Steve said. "What's Matt's middle name? Don't tell me it's Ulysses."

"Ha. No. They called him Matthew Regis Dalton. They must have sobered up when they got a boy."

"Understandable," Steve said. "Having girls is definitely cause for celebration."

He stroked her hair and ran his fingers down her spine. "Think you can sleep now?"

"If you do a little more of that... yes, I think so."

55

---

10 September 2020

CEBS Hits China, Causing Mayhem, Death Toll Unknown

From China economic correspondent *Brance Travers*

The Boston Probe, Thursday, 10 September 2020—The Cellphone Emotional Breakdown Syndrome (CEBS) that terrorized nations, hitting Washington, DC and London, England earlier this month, hit Beijing, China at 6pm local time, causing chaos in the 21.5-million-strong capital.

Dubbed *Pandephonium*, the attack hit during the evening commute when millions of Chinese flooded the massive subway system (one of the largest in the world), turning the usual relatively orderly exodus into a chaotic scrummage of emotional collapse.

Most Beijingers refrain from exhibiting anger or other strong emotions in public, but no such self-restraint was apparent when CEBS swept throughout the city, lasting for over an hour. Many flung themselves wailing onto the electrified subway tracks, while others turned on their fellow commuters with unbridled aggression, ripping them aside as they fought their way to the exits, sobbing uncontrollably and charging over any bodies already on the ground. Outside, some jumped from high-rise buildings, screaming incoherently as they launched themselves into the air.

The number of those dead or injured is not yet available but is suspected to be in the thousands.

It is likely that these extreme reactions were largely due to the digital dictatorship that maintains rigid control over the movements, communications, consumer choices and almost every activity among the population of 1.39 billion people. The system of social credits, which rewards compliant, obedient citizens but penalizes those who object or try to expose corruption, has maintained a stranglehold over the nation, quelling any resistance, and virtually immobilizing and ostracizing those who refuse to submit.

Facilitating this is the Chinese tendency to suppress emotions in favour of politeness and political correctness, although the socially enforced correctness has resulted in what some call the *art of being politely rude*. Westerners have no such qualms, although this phenomenon clearly cancels out whatever social and cultural distinctions separate nations from each other, reducing all to the common denominator of primitive emoting and a raw fight for survival.

As with Washington and London, there has been intense speculation as to who is behind these attacks and why China has been hit, ahead of other likely contenders for political assault—if that is what this is. Many analysts claimed that China would potentially have had good reason to launch such an attack on the US, for example, but that theory clearly no longer stands up. Others have posited that China itself might have wished to reduce its unmanageable population, taking drastic measures to salvage its over-burdened resources.

There are many reasons to support such theories—largely the same reasons that have resulted in the capital being particularly hard hit.

China does not have the resources to support its 1.39 billion inhabitants, many of whom do not have the means to adequately care for themselves. This has resulted in China exporting its people and setting up business in other parts of the world, such as Africa, where more than 750,000 Chinese are reported to have taken up residence. Some analysts claim that this number will increase to hundreds of millions, reducing China's natural resource problem by tapping into Africa's resources, taking the pressure off the People's Republic.

As many nations are acutely aware, China has plans to

overtake the US as the world's leading economic power by 2050, focusing on certain key technologies, such as robotics, and the exploration and exploitation of space, as well as creating a huge military build-up.

There is also endemic corruption throughout the system, enabled by the now-absolute subjugation of those who object. This makes the current CEBS chaos in the capital a potential boon or a disaster, depending on the perspective. It could be a blessing in terms of terrorizing and further controlling the population, or an added burden on an already overwhelmed system—possibly both.

However, although the breakdown of social and cultural mores could also conceivably open the door to collective resistance by the population (now that the traditional socially induced inhibitions have been stripped away by the CEBS attack), the system of digital control may once again reign, unless awakened citizens can find a way to bring it down. What we have seen so far in other affected capitals, however, is that those exposed to CEBS become intolerant to cellphone use and are unable to function in the presence of wireless radiation. This, alone, could be enough to bring down the Chinese economy as well as the digital stranglehold. China's theft of technologies and stripping of assets have not endeared it to the rest of the world, and it seems intent on becoming the leader in determining industrial standards, while upgrading its position in supply chains, away from manufacturing towards the money-making design and after-servicing stages. For years now, China has been frustrated by being the 'factory of the world', which in many cases actually means the poorly paid assembler.

As chaos swept across the capital today, the massive numbers of those affected will overwhelm healthcare systems, while water shortages (common and serious, due to heavy urbanization), as well as the high numbers of low-income earners and an aging population, will compound efforts to restore order in the city.

Many reasons indeed for China to be a popular target for those against a Chinese takeover—or for the nation itself to find a way to defuse a potentially explosive dynamic.

It will be many weeks before the full impact of the CEBS attack becomes clear and the situation is brought under control—if, indeed, it ever is.

56

It took a few days for Lucy to get set up in her new office. Nate had installed a huge shiny teak-coloured slab that took up one whole wall of her small new office, looking more like a small skating rink than a desk. It was daunting, yawning up at her, begging to be fed. She felt like an artist faced with a massive blank canvas, unsure where to begin, how to make herself worthy of it.

Conspiring with the self-important work surface was a snazzy ergonomically exaggerated chair that looked as if it required an operating manual. It was like an industrial Venus flytrap, Lucy thought, sniffing out easy prey a mile off, and she had visions of getting consumed by it if she pressed the wrong levers, the seat snapping up towards the backrest, leaving just her feet protruding, kicking helplessly as it swallowed her whole.

There was a large potted plant in one corner, helping to slightly lower the haughty tone of furniture that seemed to be awaiting the arrival of some important business executive.

Her new role as content manager for two Cordalis clients was one she would have to grow into, flexing mental and creative muscles she wasn't quite sure how to find, if she even possessed them. When she had surveyed her new terrain with a mildly terrified look, Nate had laughed, assuring her she was more than up to the challenge and would soon be bossing her clients around just as much as before, but on a slightly larger scale and with a little more authority.

She certainly seemed to be impressing *him*, but was it because he was personally smitten with her or because he could see past her ravishing good looks to some promising cerebral activity underneath?

She was still feeling floaty after their first dinner together, and the very edible *achiote* chicken had definitely enhanced his status as solid boyfriend material. But it was weird being his girlfriend and his employee, and she wasn't sure how long that symbiosis would last. Surely, one would eventually cancel out the other… but which one? She didn't want to lose her job, but she certainly didn't want to lose the man, either, since good men were much harder to find than good jobs—and finding the two together was as unlikely as… someone off the street knocking on your door and offering you employment. Ha. Well. All bets were off, then…

She and Nate had agreed to be purely professional at work, saving their personal relationship for after hours. Lucy wasn't sure that plan had great life expectancy, but Nate seemed happy to take things slowly. Despite almost a year of unspoken manly frustrations, lusting after her in the most professional way, he'd remained a perfect gentleman, although she thought he'd want to jump her bones ASAP, after waiting so long.

She appreciated having her own office, but it also felt as if she were a volatile substance that had to be contained in a small space, away from the general population.

"Didn't the others object?" she had asked Nate, since Fitz and Tracy been there far longer than her.

He assured her they didn't. He had offered them the space last year and both had declined. They preferred the open space and worked so closely together that it made no sense for them to split up.

Last week, she had decided to explain the situation to them both, waiting till Nate was out of the office before approaching them.

"Listen, guys, a quick something…"

As an opener, it wasn't exactly Gettysburg-address material, but it was good practice.

"Yeah?" Fitz kept typing.

"Shoot, Lucy," Tracy said, turning around in her chair.

"It's about Nate and me…

'Oh, that," Fitz said, typing unperturbed.

"You already *knew?*" Lucy was beginning to think she had more experience being inexperienced than anyone else she knew. "Since…?"

"For a while," Tracy said.

"Day 1," Fitz said, grinning.

Feck. Long before *she* had. She'd have to revise her male-equivalency formula, based on the well known fact that men matured more slowly than women: a man's age divided by 10 then multiplied by 7.

Beemer would understand this, with every one of his canine years equalling seven of theirs—not that that meant they were smarter than him. She needed to either revise her formula or accept that she was working with a bunch of exceptional peeps. Or… she needed a special Lucy-equivalency formula, based on her apparent cluelessness concerning men.

"He's the best, Lucy," Tracy had said. "A keeper."

Now, as the *best* man was turning to head back to his office, letting her get settled into her new space, Nate hesitated, as if tempted to offer a hug of encouragement. But he settled instead for a knowing smile and a nod that left a lot unsaid, while promising quite a bit more, later …or so Lucy told herself, using her imagination to talk herself up.

Heck, if she could do *that*, she realized, she could probably corral some words into a pleasing order for her clients.

The first thing she did, after booting up her computer and lowering her buttocks onto her hungry chair, was check the online news. She needed to get an update on any global issues that might present challenges—or opportunities—for her clients.

She clicked, scanned, skimmed, scrolled, scoffed, watched, listened, fast-forwarded, copied, pasted and concluded—all in just over 30 multi-tasked minutes.

She sat back, her chair acting pushy against her lumbar region, but otherwise behaving itself. Once she got over its overt excessiveness, she had to admit it felt pretty good—sort of like a cross between being in a glove massage and manning the console of some critically important mission into outer space.

The news was even more disturbing than she'd expected, almost exclusively focusing on CEBS—now also being widely referred to as *Pandephonium*. Moscow had been hit on Saturday, 12 September, Sydney at 9am local time today, 14 September, and Beijing was still reeling from the attack four days ago.

It was as if the rogue frequency was dancing all over the planet, avoiding detection and keeping everyone guessing about who would be next.

Please, God, please don't let that stuff hit Boston. She loved her cellphone and was once again a faithful fan, although she hadn't told Marnie that. She didn't have to tell Marnie *everything*. She had a man in her life now, but even *he* wouldn't know all her secrets. A girl always had to hold back a little something for herself. She knew *that* much. She wasn't *totally* clueless.

57

"Delsie, what was it like when the CEBS thing hit Washington?" Lucy was chatting to Delsie on Skype. She had asked Nate if it was okay for her to make some personal calls at work as she felt a bit guilty doing that on company time. "You're your own boss, now, Lucy," he had said, "so you can make your own boundaries around that kind of thing." He smiled. "These are exceptional times, though," he added, giving her shoulder a squeeze. "Go call your friend."

That was okay, the shoulder squeeze thing. Nate, being Mr Nice Guy, would have done that to any employee, even an old hag in her 60s who had bad breath, no sense of humour and never took Beemer for walkie talkies.

Lucy wanted to have a live conversation with Delsie, rather than e-mailing back and forth, and Delsie was still not using her cellphone. "I was really worried about you," Lucy said. "Did you have an emotional meltdown? I know you were upset right after it happened, but then I heard nothing for days. And all the news reports said people just fell apart, went to bits and did terrible things to themselves."

"Yeah, it was pretty grim," Delsie said. "I had a ton of emotional crap come up, but I seemed to be hit less brutally than lots of others."

"What kind of things came up …if you're okay sharing that?"

"Well, stuff about my dad, regrets, you know, and this really intense anger at him for leaving us, that kind of thing. And other kinds of regrets for my mum—not being there for her more, feeling really guilty about that."

"But did you feel like… I dunno… *harming* yourself or anything like that, like so many people did?"

"Sort of, but not really. It was weird. At first, I felt as if I hated myself. There was like this searing pain going through me, as if it was burning up stuff inside, like a ton of Clorox in my blood, cleaning me out, but then I felt different… better." She laughed. "Still crappy and exhausted, but somehow better." She paused. "But you know what was *really* weird, Luce? *Two* weird things, actually… no, *three* things! Shit. So much happened. I'm still processing it all."

"Tell me." Lucy was captivated. In Delsie's case, this *Pandephonium* thing seemed to have transformed her somehow. She looked different, in some indefinable way. Still the same friendly face that Lucy had always felt would lull her male opponents into a false sense of security in the courtroom, her petite frame, innocent blue eyes, tousled brown hair and pouty lips concealing a whippet-fast mind and a masterful ability to see all the angles.

"Well, the effect lasted for about an hour, although it was most intense for the first 20 minutes. That was when I had all those horrible feelings about my parents, plus this really sadistic teacher in high school and some bullies that I wanted to *shred* with my bare hands when I relived those feelings. God, I *hated* those evil kids."

She paused, took a breath, reflecting. "But then I started to get the feeling that law school was not what I was meant to be doing. I had, like, all these other emotions come up—gouging conflicts about the purpose of it all and who I was becoming, in the process of learning how to apply the law, no matter what I personally thought about it. When that stuff came up, I started to feel really sick, upchucking my lovely multi-coloured breakfast right there on the sidewalk, alongside lots of others sharing their menu ideas."

Lucy laughed, imagining the pavement splattered like a Pollock painting, but she could tell that her friend was having a tough time re-living her experience.

"You know how some people talk about their lives flashing before their eyes if they think they're about to die, with all their memories flooding through at once…? Well, it was like that, but in the other direction, going *forward* from where you are, rather than *up* to that moment. I had all these feelings and images—like an emotional preview about life as a lawyer and what I would have to do to be really good at it."

"Wow. Intense," Lucy said. "And…?"

"*And*… I haven't opened a text book since, although it's only been just over a week and I'm still, you know, dealing with this stuff. But, Luce, I don't think I'll be going back to studying law. There's something in me now, or maybe something *no longer* in me, that makes this feel totally wrong, like a total mis-fit for me."

Lucy was quiet, watching her friend process this realization. She was processing it with her, wondering what life would be like for Delsie now

...and if something similar would happen to her, Lucy, if she got hit with the Cellphone Emotional Breakdown Syndrome. Would she no longer want to work for Nate? Would she want to get back into fashion design or would she head off in some other direction altogether? She almost *envied* Delsie having this... epiphany, or whatever it was.

"I went to see this shrink for some help sorting it all out," Delsie said. "WashU was offering free counselling for everyone affected, so I decided, what the hell. Might as well see what else the universe had to throw at me."

"What did he say?"

"She. Actually, she said some pretty interesting stuff that really helped. She said if we have low self-esteem—I mean, fuck, who *doesn't*, right?—then we have an inner conflict between who we really are and who we were told we should be. But we suppress all our intuitive urges and dreams and stuff and let our heads decide things for us, based on logic or fear of not making the grade. So we go through life conflicted with ourselves and with each other... pretty much in conflict with life itself." Delsie gave a wry laugh. "She said all that negative programming made us build a *case* against ourselves, trying to prove that we really *weren't* good enough or worthy or whatever, because that's the crappy thinking that we had built our lives upon. Dah-dah! A day in the life of a lawyer. Always building a case against someone."

"So...?"

"So she said this CEBS thing was acting like a kind of purge of all the stuff that was in the way of our true calling or vocation or whatever you want to call it. It was putting us back on track with ourselves, once we managed to clear out all the emotional crap that had been holding it down—*if* we managed to clear it out."

"Shit, Delsie. This is life-changing stuff."

"Yeah, I know. And she said if we had trouble dealing with that big dump of negative programming all at once, showing us the mismatch between what we had become and who we really are, then we could really lose it and go nuts."

"Which is what happened to so many people who got hit with CEBS, right?"

"Yeah. Exactly. Total meltdown. Too much of a reality check for some people to deal with, seeing all that stuff at once."

Lucy's mind was reeling from all the revelations. She might need therapy herself after this.

"But, Luce, you know what was *really* freaky?"

"Even freakier than that, you mean?"

"Yeah, this bit is kind of *out there*…" Delsie hesitated, seeking the right words.

"Is this the second thing that happened?"

"Yes. But it's about my mom."

"Your mom? Is she okay? Sorry, Delsie, I forgot to ask, I was so focused on you."

"Hey, no worries. This is all pretty gripping stuff. And she's okay, thanks—much better, in fact." She took a breath. "Anyway, my mom was heavily sedated when CEBS hit, so she wasn't conscious when all this happened. She'd been given a load of medication because she was in pain and for a while, there, the doctor wasn't sure she would pull through, as she got some kind of infection and her kidneys started to fail. It was chaos in the hospital that day but she was lucky. She was out cold and in a private room, so she wasn't affected." Delsie paused. "Not *visibly*, anyway…"

"What do you mean?"

"Well, afterwards, she told me she had this… vision and she felt a kind of hot healing energy going through her."

"What kind of vision?" Lucy was on the edge of her seat, temporarily released from the body glove of her chair.

"She saw all kinds of stuff happening in her body, at the cellular level, things moving through her bloodstream, organs lighting up—stuff she didn't understand at all but she still sort of understood, on some other level, without being able to describe it."

"This is unreal, Delsie." Lucy tilted her head, unsure what to think. "Was it because of all the drugs she was on, giving her some kind of hallucination? I know steroids can cause stuff like that…"

"Yeah, that's what I thought too, but I talked to her doctor about it afterwards and he said that almost all the patients who had been sedated at that time had experienced something similar. And my mom is so much *better*, Lucy! She looks like a new woman—kinda radiant, like I've never seen her. It's… it's really something else. You sort of have to see it to believe it, and I'm still pinching myself."

She leaned forward to gauge Lucy's reaction. "You still with me, girlfriend? I haven't shared this with anyone else because it sounds so *out there*, you know? You're not thinking I've totally lost it, are you?"

"No, of course not," Lucy said, shaking her head. She knew no one more discerning than Delsie, with her razor-sharp legal mind constantly challenging every remotely implausible scenario.

"But Delse, I've got to go. I'm at work and I need to get back to it. Maybe we could chat more this evening... Hang on, though... what was the third thing that happened that you were going to tell me about?"

"Oh, yeah." Delsie was grinning. "That doctor I mentioned who was treating my mom? A very handsome young East Indian guy who seemed to take a particular interest in her case—*and* in her daughter, which is really going above and beyond, don't you think?"

Lucy laughed, her heart suspended between incredulity and wonderment for the way life sometimes split itself into two class acts—one that seemed so heartbreakingly brutal, the other like a cosmic analgesic that made all the pain and heartache fade away, leaving a fresh new love of life itself. A daily human miracle, the alchemy of a fully felt emotion.

58

16 September 2020

Sitting cross-legged on the sand under the speckled shade of a storm-battered palapa, Celle was reading *Jonathan Livingston Seagull* in Spanish. It was a delicious, uplifting read, as you'd expect from a book written by a bird, but Celle's attention was drifting. She was drawn away from the words by the balmy breeze, the lilting swoops of the frigate birds swirling above, the hot herby smell from the clifftop behind her, and the intermittent sight of Matt swimming in the gentle swell.

They were in a small cove, away from the main Sayulita beach, enjoying the peaceful solitude and calmer waters of the sheltered bay. The waves on the main beach were always boisterous and rowdy, perfect for surfing but not ideal for delicate swimmers who preferred a more genteel immersion. Celle loved to swim but only when the water was warm and flat enough that she could slice through with minimal drag and maximum view of the teeming sea life beneath her.

She had been keeping a lazy eye on Matt, who usually swam about a mile a day, the fins of his arms sparkling in the sun as he did a steady crawl parallel to the beach.

She had taken a quick dip earlier and was drying off toastily in the late-morning heat, her bronzed skin tight and gently crusted in salt.

Suddenly, she felt footsteps pounding the sand and looked up. A tall dark-haired woman was running towards her, waving her arms, looking frantic. "My… The man swimming," she pointed towards the water, "you must help him! He's drowning!"

She reached for Celle's hand and yanked her upright. "But he's fine." Celle was flustered. Who was this woman, appearing out of nowhere, telling her what to do? "I just saw him a minute ago…" She shaded her eyes and scanned the water. No sign of him.

"There, by that rock." The woman pointed at a rock jutting into the sea about 100 metres from the shore. "That's where he went down. Go!"

She shoved her towards the water and Celle stumbled, then ran like lightning into the water, flung herself forward and ripped through the gentle swell towards the rock. Her toned body was a torpedo, barrelling forward, and she reached the rock in less than a minute.

No Matt. She swivelled frantically, treading water, then tucked and dove, scanning the rocky outcrop and the sandy seabed below her. Nothing. She surfaced and scanned again, a frantic periscope. There! A hand above the water, a lifetime away.

She kicked out towards it, terrified she'd lose sight of it before she got there. But she reached him, grabbed his hand and dove under to lift him up. His face contorted in pain, legs twisted in spasm, he was paralysed by cramps, unable to save himself from sinking.

She cupped his chin and lifted him above the surface, where he heaved and sputtered, his lungs already waterlogged. Turning sideways, she rolled him onto his back, resting his head against her body, putting her left arm across his chest and under his right arm, and struck out for the shore in a one-armed, leg-powered race.

It took an eternity to get back, Matt slumped inert against her— exhausted or already gone, she didn't know. As her feet found purchase on the sand, she dragged him to the shore and, once clear of the water, fell to her knees beside him. Tilting his head back, she pinched his nose, breathed deeply through his blue lips, then pumped his chest. Again. Again. She turned his head to the side and pumped steadily. He made a choking sound, sputtering water onto the sand, and she held him on his side, rubbing his back as he let go of the sea inside him. Finally, his airwaves were clear and he lay back, spent.

They were both trembling—Matt from exhaustion and shock, Celle from adrenaline, fear and relief. She rubbed his arms, pummeled his feet and his thighs, then ran to get his towel. Shaking out the sand, she raised him up and wrapped the towel around him, rubbing vigorously till his teeth were less chatty and some colour returned to his mottled skin.

"Celle." He finally spoke, his voice raspy. "You saved me. Again." He leaned against her, slowly steadying, allowing himself to be restored.

"Mateo," she said, finally taking a breath for herself. "I thought I'd lost you." She cradled his face. "Can you stand?"

He nodded and she helped him up, his legs jerking as he stood, but he hobbled with her along the sand to the rest of their belongings. She lowered him down onto her towel, and reached for her beach bag. She had a bottle of her favourite Orangina—her one sugary vice that always tasted so fizzily divine on a hot day, straight from the cooler. She popped the lid and held the bottle to his lips. He gulped some down, sputtered, and drank again more slowly—small sips that fed his starved muscles and soothed his salted throat.

"Better?"

"Yes. A million times." He smiled, nodding his safe return. "How did you know I was in trouble?"

"There was a woman…" Celle scanned the beach, only just realizing that the woman was gone. "She just appeared on the beach and shouted at me to go and rescue you. I have no idea who she was."

"She must have seen me from the clifftop and run down the path," Matt said. "I'm sorry she didn't stick around so I could thank her."

"There was something… strange about her," Celle said, trying to remember what she had looked like. "She had this funny thing on her arm—a wrist brace or some kind of high-tech diving watch. And she had long dark hair, very piercing eyes… but that's all I remember. It all happened so fast."

"Maybe we'll see her in the village," Matt said, his words slurring as fatigue tugged at his depleted reserves.

"Let's get you home," Celle said. "Do you think you can make it back up the path?"

Matt grimaced. "I'll give it a shot…"

"Hang on." Celle reached into her bag again and brought out some dark chocolate. They always had a few squares after their swim, and she kept it wrapped in newspaper so it wouldn't melt before they got to it. She broke off a small chunk for herself and gave the rest to Matt, who munched hungrily, groaning in pleasure.

"Thank you, Mayans. Life-saving manna from heaven." He grinned, looking almost like himself. "Or should I say life-saving mamma…"

Cell smiled, gathering up her things. "We need to go before it gets any hotter," she said. "Or you could stay here in the shade and I can go and get help? Maybe bring a boat around to the cove?"

"No, it's okay… Just give me another minute for the chocolate to hit… I'm almost back."

Celle's pulse was coming back down to normal and her body was starting to chill. She knew they both needed some hot liquids as soon as possible. She drank some water from her stash and gave the rest to Matt.

He pulled on his T-shirt and shorts, and she gave him a hand up from the sand, draping his towel over his shoulders and hers over her own, as well as her beach bag, and their sandals looped through her fingers till they reached the path.

They walked slowly up the beach, feeling humbled and grateful, shaken and stirred, more loved and lucky than anyone else alive.

59

---

18 September 2020

Marnie was walking swiftly to her rendezvous. She was to go to a small café in a rather shabby part of town and wait there for Ray. It all seemed a bit *cloak-and-dagger*—really, it was just plain ridiculous, her skulking around like a spy—yet also quite thrilling. She, Marnie, was meeting a now-famous physicist and would be taken to his secret lab to possibly find out what was causing the Pandephonium sweeping the globe, terrorizing people everywhere. What other elementary teacher got to go on such a fabulous field trip?

She would be getting the scoop of the century, for which every single media outlet would pay her a fortune—enough to last her the rest of her life without having to work. But she couldn't tell anyone and would have to contain her excitement—and, if she was honest, her ego, which was bursting to tell the whole planet that she was the only one privy to what was really going on... and that *her mother* had possibly found a way to save humanity.

She could see how easily needy mortals could get seduced by such heady secrets and the lure of instant notoriety. She would have to content herself with being seduced by Steve, while basking in the silent glory of preserving her mother's legacy to mankind.

Her excitement was tempered by momentary spurts of sheer terror that curdled her innards, leaving her weak-kneed and in danger of turning to mush. But not the kind of mush she felt with Steve, the source of which was located a bit further south in her body and was far more likely to generate delicious pleasure than the heart-stopping pain inflicted on traitors to their country.

What if she got caught? Would she be shot, tortured, publicly shamed as the perpetrator, or just plain *disappeared*?

Should she have told DeeDee or Lucy where she was going, in case she never came back? *Hey, DeeDee, just FYI, I'm going to a clandestine meeting in a shady part of town with a scientist possibly involved in CEBS. If you don't hear from me again, please send out a search party.* Well, *that* wasn't going to work, was it. The whole point of all this secrecy was so that no one would know what she was up to or where she was up to it.

Ray had told her he would be watching out for her from the window of the café, but not to look pointedly at him. She was to keep on walking if he didn't acknowledge her or somehow catch her attention. She slowed her pace as she passed the window, the muscles in her neck rigid from the effort of not staring fixedly to see if he was there. Her feet still moving her forward, she gave a slow nonchalant glance in his direction, but no one signaled to her from inside, so she kept on walking. The hairs on the back of her neck stood up in prickly anticipation, fearing a sudden clasp around her throat as a secret service agent neutralized her as an obvious threat to national security.

She hadn't been aware that she *had* all those hairs back there or that they could perform such an upstanding manoeuvre. While she was pondering this phenomenon to distract herself, Ray appeared beside her, took her arm and guided her down an alleyway to a long, low building with a series of narrow roll-up metal doors along the front. He withdrew a key from his pocket, undid a large padlock, rattled up the metal slider, unlocked the door behind it, and invited her into his lab.

For a moment, there was total darkness when Ray closed the door behind them. Then he flicked a switch on the wall and the room came to life. It was a long, narrow, windowless space with a computer desk, a large old computer chair and a wooden stool along the side wall, and two large machines along the back, motors thrumming in a bass key that Marnie could feel vibrating through the soles of her feet. A large air-conditioner hummed in jerky harmony, keeping the room cool.

"Keep your coat on," Ray said, pulling out the computer chair, gesturing for her to sit.

"I'd prefer the stool, thanks," she said, sitting down. The chair felt like too big a role for her to take on.

She sat and he paced. "I've made a huge mistake here, Marnie," he said soberly. "I should never have agreed to bring you here. It was madness, exposing you to this risk. I don't know what I was thinking."

"I promise I won't tell anyone," Marnie said earnestly.

"Yes, well, I made the same promise—" He stopped himself, shaking his head. "I don't think you realize how risky this is," he said. "If this lab is discovered and its purpose exposed, you can say goodbye to your physics lessons… and everything else."

"I don't want to put you—or anyone—at risk," Marnie said, shifting on the stool. "But you said I might be able to help you…" His concern was contagious. *What was she getting herself into?*

Ray paced the room, searching for some safe route to salvaging his conscience and making this right. Lily would kill him for risking his life like this, and he had never shared the true nature of his work as it would have endangered her, too. But Marnie… she was just like her mother—so highly principled that she'd breeze right past the dangers, once she'd weighed up the pros and cons of what was involved, and head straight for the goal.

But what *was* the goal? When he saw what was happening out there, people going nuts, harming themselves and the chaos that resulted, he had to keep reminding himself what this was all for.

"Tell me how I can help," Marnie said.

"I'm not sure you *can* help, Marnie." He shook his head. "I think… what I'm doing here is more challenging than you can imagine, and it takes a toll. I guess I have moments of weakness, wanting some… support or some kind of outlet for the solitary strain of it all." He shrugged off his discomfort. The physicist asking a clueless young woman for help… He was getting really desperate.

"To be honest, it probably also represents a… tenuous if irrational sense of connection to your mother." What the hell. He knew he was trying to justify things to himself—and to Frannie, imagining her listening on some other realm. If she could hear him, he could sure use some help, right now, once she got over her fury at him confiding in her daughter.

This man loved my mother, Marnie realized, feeling his need to share what he had probably never admitted to anyone else. "I understand," she said gently. "I can't begin to be what she was, but if you tell me what you're doing, maybe I can find a way to help."

She gestured at the machines against the back wall. "I'm guessing all this has something to do with CEBS," she said, "and what my mother was doing before she died." She froze, suddenly struck by an unthinkable thought. "Was that why they died—because they were caught doing something illegal?"

"No, no," Ray said, shaking his head resolutely. "Whatever their reasons, they *chose* to… pass on. They weren't killed, Marnie."

She nodded, trying to decide if them being murdered was less awful than them having freely chosen to check out.

"So… are you… is this what's causing those frequencies getting transmitted through cellphones? You said my mother was working on frequencies for helping humans be *better,* though… Is that what this is for?"

Ray sighed, weighing his words, and they all felt unbearably heavy. "Your parents were working with frequencies that could generate certain mental or emotional states…"

"You mean like mind control?"

"No, not like that. It was much more benign and inherent to our humanness—not something foreign or external to be imposed on people." He began pacing again, his movements helping to align his thoughts.

"The frequencies were designed to elicit emotions that had been suppressed—as you know from the news and what I've shared in interviews. After decades of using cellphones, being exposed to harmful electromagnetic fields, and living so speedily, multi-tasking, and overstimulating their minds with far too many data, most people are in an almost catatonic state of overload and disconnectedness from their deeper emotions—and, therefore, from themselves." He paused, nodding to himself as he re-affirmed the true purpose of what he and Frannie were doing.

"So… what's happening is a *good* thing," Marnie said, a hopeful question in her voice.

"Ultimately, a very good thing. There is fallout, obviously, and those who have been most deeply disconnected have the hardest time dealing with the emotion-triggering frequency. They are also the ones who would most readily succumb to a complete mental or digital takeover." He took a reassuring breath, fortified by the rightness of his words.

"But it's a necessary part of shedding what is decimating our humanity and taking us to a very desolate place. Without this intervention…" he gestured at the machines, "we will self-destruct, without even realizing it. We will not survive our own dysfunction, and the dysfunction itself prevents us from seeing what we're doing and where it's taking us."

He paused, seeming to have reached some kind of resolution within himself.

"The thing is, Marnie, someone hijacked the system and—"

Pounding on the door made them both jump. "FBI! Open up!"

"Shit. I knew it." Ray pulled open a drawer, whipped out a bible and slapped it down on the desk in front of Marnie, opening it at random.

"Be reading this when I let them in," he whispered fiercely. "You're a student studying with me. I'll talk. Don't say a thing unless they ask you."

Ray unlocked the door and stood back. Two dark-suited FBI agents immediately stepped in, wielding their badges, looking incongruously like Laurel and Hardy. One was large, stocky and broad-shouldered, with closely cropped grey hair and hard grey eyes—obviously the more senior of the two. The other was fair-haired, so skinny it was hard to see what was holding up his jacket, and looking as if he'd just finished college.

"Agent Ross and…" gesturing at his colleague, "Agent Burston," said

Agent Ross. "Dr Spence, we need to know what you are doing here."

"Nothing nefarious, I can assure you, gentlemen, but if I told you, you wouldn't believe me," Ray said, looking shifty and nervous.

Marnie looked at him, horrified. Surely he wasn't going to actually *tell* them what he was doing…

"Sir, we have reason to believe that you are engaging in activities that threaten national security, and we will impound all of this here equipment, take you into custody and shut you down if you do not tell us precisely what you are doing."

"Okay." Ray slumped into his chair, defeated and resigned. He reached for a thick pile of computer printout sitting at one end of his desk, and placed it on the desk in front of him.

"I've been working on a project," he said, humbly, spreading out some of the pages to reveal endless lines of numbers. "I'm applying my skills as a quantum physicist to tap into cosmic consciousness and…" he looked up at the two agents…"are you sure you want to hear this?"

Agent Ross was getting impatient, and his sidekick was shifting from one foot to the other, looking as if he wanted to ransack the place to liven things up. "Sir, please proceed. Do not delay any further."

"Well…" Ray shrugged uncomfortably. "The thing is, Agent Ross, I'm in the process of proving the existence of God."

Marnie's jaw practically hit the desk, and Ray gave her foot a gentle pressure with one of his own.

"Dr Spence," she said, looking innocently horrified and awed by her teacher's admission, "I thought you said you would *never* divulge this information to *anyone*."

"Sir," Agent Ross said, "what *exactly* are you doing and what are these here machines for?"

"Those are the computers I use for processing the cosmic data—the frequencies, the numbers, the vibrations," Ray said, holding up the bundle of paper. "See, here…" He stood up and unfolded the first three sheets, which dropped to the floor like a shower curtain, numbers spilling the whole way down to the bottom.

"See this code?" He stabbed a finger at the centre of the paper cascade. "Can you see these patterns?"

Both agents leaned in for a closer look, squinting and trying to make out what he was showing them. Finally, they straightened up, shaking their heads.

"What are we supposed to be looking at here?" Agent Ross said.

"The patterns!" Ray stabbed at the paper again, frowning at their failure to see the obvious. "These patterns here show a definite divine presence. These numbers relate to frequencies that are entirely distinctive and are like nothing we've been able to perceive before. But, now, with quantum analyses, we can. You can even see from the shape of them that they represent something. And we've been correlating these numbers with certain sounds and certain passages in the Bible that point to a very real connection."

He turned to Marnie. "Child, what was that passage we were just reading?"

Marnie looked down at the Bible, scanning frantically for something that might make sense in this utterly nonsensical conversation. "Bring the righteous unto me?" she asked.

"No, not that bit," Ray said, frustrated, taking the Bible from her and feverishly scanning the verses, revealing flashes of colour from sections highlighted in neon-green and red markers. "It's in the Book of Revelation…"

Ray turned to the agents. "I'm concerned about this information getting out there, Agent Ross," he said. "What I am compiling here is going to change the way people perceive our very existence. How can I know that you will not reveal what we are doing here?"

Without waiting for an answer, he gestured expansively, eyes wild, looking past them to a wondrous vision of a world transformed. "Imagine," he said, "what life would be like if we had absolute proof of God's existence—*irrefutable* scientific proof." He shook his head in wonder. "This is what I've been working on behind the scenes my whole scientific life. There is no higher calling."

He shook his head at the enormity of what he was doing. "Imagine what this would do for law enforcement and for society," he said passionately. "No more wars, nations coming together to gain a deeper understanding of what we are discovering… there is no end to the good that can come from this."

He looked from one agent to the other. "Do you have cosmologists at the FBI?"

"No, sir, I don't believe we do."

Ray regarded them sadly, poor simpletons that they were. "Gentlemen, cosmology is the study of reality, of the universe, of how things work. How on earth can you *investigate* anything if you don't know how things work?"

They remained deadpan.

He eyed them critically. "Do you mean to say," he said, very much meaning to say it, "that I have needlessly shared the details of my top-secret project with you? That you are *not* here to find out about my divine intelligence project?"

"We have reason to believe that you are involved in the Cellphone Emotional Breakdown Syndrome," Agent Ross said, "and you certainly seem to have the necessary equipment and expertise. Can you prove that you are not, in fact, so involved?"

"There are thousands of quantum physicists with this kind of expertise," Ray said. "You may have heard of research scientist Linda Resnick, for example, who said: 'Physicists have finally found god in little tiny particles.' You can look it up. So, you see, it's not just me doing this kind of work." Ray spread his hands, generously including his colleagues.

"Where my work differs is in its focus and specificity. Physicists talk about God in generic terms, using the phenomenon of particle unpredictability to indicate a higher consciousness that defies the usual scientific parameters." He paused to let that sink in, allowing for the inevitable bureaucratic handicap. "People tend to think scientists are purely rational, relying on logic and the proof provided by hard evidence—probably a bit like FBI agents." He smiled. "But quantum physics exposes us to a very different realm—one where we see that science and spirituality can and do co-exist and are, in fact, *utterly interdependent*. It confirms what our early ancestors knew through their spiritual practices for communing with the cosmos, way ahead of where we are today, in terms our society's perception of things."

Agent Ross appeared unmoved, arms folded across his large chest. "How, exactly, are you obtaining this... evidence?"

"Everything has a frequency," Ray said. "Even the skepticism you are emanating now has a frequency that we can detect and quantify. But negative frequencies are low down on the spectrum, whereas frequencies of peace, enlightenment and divine intelligence have a much higher vibration. So my work here involves detecting the higher frequencies permeating the universe, to determine what, exactly, is out there."

He reached for the Bible again. "Look," he said, thumbing through the pages. "There's a passage here… I marked it… where is it, where is it…" He looked up at the agents. "There's a passage here that explains the timing for all this, too, and now is the time! It's never been more clear to me."

He was starting to get worked up, sweat breaking out on his brow, hands shaking. He pulled out a massive cotton handkerchief and dabbed at his forehead.

Marnie reached towards him. "Dr Spence, you know what your doctor said about your blood pressure. Please calm down. You can't afford to have another one of those episodes. What we're doing here is too important." She looked at the two agents imploringly. "Agent Ross, is there anything else you need to know? I could show you some of these figures on the computer, if that would help, but Dr Spence really needs to rest and take his medication."

Ray had slumped back in his seat, head down, muttering to himself.

The agents looked at each other, taking their silent measure of things.

"Sir, Ma'am, we're done here for now, but be advised that you are under observation, Dr Spence, and we may come back for another conversation, at some point." He nodded at them both. "Good day to you."

Agent Burston nodded grudgingly, looking disappointed not to have seen more action. With a final backward glance at the humming computers, the two men exited, closing the door quietly behind them.

Ray leaned back in his chair, eyes closed, exhaling a haggard breath. "Well," he said finally, "if we fail in our mission of finding God, we could probably take up acting."

Marnie gave a shaky laugh, still in shock from such a close encounter with the Feds.

Ray turned to her and said firmly, "You, young lady, are going straight home now—*no objections*—before I really *do* have a heart attack. If we talk about this further—*if*—it will be in my home office."

The walk home was a sobering one for Marnie, her pace slowed by foot-dragging thoughts. *Was Ray behind CEBS or not?* He had started to tell her about the system being hijacked. Did that mean someone else was running things?

Then he had poured all his nervous energy into fake fanaticism for a quantum god-quest. But… *was* it fake? If it was, he had certainly put on a good act, making it all sound plausible and quantumly unquestionable. But where did that leave her, their interaction and her possible involvement?

Dead in the water, it seemed, unless she could think of a compelling way to help him in his quest, once she'd figured out which one he was actually *working* on.

60

November 2020

A Day to Remember: American President Stuns Nations with Radical Policy Overhaul

From staff reporter <u>Andrea Goodman</u>

Democracy for Good—November 8, 2020. Today, Remembrance Day, the President of the United States stunned the world with a televised speech at the White House, announcing radical reforms to his administration and specific aspects of US policy, and causing many viewers and reporters to doubt his sanity.

In what was his first public appearance since he went into seclusion two months ago to recover from the effects of CEBS (the Cellphone Emotional Breakdown Syndrome), the President seemed subdued, almost humble, choosing his words carefully as he outlined the various measures he said would be implemented as soon as humanly possible.

Top of the list was the rollback of 5G and other existing wireless telecom technologies that had, he said, clearly been harming people all over the globe and had been used to undermine their constitutional rights. He said he was ashamed to confess that governments were aware of the harm but were too economically and strategically invested to change things.

Anyone supporting the maintenance of satellites transmitting 5G or other harmful radio frequencies from space could forget about ever doing business with America again, he said. In a rare show of confident humour, the President added that they would certainly not be invited for tea at the White House, nor would they be getting a Christmas card.

Other reforms outlined by the President included the establishment of an independent task force to oversee the dismantling of wireless systems and the development of safe telecom alternatives. The task force would exclude any representatives, scientists or spokespersons involved in the wireless industry, he said, and its members would be selected from among the independent scientific community, holistic health advocates and others who had demonstrated their impartiality, as well as their expertise and knowledge in relevant areas.

A second independent task force will investigate the effectiveness and viability of vaccines and other drugs, alongside studies into healthy immune-boosting approaches that rely on traditional herbal and other natural substances versus drugs from the pharmaceutical industry.

A Ministry of Human Progress will be established to develop educational programs focusing on personal development, nutrition, creativity and emotional intelligence, in addition to handling grants for small businesses working in these areas.

Priority will be given to businesses dedicated to the betterment of society and the planet, the President said, and corporations currently depleting or polluting the environment with chemicals, plastics or other contaminants would be undergoing investigations over the next two years, starting with Monsanto, American Electric Power and Nestlé, among others.

Carbon taxes are to be abolished, he said, since they do nothing to protect the environment and merely generate funds that ultimately find their way back into the hands of the original polluters.

Funding will also be designated for the development of alternative eco-friendly forms of energy and transport, and the importation of petroleum products is to be progressively reduced over the next decade, reaching 0% by 2030.

The manufacture and use of plastic packaging, toys, gadgets and other non-essential items will be severely curtailed, and phased out completely by 2026. Companies and small businesses creating planet-friendly alternatives, as well as natural systems for cleaning up marine and other environments, will be given tax breaks and other economic incentives.

The President said that, while he was open to the idea of signing the Kyoto (Climate Change) Protocol, he was more interested in promoting radical changes and taking action than in discussing strategies that typically became distorted by political or other bias. Those days are over, he said. It's time for action and America will be leading the way.

He concluded his speech saying that he had chosen Remembrance Day to mark this turning point in US history—a day that all Americans would remember as the day they began to regain their freedom and once again believe in the American Dream. It was also, he said, a time to put an end to costly conflicts and manufactured wars, and the trillions of dollars traditionally spent on military defence would instead be invested in the programs and initiatives of his revitalized administration.

In his final remarks, the President became emotional, his voice shaky as he delivered a heartfelt message to his fellow Americans:

"America has gone through a dark time in its history, with many nations turning against us because we have attacked, depleted or oppressed them. I want to live to see the day that America is loved again, that we are once again respected, admired and emulated by other nations—not for our weapons, our slang or our strategies for control, but for our innovative thinking, empowered citizens, our humanitarianism and our initiatives to elevate the human spirit towards truly *united states*."

The news has left Americans reeling from the turnaround. Many have expressed disbelief at seeing their formerly antagonistic, bumbling, arrogant, ego-driven leader transform into a human being with a heart and a conscience. Some say he must have suffered some kind of mental breakdown due to CEBS, had a brain transplant or some kind of spiritual epiphany—maybe a visitation by Billy Graham. Others claim it is just another clever ploy to dupe the voters into liking him and that it certainly won't last.

Whatever the case, America has witnessed a presidential intervention like no other. Nations around the world are debating what these radical reforms will mean for trade with the US, while American corporations are protesting the move as unconstitutional, simultaneously scrambling to clean up their acts in case the President *hasn't* gone insane and actually means business.

The wireless telecom industry has reacted aggressively, claiming the dismantling of wireless systems will cause the economy to collapse and the President will seriously rue the day he made such an egregiously stupid move at the expense of every cellphone-carrying American citizen.

Although still guardedly optimistic, anti-wireless activists, health advocates, human-rights groups, Amnesty International, environmental organizations, holistic healthcare practitioners and countless others are applauding the President's approach, saying it heralds a new era for civilisation and ushers in the kind of enlightened leadership that has, over the centuries, been tragically and progressively missing in politics.

But we should not be stunned and amazed by this. The proposed reforms are the way things *should* be and *should have been* all along. It is the way things *have been* that should have had us all out on the streets protesting, long ago.

The US President is the first world leader to re-emerge after being affected by CEBS, which he says is not the *demonic attack* that people believe it to be but is, in fact, a human reset program that cuts through all our mental and emotional crap to a mind-blowing awareness of the way things really are.

The world watches and waits for the other affected leaders—in the UK, China, Russia and Australia—to re-emerge from their respective withdrawals and share their experiences. France is also on the list, as the French President was at 10 Downing Street with the British Prime Minister when London was hit by CEBS on 8 September 2020.

What other staggering pronouncements will they make? Here at *Democracy for Good*, we are withholding comment until we see what actions are taken by our seemingly transformed US President—a man whose words and actions have, until now, generated widespread scorn, disdain and loathing. Let's see if the rubber hits the road and if that road takes us somewhere good.

Let's see if, in fact, he has become (dare I say it) *a good man*.

61

Steve was in the shower, getting ready for their trip. While she was waiting, Marnie turned on the news just as Rick Weston was starting his morning update on the CEBS situation.

"The unthinkable has happened," Rick intoned gravely. "After CEBS—the Cellphone Emotional Breakdown Syndrome—caused chaos, injury and death in all of the countries hit so far, other nations are now asking if they can get it. The extraordinary impact of CEBS on the US President has led to millions of global citizens demanding the same kind of government reforms."

He turned sideways as a live feed opened up on a screen beside him.

"We go now to our Canadian reporter, Sally Juniper in Toronto, for a sense of what our northern neighbours think about what's happening. Sally, what's the mood on the street there in downtown Toronto?"

"Well, Rick, the mood here is a mixture of excited optimism and angry injustice. Many young people, especially, are excited at the possibilities of the kind of reforms that the US President is implementing, whereas older members of the population seem extremely frustrated and angry that such measures will not be taking place in Canada—unless it also gets hit with CEBS. And they are incensed to think that such extreme circumstances are required for some sanity to prevail in politics."

"So, they actually want to get hit with CEBS? Is that what they're saying?"

"Yes, indeed. Many people are saying that the benefits far outweigh the downsides, even if there are fatalities, since deaths are already occurring as a result of misguided policies and government greed. Considering what has happened in the US, they feel cheated out of the kinds of reforms that could save lives, restore some of Canada's contaminated natural environment, put an end to senseless wars, and bring back a sense of real community, which is something Canadians really appreciate and have been missing, they say, for a very long time."

Sally turned to the passersby on the sidewalk behind her. She stopped an older woman carrying groceries in a large brown bag hugged to her chest.

"Madam, may I ask what you think about what happened in the US due to CEBS, if you know what that is?"

The woman frowned, and those around her stopped to listen in. "Of course I know what it is," she said, indignantly. "You'd have to live in a cave not to have heard about it. Whatever happened in the US, I want some of that and I certainly want it for my family—it might knock some sense into them. I never thought I'd see such a thing in my lifetime."

Beside her, there was a young mother carrying a small baby on her hip. Sally turned to her. "What do you think about this?"

Hoisting the baby higher on her hip, the young woman paused to reflect. "I think… it's probably the best thing that has happened to mankind since… I can't think when. Maybe since politics began, whenever that was?"

A young man with a guitar slung over his shoulder was shaking his head and leaned in to give his opinion. "After what happened to that man? I'm a believer."

Sally turned to him with her microphone. "You believe in the President?"

"Uh huh." He shook his head. "I believe in miracles, man. If someone like him can turn out good, then anything's possible. I'm all for this Pandephonium thing, whatever it is. Bring it on!"

The young woman spoke up again. "But how do we? Bring it on, I mean. It all seems so random and we still don't know who's doing this, so how can we get them to hit Canada?"

A small crowd had built up around the conversation, others wanting to have their say.

"No way we want that!" Two lanky teenagers jostled each other for a piece of the action. "I'm not giving up my cellphone!" one said. "My phone's, like, my life."

"Yeah," the other one pitched in. "We don't want that stuff coming here, taking away our rights."

"Thanks, everyone," Sally said, turning back to the camera and moving away from the bystanders as they continued to debate among themselves.

"Rick, what many young people—older folks, too—don't seem to realize, and what the EMF activists have been quick to point out, is that people don't have to give up internet access just bec—"

Static buzzed across the screen, distorting the image and obliterating the reporter's words. Suddenly, the screen went blank and Sally was gone.

Rick turned back to the camera in the studio, shrugging apologetically. "Well, we seem to have lost our live link with Toronto, folks, but I think we've got the gist of things." He shuffled his papers and cleared his throat to mark the end of that discussion.

"Meanwhile, in the UK, the British Prime Minister came out of seclusion this morning and made a public announcement that took British subjects by surprise, but not in quite the same way as our President here in the United States did. This report, from the BBC in London."

A screen opened up on his left, showing the British Prime Minister on the steps outside the distinctive black door of 10 Downing Street. He looked peaceful—thinner and a little less rumpled-looking than usual. He looked directly at the camera, his words slow and measured, his wife standing loyally beside him.

"I am resigning as Prime Minister. The past few months have shown me that I am not cut out for politics." He paused, looking around at the crowd gathered on the street behind the TV crew.

"I always wanted to be an artist but was afraid of being rather mediocre. Instead, I have ended up a con artist, and it would appear that I've made a complete hash of that, although I've conned a fair number." He smiled ruefully, his wife shaking her head.

"The policies I have pushed through Parliament have been egregiously short-sighted, and the whole Brexit scheme is a fiasco of a truly asinine order. Society will be much better off without me as their leader, as some of my family members will agree."

His wife clearly didn't although his ex-wife probably did, Marnie thought.

"I can only hope that my successor, whoever he or she is, has the moral fortitude to stay true to themselves and to what matters."

Marnie sat back and closed her eyes, summoning up the ghost of her mother walking with her on the beach of her dreams. Mum, did you do this? Were you behind this? Could anyone ever have imagined such a thing? I want to let myself be proud of you both, but how will I ever know what you actually did, now that you're gone?

She was still trying to process the enormity of what the President had said he would do. Shut down the wireless industry! It was inconceivable. Like a dream come true, but surely too good to be true. She couldn't imagine it actually happening. He would wake up some day soon, or his advisors would get him to see reason, and the whole mad idea would be dumped and passed off as some huge joke.

She was afraid to let herself believe that it could actually happen so, for now, she wasn't going to. She'd wait to see what happened before she got too excited.

On the TV screen, the scene had switched to the streets of London, outside the Prime Minister's residence. There was agitation, shouting, placards brandished and people chanting the Prime Minister's name.

"Mor-ris, Mor-ris, Mor-ris…"

A young male reporter standing in front of the mob was explaining the scene, shaking his head in bewilderment. "People don't want the Prime Minister to leave, it seems. Even though he has just confessed his political sins on national TV, his honesty has endeared him to the nation and people are calling for him to stay on."

He looked around him, taking in the crowd, a steadily moving loop of bodies parading in front of 10 Downing Street, its door now closed. "It's a peaceful demonstration—more a show of support and a rousing call to action than anything else—but the British people are saying they don't want some other, and I quote, uninitiated moron to step in, now that this Prime Minister has finally found some integrity and can actually see what he did wrong."

He consulted his notes. "It's quite extraordinary. People seem to see the CEBS phenomenon as a kind of rite of passage to human decency, and everyone wants a piece of it. As you can see…" he swivelled to the crowd behind him, "they are clearly uplifted and optimistic at the idea of having an honest leader, for a change. And what a change that would be, indeed, if they can get him to agree to stay on and if he stays true to his word."

He nodded to himself, on board with the task of persuasion. "This is Brian Redding, reporting for the BBC in London."

Marnie's mind was all over the place, still grappling with what had happened with Ray, and she was relieved to be getting away for Thanksgiving to get a break from all the craziness. Ray had been uncommunicative since the FBI visit, but she was determined to find some way to help him and earn his trust.

Hearing Steve getting dressed in the bedroom, she turned off the TV and relaxed on the couch, the latest news from the UK still messing with her head. She was always fascinated by British accents and amused herself trying to copy them. We ah so hahtened to see… I must make some tea… Oh, deah, I seem to have no maw bikkies…

Steve's laughter brought her back to Boston. "Love the accent, Miss Dawhlton. Are you ready to confront the clan?

"Oh, Mista Romayo, take me to Atlanna, to the wawm bosom of the sayouth…"

"You'll get lots of bosoms, alright," Steve laughed. "All the Romero women will be there, along with about 20 kids and grandkids." He put his suitcase by the door and walked over to give her a hug. "I love it that you go all southern on me when you're nervous."

"Going southern with you is a lot to be nervous about," Marnie said. It was strange that she had never made this trip to visit Steve's family when they were a couple before. But maybe they hadn't truly been a couple—more like fencing partners, dancing around each other, not quite sure of their feelings or their emotional footing.

Now they felt like a solid unit, and Marnie couldn't imagine not having Steve in her life. It wasn't that he made her feel more complete when he was with her; it was that she was more complete in herself, and being with him enabled her to see and share that. Plus, he really saw who she was. It was one thing to be physically loved and told you were beautiful, Marnie realized. But to be truly seen and understood… that was the deeper love.

"The only thing to fear is fear itself," Steve said, "…and maybe my mama, grammaw and Josie. The others are pretty tame, relatively speaking." He gave her a knowing look. "Ready?"

"Kandly take me away from all this utta madness." Marnie swooned against his chest.

"Is that a yes?"

"It's a yes," Marnie smiled, feeling a whole lot of southern promise in that tiny word. "Let's see if the Romero clan is ready for me."

"You're getting very cheeky, Mz Dalton. I think loving me suits you."

62

In Bonn, after a long day of heated debates with her cabinet ministers, the German Chancellor was watching the latest CEBS news with her husband and her dog, the latter paying rapt attention while the former snored on the sofa, flaked out on his back, the newspaper tenting on his chest.

We could do with that kind of emotional cattle prod here, she thought, rolling her eyes. Not that she'd ever dare say that to him.

At the end of the news update, just as she was about to turn off the TV, came a news flash.

The United Nations in Geneva, Switzerland, had been hit with CEBS. But, the reporter was saying, the impact seemed to be concentrated in a small area—the World Health Organization and the nearby Palais des Nations. Within WHO, two departments seemed to be particularly hard hit: the office of the Director General, and the unit responsible for guiding nations on the issue of electromagnetic radiation. Much controversy had surrounded the unit, which was run by an electrical engineer who had worked for cellphone companies, and the unit itself received funding from the wireless industry.

The head of the unit reportedly suffered a total nervous breakdown and was taken by ambulance to the CHUV, Geneva's university hospital. The DG was also seriously affected and was attempting to throw himself out the window of his office but apparently was unable to get it open wide enough for him to jump through.

He was heavily sedated and taken to the HUG—the psychiatry hospital in Geneva—for more specialized treatment, psychiatric assessment and round-the-clock observation.

In the Palais des Nations, the Secretary General of the United Nations had been attending meetings with several visiting dignitaries when CEBS hit. He too had to be taken to hospital after having what some described as a massive tantrum—going ballistic, ripping things apart, tearing off his clothes, smashing anything within reach, and roaring obscenities about the colossal sham of humanitarianism he had helped sustain, before collapsing and muttering incoherently about the countless lives lost, the endless perfidy and his own wretched, graceless existence.

It was a tortured outpouring that belied a cover-up of profoundly egregious acts, now ruthlessly revealed by the façade-stripping CEBS frequencies. There would be no return to office for the SG after this, whether he recovered or not.

Mein Gott, thought the German Chancellor. What would be revealed about *her*, if she got hit? Nothing quite as annihilating or as internationally damning as this, perhaps, but damning nonetheless. There was that very foolish decision she made a few years ago… and then that thing with the Russians. *Scheisse*. What *had* she been thinking. More eye-rolling. Since she'd got into politics, her eyeballs got more of a workout in one day than her whole body got in a month.

No point in taking any chances. She would have to get everything hard-wired—the whole country. *Schnell.*

What about those recent anti-5G demonstrations… She could spin those in her favour. She'd tell people 4G was even worse than 5G and they needed to get rid of all the wireless networks and start afresh with something *healthier*, better for the people and the planet. That might even be true, but that wasn't the point. She just needed a plausible spin to make it work. Plus, after the initial tantrums from all the cellphone addicts, it would boost the economy, feed new industries, spark new technologies and, best of all, make her look good. *Sehr gut.*

63

25 November 2020

She could get used to this, Marnie thought, relaxing into her business class window seat. Wait… She smiled to herself. Done! She was already used to it!

Steve travelled so much for his work that he'd been able to use his Air Miles for the flight. And Josie would be meeting them at the airport to drive them to their mama's place, 40 minutes outside the city. Family made life easier, Marnie mused, connecting all the things that mattered. Her heart rippled in reassurance and fear; she had never experienced the safety net of an extended family tree, but now perhaps she would. Why that should both scare and soothe her was unnerving in itself, but was surely nothing more than a fear of the unfamiliar. She could get used to it—like being in business class.

While Steve settled back to read his newspaper, Marnie tuned in to the TV news channel on her personal screen, catching up with the latest on CEBS.

Three days previously, Canada had got its wish and had been hit. Not in Toronto, as some had hoped, but in Vancouver.

A reporter was explaining how the Canadian Prime Minister happened to be in Vancouver, at the time, for meetings with the Mayor and the BC Premier, and that he, like everyone else in the 2.4 million-strong Greater Vancouver area, was directly affected.

"Now," the reporter continued gravely, "a shocking new development has come to light: the existence of a huge pedophile network involving celebrities, the movie industry and numerous elected officials, right up to the highest levels of government."

Marnie nudged Steve and gave him one of her earbuds. "Take a look at this. It's unbelievable what's happening."

Steve leaned over and plugged in, watching her screen.

"The discovery came after video recordings of the meetings were secretly released to the media, showing the cameras still rolling even as CEBS hit, capturing some of those present going into meltdown over what they had done. What the footage revealed has shocked Canadians to the core, leaving the government in a complete shambles, with the offenders crippled by shame and remorse, incapable of functioning normally or even answering questions."

Marnie turned to Steve. "Who could have known about this and then brought about the attack? It would have to be the same person, wouldn't it?"

"No idea," Steve said, "but it's interesting that there's nowhere for the offenders to hide, and none of their henchmen or bouncers can cover for them since they're affected too." He shook his head. "It's a beautiful thing, criminals confessing their sins in public and taking themselves out of the picture for the good of all."

Marnie was flabbergasted. Was this a huge coincidence or was it part of some bigger plan? Did someone, somewhere, have access to secret websites and corrupt organizations? Were they passing on this information to whoever was behind CEBS? Or was it the same person? The minute she got back to Boston, she was going to visit Ray again and find out. He knew the answers, she was sure of it.

"Seems to me," she said to Steve, "that the whole internet is being turned back on those who corrupted things and started using it for all the wrong reasons."

"Yup. Surely a sweet comeuppance," Steve said, already deepening his southern drawl in preparation for re-entry into the Romero orbit.

"Don't watch any more of the news, girl," he advised, returning to his newspaper. "You need to prepare for the impending inquisition. You'll be hugged, pummelled, questioned, scrutinized and rated, your history examined and cross-checked between the various interested parties—and they'll all be very interested in Miss Marnie. "

"I'm as ready as I'll ever be," she said, feeling terminally unready. She wasn't used to big families, or even small ones that worked well. It felt daunting to be meeting the whole clan—a public declaration of their commitment… a real test of their commitment, Steve had said, laughing. If you pass muster with the Romeros, he said, you'll be loved and pestered for life.

Marnie wished Steve could have met her parents. For the umpteenth time, she wondered what they would make of all this—everything that had happened to her, Matt and Lucy since they died, but especially this whole CEBS phenomenon.

She would watch the rest of the news update, then read her cosmology book—Quantum Wonders—which had finally arrived. The book was causing mental contortions and was not exactly light reading, although it talked a lot about light. But Marnie couldn't always fathom what the author was saying, even when explained in the simplest of terms. There was nothing simple about particle physics—or human nature, for that matter, or a single blade of grass. Perhaps she was simply dwelling in what the author called the 'darkness of the mind within a universe of light'.

"After a lull of several weeks," the TV reporter continued, "some countries have become complacent, convinced that the rash of attacks is over and things can revert to normal.

"The US President is now under huge pressure to rescind his

proposed reforms, but he is sticking to his promises and appears to have enough of a CEBS-affected entourage to support him in staying the course. It also helps that using a cellphone has become impossible for those touched by CEBS. Even being in the same room as a wireless device now has *CEBSters*, as those affected are now being called, running in the other direction."

Marnie wondered what it was like to be a CEBSter. Would she feel different? Would she be emotionally *free* …whatever that meant?

"Many devices also seem to have become defective, and the few who persevered through emotional anguish and piercing headaches, trying to make a call, found that their cellphones no longer worked.

"Some cities have set up gambling stations where people can place bets on which capital will be hit next. Vancouver not being a capital has made a lot of people unhappy."

Marnie marvelled at how some things were unravelling, exposing the very worst in people, while other things were causing a reversal of distortions, taking things back to the way they should have been all along …with one being the result of the other, she realized.

Apart from potentially seeing an end to wireless telecoms, which was mind-boggling enough, she was fascinated by the many social implications of what was happening.

In Vancouver, the reporter added, since CEBS had struck just three days ago, the exceptionally high property prices were dropping alarmingly. People selling their homes were finding it morally and ethically unconscionable to ask the astronomical prices that the market had typically borne. Some were selling their homes for millions less than they could have, simply because they knew it was becoming impossible for many families to have any kind of home in the city, given the prohibitive prices. Real estate agents have also been affected by CEBS, experiencing their own crisis of conscience, which could make it impossible for the market to ever recover. Market analysts say the whole Greater Vancouver area housing market will collapse if this goes on for more than a few weeks.

Other unexpected social phenomena had arisen out of the CEBS attacks, the reporter was saying. In the cities affected, singletons looking for a relationship were checking first to make sure their prospective partner was a CEBSter. Online dating sites even had a special category for this group so they could find each other easily.

Many marriages were falling apart—especially in cases where one spouse had been exposed but the other hadn't. Some claimed it was like having a religious experience and never being able to see the world the same way again. Others said it was like being from different planets, with no way to reconcile the gaping emotional chasm between them.

Given the reactions and repercussions through so many layers of society, Marnie was amazed that whatever was being transmitted via wireless devices still hadn't been tracked and identified. Could the telecom companies not intercept other frequencies riding their wireless systems? Surely some skilled hacker could figure it out.

Personally, Marnie didn't know what to think—whether to pray for this thing to hit Boston or be thankful it didn't. What if Steve went on a business trip and got hit with CEBS but she didn't? *What would happen to them then?*

64

26 November 2020

They had been greeted like astronauts returning from a distant planet, enfolded into the warmth and steady hum of a family on fire. Marnie could not keep track. The only identities she could hold onto after the initial onslaught of hugs and passionate greetings were Mama, Steve's mom, who clearly doted on him; Grammaw, his feisty 92-year-old grandma, whom he still called *girl*; Marietta, his younger sister, a dark-haired southern beauty who seemed incongruously shy and all the more memorable for it; and Josie, who had talked non-stop on the drive from the airport, speaking a family code that sounded more like the lyrics for a Dolly Parton song than everyday speech.

Flowing around them as they moved through the house was a kaleidoscope of life in all shapes and sizes. Screeching children chased each other through the downstairs rooms, fathers lazed in armchairs, a throng of over-heated women hogged the kitchen, standing over massive steaming pots, gossiping, teasing, back-slapping, rejoicing in the maternal matrix of love. The women clustered around Steve's Mama were like younger versions of herself, differing only in size and shape, like a set of Russian dolls—or lite versions of Oprah, Marnie couldn't help thinking. *The Oprahlites.*

The old house was itself a living entity that pulsed with generations of wear, care and non-stop laughter—three storeys of a never-ending love story.

Thanksgiving in the Romero household. Marnie felt like an alien, but tentatively observing from the sidelines was clearly not an option. When she made her way into the kitchen to see if she could help, it felt as if she might get swallowed up, never to be seen again.

But it was also delicious, winning her over as she adjusted to the lilting cadence of speech and the booming heartiness of fearless females accepting her as one of them because she was Steve's chosen woman.

Do not be fooled, Steve had joked, before heading out for a manly catch-up with his two brothers. *You might think you're just learning some recipes and helping to stir a few pots, but you'll be watched like a hawk every step of the way.*

If she was, it was part of the loving. To care enough to take the time to investigate: wasn't that what families were for? To watch out for each other, warn each other of dangers, laugh at each other's blind spots? More laughter meant fewer blind spots, it seemed. It was hard to see how you could have *any*, with this lot monitoring your every heartbeat.

Mama was at the hub, directing operations around a massive Aga stove and a chopping board the size of Philadelphia, while Grammaw sat at the large wooden table, banging her coffee mug to punctuate her edicts on the way things rightly should proceed.

"Quit bein' ugly, Glory," she told her daughter—62-year-old mama—when she joked about their neighbour falling off his roof because he farted and lost his footing.

"Mama," said Mama, wiping the tears from her eyes, "that man fell offa his roof coz he ate too many beans or he juss plain forgot to boil his peanuts."

Grammaw clucked and banged her mug, clearly loving every minute of the mayhem, and holding sway at its centre.

"Marnie, darlin'," Mama said, "come give me a hand with these here potatoes." She plonked a huge stainless steel pot on the table beside Grammaw and handed Marnie a masher. "Mash those things into submission, girl, and you can add some butter to help soften 'em up."

Marnie got gratefully to work, while the maelstrom continued around her—skilled eyes covertly observing how she shaped up in the kitchen.

"How many of you are there, if you don't mind my asking?" she said to Grammaw. She was still trying to match up names and faces.

"Lordy, I've lost track," Grammaw said, rolling her seen-it-all eyes. "Last count, there were… Glory! How many are we now, kids an' all?"

Mama held her wooden spoon in the air, testing the possibilities, and declared, "Well, my beloved Mason departed a good long while back, bless his huge heart, so it's me and my three girls, Josie, Ruby and Marietta; four men out there doing much a' nothin'—three of mine, Stevie, Mason Jr and George; then Carlton, Tonya and Rosa Lee—mine by marriage to my kids; 7 grandkids runnin' round; my sister Betsy here; Lady Gaga Grammaw; and two squibs in their cribs, soaking up the madness." She paused. "Plus, two more who had to stay home—Troy and Annamae—due to them expecting their double delivery any minute."

She turned to Marnie. "Troy is Stevie's younger brother, down in Jacksonville. He and Annamae were right sorry they couldn't be here to meet you, Marnie. They'll be having twins just as soon as we start carving up the turkey, mark my worlds."

Marnie liked that: *mark my worlds*. Mama had many, all revolving around her.

How could such down-to-earthedness be so profoundly intimate? It reminded Marnie of the potent writing in the novel she'd recently read. Here, the language was simple, yet the feelings ran deep. The throwaway words belied a solid core of forgiving acceptance, familial tributaries feeding a wide river of loyalty and inclusion that could see you through any disaster. Hot tears pricked her eyes as she pummelled the potatoes, awed by the raw power of togetherness.

A gentle hand landed on her shoulder as Marietta sat down beside her. "Don't let this rowdy bunch overwhelm you," she said, chocolate-brown eyes warmly sympathetic. The Romero women had no hard edges in word or body, that Marnie could see, but Marietta was like a solitary lily—a slender, elegant stalk in a field of dancing poppies. Yet all had inherent dignity, born of the incessant interweaving of joyful participation and graceful acceptance of life's mysteries.

Kids ranging from 3 to 14 flowed in and out of the kitchen, the teenagers guiding the smaller ones in their social graces. "Say thank you to Grammaw," and "Bethany May, you stop shoving your little brother!" All exuded the glow of happiness-fuelled health.

Potatoes finally beaten and spooned into a bowl the size of a baby's bathtub, a massive turkey birthed from the hot womb of the oven, corn grits, Brussel sprouts, green beans and cranberries ladled into serving dishes, a river of pungent gravy poured into a sauce boat, and hot cheese rolls lolling in a wicker basket… the Romeros were ready to eat.

The wave of women swept into the dining room, heaped platters borne aloft, like ritual offerings to the gods of plenitude, calling men and children to the table. Marnie carried hot dinner plates, placing them at the head of the table, and Steve appeared magically beside her, smiling his reassuring presence.

They sat together, on one side, as the family filled in the spaces around them—Mama at one end, eldest son George at the other, filling in for long-deceased Daddy, and everyone else in between. The kids had their own table, at one end of the long room, and they settled like flies on the feast, no strangers to the nourishment of well-loved food.

As she ate, warmed inside and out, Marnie felt blessed. Talk of food, siblings, babies, new beginnings and old friends filled the air, the rest of the world of no import. After the buzz of Boston, filled with cellphone-toting figures of urgent consequence, this felt like blissful freedom, untethered from binding digital cords. Not a cellphone to be seen and no social props required.

Betsy on her right, Ruby and Marietta opposite, Marnie was gently probed about her life. She talked of school, her love for the kids, the challenges of needy expectations and the wish for a simpler kind of living.

When the turkey had been reduced to its bare bones and the plates cleared away, two pumpkin pies with pecan crusts appeared to replace them. Sated on every level, Marnie wasn't sure she could do them justice, but she could no more refuse a slice of such lusciousness than she could say no to another breath.

"What all are we thankful for, today?" Mama asked, the lighthouse of her gaze scanning all assembled. "Me, I'm thankful for this here bountiful banquet, for my darlin' Mason, still with me in spirit, for my precious ever-expanding family, and for the gift of seven golden puppies, which my beloved Thelma delivered this mornin', with uncanny canine timing."

She looked around the table. "I expect y'all to take at least one or find homes for them among your friends." Her eyes settled on Marnie. "If you'd like one, Marnie, you can take your pick of the litter. We'll go see them after dinner, out back in the garden shed."

"I'd love to see them," Marnie said, wondering if Maisie might like another puppy to keep her latest Collie company. But that would involve another trip down to Georgia in a month or so, when the puppies had been weaned, so best not to commit, just yet. "What kind of dogs are they?"

"I've no idea who the daddy is," Mama said, "but Thelma is a Retriever with the gentlest of hearts." She nodded, as if the matter of puppy homes was settled. "What all else are we thankful for today?"

Josie jumped in. "I'm surely thankful that the men are going to do the dishes," she said, to much laughter.

"I'm surely thankful you're joking, like every year, bless your heart, Josie," George said solemnly. "But I'm grateful for the gesture of inclusion, which I will respectfully decline, knowing how y'all women want no men in the kitchen realm."

An old family refrain, Marnie could see, smiling at their banter.

"I'm thankful for my Carlton," said Ruby, a leaner version of Mama, with bouncy brown curls framing an innocent face and the trademark melty Romero eyes. "I just got myself set up in business with a beauty salon, thanks to Carlton here supporting me in that endeavour."

She leaned towards Marnie to explain. "Carlton's my husband, in case you're having a hard time keeping up."

Marnie nodded gratefully, as raucous delight and clapping supported this venture, and Carlton beamed at his wife.

Grammaw banged her glass on the table and cleared her throat. "I'm thankful I'm still here to be thankful," she said, to more laughter, "and that I'm about to become a great-grandma again, two times over, when those twins get here. I need a cal-cu-later," she said, "if I'm to keep up with y'all doing this brooding."

As more red wine was poured, water glasses refilled, and brandy placed on standby to wash it all down, Steve got up to speak.

The laughter gave way to silence and all eyes swivelled Steve-ward.

Marnie tensed, expecting a formal introduction and perhaps an invitation for her to stand up and speak. *No, no, please don't*, she telegraphed to Steve beside her.

"I am thankful to y'all for welcoming Marnie into the family, as y'all have done so warmly. I wish our Daddy could be here to share this time with us and to meet her. This is one special woman I have been perusing and pursuing for some time, as some of you know…" He smiled at Josie, who shot back a told-you-so smile.

"I've been trying to persuade her that it's a blessing and an honour to join the Romero clan, as it surely is, so…" He paused and looked down at Marnie, rigid with anticipation beside him.

"So, I'm thankful for this opportunity to welcome her *officially.*" He reached into his pocket and pulled out a small box. Gasps and laughter resonated around the table, Grammaw banging her glass to the beat. Mason Jr, realizing what was afoot, yelled, "Go, brother!"

Steve turned to Marnie and opened the box, revealing a simple gold band with an embedded ruby—a ring of unpretentious beauty, exactly what Marnie herself would have chosen, had she been consulted.

"Miss Marnie, would you do me the honour of being my wife?"

"Lordy, course she will," Grammaw said, indignant. "Any darn fool can see that. Now someone pass me the brandy."

Everyone laughed, but no one passed the brandy, all eyes on Marnie.

She couldn't hold her breath forever. When she finally exhaled, out came the *YES* before she even knew it was there.

65

10 December 2020

China's Resurrection: Demolishing New World Disorder?

From social correspondent Janis Nooth

China Update, **Opinion,** 8 December 2020—The impossible is happening in China, following the CEBS attack in Beijing on 10 September 2020. Arguably the world's most oppressed people, who have been subjected to an increasingly crippling digital dictatorship, the Chinese are staging a resurrection unlike any ever seen in human history.

Since Beijingers were hit with CEBS three months ago, they have daily taken to the streets, the parks and the infamous

Tiananmen Square to openly practise Falun Gong (also known as Falun Dafa)—a spiritual practice promoting compassion, truth, kindness and virtue. Formerly banned by the Chinese government for having *nothing in common with the socialist ethical and cultural progress it was trying to achieve*, this peaceful moving-meditation practice is reported to have resulted in 3,700 Falun Gong practitioners dying as a result of torture and abuse in custody, typically after they refused to recant their beliefs.

The practice is generating a tidal wave of community engagement, solidarity and innovative thinking, leading to initiatives promoting numerous green technologies, including the development of free energy for the nation's 1.39 billion inhabitants—in addition to stopping all traffic, business activities and anything else going on for the duration of the hour-long twice-daily meditations throughout the city.

The Minister for Education, Wong Wei, who was also affected by CEBS, has said that the government is now "100% committed to making China the world's most innovative, eco-friendly and prosperous nation, for the good of all." Stunning other global leaders with this altruistic approach, who for once seem to be at a loss for words, the Chinese have publicly stated that whatever innovative breakthroughs they make will be freely available to any other country wishing to adopt the same patent-free earth-friendly technologies. Their newly formed Department of Eco-Innovation is already working on free-energy generators modelled on Nikola Tesla's early inventions, and aims to have the technology up and running by mid-2021.

The former Publicity Department of the Communist Party of China has changed its name to the Department of Prosperity (*Fánróng*), while the party itself is now called simply Humanity (*Rénxìng*).

Nations not touched by CEBS are up in arms, saying this kind of *misguided, suspect generosity* will disrupt the world economy, creating complete chaos if there is no further demand for fossil fuels or utility companies.

While the US is making impressive strides in the rollout of its radical reforms, prompting some US-friendly nations to follow suit, China is clearly taking the lead in the global popularity stakes. The profound government turnaround has shown just how powerful the CEBS process is, and how positively depolarizing. The more repressed the nation, the greater the potential for transformation—from one end of the spectrum to the other. Those operating somewhere in the middle, with traditionally less draconian governments, do not stand to experience the same kind of dramatic sea change… *if* they get exposed.

For a nation that formerly had no free press or free access to the internet, this is heady freedom indeed. Many of those who had been trying to leave China but were forcibly prevented from doing so and were black-listed by the ruling digital dictatorship, now find themselves wanting to stay to be part of most exciting development humanity has ever seen.

From being the bad guys that most nations had come to fear and despise for their ruthless global-takeover tactics, the Chinese now constitute a huge force to be reckoned with—a force for good, and a growing collective consciousness that seems set to rival and outshine every other nation.

It is a phenomenon that some analysts are describing as *the tail wagging the dog*, and it remains to be seen just how well that dog is liked and trusted by the motley mongrels guarding their national territories for fear of altruism taking over the world.

66

11 December 2020

Lucy was drowning in words. In the past year, she had written about health, sports, nutrition, drugs, fashion, vaccines, CEBS, children, social media, pets, complementary medicine, sex, politics, climate change, yoga, marketing, friendship, relationships and everything in between. Rinse, shuffle and repeat. She had learned a ton of stuff. But she felt drained by so many creative capillaries bleeding off in so many different directions, stemming her artistic arterial flow.

Was she hungry for some action because she was so tired of all the words? Or had all those words created a need for physical translation, for something physically rendered? She missed the hands-on creations of fashion design—making something of her own, from scratch, rather than massaging words and ghost-writing for others. She was beginning to feel like a ghost of her former fashion-savvy self.

It was almost as if she'd been given a mini-dose of CEBS, with some creative juices thrown in, prompting her to clear out old emotions but also to think and even *talk* to herself in the most eloquent of terms. She couldn't seem to have a plain old ordinary thought without adding verbal curlicues and flowery descriptors. Was this the fate of a writer or was there something else going on? It didn't feel like a mental overwhelm—more like a creative upgrade pushing her to some higher form of expression. But the two things together—the emotional exorcising and the mental acrobatics—were definitely pushing her out of her current comfort zone.

Further confusing her hormones, and therefore her brain, was the sexual tension building between Nate and herself, beneath their professionally measured moves. *But why hold back?* What would happen if they let it rip? She had all kinds of fantasies about that, and she loved them all lustily, but what would happen *professionally*? Was she hungry for pure sex or purely for Nate? She felt ravenous for the fullest serving of him, a greedy three-course helping… because he was the only man available? No. It was him she wanted. Any others (*what others?*) should stand well back and make room for this to happen.

As she was thinking these unprofessional thoughts, Nate walked into her office and leaned against the end of her desk, one lean leg draped over the edge. *Was he on the edge too*, Lucy wondered. What would happen if she flung herself at him now, here, in the office, with no one to see, and only Fitz, Tracy and Beemer to hear some strange strangled noises coming from down the corridor? Would they come to the rescue, or smile knowingly…?

"Lucy? Did you hear what I said?"

"What? No, sorry. Come again?" She cringed at her Freudian choice of words. She had a one-track mind, or maybe lots of tracks, but they all led to one place: his bed!

"You're on another planet. Am I interrupting your work?"

"No way," Lucy said. "I never work when I'm in the office."

Nate laughed. "Listen, I was thinking we need a break. *I* need a break, anyway. What about you?"

"A break from each other, work, ourselves, the crazy world?" Might as well go for it, get things really clear up front.

Nate grinned, shaking his head at her delicious nonsense. "I thought we might go away for the weekend. Sort of officially inaugurate our relationship."

Lucy groaned, lowered her head onto her desk and banged it three times. "*Thank. You. God.* I might actually start believing in you again if you keep this up."

She straightened, turning back to Nate. "When and where and when? Oh, and *when?*"

"I thought we could go somewhere this weekend, if that works for you." Nate was still grinning, happy to have had the desired response.

"When do you want me here?" She held up her hand. "Wait. Before you answer that, feel free to punctuate the question any way you wish, as in *when do you want me, here* and *when do you want me here.*"

"I'll answer *both* of those questions, if you don't mind—in that order," Nate said, ticking off two fingers. "1: always… and 2: what about 9am tomorrow?"

"Well, I guess if it can't be *right now*, this second, in my very next lonely unloved breath, then tomorrow at 9am will be acceptable," she said, sighing dramatically. But she was thrilled. *Why hide it?* So she gave him her full-beam radiant smile—tough competition even for the Beamer–Beemer. Speaking of which…

"What about Beemer?"

"You want him to come too?" Nate cocked his head, eyebrows raised.

"Not *exactly*... I was just wondering who would be taking care of him."

"I'll drop him off at my sister's place before we head out. And I'll pick you up at your place at 9am, so you won't need to come here, to the office." He looked at her, checking in. "Okay? The timing and the punctuation?"

"I like both." Lucy nodded approvingly. "One other minor question: *where* are we going? So I know what to pack."

"It's a surprise," Nate said, smiling. "Just bring… very little."

After softly closing her office door, Lucy felt a hot wave of urgent emotion surging through her. She fell into her chair and lowered her head to her desk—not to bang it but to let the tears come. She imagined them flowing across the shiny dry bedrock of her work surface, making their salty way to more receptive soil.

She had cried for months after losing the parental pillars of her life. How could any tears remain in this newly configured existence? But these tears were born somewhere deeper—tears for self, begging to be birthed, not for someone else who had left her. They marked a new beginning, a cleansing of hidden hurts and an opening for a richer flow to fill her up.

But she wasn't over that other loss, either. Lucy didn't think you ever got *over* something like that. It was like getting teeth pulled (although she'd only lost her baby teeth, so far). It changed your bite. You could still eat, but your roots were gone. She had pulled herself through this past year, trying to digest what had happened, but mostly using her anger to grab a chunk of life and make it hers. With parents ripped away, it was like being unborn and she had to decide who and what she now was.

Her heart had been dormant while her mind held tight to the concept of safe struggles, conjuring shape-shifting words in the hope of some illumination. Now, with her heart opening up for business again, there were cobwebs to clear out, empty boxes to throw away, windows to be thrown open.

Words were not enough to describe all this. How could she tell Nate what he was to her—or tell herself—with mere syllables of sound to approximate such primal mating?

The fervent notion of nights with Nate fired up a vision of a much vaster horizon. Lucy allowed herself to dream. Emerging from the nightmare of lost parental illusions, she let herself see beyond the next deadline, to a new lifeline extended uniquely to her.

The rest of her day, which felt like a prelude to the rest and best of her life, passed in a blur of misunderstandings understood. She saw how she had been caught between two worlds, up-selling her finite mentality and down-playing her infinite creativity—and all the feelings in between. Like a young male whose voice was about to break, she was still trying to find her octave. She had a voice, but it resounded most fiercely inside her, with the outer words yet to align with the way the world might see her.

Beyond all her flippant banter and cocky indifference, she sensed an exquisite, terrifying tenderness emerging from her fractured life—for herself, for Nate, for every stalled heart—the classic artful dodging of hearts unsure of good reception.

She had been so desperately trying to get *somewhere* to achieve *something*, when all the getting worthy of being got was right here, perfectly packaged in this beautiful gift of a man.

67

15 December 2020

Matt was pondering the next chapter of his life. Where to go from here? Where did he fit in a world where almost nothing made sense? He had made a living out of reporting shams, cover-ups and betrayals. Yet he had since lived all of those things himself. Now, being with Celle was the only thing that made any sense at all, but he couldn't make a living doing that. *If only…*

He had been keeping track of what was happening in the US, with the President carrying through on his decision to shut down wireless networks. Matt couldn't fathom it, and the telecom companies were screaming bloody murder, using threats, coercion and every conceivable tactic to force his hand.

But the cell towers were coming down all over Washington, DC and elsewhere—with some states, such as California, welcoming the move and already working on alternative technologies, while others were trying to find loopholes to justify non-compliance with the new law.

Marnie was delighted, he knew, although not holding her breath, she said, till she saw the rollback happening in Massachusetts as well. Passing a new law didn't always mean it got implemented straight away or without a big fight.

Mind-blowing stuff was happening in China, and Matt had the feeling it was going to leave all other nations in the dust and take over—in the best possible way.

In France, the President reported feeling like an alien in his own country, having returned from London after CEBS had hit during his visit. Since most members of his cabinet had not been exposed, he was largely on his own, wrestling with guilt, conflict and huge opposition from within the ranks. It would be a miracle if he survived in office, Matt thought.

New Zealand's government was powering ahead with its rollback, getting plenty of support from the general population, despite huge resistance from industry. The Kiwis seemed to love their PM.

But it didn't make a lot of sense to Matt. As far as he could see, it was far better to get hit with CEBS, ride out the short-term chaos and then enjoy the benefits of a nation transformed, than to try to pre-empt a strike by rolling back the wireless stuff but getting none of the payoff… other than a less harmful telecom system, presumably.

The whole thing was a colossal eye-opener, a welcome wake-up call for corruption. Some of the stuff that had been exposed was causing a real shit storm—like that pedophile ring in Canada. It was the kind of thing his former sponsor, Travis Chamberlain, would have loved him to cover in their online report. He wondered what Chamberlain made of all this…

Where all that left him, Matt wasn't sure. While he seemed to have drilled down to a truer sense of himself as a result of all his personal crises—largely thanks to Celle—he now had no idea who he really was or what he wanted to be doing.

The pendulum has swung back to centre, Celle told him. *You need to give it a little time to start swinging again in some new direction.* Whatever that meant.

"Mateo!" Celle was calling to him from outside. "Look at this!"

He ran outside. "What?"

"Look," she said, pointing in disbelief at a glinting object moving along the packed earth towards the undergrowth. It was her tiny cellphone, a diminutive model like Celle herself, borne on the shoulders of thousands of industrious ants heading back to their nest. "How is this possible? It must be 500 times their size."

"Holy shit."

"I read somewhere that ants can carry up to 50 times their own weight, but this is going a bit too far." Celle laughed. "They're going to drop dead of shock if it rings."

"Or get hit with CEBS," Matt said.

"Then we'll have a million ants wailing their regrets all night long."

"What the heck will they do with it, if they manage to get it back to their nest?"

"Use it as a skating rink? Give it to their queen so she can call her friends on the hill over yonder?" She shook her head in wonder. "I think it's a sign. Time to let the cellphone go. What do you think?"

"Your call," he said, grinning. "But I didn't think you'd let it go without a fight, at least."

Celle shrugged. "Seeing how people have been affected by CEBS has really highlighted what's important, and living here has just confirmed it. I'd prefer to undergo a CEBS cleanse than stay dependent on some *thing*."

"I think you've already done your own emotional cleanse, more effectively and more beautifully than anyone else I know," Matt said. Something far worse than CEBS had transformed Celle into the goddess she was now. She didn't need another wake-up call, and she didn't seem to need her cellphone, either.

It was something to behold—the shiny rectangular object being carried like a royal coffin by a seething mass of tiny black bodies.

"If they survive the blasts of radiation, we could see a new strain of mutant ants," Celle said. "Rad ants. *Radants.* Sounds like a great name for a rock band."

Matt's mind was returning to his earlier thoughts. "What's next for us, Celle?"

"Dunno, yet. But something new is coming… and something old is definitely leaving…" She nodded towards her receding cellphone. "I sense some new opportunities coming out of the chaos." She put her arm around his waist. "We just have to be patient and seize our opportunity when we see it. Those little robbers certainly know how to do that. And what they're doing seems technically impossible…"

She turned to him and kissed his cheek. "Maybe there's a message in there somewhere."

68

Russian Federation Appeals for Global Leadership, Inspired by CEBS

From international correspondent _Boris Branov_

Daily Russian Times, Wednesday, 16 December 2020—Yesterday, in an emotional phone call to the German Chancellor, the Russian President declared his enthusiastic support for the new world order emerging post-CEBS. It is unclear why he chose the Chancellor for his pronouncement—however charmingly mispronounced—although the two appear to have a rather special relationship. No more cold war here; it's more likely to be warm hugs when they meet, which they regularly do.

Transported by the heartfelt fervour of his proclamation, the President stumbled over some of his words, interjecting expletives in his native tongue, but he was determined to show off his English, and the message was clear.

"I am not dis_putin_k the contreebution of other nations, or what Russia has done, over the centuries, to some of them... _Da prostit nas Bog_ [_may God forgive us_], even if some of the _svolach' and mu-dak deserved it,_" he said, sounding nonetheless deeply remorseful. "But things are _dee_fferent now, and those who have been _heet_ by CEBS must be at the frontline of this total and uncondeetional global transformation. The future ees here, ees now, ees all of us."

The Russian Federation would, he said, join China and the US in becoming a leader of excellence and human betterment.

"_My vse odna bol'shaya sem'ya._ We are all one big family," he said, "and those _leedairs_ that finally stop behavink like _cheeldren_ fightink over their toys and now grow up, thanks to CEBS, must be parents to the others to help them become the wise, mature humans we are all designed to be."

And the Russian President, it seems, is keen to play the role of big daddy, if not the benevolent godfather himself.

69

Sherry Merickson had never seen city folk behave like this—so exuberant, so chummy and *convivial*. As an artist, she'd seen plenty of bohemians and hipsters. She'd *been* one, for a while. This was Vancouver, after all. She'd even lived in a commune for a few years, during her rebellious phase—wearing tie-dyed cotton tunics and her hair in long braids. She'd also favoured black Gothic make-up, which made for an arresting look: half Hansel & Gretel, half Hell's Angels.

These days, she was seamlessly put together, all the various components creatively blending to form a pleasingly professional front.

Except for today. Today, she was encased from head to toe in white hooded overalls. Even her friends wouldn't recognize her if they passed her on the street. Hopefully they wouldn't.

Strike while the irony was hot. That's what she always said. Right now, the irony was heating up nicely and she was almost ready to strike.

What she was about to do was completely out of character. *Totally off the wall*, you might say. But CEBS had changed everyone. There was a deep hunger for renewal and it felt as if everything was up for grabs. People were loving the reversals, despite the loss of their precious wireless devices… or maybe because of it.

Everything was different after CEBS. She had been taken and shaken to the core, like every other Vancouverite—and a few thousand visitors, including the Prime Minister… or so everyone had been led to believe. Beyond the original scandal around the pedophile ring was the fact that the Prime Minister said he had not actually *been* in the city when CEBS hit, which explained why he hadn't made the same reforms as the US President. *And* why he was still in office, despite being implicated in that whole sick mess.

He had had the video footage seized by legal decree—the footage showing him apparently coming undone in a meeting with the Vancouver Mayor. Not him, he said. The recording was fuzzy but it certainly *looked* like him. He had been set up, he claimed. It was a smear campaign by the opposition, to get him removed from office.

Ironically, if it *had* been him, he would have been genuinely remorseful about any involvement, instead of doing all he could to dodge this deadly political bullet.

He seemed to have lied any way he could to absolve himself—first claiming to have been in Vancouver to discuss some projects for the city, then saying he hadn't been there at all, that he had sent someone else in his place, then… okay, he *had* been photographed that day, but it was in Toronto, not in Vancouver. Plus, he was no longer on speaking terms with the Mayor or the BC Premier—who were both gunning for radical changes—which was another sign that the PM was not a CEBSter.

Most Canadians wanted the Mayor or BC Premier to replace the Prime Minister, who was revealing himself to be a practised artful dodger, Sherry thought—a slippery politico who had mastered what she called the cluster*fuck-duck*.

Well, he could duck and dodge all he wanted, but it wasn't going to work this time. How delicious was that! Once you'd recovered from your own emotional exorcism, you could enjoy watching the whole government house of cards come tumbling down. If you got hit with CEBS, there was nowhere to hide, and you didn't want to hide—from yourself or from the truth, which usually amounted to the same thing anyway. If you hadn't been CEBSed, all your suppressed emotional angst and self-delusions were exposed for what they were and looked utterly sick alongside those who had CEBSed themselves free.

What a shame CEBS didn't act as a sleuth as well as a stripper, untangling the web of lies beneath the façade of government responsibility. But it *had* exposed the Prime Minister as *not* having been exposed—and for not being where he said he was, doing what he was supposed to be doing, since he had not undergone the inevitable CEBS purge and remorseful remediation.

The plot had thickened so much it was like a murky swamp of quick sand with no discernible beginning or end. It made everyone wonder what else he was lying about—or, to make things easier, and since news clips had to be kept short, when had he actually been telling the *truth*?

Apart from all that, though, the CEBS effect had felt perversely good to Sherry, in an *excoriating* kind of way that left her feeling lighter. She had weighed herself a few months later, and she *was* lighter. Did emotional angst actually have weight? It certainly felt that way when you had emotional baggage.

CEBS had left people feeling liberated and fiendishly daring. She could see them practically rubbing their hands in glee as they pondered some outrageously creative idea or new project that would blow people away. She could relate. That's exactly how she felt. Which was why she was doing what she was doing.

But the *best* part was that she no longer cared about getting caught, punished, fined or even imprisoned. Fear of authority had gone out the window along with all the other life-stalling insecurities. She still might not want to linger in dark alleys at night, although she probably *could*, now that everyone was so much more decent.

CEBSters had none of the withdrawal symptoms that many others were grappling with, now that cellphones were no longer used in the city. But those who had returned to the city, having been away from home when CEBS had hit, were having a hard time adapting, sometimes going out of town again just so they could spend time on their cellphones.

Many of those who had been affected by all the wireless radiation in the city returned after WiFi had been banned in all public places and cell towers were being progressively dismantled. There was the added plus of property prices coming down, which meant that the city had essentially reverted to the way it was 30 years previously.

But the PM hadn't yet brought about any of the reforms that the US Pres had—and wasn't likely to, if he hadn't actually been *CEBSed*—which had annoyed a lot of good people. Plastic containers and packaging were still in use, for example, when there was simply no excuse for that toxic indulgence to continue.

It was doubly ironic that the mural she was doing would be covering up the previous one of killer whales—not the kind of killers that needed to be erased, and these sentient mammals were also the ones suffering the most from all the toxic human detritus in the oceans.

Which brought her back to her mural.

She had been commissioned by the city to do a healthy, happy, hopeful scene, reflecting the new sentiment of expanded possibilities and greater community generated by CEBS—something uplifting to kick off the new year. Her proposal for a vibrant scene in Stanley Park, with dynamic community activities and interaction, had been enthusiastically accepted and she had been given a month to complete the project.

Now, standing on the scaffolding, facing her vast concrete canvas, she was putting the finishing touches to her masterpiece. The huge blue tarp flapped behind her in the breeze, sheltering her from the cold ocean air and keeping prying eyes from seeing the final product until she was ready.

It was now 6am, and commuters would soon be on the move. This would be the first thing they'd see as they drove over the Granville Street Bridge to get downtown.

An official unveiling had been scheduled for next week, but she wasn't going to wait for that. Her friend Pete had just arrived with three other guys to help her dismantle the scaffolding, and they would leave the tarp pinned up to the wall at the top until they had taken down all the poles and planks. Then they'd pull the tarp off and all would be revealed.

They worked together, going as fast as they safely could, finally removing the last pole just before 7am. The sky was starting to brighten and they could hear the first rumbles of traffic coming over the bridge behind them.

Sweaty but exuberant, they stood back to gauge the full effect.

The scene showed an emaciated African child kneeling on the ground, lapping from a murky puddle as water cascaded from a height beside him. But it wasn't the kind of water you'd want your child to be drinking... and it wasn't coming from a spring, fountain or waterfall. It was spurting out of a large naked penis, clutched by the meaty hand of a man in a suit, his other hand holding a plastic bottle of water to his lips as he drank lustily, head thrown back.

Someone caught with his pants down, so to speak. Another lovely irony. It wasn't obviously anyone in particular, although people would speculate. *The owner of Nestlé?* It couldn't be the Prime Minister... *could it?* He'd been photographed recently at a conference, drinking from a plastic water bottle in a similar pose. Surely, no one would dare do such a thing. But if you looked at it a certain way, if you squinted... it *was* him.

The original painting wasn't one of hers. It was by her artist friend Luigi who had given her permission to use it this one time. Not that it would be up there for very long. But Luigi could never resist the chance to share some of his shockingly subversive art. He had gleefully agreed to collaborate.

Sherry stepped back to admire the effect. Luigi would be chuffed. She pulled out her tiny digital camera to capture the moment. And she suddenly thought of LSD. God, Lucy would love this blast of civil disobedience. *Randy rebellion*, she'd probably call it. Suddenly she missed her old school friend. She'd have to get in touch and send her this.

As she stood on the sidewalk looking up at the shocking mural, she heard the first inevitable screech of brakes as the early-morning commuters came over the bridge. She braced, waiting for it. *There.* A nice satisfying fender-bender *crunch* as two cars collided. There would be a lot of that, this morning—followed by some deliciously heated debates over what it all meant, who on Earth had dared do such a thing, and what would happen now...

Yes, she thought. CEBS had set her free—fear-free to do whatever the hell she felt like doing.

Right now, she felt like celebrating. She was ravenous.

She turned to Pete and the gang. "Breakfast at The Fairmont?"

70

20 December 2020

When he got back from the beach, Matt put the fruit and fish in the fridge. He had stopped at the market on the way home and Celle had gone ahead. He could hear her singing in the shower, cleaning off after their swim.

There was a typed sheet of paper on the sofa—something Celle must have printed out. She had obviously left it there for him to read. He sat down and scanned the contents. Not the kind of thing he'd normally be interested in, if the heading was anything to go by.

A Charter for Cosmic Humans

What the hell was this about...? He began to read.

I am from no place, no time, no space, no one, no name, yet you-me-us—a dreamer, visionary and archangel, reversing a derailed evolution and the meltdown of a beleaguered Earth, wounded hearts and smarting sickening souls.

This is a charter of inspiration for a future we dream of living, while dwelling in the shallow graves of unconsciousness, diminished by the regulators, inside and out, in the dead zone of digital denial—the burial that comes long before death, the electronic never-game that nobody ever wins.

Yet we never ask: *Why have we lost consciousness?*

Celle wrote this? Please, no. Matt had a sinking feeling in his stomach. He wasn't sure he could handle this kind of way-out spiritual stuff from his... Was this the kind of thing earthly angels wrote? Or goddesses? But Celle was firmly grounded in the earth, not woo-woo like this. Wasn't she?

He continued reading, the sound of the shower still running in the background.

This is a quantum revelation that comes through cosmic dreaming, where all things are possible—a way back from the bridge to nowhere, the electronic sprawl, where no one can connect.

This is a story of unimagined unfolding, of stellar game-changers driving the difference engine—a cosmic comeback for superhumans, igniting in them a passion for enlightened agency, conscious evolution and quantum potentiation, as we get down to the wire that is now wireless and deadly.

This is not just for the movers and shakers who try to inspire the masses to power up and wake up, to shake down and take down the digitized existence that may soon be no more than a smart-assed robotic ant on a pale and lifeless planet.

This is a story to awaken sleeping matriarchs and thwarted men, to share the recognition of true humanness, to reject the creeping, slow-motion apocalypse, to refute the faceless fumes emanating from stinky social media with all the blinkered acceptance of digitally destitute lives.

This is an urgent invitation to all who want to thrive, to come back from the brink, to dispel the dreaded nightmares, to end the dance of dysfunction through the wastelands of futile feardom, living only our darkness, spirits growing fainter, forgetting the wisdom of antiquity, futures past, the universal multiversal mind.

What will it take to overcome the renegade reign, the data thieves, the certain kiss of digital death... as we approach zero?

Shit. Matt felt sick. Was this what it was like for couples, when one had been CEBSed and the other hadn't? And they could no longer relate, one having spiritually *evolved*, and the other not...? As far as Matt knew, they hadn't been hit by CEBS, but Celle hadn't needed that for *her* transformation.

He took a deep breath, exhaling loudly. What kind of insecure fucking control freak *was* he, anyway? To be so shaken by this, just some words on a page. So *what* if she had written it? Celle never judged *him*. She supported him in being himself, even if she didn't always agree with him. He really needed to get a grip.

He read on.

As quantum questers in the overworld, Wi-fried in the underworld, and too long on the sidelines, feeling more and more like phantom entities, we must birth anew. We must come back up from down under.

Will you explore your higher powers, feel the pulse of cellular renewal, know the potency of humanness, embrace the search for quantum genius in all the sparkling photons of the unifield, and be the talisman conferring supernatural persuasion in those too blinkered to see?

This is a lifeline for lifetimes, restoring our godness, the negation of sedation—a true tragedy when you know where the evidence *lies*, with the truth almost too far gone...

The quest is in the question: *How far must we now go to save our world?*

Celle came out of the bathroom, towelling her hair. "You found it. What do you think?"

"Did *you* write this?" Matt looked at her, stricken.

"Would it be the end of the world if I did?"

Maybe the start of a new one, but without him in it... "Please tell me you didn't write this..."

"Okay. I didn't write it." She looked at him innocently.

He wasn't convinced. "There's no name on it."

"I took out the author."

"What... he's lying dead in a Mexican ditch somewhere?"

"Hardly my style." Celle laughed. "Would my murdering someone scare you less than me writing that thing?" She smiled at his frozen expression. "The Australian Prime Minister wrote it, when he emerged from his CEBS retreat, and now he's travelling around the continent preaching his new cosmic gospel."

"Are you serious?" Matt ran his fingers through his hair. "I'm concerned about this," he said.

"Concerned about the Aussie PM?"

"No. Concerned about my reaction—how I felt when I thought *you* had written it."

"You looked scared shitless." Celle seemed unfazed. "Mateo, I think you need to *come back up from down under*. That petrified look really doesn't suit you." She sat down beside him. "I thought you'd *wrap your laughing gear round that*," she said, in her best Aussie accent.

"It is... *different*," he said, his heartrate slowly returning to normal as he reassured himself that Celle was still Celle and not some etheric prophet who would transcend the need for someone as... *unevolved* as him. Or was *he* afraid of being affected by this stuff... of having his own *transformation*? Even that word made him queasy. It seemed unmanly, something *done* to him, beyond his control... He'd read somewhere that when people who'd been hit with CEBS shared their experiences with others, in conversation or in writing, it changed non-CEBSters, too. Was that—

"I bet the Sydneysiders love it," Celle said, interrupting his rabid brain rant, "since they all got hit with CEBS."

Matt took another deep breath to clear his head. "Yeah. But I doubt the PM will be greeted with open arms by the rest of the Aussies, when he goes walkabout on his quantum quest."

Celle laughed. "I can just imagine the reception he'll get, in the outback: *Tell your story walkin'*. Isn't that what they say, down under?"

"Yeah." Matt smiled hesitantly, warming to the theme. "*On yer bike.*" He paused. "What's that other one...? Oh, yeah. *Buckley's chance.*"

"I don't know that one."

"It's the Aussie way of saying *fat chance*—zero chance of something happening. It refers to some Buckley guy—an escaped colonial convict who lived for years with the Aborigines in the 1800s, despite everyone saying he'd never survive."

"I like that story," Celle said. "And I'd say the PM's chances are every bit as good, despite people's resistance."

Matt wasn't so sure—about Buckley, the PM or himself.

"Look, I hadn't planned on trashing the guy," Celle said. "He's entitled to his ideas and this is pretty potent stuff. It may be a bit *other-worldly* for most people, but it all makes perfect sense if you translate it into simpler language. And it might improve the *cosmic* climate, which would improve the continent's and everyone else's."

She turned to look Matt in the eye. "I was curious to see what you thought of it… if it touched something deeper…"

"Which was *really* why you printed it out…"

"Yes." She shrugged. An innocent sharing.

Matt bristled, feeling vaguely manipulated. "Well, it didn't," he said, resolutely. "*Touch* me, I mean."

"Okay," she said, lightly. "Although you did seem kind of shaken after reading it, and I don't think it was about *me*."

***

In Auckland, reading the *charter*, the Kiwi Prime Minister was laughing so hard she wet her pants. This was more like a *farter*, she thought, clutching her stomach. For sleeping sheilas and their messed-up mates…

Sondra, her PA, had printed it out and handed it to her, without comment.

"It's a load of cosmic claptrap… pure codswallop," the PM said. "I mean, he sounds quite *mad*… doesn't he?"

Sondra was staring at her strangely, either because *she* was a closet *cosmic human* or because she thought her *boss* had lost it.

The American President will be fawning all over this, the PM thought. *They'll go on cosmic crusades together, converting everyone…*

Sondra glared at her, tight-lipped, arms folded across her tidy chest. "He's not so far off the mark, you know."

The PM stopped laughing and looked at her assistant. "You believe in this stuff?"

"Everything he says is based on quantum physics. It's pretty much the way things *are*, actually." Sondra seemed sternly miffed—a far cry from her steady neutral self.

"I didn't know you were religious, Sondra."

"This has *nothing* to do with religion," Sondra practically hissed at her. "Quite the opposite."

Crikey. She'd obviously touched a nerve, the PM thought.

"I'll just go and… freshen up," she said, walking tight-legged down the hallway to her bathroom. Good thing she'd worn a skirt and had been standing up when she had her laughing fit. She could feel Sondra's eyes on her as she went.

As soon as she closed the bathroom door behind her, she let out another bellow of laughter, caught sight of her mad face in the mirror, and laughed even harder. God, she thought, there was nothing like a good laugh to bring you back down to… earth. Someone should tell the poor man he's dreaming. He's obviously had a fair suck of the cosmic sauce…

She heard the front door close… rather *pointedly*, she thought, falling into another fit of hysterics.

Then she caught another glimpse of her contorted face in the mirror, sobered herself and looked closer.

If that charter-thing was such utter crap, why the fuck was she crying?

71

---

23 December 2020

Marnie was having a hard time keeping up with her own evolution. Every time she thought she had finally found firm footing, the ground shifted again, throwing her off balance. All over the world, things were changing in freaky and unpredictable ways, and every aspect of her personal life seemed to have been vigorously shaken and stirred over the past 12 months.

Millie was in California again, doing more training for her sound-healing practice. DeeDee was in the Bahamas with Jordanis, her new man. Both would be gone for the next few months. Lucy and Nate were planning to start up a new design business, with creative input from Tatum-the-wunderkind. Matt and Celle had opened up an organic-food cooperative in Mexico and did not plan on coming home anytime soon. That probably *was* their home now. Marnie could understand why they wouldn't want to come back.

And now this.

When the Thanksgiving whirlwind had finally calmed and she had wrapped her head around the idea of getting married, Steve seemed to instantly shift gears. He was getting tired of all the travelling for work, he said, and wanted a change. Would Marnie move to Georgia with him to start a new life?

Well, a change was one thing but that was more like a bombshell. Go southern? Be regularly engulfed in the Romero bosoms and almost certainly plump up her own?

But what would she *do* there? She wasn't ready to give up working and spend her days perfecting her corn grits. And what would *Steve* do?

He had already thought it all through. He wanted to go into business with his brother Troy in Jacksonville, and he was sure Marnie would find a teaching position that she'd love.

Since then, she had been vacillating giddily between being excited about the possibilities and the fresh freedom of a new beginning, and feeling nauseous, claustrophobic and terrified of losing control over… what? She wasn't sure, but she didn't want to lose it, whatever it was.

"You're just afraid of losing control over your own choices," Steve had said, laughing. "As if that will ever happen. You'll be taking *you* with you, remember," he said. "The strong-willed Marnie I know and love will never allow herself to be taken over—not even by the formidable Romero clan."

"Well, I got won over by *one* of them," Marnie had said, hesitantly open to being reassured.

"Being taken over and being won over are two very different things," Steve said firmly. "You might ultimately end up in the same place but *you* will have taken yourself there and you will be there on your own terms—free to stay or go as you wish." He had looked at her seriously, knowing this was the clincher to her commitment. "You will always have choices, darlin' girl—even more choices, I hope, as my partner in building a new life we both love."

When he put it like that, it seemed like a good thing, and she *was* ready for change. Hadn't she been going on about this for months, writing about it in her ideal-life journal? Maybe this was a new door opening as a result of all that positive focus and intention. Her dad would probably have told her to *go for it*.

She was definitely more *for* than *against*. She just needed to wrestle with her inner demons a bit longer and reassure them of continued independence and expanding possibilities.

But where the heck was Ray? She felt uneasy about leaving Boston without knowing what was going on.

When she had returned from Georgia, she had gone to Ray's house to get some answers. This time, the door had been opened by his wife Lily, looking about as pleased to see Marnie as if she was a Jehovah Witness.

"You're the girl who came for physics lessons," she said, arms folded across her chest like a *no entry* sign.

"Yes. I was wondering if I could talk to him for a minute."

"He's not here," Lily said. "He's gone."

"Gone?" Marnie's heart lurched. Gone as in *dead*, as in *found another woman*, as in *the FBI took him* or what? "Gone where?"

"Not that it's any of your business…" Lily said, hesitating. "But I don't know. I don't know where he's gone or what has happened to him." She looked at Marnie accusingly. "Do *you*?"

"Me? No. That's why I'm here… I… Is there anything I can do to help find him?" Marnie knew what it felt like to have someone disappear without a trace, leaving no target for your worry, anger and frustration.

"Not unless you have some idea where he is." Lily seemed to be steeling herself against an unwelcome reality. "I think he was working on something that got him into trouble, and he's either gone into hiding or been taken."

Marnie got the feeling she was the #1 suspect in this case, or at least somehow responsible for Ray's disappearance. Maybe she was, if she had led the FBI or someone else to his lab. She felt sick. She had promised to *help* him.

"Taken? Who would take him?"

"*You* tell *me*." Lily challenged her with another lawyerly look. "You were here every week, talking about *something*, when I was out. And I'm not convinced it was just ordinary physics."

"I wish I could tell you," Marnie said, realizing she sounded exactly like Ray when he dodged her questions. "I have no idea where he could be." She hesitated. "Have you called the police, the FBI, anyone?"

Lily snorted. "And say what? My rebel scientist husband has gone missing. Have you got him?"

"Um, yes. Have you tried that?"

"Do you realize how many husbands—and wives—walk away from their spouse every day? The police take no notice and they have bigger things to worry about." Lily looked desolate, hardening to the possibility that she might not see Ray again.

"It might be worth calling the FBI," Marnie said carefully. "Ray mentioned that they considered him a *person of interest* in the whole CEBS thing, given his expertise and all his TV interviews."

"I wouldn't know where to start or if that's even a good idea." Lily looked overwhelmed at the thought of tackling that mammoth, impenetrable organization—and maybe attracting attention to herself.

"I could try calling, if you like," Marnie said. *What were the names of those two agents who looked like Laurel and Hardy?* If she could remember, she could try to reach them.

"If you want," Lily said, shoulders sagging in defeat. "But don't involve me. I've been excluded from his work all these years and I don't want to get dragged into it now."

She took a breath, unfolded her arms and closed the door in Marnie's face.

Marnie had made her way home, lost in thought, trying to dredge up the names of the FBI agents. She had been so freaked out when they showed up at Ray's lab that she hadn't consciously registered their names, but maybe her subconscious had. She would see if the names came back to her at night, when she did her daily mental filing and processed things she didn't even realize were locked away in her memory banks.

In the meantime, she had some big decisions to make about her life, but it was beginning to feel as if things were unfolding beyond her control and all she could do was go along for the ride, hold on tight and see what happened next.

72

OHMYGODLUCY!

Sherry had never bothered much about punctuation. Life was all about the poetry, creativity, artful living… and dodging, when required. There had been a passionate reaction to her mural and she'd only just come back down to earth to e-mail Lucy and send her the photo. She'd expected *passionate*, but not in her *favour*. Anger, public condemnation and a hefty fine—yes, but not this groundswell of gleeful delight at what she had done.

Must talk! Lots to share. See attached pic. Skype me! sox

Lucy did, and it was the first time they'd talked since Sherry's move to Vancouver in mid-2019.

"Dalton, how the hell *are* you? I haven't heard a single sound bite from you since high school." Sherry looked animated and was practically bouncing in her chair. Lucy had never seen her so jazzed— eyes on fire but without the raccoon make-up or any of her former laid-back hippie demeanour.

"Yeah. Sorry. After what happened with my parents, you know…"

"Of course. Delsie told me. I e-mailed and texted but never got a response." Sherry brushed it aside. "Look, I totally understand. I wanted to be there for you, you know? You must have been in shock. *I* was in shock when I heard." She paused for a breath. "How are you now? Not that you ever get over something like that…"

"I'm… okay," Lucy said, realizing that she was, more or less. Most days, more than less. "I put fashion design on hold, for now. I've been working for a communications company writing copy on health-related stuff. But I'd prefer to hear about you. Much more exciting." Ugh. Lucy didn't like how that came out. Pathetically self-pitying. "We can talk about me another day," she amended. "What's this photo you sent? Wasn't that the mural that caused such a scandal in Vancouver last month—a painting of the Prime Minister peeing into a puddle… by some guy, some artist called Shermer?"

"Ha. Think about it… Sher… Mer…"

"Shit. That was *you*?"

"Yeah. Sherry Merickson—*Shermer*. You know how west-coasters *love* progressive, edgy stuff. I was sure the mural would be whitewashed as soon as the city authorities got wind of it. But everyone *loved* it! They all want it to stay up there till the PM is toast—well and truly *gone*. And they're still trying to figure out where he was and what he was doing if he hadn't been where he *said* he was, doing what he was *supposed* to be doing, and why he'd needed to lie about what he actually *had* been doing, which was probably far worse than the lie itself."

"Feels like a political pirouette that most people will be too dizzy—or too digi-ditzy—to figure out," Lucy said, not sure she could keep up with her fired-up friend. "Apart from all you switched-on Vancouverites, of course."

"Well said, Dalton. No more spin at the top. The truth is so *refreshing*, isn't it?"

Lucy knew she wasn't expected to answer—and wouldn't have time to.

"Speaking of which…" Sherry continued, "people are asking me to *Shermer* lots of other shady officials. No shortage of *them*, especially in Ottawa, although not so many in Vancouver, since the CEBS clean-up.. I've become a verb, Luce! Who'd have thunk it?!"

"Shermer…" The name was ringing a faint bell in Lucy's head. "Isn't that the American skeptic guy? The science writer who defends free speech and explores pseudoscience and paranormal stuff?"

"Never heard of him. Sounds like my kind of guy, if he's defending free speech, although I'm skeptical about people attacking the unconventional—if that's what he does. I'll take *paranormal* over *normal* any day." She paused to take a normal breath. "Since CEBS, Vancouverites love debunking pseudo-truth and graphically exposing public offenders who have got away with murder for far too long. Giving them a *visual flaying*, is what the media called it when the mural went up—a *shermer*."

"So… *you* painted that…" Lucy still couldn't quite wrap her head around it.

"Well, the original was by my artist friend Luigi, reproduced with his permission, but I put it up there."

"Wow. That's amazing, Sherry. You've really made your mark."

"Hey, no one's more surprised than me. Luigi is loving this, too. We're collaborating on some other shit-stirring stuff to really get things moving." She paused, shaking her head in wonder. "This place is unreal, Lucy. The whole city is pulsing with possibilities and *no one* is using a cellphone. I'm pretty sure it's the end of wireless technology— for Vancouverites, at least. In this expansive new scheme of things, they know something better is already gearing up to take its place. And the benefits so vastly outweigh the downsides, which aren't really downsides at all, once you see past all that old stuff. Everyone is sharing ideas, inspiring each other, coming up with all kinds of new stuff. It's *electrifying*."

"I can see that," Lucy said, smiling. "You seem totally wired."

"Yeah, fully wired, no more wireless! That's the beauty of this whole CEBS thing. It's brought everyone back down to earth in a very real way. The pre-CEBS world seems so *alien* now, you know? When I think how *I* used to feel like an alien visiting some strange corrupted planet."

"You *were*!" Lucy laughed. "It must be great to no longer be in the minority—in Vancouver, at least."

"It is. Before CEBS hit the States and started the turnaround, all that fear-mongering, confinement and control really did a number on people's sense of power over their own lives. Not that they ever had *much*, thanks to all the diligent *regulatory* bodies, such as the FCC— not the F-ing Federal Communications Commission— but the other one, the Friggin' Catholic Church, which was a far more ungodly form of communication, indoctrinating everyone into feeling sinful, subservient and a total waste of space."

"I remember how fervently you loved trashing religion." Lucy laughed. It felt good to get a dose of Sherry's rebelliousness. She hadn't lost *that*, Lucy was glad to see. If anything, she'd found the perfect platform for it.

And she was on a roll. "Feardom and freedom—they are total *opposites*. People have no *idea* what real freedom means, and they never will unless they dump the fear." Sherry had obviously got rid of hers, Lucy thought, which made her wonder how much fear was cramping *her* style…

"That's what CEBS does for people, Lucy. It purges them of all that crippling crap that gets in the way of living *full on*. You can't *imagine* freedom—you can't feel it, know it, share it or *be* it unless you totally shed the fear."

Lucy was starting to feel downright boring, and a little *pissed off*.

How come *she* hadn't got hit with CEBS and launched a whole new fearless life like Sherry had...

"When the fear is gone," Sherry was saying, "you get to see just how much power you really have. And you get to see the truth. You cut right through all the crap and see what's real—in people, too. It gives you a fierce clarity and instant bullshit-detection, with zero tolerance for the same sick old games, including your own. We all have this powerful inner freedom and it's been there all along, but the fear blocks it out—*locks* it out—so you can't see beyond it. And there is *so much* beyond it."

She paused, sensing Lucy's absence.

"Lucy? You still with me?"

"Yeah. Sorry…"

"What is it?"

"I'm just… I feel I'm stuck in some tragically normal, plodding existence, just trying to..." Lucy wasn't sure what she was trying to do, but her life seemed almost *stationery*, compared with Sherry's dynamic adventures. She wasn't exactly pushing the envelope… More like pushing paper and promoting someone else's success… Even that *thought* felt old. Hadn't she been here recently, in her head, questioning the viability of her life?

"I totally get that," Sherry said, "but the reason I got in touch was because I knew *you* would get this, Dalton. And you *do*. You're very much a part of this process. I don't know how or when, but I do know you are destined for something great to come out of this. And you won't need CEBS to launch you."

"I don't see that at all." Lucy sat back, arms folded across her chest. She *wanted* to believe it, but where was the evidence? It certainly wasn't in her current sorry life. This was just some west-coast pep talk from a friend taking pity on her—

"Okay, enough pity-party crap, Dalton. This is not your style." Sherry narrowed her eyes and looked pointedly at her laptop camera. "You were the first person I thought of when I did that mural. *Lucy will totally get this*, I thought. *This is exactly her kind of thing*. You were always the spunkiest, most outspoken kid in school. The biggest brat, too, but that was part of your charm. I didn't know anyone like you. Please don't tell me that girl is gone."

Lucy felt her spine tighten. In resistance? Or was that some of her spunk coming back? She felt taken aback but also deeply *stirred* by

Sherry's words, as if some dormant sediment that had settled over her soul was being shaken off. But she felt shaky, unsure about what this all meant for her, if anything…

"Who the hell *are* you and what have you done with my friend Sherry?"

"Yeah, yeah. Be flippant and deflect it all you want, but that's actually what *I* should be asking *you*. So, has that girl gone? Am I wasting my breath?"

"I'm not sure." Lucy took a breath, so it wouldn't be wasted… and that thought made her smile. "I hope not. I'm just not sure where she's hiding out, right now."

"Listen, Luce." Sherry's voice softened. "I know you've lost your parents and that's bound to rock your foundations, but I also know your mom left you a unique legacy—a big chunk of intelligence, wisdom and kick-ass determination to do something extraordinary, unconventional, mind-blowing. You can't just roll over and die. I'm here to tell you to get your act together, girl. Kick that cute little ass of yours into gear and get ready for some meaningful action. Don't make me come down there and *Shermer* you, okay? There's a whole new world emerging and you, my friend, are most definitely a pivotal part of it."

73

---

24 September 2019

She had felt the loss long before the losing, just as she had loved her offspring long before they sprang from her body. This conscious countdown was a killer, in every sense. It brought a throbbing awareness of every breath and heartbeat, of neurons firing frantically in her brain, of life still wanting itself, of each remaining second magnified into nothingness.

Hugging her knees, Frannie sat gazing into the flames. She felt hollowed out.

Daniel squatted down on the floor behind her, legs on either side, bathing her in the river of love that he was. She should have floated a whole lot more in that river…

"What are you thinking?"

"That we should have done more of this," she said, her arms overlapping his and squeezing—the Morse code of touch.

"This feels perfect, as always, and we've still got a few hours left," he said, his chin on her shoulder. "What else is going on in that brain of yours?"

"I did something silly."

"You, *silly?*" Even that sounded like a loving invitation to be more of herself.

"I left something behind for Marnie."

"After the six three-hour lectures you gave me on not leaving anything behind…?"

"I know, I know. It was a risk, but I thought just one small inanimate thing would be okay…"

"What did you leave her?"

"My old travel alarm clock."

"You must have had a reason for leaving her that old thing."

"Not really. It was sentimental… and stupid." Frannie sighed. "I suppose I was trying to give her some kind of subliminal message about time… that it was just a matter of time before…"

"Before what?"

"Before she could… forgive me. Or maybe it was just a way to let her know I loved her and wanted to give her some tiny piece of me."

"You don't think she knew you loved her?"

"No. I don't think she did." Frannie turned sideways to face him. "Daniel, they are going to *hate* us," she moaned. "They won't understand and they will never forgive us. We will have deserted them and they will never know why."

"I know," he said, holding her close. "But we're doing this for them, so they can have a life," he said. "That's what you've been telling me all along, so they will survive, even if we don't."

"But we've had so little time with them *now*," she wailed. "We've been so busy trying to save them for the future that we've barely been with them in the *present*. And that's all they've got. What kind of parents *are* we?"

"The kind who sacrifice everything for their children, which parents have done since the beginning of time," Daniel said, "only other parents just have plain old time to work with, whereas we've been able to cheat and give our children a chance they would never otherwise have."

"Should we tell them?" She looked at him hopefully. "Before we leave?"

"Frannie, you know we can't. If we weaken now and tell them, it will all have been for nothing—and they won't survive what's coming. You know how this works. *You* taught *me*. There are only certain algorithms we can use to make things right for the future."

"Is there any way we could rework the numbers to create a different outcome or timeframe? So that we could stay with them and not have to… die?"

She knew the answer to this better than he did, but she was desperate, anticipating the pain that Marnie, Matt and Lucy would go through—pain that *they* would cause them and not be able to lessen.

"Sweetheart, we've spent the last five years working the numbers, looking at all the possibilities, and we've narrowed things down to what we've got now."

He hugged her tightly, trying to infuse her with some of the certainty she had shared with him when he'd had all his initial doubts.

"You've gone into the future and checked out every possible permutation and this is the only one that's going to work."

"But how will they manage without us?"

"You know they will manage," he said, turning her to face him and smiling. "You've already seen that, on your travels, so you know they'll be okay—thanks to you, Frannie."

He looked in her eyes. "How many parents get the opportunity to do that?"

"But *they* don't know that," she said, her sobs making her hiccup. "And we can't leave them anything!"

"I know, I know," he said, stroking her back. "I wish it could be some other way."

His chest was starting to ache. "You know we have to remove all material trace of our existence, except for them, Frannie."

"But we can't even say *goodbye*," she said, her hand clutching his chest, trying to absorb some of his strength.

She was getting herself worked up and Daniel could see the deep fatigue in her eyes.

'Sweetheart," he said gently. "I wish more than anything I could make this right for you, for us and for them, but we've done everything we can, and you have been extraordinary."

He held her at arm's length again, looking her in the eye.

"Frannie, you are the most amazing woman on the planet," he said, his voice catching. "What you have achieved is phenomenal—far beyond what we originally envisioned."

She was shaking her head as if none of it mattered now. And it didn't—not for them, anyway.

"Daniel?"

"Yes, Frannie…"

"Do you *really* think it's going to work?"

"Which bit?"

"All of it… especially the last bit."

"Fuck, I hope so," he said, just to make her laugh.

She did.

"All our calculations worked before," he said, gently. "You always landed more or less in the right place, and came back to me with all your bits intact, thank God. We can't know for *sure* that what we've set in motion will work. We just have to trust that the numbers, the algorithms and the portals are as accurate as before. That's all we can do now, Frannie. Trust."

"I know," she said, resting against him. All the same old quantum questions, asked again for the very last time.

"You know, I'd prefer to have had these past 35 crazy, wonderful years with you than 60 years with a hairdresser," Daniel said, desperate to make her laugh again. "Even a really good one, which I could definitely use, right now." They'd been so busy with their work that his hair was almost down to his shoulders.

She grunted. Was that a laugh or a groan?

"You remember the granola?"

Her breathing shifted. He felt her smile. She remembered.

Frannie used to make him the most delicious granola, with oat flakes, blackstrap molasses and lots of mixed nuts, filling the house with the most tantalizing smell when it was baking in the oven. She didn't like oats but she used to pilfer the roasted nuts during the day and, in the morning, when he had his dish of granola with coconut milk, he would wonder why the ratio of nuts to oat flakes seemed to have changed.

He finally figured out what she was up to and started leaving her

Post-it notes in the granola jar.

I'm watching you…

The next morning, more nuts had disappeared and there was a different note in there. *Just checking it's still fresh…*

He left another note. *It's fresh!*

The nuts were down by half, and there was another note the next morning. *I don't know who you are or what your game is, but I haven't been anywhere near this stuff.*

This went on for a while and Frannie continued to pilfer his granola nuts even when she roasted a separate batch of nuts for herself. "They're just not the same," she said. "Something changes when I make them for you."

"*Your nuts* do not change the fact that *you're nuts*," he had said. "I think that tells us all we need to know."

He laughed quietly and felt her lighten against him.

He kept going. He so wanted her to go out happy—or at least reconciled.

"You remember when Lucy was born?"

She shifted against him again as she relived the memory.

"She was so *fast*, popping out with barely any warning, and then looking up at us as if to say, *What's your problem? You've known about this for nine months. Get a grip!*"

Frannie laughed, and Daniel hugged her close, marveling at the miracle of life and all they had shared.

"She was feisty, right from the start," Frannie said.

"Just like you," Daniel said.

"I was prickly, wasn't I."

"*Was?*"

She laughed, loving him for always trying to make her laugh, from the very first awful joke he told her about quantum physicists, when she went to his party—his *particle*—where it all began. But then didn't everything start with a particle?

"You remember, when we met," Daniel said, as if reading her mind, "you told me you wanted to achieve something that defied reality and gave people something they didn't even know they needed? Well, you did it. And you know what will happen if we don't intervene."

He had raised all these same objections with her, countless times, and she had countered with all the same arguments …except that she had seen the future long before he had, and he'd had to trust her when she said that things needed to be this way.

But, now, having gone with her the last time, when they had finally figured out how to get *him* into the future so he could see for himself, he no longer doubted her. Not that he ever had; it was more his own judgement that he questioned, given the enormity of what they were doing.

She sat back, a hand on his heart, looking into his eyes.

"Daniel, there's something I must tell you," she said, and his heart almost stopped. Was she finally going to admit to having done something in some future time she had visited?

"I do love you, you know," she blurted out, rushing the unfamiliar words. "I don't know why I've been so stingy with these words for so long, but…"

In 35 years of being together, she had never said those words to him. Daniel felt his throat constrict and could not respond. He knew she loved him, but hearing those words now, right before they ended their lives together, felt like a horrible irony, yet a fitting end to an extraordinary relationship. His heart was battling with more love and more pain than he felt he could handle.

If only they didn't have to die. Now that they had finally managed to resolve things in their work, he desperately wanted more time with Frannie—quality time for just the two of them, without needing to focus so much on saving the world. The thought of losing her and abandoning their children felt like a crushing nonsense.

If he hadn't needed to be strong for her, he wouldn't have been able to do this. But none of this would ever have been possible without her, and their children would never have existed.

Was it better to have had them, just long enough to get them to adulthood, and then have to leave them, rather than never having had them at all?

It was the age-old question: *Was it better to have loved and lost then never to have loved at all?* Maybe, but it didn't help at all. Not even a quantum bit.

PART 3

74

September 2022

CEBS Supplement, September 2022 Update: Where are we now?

After the initial euphoria following the US President's post-CEBS proclamation of positive reforms in 2020, some harsh realities had kicked in.

There was the inevitable backlash from the wireless industry, amid fears of a global economic collapse, which the President had said would be short-lived, since he was not doing away with telecommunications, merely the wireless component. He turned out to be right, although we have seen two years of massive upheaval, political back-pedalling, a media feeding frenzy and dissent from certain human-rights groups.

But what the President had not anticipated was the need for a massive nationwide rehabilitation program to address *chronicomia*—the physical and emotional addiction to wireless devices, which afflicted the majority of the population, especially young people. Recovering from the condition involved extreme withdrawal symptoms, intense anxiety, agitation and depression, as well as manic mood swings and personality disorders.

Psychiatrists, clinical psychologists and other medical professionals had estimated it would take up to two years for the condition to be fully resolved among the population.

However, a small percentage have been unable to bounce back and remain removed from the rest of humanity, on the fringes—similar to the former environmental refugees affected by wireless radiation, who had been effectively excluded from participating in normal life.

By the end of 2021, it had become clear that the CEBS attacks had ceased but something else seemed to have taken their place. There was speculation that a new wave of positive frequencies was somehow being transmitted through the air, since CEBS had only hit a handful of capital cities and could not account for the radical worldwide shifts that had followed.

A global renaissance was sweeping the planet, with an explosion of creativity, innovation and expansive thinking. Despite this renewed exuberance for life, the world seemed a lot more peaceful. Since the agitation, distractions and speediness of non-stop wireless connectivity had been reduced, people had slowed down and become more present, sitting quietly in nature, making time for each other, making eye contact and talking to each other in cafés, checkout lines and on public transport.

In fact, people seemed *transported* in some way, lifted out of their former distracted self-absorption and landed back inside themselves.

The CEBS acronym had been adjusted to reflect the more uplifting, transformative frequencies. It was now known as the *Conscious Evolutionary Broadcasting System*, or just CEBS2.

Those who had not been hit by the original round of CEBS were nonetheless dealing with physical and emotional fallout triggered by the later frequencies. For those who had been deeply programmed or repressed in some way, it could still be a brutal emotional exorcism. For most, though, it was a gentler, slower process—more like the delicate low-temperature cycle of a washing machine, compared with the intense 90° industrial-strength purge of the first CEBS attacks. Some described it as an invitation rather than an enforcement or, among the techies, a natural defrag and reset rather than ripping out the motherboard.

The various CEBS frequencies had been identified in mid-2021, but no one had yet managed to trace the person or persons transmitting them. Back in 2020, amid widespread outrage and fear, there had been calls for the perpetrator's arrest and worse. Many wanted that man or woman to hang for what they had done. Now, if they ever did manage to track down those responsible, people were far more likely to celebrate and honour them—to thank them for giving them back their lives.

75

Sometimes, Lucy had to almost pinch herself to make sure this was real, that this was her *life*. When she looked back on all that had happened since her parents died, she could hardly believe how much she had changed. Just five years ago, she had been an angry, petulant mess, ready to end her wretched empty existence. *Now* look.

As she gazed at the precious gift in front of her, here in their new home, she felt the powerful wave of emotion that regularly washed over her like a tide cleaning a beach. Awe, gratitude and a faint ache of sadness that her parents could not be here to share such moments.

It always made her smile remembering how she had surprised Nate, shortly after their first successful year with their new online business. She had just finished processing an order for a store in California, and was in the living room drinking her favourite decaf organic coffee, when Nate came in to join her.

He flopped down on the couch beside her. "So, what's your next project?"

"Mmmm… I think maybe… making baby booties."

"What?" He looked at her, eyes wide, computing the possibilities. "You mean…?"

Lucy smiled, relishing the sharing of a woman's most potent secret.

Nate shook his head, taking a deep breath and holding it *for-ev-er*, it seemed to Lucy, who was holding her own.

"No!" he exhaled emphatically. "This is *not* okay, Lucy. I absolutely forbid it."

Lucy froze. *Nate*, doing the classic man-runs-for-the-hills manoeuvre at the notion of a b-a-b-y?

"No way," Nate said, glaring at her. "What are you *thinking*? We'll get *Tate* to design a special pair—the most unique booties in the world, for the most amazing child on the planet, born to the most amazing woman, married to the most amazing man."

Lucy collapsed back onto the cushions. "Those are going to be *some* booties."

"Yes," he said, beaming, "and then everyone will want them, so that probably *will* be your next project… until the bambino arrives to take those booties for a test drive."

Their son Charlie was born on 24 September of 2021—the same day that Lucy's parents had died in 2019. Lucy wished he had arrived a day sooner or later, so she wouldn't be reminded of their absence every time she celebrated Charlie's birthday, but it was hard to have any regrets where their little boy was concerned.

From the moment that little bundle of joy had blasted into their lives, he had been stealing the hearts of all who met him. Precocious, inquisitive, demanding, turbo-fast and wickedly funny, he was a mini-replica of his handsome dad.

Even as an infant, Charlie seemed very aware of his surroundings—and almost adult-like in adapting to his new environment. After the first few months, he began to sleep right through the night, rarely waking them in the bleary-eyed hours, wailing for food or attention, or even just to exercise his lungs, which worked fine and needed no additional workouts. Lucy had often suspected that some babies, especially those who were neglected or simply didn't get enough bonding time with their parents, did everything they could to make it clear that *they*, the babies, were now in charge of the household and would, forever more, be the centre of that little biosphere.

Charlie was certainly at the centre of theirs, and it was a happy, mind-expanding universe. For Lucy, watching her son grow was like seeing time-lapsed photographs of a budding flower. He seemed to be growing on a timeframe all his own, completely disregarding all conventional directives on how babies should develop.

A year after officially *inaugurating* their relationship at the lovely country inn where Nate had taken Lucy in December 2020, they had moved to Rhode Island, to a four-bedroom house on the outskirts of Cranston. With a large garden, lots of parks, yet easy access to amenities, it was a good spot to raise a family—and run a home-based business. It was perfect for dogs, too, but Beemer had died in his sleep at the age of 15, shortly before they left Boston. They both still missed his wise, faithful presence and decided to wait a while before getting another dog.

Nate's parents, Nancy and Brandon, had sold the Boston townhouse and given Lucy and Nate this new home as a wedding present. They felt blessed, with family life unfolding like a huge gift-wrapped package all around them.

Lucy had enjoyed getting to know her in-laws before she and Nate had left Boston. And they seemed as enamoured with her as she was with their son. A perceptive woman who seemed profoundly at peace with herself, Nancy was a fount of earthy wisdom and practical solutions. After Charlie was born, when Lucy had shared her concerns about him potentially being more than she could handle, Nancy had hugged her and told her just to hold on tight and enjoy the ride. Nothing was more exciting than joyful genius and creativity, she said, and Charlie had an abundance of both.

Brandon was a quiet man, with well-considered words and a wry smile. Lucy thought of him as deep and reflective, prone to consulting his vast mental archives before offering up his own brand of wisdom, whereas Nancy was more present to the humans around her, more ready with her laughter and cookies. Lucy loved them both and could see where Nate got his solid goodness and quiet self-confidence.

The whole Dalton clan seemed to be going south, which suited Lucy just fine. If she could just get Matt and Celle to come for a visit, her world would be complete. Well, as complete as it was ever likely to be, *sans* parents.

Their online business, Cordalis Creations, was now making a nice profit, with a percentage going to Tate for his designs, all of which bore his trademark signature over a pocket, along a seam, or on the collar, depending on the style of the shirt.

At the advanced age of 11, Tate was still in high school but was allowed to spend Saturdays working on his designs and creating patterns. His dad helped him scale them up for M, L and XL sizes and his mom sourced unusual fabrics to keep things original.

Lucy was production & design coordinator; Nate was marketing manager; and they had a manufacturing and fulfillment centre in Mexico, coordinated by Celle.

The Shimmer was one of their best sellers. In a deep cerulean blue, made of super-soft brushed organic cotton, the shirt had a mandarin collar and was worn out over jeans (*not* tucked in, Tate insisted). It had shimmering silver threads running vertically through the fabric, with occasional bright-red threads scattered throughout, and Tatum's signature in red on the collar.

Tate usually named the shirts when he designed them, although Celle sometimes suggested an alternative when she went to check the production line and saw some of the shirts being made in the Mexican factory. Zenith was one of hers, blending Zen-ness with the height of fashion. It was made of a soft bamboo fabric in a solid forest green with textured undulating horizontal patterns worked into the fabric to give the illusion of waves. Tiny gold flecks crested some of the waves like sunlight glancing off breakers.

Lucy was loving the creative challenges, but Charlie was her best creation ever. Already, he was demonstrating his own unique streak of genius and seemed to have inherited the prodigious genes of his uncle Tate, plus a few of his own.

They first noticed it shortly after Charlie's third birthday. It seemed like a fluke and they forgot about it for a while. He was playing ball with Nate in the back garden when he kicked the ball straight up into the air. It kept on going, up, up, up for an impossible distance, until it was the size of a golf ball in the sky. Nate watched, stunned, as the ball remained suspended for several moments, eventually coming slowly back down to earth, like a space ship coming softly to rest on the ground.

Nate turned to his son. "Charlie, how did you do that?"

"Dunno." Charlie shrugged, grinning. "I just kicked it."

"It was freaky," Nate told Lucy afterwards. "It was like a super power or something, as if Charlie was somehow controlling the ball and keeping it up in the air like that."

Charlie had started kindergarten a few months previously, which freed up Lucy's mornings. She was now working on their new line of shirts for children. If that went well, they planned to expand their offering to include women's shirts next year.

They soon noticed other super-normal things that Charlie could do without even realizing. For him, it was normal. For Lucy, it was scary. *Was he a little alien transplant or just supremely gifted?*

After only three months at kindergarten, Charlie could read, write, spell and count. But it wasn't just books he could read; it was people. With just one look, he could tell what they were thinking and feeling, which reminded Lucy of the way Tate had picked up on his uncle Nate's emotions when she'd first met her future nephew. Maybe this new generation of kids was tuned in to some other dimension that gave them access to a higher form of intelligence.

And it wasn't just the alphabet that Charlie could write, but full sentences in a grown-up longhand—although he was far more likely to speed-type on her laptop, which was a skill he seemed to have learned on his own. As far as Lucy knew, they weren't yet teaching touch-typing in kindergarten. As for counting, he could multiply, divide and find the square root of three- and four-digit numbers… in his head.

The kindergarten teacher told Lucy she needed to find another school for her dauntingly gifted child.

Charlie seemed to agree. "Mum, she talks to me as if I'm a baby, so I told her she had to talk popper senses."

"You mean *proper sentences…?*"

"Yeah." Charlie laughed. "But I was just using baby talk for her sake."

The irony of this kept Lucy bemused for days, alternately laughing to herself at the idea of her little boy outsmarting his teacher (probably why the teacher wanted him to leave), and trying to imagine the kind of proclamations he would deliver when he was 20.

Lucy kept in regular touch with Delsie, who was now practising psychotherapy in Colonial Beach, Virginia, where she had moved to be closer to her mom. After giving up her law studies, following the CEBS attack, she had decided that addressing conflicts and problems *before* they turned into lawsuits would save everyone a lot of heartache and money.

Given her own personal experience with CEBS, Delsie knew the kind of breakthroughs that could occur when certain emotional elements were addressed, and she had developed her own version of the CEBS process, which she called Conscious Emotional Breakthrough System. She had only been in practice for the past year but already had a full slate of clients.

She had come to visit, shortly after Charlie was born, to officially accept her role as godmother. Not something Lucy really believed in, but Delsie insisted. She wasn't religious either, but it was a good excuse to lay claim to this little man in some official capacity. As if she needed one, Lucy told her fondly. She would be more like his auntie than anything else.

Now, as Lucy watched her super-smart son reading a novel on the sofa, she wondered what other miracles life would send her way—and whether she could handle any more. *What if she and Nate had another child like Charlie?* They could probably give up working altogether, for starters, and just let the kids invent things that made millions. But how do you parent children that are a thousand times smarter than you? What the heck happened when they were teenagers and knew more than you did about… everything?

She'd talked to Delsie about it, trying to get to grips with the unsettling phenomenon of being outsmarted by her own tiny kid—who should, at this tender age, be learning how to read three-letter words, not read minds or do mathematical calculations that were way beyond the brainpower of both parents combined.

"I'm seeing something similar happening with a few of my younger clients," Delsie said. "At first, I wasn't sure if it was some futuristic thing or from our ancestors or new parts of our brain developing or what."

"And?"

"As far as I can see, it's all of those things." Delsie laughed, delighted by the infinite possibilities. "It's as if some dormant part of the brain is being activated, enabling us to tap into all kinds of faculties that seem freaky but are really just part of being more highly evolved—something our early ancestors were able to do much better than us. We normally use only a tiny fraction of our brains, and even *that* gets distorted by social conditioning and emotional issues."

Delsie was convinced the positive changes were related to the whole CEBS phenomenon *and* the new telecom technology. Ever since Gravizone had replaced wireless telecoms, she had felt a shift—and seen it in her patients. *Was this new technology also transmitting something beneficial, on the heels of CEBS?* She had to wonder. "Even those who were never hit are different," she told Lucy. "I see it in other patients. Have you noticed this, Luce? Do *you* feel different?"

"Different how?"

"Just… more tuned in, somehow… more aware, more intuitive and more connected to yourself."

Lucy thought back to her meltdown and the swell of emotions, insights and realizations that had hit her when Nate said he wanted to officially launch their relationship. That *was* different. *She* was different.

"Yeah. I think I know what you mean. I've changed a lot. But having Charlie kind of eclipses some of my own revelations, you know? Although he also accentuates them, and causes some, so he's very much entangled in my evolution."

"I think you have changed tremendously on your own—without the CEBS hit. Maybe Charlie is your own personal growth booster."

Lucy laughed. "He sure is that. You can't sit around reading magazines or filing your nails when your 3-year-old wants to talk about the Fibonacci spiral or the nature of reality."

"He's something else, my little godson," Delsie said. "But you're not alone. I work with two kids a little older than Charlie that are scarily smart, and I'm writing up some case studies that I'll publish later to see if other therapists are seeing the same thing in other countries."

It was reassuring to know that Charlie's genius might be part of an evolutionary phenomenon, although it didn't really help in terms of everyday parenting.

But Delsie's support and input always brought Lucy back to a more centred perspective where she could keep loving the immense gift of Charlie without being daunted by his greatness.

"Don't forget he *is* just a kid," Delsie said. "It's easy to forget that when he's such a brainiac, but he still needs hugs, stories, games, playing ball with his dad, going camping and doing other fun stuff, just like normal kids. Maybe even *more* than normal kids, just to balance things out."

"Yeah. Thanks. That makes sense, and we *do* have lots of laughs."

One of the many things Lucy still found disconcerting was the way Charlie could telepathically pick up on what she was thinking. She could communicate with him via her thoughts, without using words, although he always had to respond out loud, since she was not *quite* as evolved as he was. She could call him or reprimand him without having to shout or figure out where he was, which was handy, although sometimes he pretended not to hear her.

Then she would say it louder in her head. "*Okay, Buster, I know you're getting this. Get your ancient little 3-year-old butt in here, right this minute.*"

Charlie would arrive, grinning. "No need to yell," he'd say, and she would drop her wooden spoon or whatever she was doing, and chase him around the house. Charlie would run, squealing, as fast as his little legs would carry him, which wasn't very fast. She might not be able to keep up with his phenomenal brain, but she could still out-run him and she would take full advantage of that for as long as she could. When she caught him, she would grab him and wrestle him to the ground for a thorough tickling, and Charlie would giggle and shriek like the little kid he actually was. And that was the most precious sound Lucy could possibly imagine.

Delsie had asked her to keep a diary of spectacular stuff Charlie did, so she could include it in her research. The last time they had chatted on Skype, Lucy had shared the latest.

"One thing he did last week really blew me away, Delse. You know how he can read our minds and know what we're thinking? Well, I told him I didn't like it because then his dad and I had no privacy. So he said he'd block anything that was personal and not intended for him."

"Shit. How the hell does he do *that*?"

"I don't know how he does *any* of it, and he couldn't explain it to me—not in a way that my simple brain could understand, anyway. Imagine. A 3-year-old kid creating boundaries to protect his *parents*. It's just so friggin' *ass backwards*."

Nate was a lot more relaxed about it all, but he was used to his nephew Tate being freakily smart, so perhaps it was a family thing. Definitely something that came from *his* genetic line, not hers, Lucy was pretty sure. He told her not to worry, that things would level out and she'd get used to this new super-normal and could have fun with it once she relaxed.

She didn't know whether to feel honoured to have such a child prodigy, or cheated out of savouring the precious moments in the evolution of a child on a more normal developmental schedule. Not that she'd had any experience with so-called normal children. It was just that her expectations—the ones she hadn't even had in the first place, given the perfection of the little human she had produced—had been wildly exceeded. That was supposedly what every parent dreamed of, for their children, yet it was surprisingly confronting. Charlie's brilliant brain sometimes made her feel like a big lumbering dinosaur. She felt as if *she* should be at school learning basic life skills while he stayed at home and ran the business or a bank or the State of Massachusetts.

"It's nothing to be afraid of, Mum," Charlie said. "It's just neurons firing in the brain."

"But you're way ahead of me, sweetie," Lucy said. "I'm afraid I won't be able to keep up with you, and you'll get married when you're 10, then invent a photon-powered space machine and go off exploring new galaxies, leaving your mum light years behind you."

"I can teach you how to be brilliant," Charlie said. "It's easy. Grandma showed me how."

"I didn't know Grandma Cordalis was teaching you that kind of thing." Lucy was surprised. Charlie hadn't spent much time at her in-laws' place, now that they had moved out of the city, although he loved hanging out with his cousin Tate, who sometimes came to visit.

"Not *that* Grandma," Charlie said, looking at her knowingly, and Lucy felt her heart go still. "The other one. *Your* mum."

Lucy sat down fast. On the floor. So she couldn't fall any further. In case she keeled over. From shock.

"It's okay, Mum. I know she's dead," Charlie said reassuringly. "We just talk on another dimension, you know?"

Of course. Silly her. How come *she* hadn't thought of doing that.

76

February 2025

Reading about quantum phenomena always made Marnie feel a little closer to her parents. She sometimes wished she had taken more of an interest in their work when she was growing up. But she also understood why she hadn't. They could have been designing rockets to Mars and been on TV every night, but that doesn't impress a 10-year-old who just wants her mum to show her how to make cookies, do her hair, or make popcorn and watch movies together. She could understand what it must feel like for the kids of celebrities and actors, who got none of the accolades their parents got, while needing the attention and recognition all the more.

Marnie had officially given up trying to make sense of what had happened to her parents. Every time she had tried to get in touch with someone who might have some information, she had hit a dead end. Their former neighbours Doug and Maisie knew nothing and were as shocked and clueless as the rest of them. When Marnie had finally made her way to the archives office at MIT to find out about her mother's former college roommate, the office was closed because the archivist was on maternity leave. *Didn't they have someone else to take over?* She finally found someone to open up but the girl knew nothing about the filing system and Marnie hadn't been able to get past Go.

The search for information on the shell company MLM had been disastrous, with Jed getting killed and their one lead gone with him. Dr Pemberton had been a waste of time, although the ride on his Ninja had livened things up a little. And Ray... well, Ray had turned out to be an exercise in frustration, providing lots of tantalizing information but never quite enough to get the complete picture... and then disappearing altogether. Case closed. Two years after her parents' death, she had no leads and no more energy to pursue things.

It had been tough to give up her teaching job, and the send-off by the kids had been heart-breaking. They had all brought her little gifts—even Stuart Smith, who gave her a tiny wooden carving he said he had done himself. Marnie wasn't sure what it was but he said it was a bear, like the one his dad had shot on a hunting trip. Sasha had written her a beautiful poem, presenting it to her with brave tears un-shed. Isabelle had been teary also, saying she didn't want her to go, holding onto her pant leg while Marnie was talking to Isabelle's mother. There was a card the size of a pillow signed by all the kids, with lots of smileys, hearts, kisses and wildly scrawled names.

The Principal, Leslie Vauxhall, had been sorry to see her go, but her former Friday stand-in, Alison Marsh, was taking over the position and Marnie couldn't have hoped for a better replacement. The kids already knew and liked her, so Marnie felt slightly less awful for leaving them. The staff had given her a small farewell party on her last day, toasting her with wine and a small gift they had bought together. Marnie felt a *déjà vu* flutter in her chest as she unwrapped the small weighty object. It was an exquisite antique alarm clock in burnished gold, on three stocky little legs, with an old-fashioned bell on top. It brought tears to her eyes, for reasons she could never explain to her colleagues, and she thanked them hoarsely.

Finally emerging into the late-afternoon sunshine, she had pushed through the school's main door for the last time, legs shaky, heart hammering, vision blurry, like a foal just born into a whole new world.

Now she had a new life and had left all that old stuff behind. She loved their new home outside Jacksonville and had been happy to take time off while they got settled. Steve and Troy were busy building their business and were turning out to be a dynamic brotherly duo.

By early 2022, though, Marnie was ready to get back to work and had got a job in a private kindergarten school that embraced the principles of whole-person development. The kids were aged 3–6, their tender unfiltered hearts wide open for ideas, play, laughter and hugs. No WiFi, no emotional angst, no parental constraints or recriminations. Bliss.

She hadn't realized how much energy it had taken in her previous job, trying not to get upset when the kids had issues. All the politics, parental pressure, soul-destroying expectations and too little of what really mattered… there was none of that here. Parents still wanted their kids to do well, but it was more about cultivating their unique creativity than pushing them to perform in a certain way or get good grades.

With this new job, Marnie was seeing the power of teaching the whole person, in a healthy environment—and having that process supported and continued by the parents at home. Pushing for academic achievements without helping kids discover their own innate gifts could only ever produce unhappy, dysfunctional performers who either succeeded or failed, according to their parents' standards. There was very little love in that kind of education, Marnie thought. Most parents loved their children, but their own neediness and unfulfilled dreams could create horrendous pressure for fragile offspring dependent on their care-givers' approval.

The US President had followed through with his reforms and most of the cell towers had come down. It was beyond anything Marnie could have imagined, and Steve teased her, saying she had surely played some cosmic part in it, just by being so darn determined about the world needing to give it all up.

Him giving up his cellphone had meant the world to her, deepening their relationship and sharpening their awareness of how they were living. Marnie was convinced that this was what had led to Steve wanting a simpler life, closer to family and the things that really mattered.

It was fascinating observing the rest of the world slowly transform as people were forced to give up their devices. CEBSters did it willingly, but the others kicked and screamed all the way to the cellphone-recycling centre.

Cellphones had been phased out, but a whole new brand of social reintegration programs had sprung up, promoting emotional intelligence in the workplace and 'tiered teaming' in local communities, which involved teams made up of every age group, from the very young to the octogenarians.

Young people especially were coming up with all kinds of inspiring innovations in eco-excellence, Earth-friendly packaging, technologies for converting the world's plastic waste back into clean fuel, and water-powered vehicles. There were new forms of sports using high-tech inventions such as the GraviTass—a spherical oscillating ball that players had to keep suspended in the air using the power of their minds.

Life truly was a whole new ball game.

77

May 2025

Matt could now sing, joke and love just as easily in Spanish as English, and a lot more passionately. While Italian had always struck him as a demandingly romantic language, every rich vowel sounded, Spanish was gentler, more sensual—like a shallow stream flowing over time-rounded river stones, compared to the white-water rapids of Italian. And English seemed harshly guttural, a language for more practical, logical living.

His soul felt lighter with every day he lived here, his words more lyrical and his whole demeanour more relaxed and fluid. Even his laugh sounded different. But then he had a lot more to laugh about now than before, so he was much better at it—and all the better for it.

Mexico was emerging as another exemplary Earth-friendly leader, developing a large market for its bamboo products, alternative energy systems and biodynamic farming. It received funding from the US for many of its eco-friendly projects and for training visiting manufacturers wishing to emulate Mexico's innovative model in their own countries.

Following China's cue, the US President claimed that focusing on global eco-excellence and international sharing would ensure that there was always more than enough for everyone and that resources were respectfully managed. *Eco-sharing* had become the new buzzword, replacing the carbon tax, which was money that went right back into industry and did nothing to reduce the pollution the carbon-tax-payers were causing.

People had asked what the US would do if it was attacked, now that it had disbanded its military forces and was investing that money into educational and other human-excellence projects.

"Why would anyone attack us?" the President asked, in one of his regular public updates. "The time for war and conflict is over. We must collaborate and cooperate if we are going to survive. All nations working with us are friends of the US and will from now on be treated with the greatest respect and consideration. We are working closely with our southern neighbours in Mexico, doing our best to make up for our egregious abuses in the past, and they are being extremely gracious in forgiving us. In recognition of this, we are supporting some of Mexico's Earth-friendly programs and helping them create employment for the many millions who have remained in poverty for far too long."

But what about *us*, Americans inevitably asked.

"Of course, we are doing the same for our own people," the President said, "while cultivating synergies and free trade between our two great nations. A win–win is the only kind of win for us now."

Matt and Celle were riding the wave and loving it. Matt worked in the organic-food co-op they had set up, and Celle helped, while also managing production of the Tatum line for Cordalis Creations. The money they made was almost incidental, since the work itself was so gratifying, uniting communities, creating jobs and generating heartfelt solidarity in community, health, innovation and shared ideas.

They were also meeting lots of like-minded creative bods—native Mexicans as well as expats and visiting foreigners—all of whom were inspired by what they were doing and wanted to be a part of it.

It reminded Matt of the classic Mark Twain story about Tom Sawyer painting a fence. Instead of treating it like a chore, when he would have preferred to be playing with his friends, Tom had acted as if he was having the time of his life, which prompted all his friends to pick up a paintbrush and join him.

Here, though, they didn't have to pretend. They *did* love what they were doing and that love was clearly contagious.

The old, cynical Matt would have scoffed at the notion of freely sharing ideas and wanting nothing in return. He would have looked for the *hook*, the sell-on from the initial *free offer*. Now, it seemed like the most natural thing in the world—the way things were always meant to be.

The air was cleaner, the light sharper, natural aromas stronger, colours more vivid. The noisy rust-buckets were being phased out and replaced by spanking-new vehicles called ZipVs or Swaves, depending on the design and manufacturer. Matt almost missed the raucous revs of the motorbikes, which had become a familiar backdrop to the animated industry of life. Now, vehicles swished silently past, powered by water—more likely to put you in a meditative state than grate on frazzled nerves.

The ZipVs (Zero-Impact-Power Vehicles) were his favourite—sleek two-person porters that looked like small horizontal rockets with doors that opened skyward. Swaves were a bit more expensive and less common here. Shaped like a vertical wave, they were more like the old SUVs, with room for four, and space for luggage under the two seats at the back, so the passengers sat higher than the two front seats, encased in a natural polymer bubble, with a clear view on all sides.

Before Charlie was born, Lucy and Nate had come to visit and check out clothing factories. Marnie and Steve had come down on a separate trip. All four had marvelled at how beautifully Matt and Celle had created their perfect niche. Matt knew how they must have looked to the more sun-deprived northern-dwellers. They were both tanned, toned and healthy, and Celle looked like a movie star with her platinum-blond pixie hairstyle and blue eyes against sun-kissed skin.

Matt and Lucy had gone for long walks on the beach, and Lucy told him he seemed solidly himself—forcefully yet quietly present, with no rough edges or inner agitation. It was a nice reminder that he was no longer that unhappy agitated man who reported on corruption and failed to see the extent of his own.

Mexico now felt like home, and home was a large house on the hillside overlooking San Pancho—a small village about 3km north of bustling Sayulita. Smaller, quieter and less developed, it was a peaceful haven after the touristy buzz of the larger town.

He and Celle had tried to have a baby but it hadn't happened yet. He wondered if the trauma of her brother's abuse and the loss of that first baby had blocked any further procreation. They talked about adopting but Celle said she wanted to give her body a little longer to be fully at peace with itself, and that it would know when it was ready to open up again. When it did, she said, she would *also* like to adopt a little Mexican baby or two, from the many thousands of orphans in need of a loving home.

"There's something in the air," Celle said, referring to the new ethos of giving, sharing and loving the connections. "Can't you feel it, Mateo?"

It was a question she often asked and he wasn't sure of his answer. Yes, their world was transforming, but was it because he himself had transformed (thanks to having a goddess in his life), or had this new vibe been part of his metamorphosis?

Whatever the case, he was having a hard time remembering who he used to be.

"The best possible news," Celle said, "because it confirms you are no longer that lost man."

A dysfunctional life and persona, gone for good.

78

June 2025

Dr Ravi Suranjit stood transfixed in front of the image. He could not believe what he was seeing.

On the backlit wall screen in his office was the final follow-up plasma polymer scan of Selma Roman's brain. Mrs Roman, 57, had been progressively degenerating from Alzheimer's prior to CEBS. She had been unconscious the day CEBS hit, but she was one of several patients at Washington Hospital Center who had made a miraculous recovery that day—a *complete* recovery, with zero residual damage or evidence of disease showing on her scan.

Not only that, but the part of her brain that had been most affected—the hippocampus—which the disease had caused to shrink by about 25%, was now about 25% *larger than before*, with a great deal more electrical activity than normal, even for a young person or even a child.

He loved Selma Roman, not just because she was wise, kind and funny, constantly singing his praises for having provided such expert medical care, and not just because she had produced Delsie—the woman who had stolen his heart the day she came to visit her mother in hospital and had been the love of his life for the past two years. There was also Mrs Roman's stellar cooking, which he enjoyed at least twice a month and would make any Indian grandmother proud.

While all of that was miraculous enough, it wasn't the main reason for his awe and wonder now.

He remembered reading years ago about a practitioner in France who specialized in food allergies and had found a way to detect and treat them. He had taken a few hairs from his patient's head and looked at them under a microscope. When the patient, sitting in the same room, then held a particular food or supplement in their hand, the hair under the microscope responded.

But *this*… this was something else.

It seemed like a similar kind of remote intelligence, confirming the quantum theory of non-locality, whereby particles remained connected and interactive, even if separated by vast distances. But this was an inanimate image, not a piece of tissue… wasn't it?

He had been studying Selma Roman's brain scan, reflecting on how the healing had come about. He had been going over the options in his head—all the things that had been tried in the course of her treatment, the medication she'd had, the course of CBD and several other things. It was more a mental cataloguing of her treatment, confirming what he already knew, since he was convinced that CEBS had somehow healed her.

But when he actually *thought* about CEBS, as he studied the brain scan on his wall, the scan had responded. He had almost fallen over backwards in shock, jerking away from the image as if it were some kind of alien that had invaded his office.

When his heart had slowed to a mere 120 beats a minute and his head had stopped pounding, he approached the scan again. He thought about CEBS… and the brain lit up, sparkles dancing in the neocortex, which he knew controlled sensory perception, cognition and language, among other things.

He leaned forwards and flipped off the light switch. Surely, the light was playing tricks on his eyes. He thought of CEBS again and the image lit up. He didn't even *need* the light behind it.

He reached sideways towards his desk, fumbling for his Gravijot, not wanting to take his eyes off the image. He needed to document every second of this eerie, unbelievable, phenomenal event. Later, it would help to convince his residency supervisor—and himself—that it had actually happened.

What if he asked it some questions? The neocortex lit up again. Ravi gulped, his throat dry, sweat trickling down his spine. *Was the brain scan actually talking to him?* It sparkled again, in the same area.

Holy shit. It was.

Sparkles now in the lower frontal lobes of the brain, which Ravi knew was often associated with humour. *Was the brain* enjoying *this interaction?* Another mini light show.

With the palm of his hand on the Gravijot, he began recording all his thoughts and questions, as well as what was happening on the scan in front of him.

Still looking at the image, he leaned towards the door, only an arm's length away in his tiny office, and turned the key in the lock. He did not want any interruptions. He was going to have a… *conversation* with Selma Roman's brain scan and see what happened.

What the hell he would do after that he had no idea.

For now, this was almost more than his own brain could handle, although his professional fascination was taking over, pushing panic to the back of his mind, to the primitive brainstem, where it belonged. He was feeling giddy and needed to breathe and calm himself so he could process things properly and document what was happening.

One mind-boggling step at a time. He could keel over afterwards, drink a stiff whisky, run naked down the corridor—whatever it took to capture the magic of whatever this was.

My God. The possibilities… people in a coma, children who couldn't yet talk, animals, maybe even trees or other forms of life…

The plasma scan seemed to be connected to Gravizone, universal intelligence, non-local information, everything that was out there. Maybe he could ask it questions, see if it responded with yes or no answers.

The neocortex lit up again. Was that a *yes?* Another sparkle.

What about a no? Nothing.

So, it only responded to questions that could be answered with a *yes…* Shit. That still left a whole universe of possibilities for him to work with.

Then he had another thought. *What if Selma Roman was aware of this happening and was herself talking to him via her brain and the scan?* He would have to call her after this—or maybe *she would call him.*

If he hadn't switched his specialization to neurology instead of pediatrics after CEBS hit, he would not be witnessing this unfolding miracle. He'd be delivering babies, counting fingers and toes, with no inkling of what was going on inside their brains.

The front of his shirt was clinging damply to his chest, but he barely noticed. To be alive at such an extraordinary time, to be given such an evolutionary gift... It was enough to make a grown man weep with wonder.

79

November 2025

It was the last packed box left over from their move four years ago. They needed the space and Marnie decided that today was the day to finally unpack it and start decorating the spare room.

It contained some reference books, her stuff from school, the gifts from the kids, the card they had all signed, and the clock...

This clock thing was haunting her. She lifted it out, turned it over and wound it up. It was reassuringly solid, nothing like the plastic digital clocks the Chinese had churned out for years but were now no longer in use—and no longer allowed in the States, because of the ban on plastic.

It reminded her instantly of her mother's clock, which sat on a shelf in the living room, still stuck at 3 o'clock and never wound. It was disturbingly similar, but this one was simpler, with none of the digital 'petals' around the rim that the other one had.

She put it on the small bookcase against the wall. She now regretted winding it up, as its intrusive presence reverberated throughout the small room.

She looked inside the card, smiling at the names and the memories. Most of the kids would be 13 now—young teenagers. She wondered how Sasha was doing, if she was still writing... and Isabelle, if she had toughened up a bit. Had Stuart joined a neighbourhood gang, and was Sebastien baking cakes for his mom? So many tender lives that could go in any direction, depending on the grief or guidance along the way. The card was a keeper, but it would be laid to rest on the top shelf of her wardrobe, like a giant passport to another world.

Next, she pulled out a newspaper clipping about Ray. Just before they left Boston in mid-2021, he had resurfaced. She only knew because he made the news again—this time, because he had developed an advanced gravity-driven communication technology he had been working on with Russian scientists. That was where he had been: *Russia*.

She had worried about him for months. It would have been nice to know he was okay. *A short note or something, Ray? Did you even think of me?*

There was a subtle tingle in her brain, like a synapse firing—not that she'd ever consciously felt or noticed one ever firing before, among the millions that did, every second, but she imagined that was what it was. Yet it was more like the click of an old-fashioned switchboard putting through a call, and she suddenly heard Ray's voice.

Marnie, it was to protect you, to keep you safe. Hang in there. We will talk soon.

Then he was gone.

Was that real? Or just her ego reassuring her?

She scanned the article again. Dr Raynor Spence had been in Russia, he claimed, working with Russian scientists on a new technology for using gravitational waves to transmit voice, data and other information. It was something the Russians and Germans had been working on for years, apparently, and he had helped them take it to the next stage of development and commercialization.

He had been hailed as a hero for saving the population from the dreaded prospect of not having mobile telecommunications. Not that other systems weren't being developed, but this one had looked the most promising and now, four years later, was the one being used all over the US and elsewhere.

Despite feeling hurt at being left in the dark by Ray, Marnie loved what he had done. The Gravizone technology required no transmitter and generated no electromagnetic pollution. Instead, it used naturally occurring standing gravitational waves for information transfer— natural frequencies that couldn't be sold, acquired or monopolised. Because the gravitational waves organised all particles in the universe into synchronous oscillations, transmission could be instant.

She didn't understand all the technicalities. All she knew was that it worked and everyone loved it.

The system had a range of up to 2,000km, so far fewer devices were needed, compared with the multitude of cell towers before. And it was free. All you had to do was buy your own personal device, called Gwen

(Gravitational Wave Evolutionary Nexus) for making/receiving calls or sending/receiving data. It could also be hooked up to a computer.

No monthly bills, no radiation, no pollution. *What's not to love?* The wireless industry was trying to find ways to cash in on the new technology but not getting very far. They were quick to start making personal devices for sale, but the system itself was available free to anyone who wanted to use it, so there was nothing to be gained by trying to create a monopoly. It simply wouldn't work.

The old cellphones seemed ridiculously crude and clunky, compared with the new technology. Phones were no longer *phones*. Gwen was changing the way people communicated, while expanding their brains' capacity to connect with others, and upgrading lives mentally, emotionally and spiritually. It truly was evolutionary.

80

11 March 2026

Lucy was waiting for the call, nervously pacing the kitchen, sending good vibes through the airwaves. Marnie was in hospital. She had gone into labour the day before and Steve had called to tell her they were getting close. Any time now.

"It will be another hour, Mum," Charlie told her, and he turned out to be right, almost to the minute.

Steve called, jubilant. It was a girl. Mella Rachel Romero was born at 8pm on 11 March, with the acceptable number of fingers and toes, and a smile to make a proud father weep.

It had been a long labour—almost 24 hours—but Steve said Marnie was fine. Exhausted, but radiant with happiness and relief.

Lucy was euphoric and danced around the kitchen with Charlie, who dissolved into fits of giggles. There was nothing more powerful than giving birth to a perfect little human being.

Charlie had arrived very quickly and easily, and Lucy was amazed he hadn't popped out onto the delivery table and immediately asked, *What's for dinner?*

He did everything fast, which meant that they had to, too. Their engagement had lasted about five minutes because Charlie seemingly couldn't wait to be conceived and let loose in the world.

"You've been doing everything fast ever since," Lucy told him.

"Life is short, Mum," Charlie had said… at 5 years of age.

Was he being philosophical or did he have a sixth sense that he would die young… or that she *would?* Was he like that guy in the movie who was psychic because he had a brain tumour?

Why was greatness suspect, when stupidity was accepted as normal and seemed infinitely more reassuring? That said a lot about why things in the world had gone so wrong for so long, Lucy thought.

Charlie delivered fresh surprises every day—the inevitable mental exodus from his immensely fertile brain. He now called Nancy and Brandon *Grancy* and *Grandon*, refusing to use the baby terms *Grandma* and *Grandad*. He had no time for *auntie* or *uncle*, either. He was far too grown-up and creative for that. And it was clear he got a kick out of inventing names, concepts and whatever else his mind trawled through with its massive neural net.

Nancy was right; he *was* a joyful genius, rejoicing in every quirky spin he could put on the universe, his playground.

What would he have called her parents, Lucy wondered. *Grannie and Graniel?*

Yes, Charlie said, reading her mind. *That's exactly what he called them.*

After he had dropped his bombshell about communicating with her mum, Lucy had sat him down for a serious talk.

"Tell me how you do this. How do you connect with… Grannie?"

"She's just *there*, you know?"

"No, I don't. Explain it to me."

Charlie paused—probably searching for some simple way to explain this so her simple brain could understand, Lucy thought.

"You're not that simple, Mum," he said, grinning. "You just have lots of worries and stuff in the way. Makes it hard to get a clear signal."

Lucy tried to empty her mind, so he could focus on what she needed him to explain and so she could take it in.

"You know when you think of someone and then they call you?"

"Yes." Lucy could certainly relate to that. It had happened many times, especially with Nate and Marnie.

"Well, it's nothing like that," Charlie said, rolling on the floor and laughing himself silly.

"Not funny, wise guy," Lucy said, laughing anyway. "Stop stalling and tell me how this works."

"It's *kinda* like that, but you have to use a part of your brain that you don't use for other things."

Lucy groaned. "I have *no* idea what that means. What part of my brain and how do I use it?"

"Okay. Think about thinking. You use a certain part of your brain for that. Think about what you're going to make for dinner and see where you feel it in your head. Think of a really complicated recipe and how to make it."

"Trust you to always make it about food," Lucy said, but she closed her eyes and thought about *croissants*, which she had never managed to make successfully. She could feel herself frowning, thinking about the process.

She opened her eyes. "I'm also *remembering* the recipe, though, not just thinking about it. Is that different?"

"Nah. Doesn't matter," Charlie said. "Where do you feel it?"

Lucy closed her eyes again and thought hard about that finicky pastry that never turned out right, no matter how many times she tried. She just didn't have those natural baking genes like Marnie did. *But where was she feeling it?*

"I think it's here," she said, pointing to her forehead.

"Now think about being on the beach. Nobody there. No noise. Sun. Hot. Waves. Just feeling, not thinking. Where do you feel that?"

"I'm not sure," Lucy said, perplexed. She was failing miserably at this test.

"Do you feel it here—" Charlie pointed to his head "or here?" He pointed to his chest.

"Ah. Trick question. I think I feel it in my chest."

"But the heart tells the brain what to feel, so the feeling can sometimes start in the heart but then the head tells you what's going on."

"Right. Simple," Lucy said, feeling thick as a brick. *Wasn't it supposed to be the other way around?* "But when I'm feeling a big fat love for you here," she thumped her chest, "and my heart feels as if it's bigger than usual, I don't need my brain to feel that, do I?"

"No, but you need your brain to tell you it's love—at least, you did the first time it happened."

"How come you know all this stuff?"

"It's out there." Charlie waved vaguely at the air. "Everyone can get it. You just have to know how to access it."

Lucy sighed. "It's hopeless. I'm telepathetic. I'm never going to get this."

"Mum, you're worrying again and that uses the wrong parts if you want to do this other thing."

"So I need to use my heart, not my brain?"

"Yes and no."

"Could you keep it simple, please?"

Charlie gave her a look.

"Okay. I get it. It doesn't get much simpler than yes and no." Lucy rolled her eyes.

"See? You just did it."

"Did what? Read your mind? No way. I just know the way your clever little mind works."

"We can practise a bit every day, if you want. First, you need to teach your brain to relax, so you don't push away all the things trying to come in. Just worry less, Mum."

"Okay, Buster, you do the dishes after dinner while I practise relaxing my brain. Deal?" She looked at him. "That's one thing you *can't* do with your mind, right? You have to actually *wash* them or put them in the dishwasher."

Charlie groaned. "How come I have to do extra work when I'm helping you get smarter?"

"Because when I'm smarter I'll be able to think of even more things for you to do while I do less. See? I'm smarter already, thanks to my amazing teacher."

81

Dawn was peeling back the last of the purple night when Charlie came into their bedroom. Lucy was dreaming about living at Westfield when he gently shook her shoulder.

"Mum. Wake up," he said.

"What…?" She was groggy with sleep and dream-warped memories.

"Marnie's baby is dying," he said, and she was instantly awake. Bolting upright, she turned to Charlie, Nate stirring beside her.

"Mella has a virus and she's going to die if we don't help her. Grannie told me."

"What?" Lucy couldn't make sense of what he was saying.

"You need to call the hospital, Mum. Now. Get up." He pulled back the covers and grabbed her arm.

Lucy reached back for Nate and shook his shoulder. "Babe, wake up. We need to make a call."

Leaping out of bed, she grabbed her robe from the back of a chair, tying the sash as she and Charlie raced down to the kitchen.

"What should I tell them, Charlie? What do you see? What do they need to do?"

She reached for Gwen, said the name of the hospital, got immediately connected and told them it was an emergency relating to baby Mella Romero, born yesterday. She needed to urgently speak to a doctor on duty in the neonatal ward. Questions ensued as the operator tried to assess the urgency.

"Mella's mother is my sister. Do not waste another second, please. Put me through to the doctor now."

On hold, she paced back and forth, while the operator tried to reach a doctor.

Charlie was sitting on the floor, his face in deep concentration.

"Tell me, Charlie," Lucy said. "Tell me what to say to the doctor."

"Tell him it's a virus affecting her here—" he pointed to his throat "and that it's blocking her breathing."

"Hello? This is Dr Patrice. Who am I speaking to?"

"My name is Lucy Cordalis. My sister Marnie Romero gave birth to a baby girl yesterday, Mella Romero, and… could you please go and check on her immediately? I can't explain now, but I think she has a viral infection that is affecting her breathing."

"Mrs Cordalis, how do you—"

"Please, I will explain afterwards. If you don't act now, Mella may die. Please. Go check on her. Check her breathing. This is serious. If this baby dies, I will hold you personally responsible." She took a deep breath. "I will stay on the line till I know she's okay. Please come back and tell me."

"All right, Mrs Cordalis. Give me a few minutes…"

Charlie was gesturing urgently. "Do not give her penicillin," he said. "She is allergic to it. Tell them!"

Lucy had no time to ask him how he knew. "Wait! Dr Patrice. If any medication is needed, do not give her penicillin, okay? She is allergic. It… runs in the family. I think my sister may have forgotten to tell you."

"Understood. I'm going to hand you through to the nurse's station, Mrs Cordalis, while I go check on baby Romero. I'll be back shortly."

"Thank you, thank you," Lucy said, but the doctor had already gone.

"Mrs Cordalis? This is Marion, the night nurse. Dr Patrice will call you back shortly if you give me your number."

"Could you put me through to my sister, Marnie Romero, please? While I'm waiting? I need to speak to her urgently."

Nate was beside her, rubbing her shoulders, speaking in low tones to Charlie, who was filling him in.

A long wait of precious seconds. Then… "Lucy?" It was Marnie.

"Marn! Go check on Mella. Charlie thinks she has an infection that's affecting her breathing. I just spoke to Dr Patrice and he said he was going to check on her straight away. Go! Call me back after, okay? "

Lucy zoned off, heart racing. She leaned her head against Nate's chest. "I don't know whether to pray that Charlie is wrong or right," she said, beckoning to Charlie to come to her.

"You okay, Bud?" Nate asked his son.

"Yeah. I'm not wrong, Mum. If he's a good doctor, he'll save her. But Grannie and I have been sending her some help anyway, just in case."

Nate led Lucy to the table and got her to sit while he made coffee.

She watched the clock, holding Charlie against her. It was 6.35am and she had called at 6.15… *Had they got there in time? Had they found something wrong? Was she okay?*

Gwen beeped, making them all jump. Lucy leaped up and zoned in. "Marn?"

"Lucy. She's okay. Thank God. She has an infection and she was turning blue when they got to her. But she's on oxygen now and they're trying to figure out what medication to give her. How did Charlie *know*?"

"I don't know, Marn. I'm just so thankful he did. And he said she's allergic to penicillin. Hang on."

She turned to Charlie. "You were right, sweetie. Of course you were." She pulled him close, feeling his small body trembling. "Do you want to speak to Marnie?"

He nodded, reaching for Gwen.

Lucy could hear Marnie sobbing. "It's okay, Marnie," Charlie said. "She'll be okay now. Tell the doctors to give her something natural and—" he turned to Lucy. "Mum, what do you call those things they used to give people against diseases?"

"Vaccines, you mean?"

"Yeah," he said, turning back to the call. "Marnie, no vaccines or stuff like that. Mella is very sensitive to all that stuff. Tell the doctor, okay?"

Not waiting for an answer, Charlie thrust Gwen at Lucy, and ran from the kitchen.

"Marn?"

"I've got to go and see what they're doing, Lucy. Later."

Lucy zoned out and slid down the wall to the floor. Nate came and sat beside her as the coffee sputtered into its pot.

"You okay, sweetie?"

"Yes. No. I have no idea." Lucy felt drained, but she needed to go check on Charlie. "I'll just make sure he's okay," she said, getting up slowly. "Could you make breakfast, babe, please? I think we all need some hot food."

"I'm on it," Nate said, helping her up and rubbing her cold hands.

Upstairs, Charlie was lying immobile on his bed.

"Charlie, talk to me," she said, sitting beside him and stroking his damp forehead. "What's going on?"

"Juss tired…" His words were slurred and he seemed on the edge of sleep… or collapse. Lucy wasn't sure which. "You sure you're okay? You want to have breakfast with Dad and me? Or just sleep?"

"Sleep," he said.

Lucy pulled the comforter over his small limp body. He was hot but not feverish. Connecting the way he did, tapping into whatever dimension gave him access to precious life-saving information, must have taken a huge amount of energy. She brushed damp dark curls off his face.

"Want me to press?"

Charlie sometimes asked her to press on his head and then abruptly release, as this seemed to have a decompression effect, releasing some of the pressure in his phenomenal brain.

She placed her hands gently on his head and pressed down. "And release, or just press?"

"Press…"

"Okay, sweetie."

She held the pressure for a few moments, eased back, and then gently pressed down again. He groaned with relief.

One more time, then she lay down behind him, one cool hand resting gently on his head as his breathing slowed and steadied.

"I love you, Charlie Cordalis," she whispered to his sleeping form. "You are the most amazing little person ever." Somewhere, on some level, she knew he heard her.

Nate came up to check on them both.

"I brought you some hot lemon, honey and ginger. You need some sugar after that shock."

"Perfect." Lucy sat up carefully, so as not to disturb Charlie. "*Two* psychic men in my life. What more could a woman ask for?" She was joking but close to tears. It had been an intense and scary start to the day. She sipped gratefully, the hot liquid softening the knots in her stomach.

"Okay?" He meant her and Charlie.

"I think so," she said. "I'm sorry we dashed off and left you to figure things out, sweetie. I had to move fast and didn't have time to explain."

"I know that, Luce. I'm just glad you acted so quickly. It took me a few minutes to catch up." He looked at his son, his face softening in gratitude and pride. "You two have a special connection," he said, but there was love and pride there too, no jealousy.

"Yeah. He's miraculous, isn't he?"

She felt Charlie's forehead one last time. Cooler now, approaching normal—normal, at least, for their paranormal son.

82

It was market day in San Pancho—a noisy, convivial event in the square, stalls piled high with aromatic fruits and vegetables, misshapen roots protruding from hessian sacks, pungent powdered spices piled into multi-coloured pyramids, roasted peanuts in twists of newspaper, squawking hens and roosters in wooden cages, vendors shouting to each other, mangy dogs scavenging for scraps. Raw life, Mexican style.

Celle and Matt were buying fruit at one of the stalls when it happened. Beside a mound of lush papayas, as Celle was reaching for a mango, a spider dropped from the awning and landed on her arm. She screamed, went white as her hair and fell to the ground.

"¡Dios mío!" The old woman behind the stall clutched her heart. "*Es una reclusa parda.*" A brown recluse spider.

"Celle!" Matt fell to his knees beside her and shook her gently. "Celle!" The spider was gone but Celle's left wrist was swelling into a marbled lump.

Matt felt for her pulse. Very weak. He pumped her heart. Felt again. A faint scintilla of life. He tilted her head back, pinched her tiny nose and breathed into her mouth. Felt again. Nothing. She was gone.

"No, no, noooohh!" He howled in pain, his whole reason for living gone in just a few seconds of insouciance.

Someone was tugging urgently at his shirt and he shrugged him off. More tugging and a small boy of 5 or 6 pushed himself in front of him, holding out his hand. "*¡Tómalo!*" Take it. "*Toma mi mano.*" Take my hand.

"*¡Vete!*" Go away!

The little boy slapped Matt in the face, his dark eyes fiercely urgent. "*Toma mi mano. Hay una mujer espiritual aquí para ayudarte.*" There is a spirit woman here to help you.

The boy grabbed Matt's left hand and clutched it in both of his own, using his shoulder to push Matt towards Celle's swollen wrist.

"*¡Chupa la herida! ¡Chupa el veneno!*" he commanded, his hot little fists squeezing Matt's hand like a vise. Suck the wound! Suck out the poison!

Matt obeyed like an automaton, grasping Celle's narrow wrist in his mouth and sucking with all his might.

"*Escupirlo*," the boy commanded, and Matt spat—a greenish mucous falling on the pavement beside them.

"*¡Más! Otra vez!*" *Do it again!*

Matt sucked and spat again, and again, until his throat ached, all the while gripped by the little boy, whose fists were making his hand throb like a hot broken bone.

"*Golpea su pecho*," the boy commanded. *Thump her chest.* "*Asi.*" Like this. He released Matt's hand and made a fist, pumping the air in downward motions.

Matt thumped Celle's chest as hard as he dared. Two, three, four times…

"*¡Alli!*" The boy pointed. *There!*

Her chest rose and Celle gasped, sputtering into consciousness.

"Celle!" Matt pulled her to him, his hands throbbing and his heart about to burst. "You're alive! You're alive! *Mi amor*, I thought I'd lost you."

She looked at him, unfocused.

"Can you hear me? Are you okay? Celle?"

The boy was beside him again, holding out a paper cup of some bright-green liquid.

"*Dale esto,*" he urged. *Give her this.*

Matt took the cup and held it to Celle's lip, holding her head up with his other hand.

She drank and seemed to revive, the colour returning to her cheeks and the light back in her eyes.

"Mateo, I saw her," she said. "That woman."

"What woman?" *Was she delirious?*

"The woman who appeared on the beach the day you almost drowned. The one who saved you."

"She was here?" He looked around. He had been so consumed by bringing her back to life that he wouldn't have noticed if the entire Mexican army had surrounded them in the meantime.

But there was no one there apart from the old woman from the stall, who was shakily crossing herself, the boy, who he guessed was her grandson, and some useless nosy tourists now moving on.

"No, Mateo. She came to me as I was… going to the light. She sent me back. She said… she said she didn't save you just so you would get your heart broken by me dying." Celle smiled in dazed wonder. "She must have been an angel."

The boy seemed to understand some of what she said. *"La mujer,"* he said, nodding. *"La mujer del espíritu. Ella vino a través de mí también."* *The spirit woman. She came through me also.* He turned to Matt. *"Ella me dijo que tomara tu mano para salvar a la novia."* *She told me to take your hand to save your girlfriend.* He looked earnestly at Matt, waiting for recognition. *"Tu mami,"* he said, patiently. *Your mother.*

As they walked slowly home, his heart in turmoil, Matt kept turning to check that Celle was real. She was back, here beside him, his luminous angel, once again creating heaven here on earth. He squeezed her hand, his own still throbbing hotly from the little boy's grip or his mother's ghost or whatever had saved them both.

That was three near-deaths in his family. First his own, then his niece—little newborn Mella—and now Celle. Enough already. He knew the power of loss and redemption. Each time, there came a deepening gratitude for the life they shared on this pulsing planet, finding its way back to balance as humans regained their humanity and found each other again. As his extended family extended further, he had more to lose but also a lot more to love. Which meant he had even more to laugh about. And he *so* needed to laugh—to release the ball of terror from his gut, to lift Celle into the air like the divine sprite that she was, to savour every precious atom of her being and his.

83

September 2026

It was far too long since Marnie had seen her friends and she felt strangely dislocated, all her familiar moorings gone. Millie had moved to California in late 2021 after falling in love with a Santa Barbara chiropractor by the name of Barrington Blest.

Marnie had visited her in the summer of 2022, before starting her new Jacksonville job in September. Millie was blissfully happy and in her natural element, surrounded by healthfood stores, practitioners of every conceivable healing modality, and endless beaches. She had set up her own sound-therapy practice and seemed to be hitting all the right notes.

DeeDee Melina King had been all over the map since meeting Jordanis King in 2020, travelling to exotic places and still doing her own work in Japan and elsewhere. Now, they seemed to have settled in the Bahamas—if DeeDee could ever be said to *settle*. She had resisted becoming *Mrs King*, seeing no reason to surrender to the archaic ritual of marriage, but then they had the twins in 2024 and everything changed.

"I'm expecting epic names," Marnie had told her when they zoned in. "Romulus and Remus or maybe Atticus and Alexander."

She could practically hear DeeDee rolling her eyes. "I hate to disappoint you, girlfriend," DeeDee said, a sardonic smile in her voice, "but we decided to go with plain old Quillon and Osiris."

Marnie was concerned. "Do you think it's fair to give them such boring names?"

"I'll send these two to stay with you for a while—maybe a year or two," DeeDee said, "then you'll see how boring they are." As if she ever would, Marnie thought, knowing her friend treasured every second of double trouble with her boys.

There was nothing remotely boring or disappointing about either of them, which was handy because Marnie had no idea which one was which. DeeDee had sent photos and the boys looked like miniature African princes, with DeeDee's striking eyes and mocha skin, and Jordanis's strong features. Marnie could imagine how DeeDee must have looked when she was pregnant—like the prow of a ship cleaving through the water as everyone made way for her magnificent twin-filled form.

The two-year-olds were already learning to sail with their dad and DeeDee said they were all coming for a visit soon—maybe on the yacht—so she'd better get ready.

Mella was now six months old and growing like a hothouse tomato, with cherry cheeks dimpling deliciously when she laughed her easy laugh. Marnie found her breathtakingly beautiful—a delicate blend of herself and Steve, yet with her own feisty personality. There was no trace of her early illness but Marnie remained on the fragile fringe of alertness, watching for any hint of wilting.

"I sometimes wonder if Mella is too soft a name," she said to Steve, one evening over dinner. "If we should maybe use Rachel, instead."

"What do you mean, *soft*?"

"Well, you know, based on the numbers idea." Marnie still wasn't sure she believed in that stuff, but there was no harm in covering all the bases.

"You've already looked up the numbers, I'm guessing." Steve smiled. "So why don't you tell me."

Steve knew her so well, which was fine… *most* of the time. "Mella is a number 7, which is supposed to make her spiritual—an investigator and a seeker—in terms of who she is or will become."

"Sounds a bit like her mama," Steve said.

"She would also have a deep love and strong sense of responsibility for family, in terms of potential or inner resources."

"I rest my case," Steve said. "Nothing much wrong there, far as I can see."

"But then the name Rachel is supposed to be about independence, leadership and creativity, with the potential to be a good healer and nurturer."

"And the problem is…?"

"I just wondered if the name Mella made her more sensitive… *if* any of this stuff makes any difference at all."

"You mean, was that why she got sick and nearly died?" Steve looked at her tenderly. "That's what's really worrying you, isn't it?"

"Yeah. Maybe." Marnie took a breath, relieved to have finally expressed the ongoing worry. "But *why* did she get sick, Steve?"

"Why does anything happen, darling girl?" He spread his hands, including the world.

"And the answer is…?"

"You think I can answer that cosmic question?" Steve laughed. "Why don't you ask Charlie. He's far more likely to come up with a solid answer."

"I will ask him. But I'd like to know what you think, you being the numbers guy who claims everything comes down to numbers."

Steve sat back to reflect, feeling the weight of the question. "I'm afraid of giving trite answers," he said. "Like it's a numbers game or there's some bigger picture we don't understand yet."

"But you don't think it *is* a numbers game."

"No, I don't. Not in a case like this."

"So there probably is some bigger picture, like with my parents, right?"

Steve nodded. "Yes, but why don't you ask Charlie?"

"Okay. Good idea. Thanks, sweetie."

"For what? I don't have the answer."

"I know. But you respect me too much to give me any old answer, even though you really *wanted* to come up with one to impress me."

"True." Steve smiled. "Go check with cosmic Charlie and see what he has to say."

Marnie got up, trailing an arm across Steve's shoulders and kissing his neck on her way to the kitchen.

Gwen sat on the kitchen countertop, a crystalline sphere that seemed to glow from within. She could be anywhere, but they kept her in here—probably just out of habit, having had a corded phone for so long. Marnie always thought of Gwen as female, even though it was just a piece of technology. Somehow, it felt more sentient than that— like a gentle intelligent presence emanating wisdom, understanding and support. Not like the old cellphones, which were part of a highly controlled commercial network, feeding you stuff, getting you hooked on products, *likes* or whatever else might seem to fill some unmet need but always left you wanting.

This was more about tapping into consciousness and higher states of mind, stretching your brain to co-evolve with all of Gravizone—the infinite matrix of natural gravitational waves pervading and supporting the entire cosmos… and everyone in it.

She thought Charlie's name and waited for him to respond. She was getting good at this. At the beginning, she had to say his full name and location, *and* think of him, so the zone would detect his electromagnetic signature and connect her to him.

Now, the thought was enough, so she seemed to be evolving in *that* respect, at least.

After a minute, his grinning face appeared on the globe. "Marnie, it's an interesting question," he said, "but I think you already know the answer."

Would she ever get used to her freakily smart nephew, anticipating her questions—and probably even her call—without her saying a thing?

"Yeah, you will," he said.

She sighed. "So, brainchild, what is the answer? I don't think I know, otherwise I wouldn't call my 5-year-old nephew and humiliate myself unnecessarily, would I?"

"Yeah, you would, cos you're not sure. But you do know."

Marnie paused, took a breath. Charlie was so smart he knew her brain's capacity better than she knew it herself. Which was mind-boggling, because he obviously thought she was smart in ways she didn't feel smart at all, yet his smartness made her feel unsure of herself and question her own wisdom, but also reassured her because he always knew what he was talking about. Then she got dizzy trying to make sense of it all.

Charlie laughed. "Don't forget to breathe," he said. "Your brain needs oxygen to work properly."

"If only that were enough." Marnie laughed too, taking some noisy deep breaths.

"Think of the question again."

Marnie thought it. *Why did Mella get sick and nearly die?*

"So, what's the answer?"

Marnie was about to say she still didn't know, but Charlie interrupted.

"Pretend you *do* know. Close your eyes and let the question float. Imagine it going out through Gravizone, where all the answers live."

She did. *Why did Mella get sick and nearly die?* She imagined her question floating out there, through the ethers, permeating the cosmos, formulating a response and coming back to her as wisdom.

Instead, a jumble of thoughts and other questions filled her head. *Why did she, Marnie, get born and not some other zygote in her mother's womb? Why did ZipVs not collide on the street? Why had all the cell towers come down, defying all the odds that it would ever happen?* The thoughts seemed endless, generating far more questions than answers.

She opened her eyes and looked at Charlie. "I don't get it," she said, "even though all those questions seem to have something in common..." She trailed off, totally flummoxed.

"They are the answer," Charlie said.

"Okay, listen, I know you want me to get it myself, like the good little guru you are, but could you just tell me?"

"What do all those things have in common?" Flattery never worked on Charlie.

Marnie groaned, closing her eyes again to focus. *Because they were meant to happen… because someone wanted them to happen.* The thought came unbidden but it sounded more like a Japanese koan than an answer.

"Is that it?" she asked Charlie. "She got sick but didn't die because she wasn't *meant* to?"

"Yeah, sort of."

"But that doesn't explain why she got sick in the first place." Marnie was getting frustrated.

"What was the benefit of her getting sick? What happened?"

"You got to show everyone how amazing you are by saving her? Is that it?"

"Don't think about me. Think about Mella. And you."

Marnie thought back to that awful time and how scared she had been. She sensed some cosmic dance, choreographed beyond her awareness, determining how life unfolded. In almost losing Mella, she had felt the preciousness of life, but she had *already* felt that… She hadn't needed her baby to almost die to feel that.

What about Mella. What had happened for her? *Had she thought of not staying? Did she not like what she found when she arrived but decided to stay because Charlie pulled her back into her body? Did she have some higher purpose that made her decide to stay?* Such thoughts were ridiculous for a newborn.

"I think it's something to do with evolution," Marnie said. "Right? Charlie?"

Gwen glowed mutely. Charlie had zoned out.

84

November 2026

Lucy was thinking about words and how crowded out they used to be, pre-CEBS. She had written and plied so many—to convey a message, convince a client, produce a sale. It was a pressurized world where all the spaces got filled in. If you dared draw breath, you would lose your place in the queue. It wasn't conversation. It was a traffic jam of thoughts trying to get home, like horns blaring, regardless of who else got drowned out along the way.

Now, there was more mental space, time to pause, reflect and assimilate. People could have a thought, float it out there, let it breathe and allow it to settle in some fertile foothold where it could take root and grow. A thought ultimately becoming a thing, as all thoughts do, just as anger could become an ulcer or frenzied haste created a vacuum that couldn't be filled. With fewer words being used, they once again had more meaning. They resounded more clearly in a peaceful mind, with space for them to echo back and be heard again, before a flood of others washed them away.

While she was sitting at the table in the living room, having these thoughts, Charlie came to her and said *yes*, that was exactly what you needed for higher conversations to happen.

"You mean like with Grannie," she said.

"Yeah, and others— like Mella, when she was sick."

"She communicated with you? A *newborn*?"

"No, Mum, it's not like that. It's like… when your mind is really quiet you can hear things you don't hear if you're really busy or worried. Sort of like how people used to listen in on cop radio chatter in old movies."

"So, it's like meditation?"

"It's more like creating an antenna in your brain, so you can transmit and receive messages."

"O-kaaay… but how?"

"Mum, you're always asking how instead of just doing."

"So just doing *is* the how?"

"Yeah. It's like how it used to be on that Facebook thing before it crashed, when people had friends they chatted to a lot. They got to see stuff posted by those friends because they had a kind of virtual connection. It was an algorithm, but it's the same thing."

"You're 5 years old. How do you know how things *used to be* on social media?"

"What you know, I can sometimes remember."

"So, I'm like your personal database of archives. And I thought I was just your plain old mum."

Charlie grinned. "Yeah. It's handy. And if you're close to someone, it's easier for me to connect to them."

Lucy was thinking about what had happened to Celle. "So, because I'm close to Marnie, you picked up on Mella, but because I'm not so close to Matt, you didn't pick up on Celle?"

"Yeah, but she was taken care of anyway. She didn't need me."

Charlie looked at her and rolled his eyes. "You're worrying again. Let's just practise, okay?"

"Okay. What do I do?"

"I'll go into the kitchen and send you some thoughts, and you try to connect with me. Okay?"

Lucy sat on the couch, closed her eyes, took deep breaths, emptied her mind and then thought of Charlie. Colours swirled in her head. She tried not to imagine what he might send her… *but how would she know the difference?*

Don't analyse it, she imagined him saying. Or was that just her own mind advising her?

Breathe. Allow. Relax. BAR. She'd have to remember that…

Tune in to Charlie, she told herself. Just let him through. More colours swirled. Suddenly, through the colours, she saw a place take shape, a town, with dark sandy colours… a place in the desert? She didn't recognize it, but there was something familiar about it. She saw cacti. Wooden houses and storefronts. People dressed in colourful loose clothing. Was this a real place?

She got a strange sensation in her gut—a knowing or a sense of something she didn't want to know because it felt scary. *What the hell…?*

She wanted to stop. She opened her eyes, got up and went into the kitchen.

Charlie was sitting on a bar stool, swinging his short legs, an impish smile on his beautiful little face. A bar stool… was that a coincidence?

"That's part of it," Charlie said. "You want to know what that place is called?"

"What? Was that you?"

"Yeah. That place you saw. Do you know what it's called?"

"No. I've never seen it before. Is it a real place?"

"Yeah. I think Grannie has been there or she just liked the name." Charlie leaned across the countertop and pulled a sheet of paper towards her. On it was written one word in red marker.

SEDONA.

85

"What about population?" The roasted vegetables were making their second round of the table and would not survive a third—not with Troy tucking in so enthusiastically, despite talking almost non-stop. He and Annamae were having dinner at Marnie and Steve's, discussing population, food production and CosmiCrops—the thriving eco-food business Troy and Steve had started five years ago.

Mella was sleeping peacefully upstairs, and 6-year-old twins, Chester and Rosie, were in the den playing an interactive Gravigame. Already smart kids, they were activating new parts of their brains and creating new neural networks that enhanced their mental and spiritual abilities, according to the results being documented via the Gravizone evolutionary system.

Compared with Steve's football-player physique, Troy was more like a greyhound ready to rip around the racetrack, although definitely a *well-fed* greyhound, Marnie thought, fondly. No skinny ribs in evidence. Annamae was similarly slender, with just enough gentle curves to stop her from catching on the furniture.

Marnie had enjoyed getting to know them and the twins when she and Steve had moved to Jacksonville in early 2021. They had dinner together once a month, alternating between the two houses. But something was not quite right between her brother-in-law and his wife. Marnie sensed a tension, some kind of resentment between them, although they were always polite to each other when they socialized.

"Everyone thought population was going to be a huge issue, despite all the good stuff governments are doing," Troy said, "but things seem to be rebalancing anyway."

"It's happening all over," Annamae said. "Deserts are becoming wetter, weather extremes are less common, the air is cleaner, and the polar ice caps are growing for the first time in modern history."

Annamae had studied meteorology for two years before getting pregnant with the twins and having to give up her studies. Now that the climate was changing in such radical, fascinating ways, she was getting back into it, studying from home. She was also exploring community projects for taking advantage of newly cultivatable land.

"Why *is* that?" Marnie often felt quite giddy at how unbelievably good things were. "It's the polar opposite of how things were before—" Groans from around the table at her pun. "Yeah, sorry." She grinned, not sorry at all. "Just six years ago, almost every aspect of life was getting worse rather than better. Now, it's the other way around. Surely that's not just because of all the positive reforms, is it?"

"Partly, I think," Steve said, pouring Marnie's homemade rocket sauce over his vegetables and quercia.

"But doesn't that mean there'll be more people, since the environment is more hospitable and people won't die of hardship or crop failures, like before?"

"Plus everyone's healthier," Annamae added, "living longer and better."

"So… how come the population isn't expanding even *more*, rather than reducing?"

"It is still expanding," Steve said, "but it's distributed more evenly, without as much urban congestion as before. There's actually plenty of space for everyone."

"Because food is now being produced more naturally and closer to home," Marnie said, nodding to herself. "Sorry, sweetie, but I still don't get it. With healthier people, more stable climate, greater self-sufficiency, won't there *eventually* be more people than the planet can tolerate?"

"When the natural balance is restored, things have a way of stabilizing, or so they say," Steve said. "I guess we'll just have to wait and see."

"Population dynamics are changing too," Troy said, describing an arc with his briefly empty fork. "All over, people are having fewer children but living richer lives. They're more focused on quality than quantity."

"But lots of people still want big families," Marnie said, looking pointedly at the two Romero men.

"And I guess there'll always be natural disasters," Troy said.

"Like having twins, you mean." Annamae smiled wryly.

"Woman, mind what you say when the progeny are within beaming distance," Troy said. There it was again, Marnie thought. Troy made it sound like a joke, but his tone implied something else. He turned back to Marnie. "I meant climatic events or other phenomena that periodically reduce our numbers."

"I'm not so sure about that any more," Marnie said. "All the insect plagues, epidemics and viruses we've had in the past have been manmade or introduced where they shouldn't have been. Haven't they?"

"That or due to unhealthy ways of living," Annamae said. "I'm convinced the Earth is collaborating with us—sort of loving us back into balance, as we make all these positive changes and finally start putting the planet first, again." She paused, reflecting. "All that new age stuff from before, with people *finding* themselves and figuring out how to have a fabulous life without thinking about the planet... it all seemed so self-centred. To me, it made no sense to put people first like that. It's like saying babies should decide what's best, when they could barely survive a single day without their mothers."

"It's true," Marnie said. "You'd see people meditating and doing all kinds of stuff to have a healthier life, yet still using a cellphone."

"Scratch my theory, then," Troy said, spearing a pile of browts and twisting them around his fork. "These are great, bro. What have you been adding to the flats to get this taste and colour?" Troy held up his fully loaded fork, observing the browts' rich texture and deep maroon colour.

"Don't look at me," Steve said. "Marnie does all the tweaking now."

Browts were their most popular product—a new kind of hydroponically grown superfood. It was a green vegetable full of nutrition, "*with all the essential amino acids and vitamins for building strong minds and bods*," Troy had proudly told her, when he and Steve had grown their first batch.

Blending the benefits of broccoli, spinach, bean sprouts and hemp, browts grew in a mad tangle of tiny shoots that always made Marnie think of old electrical cables. She loved them anyway, and they definitely delivered their own kind of energetic charge. Crunchy, moist and slightly peppery, with hints of rosemary and oregano, browts required no cooking and grew in a matter of days. When the shoots were just starting, you could add all kinds of natural cosmi-nutrients to the water to create different health properties and effects. This week, she had added purple powder and trace minerals.

Troy and Steve had started CosmiCrops in 2021, creating oxygen-producing crops alongside a new system of hydroponics that could be used even in hot, arid countries. Browts were now grown and consumed worldwide, and the brothers were working on a range of other biodynamic fruits and vegetables, sometimes combining the two, as with crowberries.

These were one of Marnie's favourite vegi-fruits—shiny round black berries blended with hazelnuts and rich in chlorella, antioxidants and so many other nutrients that even Marnie started to yawn if Steve ran through the list.

"Just give me a bowlful every day," she said. "They're so good I can't seem to get enough of them." After eating them, she looked like a scary black-toothed Halloween witch when she smiled, sending Mella into fits of giggles.

Most babies would recoil in terror and bawl their eyes out. Marnie even scared herself when she looked in the mirror. But Mella seemed to have decided to be totally safe in this life, living it lightly, trusting in her existence. Nothing seemed to faze her.

From software analyst to eco-foodie: Marnie still marvelled at how seamlessly Steve had made the shift. And he was thriving on it. They all were. Marnie had never felt so healthy and she could see the effects on Mella also, her eyes luminous and alert, cheeks rosy, tiny teeth strong and fiercely white. No fevers, no colic, no childhood illnesses.

They had been lucky to have had Dr Patrice as her pediatrician when Mella got sick. He knew exactly what to give her as a natural alternative to the harmful pharmaceuticals routinely given to babies in the past. Thanks to him and Charlie, Mella's life had been saved—and, ironically, she had ended up getting the best possible start in life, with immune-boosting nutrients that fortified her body, instead of drugs designed to kill bacteria, good and bad.

Now that almost everyone had a Hydropon unit, they could grow their own food. And with all the free energy for heating or cooling greenhouses, you could grow practically anything. Food grown locally meant less transportation, fresher produce and healthier processes, which Marnie loved. It also meant far less shopping, and the huge market for packaged cereals and processed foods had collapsed practically overnight, following the introduction of the President's new program.

"Not everyone is happy about the reforms," Annamae said pointedly, which made Marnie wonder if *she* wasn't entirely happy about them. "Look what happened with all those riots last year, where people in three different states protested having to give up junk food and not being able to eat what they wanted."

"Yeah, but it was the same with smoking, wasn't it?" Troy seemed keen to defend the positive changes that had made CosmiCrops so successful. "There were lots of riots when smoking was banned, but everyone accepts it now." He gestured around the table with his fork, a conductor leading his orchestra. "Just takes time, you know?"

"Some people say they have the right to choose what to eat," Annamae persisted. "Like they have the right to choose the kind of medicine or healthcare they want to use."

"But eating junk food harms everyone," Troy said, turning to her. "And it *costs* everyone, creating all kinds of diseases that put a burden on the healthcare system. So it's not as if their choices are independent, affecting no one else."

Maybe this was the source of the tension, Marnie thought—or maybe it was something else and this was just how Annamae's frustrations came out. She'd had to give up her career to become a full-time mother, while Troy kept forging ahead. Maybe that was it.

"It does take a while to adjust to all these new textures and flavours," Marnie said, diplomatically. "I already loved this kind of thing, so it wasn't much of a shift for me. But people on low incomes could only afford junk food, or didn't know any better, and then ended up addicted to it."

"You can blame the fast-food industry and government for that," Troy said vehemently.

"That's not helpful," Annamae said. "And you're missing the point."

"What *is* the point, then?" Troy turned to face her, a challenging look on his face. This was a side of him Marnie hadn't seen before, and she wasn't sure she liked it.

"The point is *freedom!*" The word was unleashed with such passion it was clear she was no longer just talking about food.

Steve laid a gentle hand over Annamae's. "*That* is a lot more interesting to me than talking about food, which we do all day anyway." Marnie nodded agreement, while Troy stabbed his vegetables with his fork, his face averted. "Freedom is what this is all about."

It's all that really matters, Marnie thought—the freedom to nourish and heal yourself, to love and to *be* loved, without old plaque-forming mental programs clogging the highways to your heart.

Before CEBS, emotional angst was fed three square meals a day by the toxic workings of a distorted humanity, numbly heaped upon existing old wounds. Now, people were healing from the world they had left behind, yet still carried with them in some small measure. It was a healing propelled by the CEBS evolutionary imperative—a one-way upgraded passage, rather than the constant recycling of an expanding pain.

Annamae was bristling, her cover blown and uncomfortable now that the focus was on her.

It's about time, isn't it? Marnie thought. "What does freedom look like for you, Annamae," she said, "in this brave new world where everything seems possible?"

Annamae lined up her knife and fork on her plate, then folded her napkin and placed it deliberately on the table. "I want a divorce," she said.

When had life become a spectator sport? Marnie wondered, her mind playing for time while it processed this startling input. They knew so little about each other, really—merely skimming the surface of each others' lives. In earlier times, the whole tribe would come together to discuss a marital rift, which affected everyone. Now, despite all their newfound humanity, people didn't always know how to deal with this, or prevent it from happening in the first place.

The drumroll of *divorce* had charged the air with an almost tangible portent, bringing all digestion to a halt. Even the den had gone quiet, the twins telepathically poised for the sequel.

Troy's fork clattered onto his plate, like a baton thrown to the ground, the orchestra now silent.

"That sounds like a good idea," Steve said, shocking them all, especially Annamae.

Troy looked close to tears, staring at his plate, gritting his teeth.

"Why?" Marnie said, unsure if she was asking Steve or Annamae.

"Why not?" Annamae said. "I've totally lost myself in this relationship, and nobody seems to have noticed, least of all me."

"Certainly some time out could be a good thing," Steve said.

It was a wise strategy, Marnie realized. Annamae needed support, not resistance.

Troy glared at his brother, then got up abruptly, flinging his napkin onto the table and striding out the patio door into the garden.

This was a scene from old-world dysfunction, Marnie thought. Troy was better than this. Steve would talk to him. No, *she* would. Now that she was a mother, she was more engaged with the fragility of existence. She thought of the plants they grew in their business, how life emerged so fast. Like the earth being born each time, a Groundhog Day of creation. All in that frozen moment, as she sought a way home for a wayward heart.

"I've stopped loving him," Annamae said.

"I'm not so sure," Marnie said. "Maybe it's you you've stopped loving."

86

---

1 December 2026

They were having a horrible argument. It didn't happen often. When it did, though, it was usually fiery and often about Charlie. This one was the most heated and dreadful they had ever had.

Shortly after Charlie's sixth birthday, they had woken up to discover that Charlie was... normal. His super-human capacities seemed to have dissipated, leaving behind a normal kid doing all the normal things kids do, with all the persistent *whys*. *Why can't I? Why must I? Why?* Plus the usual crankiness of growing kids, complaining about their homework, not wanting to do any chores...

It was the most devastating, crushing come-down Lucy had ever experienced, and she was torn apart, unable to process the reversal.

Nate was furious with her. "You've complained all along about him being so smart you can't keep up and how challenging it is for you. Now that he's a healthy, normal kid, that's not okay? How do you think that makes him *feel*—to be normal and for that not to be *okay?*"

"It's not that." Lucy was sobbing. "It's just that... he was so *extraordinary* and I felt so conflicted at the beginning because I felt inadequate... But then I grew to admire him so much, and he made me stretch myself, so I was becoming a better person because of him— this little boy who made everyone think deeply and ponder the fabric of life and the bigger questions people rarely ask themselves."

More sobs. "He was teaching me so *much*, Nate, opening up a whole new world of ideas, colour, layers, hidden meanings, our deeper selves.

I just can't bear it that—"

"Mum… Mum, wake up. You're dreaming."

Still sobbing, Lucy opened her eyes. Charlie looked concerned, his little forehead creased into a frown.

"Another emergency?" She gasped, still caught between two worlds.

"No, Mum. You were just dreaming. Everything's okay. I'm okay."

"Oh, thank God." Lucy sat up, wiping her cheeks. She leaned back against the pillows, pulling the comforter around her. *What a horrible dream. Thank God it was just a dream.*

Nate was in Mexico, she just remembered, checking on production of their clothing lines for kids. Tate had gone with him and Lucy knew they'd have a blast with Celle and Matt, surfing, swimming, maybe some zip-flying.

The three of them would go as a family next time, as Celle was dying to meet Charlie. That always made Lucy smile. She was *living* to meet him, thanks to Charlie. But it was as if Matt and Celle lived on another planet from which they found it hard to return. Lucy could understand, sort of. It was another world down there, although life here in the States was pretty spectacular since all the CEBS reforms, with Mexico benefitting hugely. Still, there really wasn't much to come back for, except family. *But wasn't that enough?*

Charlie still looked troubled, spooked by her tears.

"Are you too big to climb up here onto my lap?"

He shook his head, scrambling up and plonking himself on her legs, leaning back against her chest as she wrapped her arms around him.

"Why were you crying, Mum? Was the dream really bad?" He seemed on the verge of tears himself. Her conflicting emotions sometimes made it hard for him to read her, which he found unsettling.

"It wasn't a nice dream," she said, her chin resting gently on the top of his head.

"About me," he said, matter-of-factly.

"Yes."

"Tell me. I want to know the bits I couldn't see."

"Well, it was…" *What to say, without making him feel conflicted?*

"About me being normal," he said.

So he'd picked up on that much. "Yeah. In the dream, I woke up one morning, and you were just like every other kid. Still the Charlie

I love more than anything, of course. That will *never* change. You were just… different."

"Why were you so upset?"

"Because… I think it was just a shock, you know? And you've taught me so much, Charlie. I've discovered a lot about myself, and I think maybe I've put pressure on you, without realizing it. Not feeling smart enough to be your mum, which must feel weird for you. Right?"

Charlie grunted.

"So sometimes you end up being like a parent, because you're so smart. I'm not sure I know how to fix that, honestly… Or how to be a better mum…" She felt close to tears again. The dream had dredged up deep emotions she had obviously suppressed.

"I'm sorry, Mum."

"Nothing for you to be sorry about, sweetie." She hugged his little chest.

"Yeah, there is."

She paused. "Did you send me that dream?"

"Sort of…" He wriggled round to face her, looking scared. Not a look you often saw on Charlie's face.

She wasn't going to scold him. He had done this for a reason. "Why, sweetie?"

"Sometimes you seem unhappy, maybe 'cause of me."

"Because you're so smart?"

"Yeah, but more because you don't think *you're* smart."

"So you think I don't like myself much because you're so much smarter than me." She was thinking out loud, processing as she went. "And I was sort of using you to make me feel bad about me."

He shrugged.

"You're right. Not nice. I deserved to have that dream." She pulled him into a hug. "Good thinking, kiddo."

She could feel his tummy relax. He needed this conversation as much as her. It was easy to forget that he sometimes needed reassurance, despite being so intelligent.

"Charlie, I am in awe of you, sweetie. You are the most incredible, humbling gift I could ever have wished for, even though I never even knew such a thing was possible."

"Which means…"

"Yes, okay." She smiled. "I must be pretty wonderful too, then, right? To have produced the miracle of you?"

"Yeah." That seemed to make him happy, which made her heart turn over. She needed to love herself more so he could relax and not feel he had to be less than *he* was, for *her* sake—or more, to make up for her not feeling up to snuff. How twisted hearts could get when they felt insecure.

"There," he said. "That's where more love needs to be."

She nodded, hearing the echo of her own recriminations. "It's an old habit."

"Already too old," Charlie said.

"Yup. Got it. New story: I'm doing a *phenomenal* job of raising such a brilliant child, and I'm constantly *gobsmacked* by my own brilliance, even giving myself wake-up calls in my dreams."

Charlie laughed and Lucy breathed in his heady *haps*, as he called them. He had missed the whole internet apps craze, but he knew about it. *We need haps not apps*, he had told her. More happy, less appy.

"How do *you* feel about all this, sweetie? Being so smart must be lonely, even though we love you and you have Tatum and… Grannie." She wanted to know more about that special connection, but now wasn't the time.

"I can't always read your mind," Lucy said, "but I always want to know what you feel or if you're ever upset. Even if you think that might upset *me*, okay? I insist."

He nodded. "'Kay."

"Tell me what's going on inside this fabulous noggin." She tapped his head with her knuckles.

"I don't like the new school."

"Why not?" Charlie was now going to a special school for gifted children. He had seemed happier. *Had she not been paying attention?* "Because it's for special kids?"

"It's the other kids."

"Because they're smart?"

"Yeah, but they think being smart makes them special, which makes them not so nice."

"Not so nice how?"

"Being smart here—" Charlie tapped his head—"doesn't always make you smart here." He tapped his chest.

"You're right," Lucy said. "I guess it can make some people mean, if they're not *really* smart. Like we were talking about before, about getting a swelled head?"

"Yeah." Finally, the grin was back.

They had laughed over that. Nate and Lucy had been in bed one evening, and Charlie was in his room down the corridor, still wide awake, reading... but eavesdropping, as he sometimes did, if they were talking about him and forgot to say PRIVATE.

This time, though, they knew he was listening and were taking advantage of it.

Nate had been joking, but he also sort of wanted to make the point, just in case. "Charlie would be so obnoxious if he became big-headed and full of himself," he said to Lucy. "Wouldn't he?"

Big sigh from the other room. "I thought you said I was smart."

"You *are* smart," Nate called back.

"So I would *know* that."

"Yes, but we tell you so often how smart you are and how much we love you that it might go to your head."

"*Everything* goes to my head, but that doesn't mean I turn into an arrogant, egotistical, demanding, self-centred, obnoxious little prick, does it?"

"Whoa, buddy," Nate said. "Or a foul-mouthed one!"

"Yeah. Okay. I just wanted to make the point, like you made yours." They could hear him grinning.

"We got it, Charlie," Lucy called out. "You are the most selfless, generous, funny, endearing, wise kid two parents could ever be humbled to have."

Nate still needed to be the boss. "But no more swearing, okay? We've got to have *some* rules around here, even if you make and break most of them."

"Yeah, okay."

Lucy smiled, remembering. Charlie did not have a swelled head, thank God, but some of the kids at his school obviously did.

"So, are the kids mean to you?"

"They're not kind, you know? Not like CEBSters."

"I hear you. Those guys have their hearts wide open, don't they? We all need to let ourselves do that more." She breathed in a reminder. "So how are they not kind? Do they bully you or what?"

"It's not like that. It's more that they do almost everything with their heads and don't use their hearts to apply the stuff they know."

"You're very wise to see that, Charlie. Before you were born, the whole world was like that, only a lot worse and with very little intelligence. Things are getting better, but maybe it's hard for some kids to get it right, especially if their parents push them to be super-intelligent, instead of emotionally intelligent."

"Yeah."

"Maybe you could help teach them that."

"I don't want to always be teaching other people to be smarter."

Lucy gulped.

"I don't mean you, Mum. We have fun, you and me. But I don't want to be a teacher at my own school."

"Kiddo, you could *run* that whole school." But that wasn't what he needed to hear. "What would help, then? How can we fix this?"

"We need a school for gifted hearts, not just gifted heads."

Do we ever, Lucy thought. *A happiness school.* The idea made her heart smile.

87

10 December 2026

CosmiCrops was taking on a whole new meaning for Marnie. She had always loved being creative in the kitchen, concocting new dishes using good organic produce. But *creating* new foods was something else, and it was exciting. She remembered telling Steve a year ago that she wished there was a food that provided some of the same marine nutrients as fish, which were no longer being farmed in the same way. Five months later, he had presented her with a basket of chorlies.

Like cascading seaweed vermicelli, chorlies were rich in iodine, vitamins, minerals, chlorophyll and omega-3 oil. They grew like a soft curtain of green-and-purple braids, and they were delicious flash-fried to a crunchy crispiness in a little sunbean oil.

This new oil had turned out to be highly nutritious, with subtle hints of lavender and mint. Sunbeans themselves could be sprouted and eaten raw. When cultivated for their oil, the plants produced tight profusions of small yellow blossoms, leaning towards the sun. *Sun stalkers*, Marnie called them. Similar to the sunflowers that used to be grown in vast fields for their oil, sunbeans had the advantage of producing ten times the yield from their fast-growing flowers, which generated brain- and hormone-enhancing properties, while boosting energy levels and mental clarity.

But what Marnie found truly amazing was that each of the new cosmicrops activated and enhanced particular parts of the brain and certain aspects of the heart. She was starting to get an intuitive sense of their unique properties—not just how nutritious or tasty they were, but how they actively promoted personal evolution.

Perhaps Troy needed more of his own home-grown goodness. A daily dose of chorlies, which were good for fortifying wavering hearts and softening those that had hardened. Or quercia, which helped shore up the courage of edgy innovation, stretching minds beyond their former frontiers. But also some sunbean oil, which got molecules meshing in a matrix of assertive masculine action and grounded feminine allowance, forging the timeless union of cosmic complements. Definitely good for relationships.

He would benefit from all three, Marnie decided, and Annamae probably would too. Everyone would, in fact, now that she thought about it. In the old dysfunctional world, so many hearts had been hurt, protective body armour worn like a business suit, and the whole male–female balance as off kilter as the depleted planet itself.

It reminded her of an expression she once heard: *We teach what we most need to learn.* Perhaps we should learn what we most need to grow, she mused. Not just foods to feed the body, but foods to heal and grow the heart and brain, while leveraging the intelligence of both. Marnie couldn't think of anything more rewarding than conscious creative expansion of one's own body and life.

She was telling Lucy about some of the new foods when they last zoned in for their weekly chat.

"It feels a bit like playing God, Luce, creating new species."

"Could I please order a blue-spotted, weed-eating miniature giraffe for my back garden?"

Marnie laughed.

"It *is* wild what we can do now, Marn, kind of like evolution on fast-forward. But it's not like genetic engineering, right?"

"It's nothing like that, Steve says. And GMOs are no longer allowed anywhere, as far as I know, although a few countries are still catching up."

"So how does it work, creating new kinds of foods?"

"I still don't really understand it, and it feels almost creepy being able to create things so fast. They use a special culture medium for growing things—with stem cells taken from nature and then enhanced with cosmi-nutrients and herbs or spices or probiotics, so they're good for digestion and the immune system."

"Food becoming medicine."

"Yes. Like it used to be."

"But you always ate perfectly before anyway, so this isn't a big shift for you."

Marnie laughed. "I wasn't the angelic foodie you seem to think I was," she said.

"Compared to *me*, you were," Lucy said. "I don't think I ever saw you pig out once."

"Oh, I pigged out. Just not when anyone else was around."

"But you always seemed so calm and so on top of things, while I was having melodramatic meltdowns after Mum and Dad died."

"You just had a different way of expressing stuff and getting it out of your system."

"But how did *you*, Marn? How did you process all that stuff?"

"I don't know, Luce. I think helping you and Matt get through it helped me, too. And then there was Celle. Plus, I did all that body-tuning work with Millie, which cleared out a lot of old patterns."

"So even though we didn't get hit with CEBS, we seem okay now, don't we?"

"Yes, we're okay, Luce." Marnie smiled. "There's lots of good stuff coming at us through Gravizone—healing frequencies that make it a lot easier to let go of old stuff. We've all done a heck of a lot of that, even without CEBS."

"Yeah. And having our own family heals things, too." Lucy sometimes felt as if she had already lived a whole lifetime in just six years. "So, what's this new food—*quercia?*—that you mentioned last week?"

"It's a new protein, one of Steve's favourites," Marnie said. "It's an Italian word, meaning oak, pronounced *kwair-cha*, which almost nobody gets right." She tried to remember the process. "I think they started out with stem cells from acorns that they cultured in their special medium, combined with *gorlum*, I think it's called… a fibrous substance they got from the bark of the tree."

She paused, reflecting. "Anyway, they cultured the two things together and came up with a new kind of complete protein that looks a bit like textured bamboo, but tastes really nutty and substantial. You can barbecue it, grill it and use it raw. Nothing like tofu, you'll be glad to hear."

"Ugh, yeah. I never could stand that stuff. It always felt and tasted like putty, to me," Lucy said.

"And was about as nutritious."

"It's brilliant what you guys are doing. You must be proud of Steve."

"It's a whole new world, Luce. Who'd have thunk it…"

"Yeah. Six years ago… you and me and Matt in your little place in Brighton, in bits after Mum and Dad died. If they could see us now, Marn. They'd love all this innovative stuff, wouldn't they?"

"I was thinking the same thing," Marnie said quietly. "I wish they were here. I think they'd be proud of us, Luce. I like to imagine that, anyway."

88

---

20 December 2026

In Rome, the Pope was crying. He was on his knees in his chambers. Nothing unusual about that. What was slightly less typical was his attire: baggy jeans and a knobbly old sweater that looked as if it had belonged to Moses. His white robes were strewn across the floor, his red satin mozzetta snaking through them like a river of fresh blood.

His ring had ended up under a dresser somewhere, after he had flung it at the wall. How many hapless supplicants had kissed that duplicitous ring in the hope of some kind of redemption? He was the one who needed redeeming. He was a fraud. He was no more a successor of Peter than he was Mother Teresa. He was nobody's *eminence*.

He had been vomiting all night, trying to expunge his shame. All the papal repasts of the finest ingredients and vintage wines from the

Vatican cellar seemed to be lodged in his belly, repeating on him like old garlic; bile and acid corroding his insides.

Over 1,700 years of indoctrination and iniquity, contaminating the human psyche and the planet: it made him want to retch all over again. *Abbiamo rovinato tutto il mondo con questa maledetta finzione di redenzione. We have screwed up the whole world with this cursed sham of redemption.* No Pontiff had ever uttered such profanities—not out loud, at least.

Humanity had been evolving naturally until the Church corrupted it, imposing a hierarchy of subservience that left hearts and spirits out in the cold, homeless and rejected as unworthy.

How could he even begin to undo the distortion? The natural order had been so thoroughly disrupted, even within the Church, with priests and nuns denying themselves pleasure and believing themselves to be unclean and undeserving of love—and then abusing others because they themselves had been dehumanized, branded innately sinful. It went against the essence of love itself, which he was convinced made up the very fabric of the cosmos.

It had begun to feel wrong to him some time ago, his unease growing steadily in the past ten years, particularly. People seemed increasingly robotic, as disconnected in their religious convictions as they were from each other, in their everyday lives, immersed in gadgets and no longer really seeing or caring what was happening around them.

The early Church had done a masterful job of inducing blind acceptance among the masses, programmed from birth to defer to the power of the church and deny the power of their magnificent selves. People were now so deeply programmed they probably wouldn't believe the truth if the liars themselves confessed it.

He was reeling from all the inner revelations. He didn't understand why Rome itself had remained untouched, but CEBS—or CEBS2, its slightly gentler successor—had hit the Vatican like the storm of the century, blasting through the pomp and ceremony, the daily rituals, and slamming him with truths that he had hidden even from himself. It seemed appropriate. It was time for this massive institution, like so many others that had become big business, to be dismantled and replaced with something more enlightened, unifying and soul-enhancing.

How many of his fellow clergy concealed their own spiritual

emptiness beneath their religious garb? Most of them, it seemed, if the mayhem he could hear all around him was any indication. Chanting time-worn refrains did little to heal splintered hearts, merely echoing through the catacombs of uncertainty and drowning out the cowering inner voice so long ago suppressed.

There were few groups more principled or uptight than the clergy— more *anally retentive*, the Americans would probably say. Or more *venally retentive*, he might say, if he were a cynical man.

He felt hollowed out. Hallowed, no. Had he ever felt hallowed? He had tried to remain humble. But CEBS, with its soul-scouring force, stripped away all façades, all constructs that lacked a loving cosmic backbone.

Yet he did love the people. He just hadn't been at liberty within the traditional constraints to help them love themselves. But he hadn't tried hard enough. That would weigh heavily on him forever more.

He could see it now, how divisive all religions were and how much damage they had done. What did he really stand for, anyway? How had he personally enriched the world? He could no longer tell. Since CEBS had struck, he could only see the missed opportunities, the lost souls and all the pain—his own and the pain of the people. *POPE* seemed synonymous with *prevention of personal empowerment*.

He still believed in God, but all the ritualistic trappings felt more and more like an encumbrance, the older he got. Like scaffolding around a building completed and perfected long ago, obscuring its beauty and essence and keeping it perpetually propped up, when the need for support was long gone and only got in the way. Was that what religion had become—a prop that got in the way of humanity?

There was no need for such a complicated superstructure when the truth was simple. Humans and God, with nothing in between. What could be simpler or more honest than that? There was no money or power in it, of course, in a world that seemed constantly ravenous for both. Not a commercially compelling *raison d'être*; more of a *raison de ne pas être*.

You could shock yourself with what you kept locked inside.

Like Carlotta. The love of his life, buried deep, like a diamond formed at the core of the Earth, a precious gem that never got to be seen or enjoyed, least of all by him. Where would she be now? Married, widowed, dead of a broken heart?

His own heart felt wretchedly heavy and in need of its own salvation. The coffers were filled to overflowing, thanks to other lost souls trying to buy their way back into God's favour, when they had never lost it in the first place—merely been *told* they had, by the biggest spin doctors in the history of mankind. The history of man*cruel*. That was what the Church had done: bred cruelty among men, teaching by example, condemning and slaughtering those who refused to submit to their oppressors and to convert to an alien god that went against every cosmic principle mastered in the spiritual schools of antiquity.

People had turned against themselves and each other, convinced by the Church that they needed perpetual intercession, which kept them forever locked in a cycle of false hope and self-rejection. They had spent generations destroying themselves, derailed and bereft, constantly seeking to fill the inner void created by the hijacking of their spiritual autonomy and heart-centred essence.

But he had wallowed enough. Three days of grief and self-recrimination had left him haggard—unshaven and unkempt, more like a beggar of alms than a leader of men.

It was time to face the people and confess. It was time to give them what they really needed and deserved.

The Vatican was one of the wealthiest institutions on Earth, worth almost $15 billion. Perhaps he could do something good with that.

A different kind of Christmas present for the world.

89

21 December 2026

"God, have you seen this?" Marnie was reading the CEBS supplement from the newspaper they were sharing, getting an update on the situation. She was glad that *some* things hadn't changed and you could still buy a few physical newspapers, as well as her beloved books.

"God sees all, I think," Steve said, looking up from the sports section. "Tell me."

"The Pope says he's dismantling the Catholic Church." Marnie shook her head in wonder. "I'll read it to you."

As has happened to so many of us around the world, CEBS has brought me to my senses—to a deep awareness of what we have done to our planet and how we must now evolve in new ways.

This is a time of reclaimed freedoms and truth. It is a time for humanity to regain possession of its wholeness and to take back responsibility for what it was forced to surrender many generations ago.

I seek forgiveness from our ancestors, from current generations, but most of all from myself. No one can absolve me for my part in what has been done, and I have learned that absolution, like forgiveness, comes from within. No one can give us either of those things. Full responsibility for self is what we must all now reclaim and embody to the very best of our physical, emotional and spiritual capacities.

Over many generations, the Church has gained tremendous power, at the expense of humanity. Now, it is time for the people to be supported by the Church—not maligned or condemned for being sinful, but celebrated for being blessedly human, in the fullest expression of all their spiritual splendour and rightful autonomy.

The choice of what to believe and who you want to be is yours—and always should have been. I cannot set you free from all the religious constructs implanted in you. I can simply tell you that you *are* free, and that the early Church did us all a great disservice in preaching falsehoods about a god created in our image, rather than celebrating and elevating our humanness in a universe of infinite loving intelligence.

The Church as we know it can no longer be. This is not about renouncing God, but fully knowing and accepting ourselves, which inevitably unites us with the creative intelligence that pervades the cosmos and interconnects us all. We are all one. Along the way, we were forced to betray that spiritual union. Now, it is time for us all to come together—all faiths, all cultures and all races—to share in the common purpose and privilege of creating a world inspired by love.

"Holy shit," Marnie said. "What the hell will happen now?"

"All hell will probably break loose." Steve looked unruffled.

"But this is a *good* thing, right?"

"You're asking me? After what the good man just said about thinking for ourselves?" Steve turned to face her, smiling. "What do you think?"

"I think… I'm shell-shocked. I think this will turn the world upside down. But I think it *is* a good thing and it has been a hell of a long time coming."

90

March 2027

There was always a soft sea breeze floating up from the coast, keeping them cool with spray-spangled air, wafting the scent of hot herbs and dry earth through their open windows. Their house on the hill was a haven of tranquillity and a place for expansive thinking, with the endless Pacific Ocean laid out below them and the horizon stretching into the distance.

At dawn each day, Matt sat on the deck as the vista emerged from the muted sky, his brain slowly gearing up for the running of his body, while his higher mind contemplated the infinite possibilities constantly unfolding around them. With things evolving so fast, he needed this daily dose of stillness to integrate things.

At certain turbulent times of year, a fierce storm swept across the ocean, scouring the hillside, sucking the breath from your body and dispelling any lingering illusions about who was really in charge.

He still sometimes felt a shaky vulnerability—an irrational fear that it could all get swept away in an instant. After almost losing Celle, he took not a single moment for granted.

Yet here they were. Healed and whole. Living an unimagined existence, with a brand-new family. Love and beauty, moving the world along, one heartbeat at a time.

Life had changed completely after Celle had fully recovered from the near-fatal spider bite. They had returned to the market to find the little boy who had saved her, to thank him properly and bring him a gift. He had been scantily clad in threadbare clothes, and Celle had brought him some Tatum T-shirts for kids—colourful designs that worked well among the vibrant rainbow fabrics worn by young Mexicans.

But the boy was nowhere to be seen. They went back to the old woman's fruit stall and asked her where her grandson was.

What grandson? She had no grandson. Only a too-busy daughter in Mexico City who rarely visited.

But the boy… Who was he? Was his family here? Did he live nearby?

The old woman had no answers. See Sallee, she said, in Sayulita.

After several more rounds of questioning, it became clear that Sallee was Sally Miggs—a Canadian who worked with a volunteer organization in Sayulita, caring for homeless and orphaned children. They should ask her if she knew where the boy was. Near the juice bar, she said, opposite the school. Look for the Amados sign.

Did she know his name, Celle had asked.

Migué, the old woman said. That was all she knew.

They hurried back up the hill, got the ZipV and drove to Sayulita as fast as they could. Celle was distraught, convinced now that the boy was homeless and might be gone for good, untraceable among the many orphans that hid out in the villages, scrounging for scraps and begging from the tourists. How could they not have realized this? They should have paid more attention when he saved her life. Instead, they had left him standing there and gone home to their nice house on the hill, oblivious to the boy's aloneness.

They found Amados down an alleyway beside the juice bar—a shack-of-an-office, with two desks, a phone, an arthritic ceiling fan, a middle-aged Mexican woman methodically typing on an old computer, and a smiling over-worked-looking young woman surrounded by a small thicket of skinny children, all talking and laughing at once.

Matt and Celle waited while the woman finished with the kids, finally ushering them out a back door to a kitchen in the alleyway where they would get lunch.

"Hi. I'm Sally. Can I help you?"

"I hope so," Celle said. "We're looking for a little boy called Migué, probably no more than 5 years old."

"Are you… family?"

"No, but we're concerned about him. He saved my life last week at the San Pancho market, when I was bitten by a spider, and we were trying to find him to thank him. But then we found out he's probably an orphan and…" She spread her hands. "We'd like to help him." She looked at Matt. He nodded. "Maybe give him a home." Her voice caught, eyes misting. Her heart wanted to jump out of her chest and take over the conversation. She suddenly realized how much she wanted to find this boy and love him the way he had fiercely loved her back to life.

Sally looked at them both, considering. "We help feed and clothe homeless kids and try to find family members, if they have any," she said, gesturing at the woman typing, "but we're not an adoption agency. You would have to go to the city, to Puerto Vallarta, for that."

Celle felt her shoulders slump. "But do you know the boy? Do you know where he might be?"

Sally hesitated, then suddenly smiled. "Yes," she said. "He's right behind you. We give him lunch every day and he just walked in."

They turned, and there he was. When he recognized Celle, his little brown face lit up in delight, and he ran to her, clasping her legs. "*Mujer araña*," he said, laughing. *Spider woman*. Celle thought her heart would burst with unbounded joy, and Matt was staring fixedly at the ceiling, eyes brimming and threatening to spill.

Four months later, after surprisingly little paperwork, thanks to the magic of Sally Miggs, Migué was their legally adopted son. Five months after that, their baby girl Surinaya was born… exactly nine months after Celle had got her life back.

Suri had instantly mastered the rules of life. Rule #1: Be happy. For now, she seemed content with that primary guiding principle, thrilled to have landed on Earth. Her little body thrummed with happiness, smiles creasing her plump cheeks, big blue eyes like whole planets looking right into your soul, and arms reaching for whatever they could grasp—hugs, hair, food or just thin air, for the sheer joy of flexing her brand-new digits.

She also knew how to enthusiastically take in food and then let it all go. Complete freedom of expression and expulsion, Celle said, laughing. They could sit and stare at her for hours—and sometimes did.

Migué loved her with a tenderness that made Celle's heart ache for the parents who had lost him, given him away or abandoned him, for whatever tragic reason.

Now, in the crisp new air of a March morning, Suri surfaced from her distant dreams, rediscovered her lungs and responded to the ancient call for sustenance, declaring her right to have an impact on the world.

Reaching for the tiny bawling body, Celle suddenly remembered something the spirit woman had told her when she almost died from the spider bite. *Your baby can come now.*

Just as the spider venom had been countered in her blood, the clenching of her ovaries had dissolved, the door to procreation swinging gently open once again.

As Suri sucked liquid life from her mother's breast, Celle was suffused with the interconnectedness of things, the indivisibility of life, the riches multiplied by a grateful heart.

LOVE x GRATITUDE x TRUTH surely formed the cubic footage of the cosmos.

91

April 2027

Nate was gently squeezing her shoulder. After a fragmented night, she was only lightly asleep, aware of the ridiculous dream she was having.

"What is it, Nate? Why did you wake me?"

"You were crying in your sleep."

"I was not. My eyes are completely dry."

"Well, it sounded as if you were crying, so I thought I'd do the caring-husband thing and wake you."

"I wasn't crying."

Nate was unfazed. "*And* you were talking in your sleep… something about the police."

"Are you sure *you* didn't dream this?"

Nate laughed. "What were you dreaming about, anyway?"

"There was this stupid swimming pool with only one length…"

"Aren't all pools only as long as they are long?"

"You could only swim one length—one *stroke*, I mean." She was still groggy.

"Are you sure you weren't just swimming across one length widthways and not down it, the long way?"

"No, Na*than*iel. It was square, only one stroke long in either direction."

"Except diagonally. You could have swum at least a stroke and a half that way…"

"It was just a stupid dream and I wouldn't even have remembered it if I hadn't been WOKEN UP."

"In future, I'll let you cry and moan and call for help in your sleep, even if it wakes ME up."

"Now I *know* you dreamt this. Nothing wakes you. And you're far too wide awake and chatty to have just woken up."

He grinned, obviously enjoying this.

"What does the dream mean? Symbolically."

"That we need a bigger house?"

"Why? We're the same number of people as when we moved in."

"But it feels smaller."

"Yeah, but so do your jeans."

Lucy swatted his shoulder.

Charlie laughed his maniac laugh in his room.

Lucy called out to him. "Would you stop beaming in to your parents' dream analysis?"

"I wasn't beaming. The whole neighbourhood can hear you. Marnie in Georgia can probably hear you."

"Ha. Very funny, the two of you."

"Is it nearly time for you to get my breakfast?" Nate asked sweetly.

"No more breakfasts. I'm on strike."

"You're never going to eat again?"

"Not after what you said about my jeans."

"You're still half-asleep, not thinking clearly. Those jeans have clearly shrunk. And I'd really love some of your Chorley Crunch with eggs…"

"Me, too! Nobody does it like you, Mum."

"What does a woman have to do around here to get some sleep?"

"Cook meals, do all the housework, run the business, care for the children… Just the usual stuff. What's the big deal?"

"Mum, maybe someone's going to have a *stroke*. Maybe that's what the dream is about."

"Yeah. Me, maybe, from being so sleep-deprived," Lucy said, although she didn't like to joke about illness.

"Dad, is it possible for someone to have a stroke because they didn't get a proper breakfast?"

"You know, Charlie, it *might* be. Have you thought of becoming a doctor when you grow up, next year?"

Charlie laughed. Then, in his best palm-reading voice: "*Mrs Cordalis, I see a malnourished child in your future...*"

"That does it. You two are going to go make breakfast and bring it up to me, the way loving husbands and children sometimes do, if they know what's *really* good for them."

"Dad, be careful."

"The boy has a point."

"Go."

"Charles, you heard your mother. Let's go."

Nate kissed her neck and whispered mock-menacingly, "I'll be back..."

"Come bearing food."

"I'll come baring something..."

Lucy laughed, rolling over and hugging the blankets around her.

Nate swung out of bed and pulled on his sweats. Charlie was already dressed and on the landing, bouncing on his toes, full of energy and loving every second of being the smartest kid in the house.

Mum, Lucy thought wistfully, *you missed this. You could have had this kind of fun with us when we were growing up.*

She couldn't communicate with the ghost of her mum the way Charlie could, although she was getting good at beaming with him. Nate was, too. But she and Nate hadn't mastered it between them yet, although that was fine with Lucy. No way did she ever want kissing or intimate stuff to be replaced by psychic beaming. Certain kinds of messages were definitely best transmitted the old-fashioned way.

And no one had yet invented Gravi*hugs*, which was probably just as well. Some things just weren't meant to be gravitated.

Lucy sighed and tried to sink back down into sleep. Too often, lately, her dreams took her back to Westfield, where she really didn't want to be. Now that they lived in Rhode Island, so much closer to where she had grown up, she was aware of Westfield's presence in the background. But she hadn't wanted to go back to see it, or even to visit Doug and Maisie, which would have meant driving past.

Even the stupid swimming-pool dream was better than being back there, with all those memories—all the more poignant now that she had her own family.

If only her parents could be here to share this with her. Then they *would* have fun together. *That* was a dream worth having... She dozed, dreaming that impossible dream, the sounds of love and laughter echoing up from the kitchen below.

92

May 2027

Marnie was still in shock after receiving Ray's message. It had taken her a while to access it as he had used an encryption process requiring her to log in to a protected site using two different passwords: her middle name, Astrid—*How the heck had he known that?*—and his wife's first name, Lily.

After years of no contact, she was hugely relieved to hear from him, but it had been devastating to read what he had been through.

He told her he had been working with three other scientists—a Russian and two Germans—developing the gravitational-wave telecom technology now being used worldwide. But they had been arrested by what Ray referred to as one of the *military acronyms*—CIA, FBI? Marnie wasn't sure—before they could launch the system they planned to roll out.

Marnie thought back. That must have been just after the newspaper article about him working with the Russians—the one she had clipped and packed in one of her boxes before leaving Boston.

The scientists were accused of scientific fraud, their research classified as *pseudoscienc*e in a civil court with zero scientific scrutiny or oversight. Despite letters of support and testimony from NASA and ESA scientists, as well as from the Russian Academic Society and other well-known international scientists, everything was rejected. The judgement against them was made *in absentia*.

Then they—whichever foul creatures *they* were, Marnie still couldn't tell—confiscated the scientists' computers, measuring instruments and prototypes, hijacked pending patents and put the four scientists together in a solid metal box measuring 8 cubic meters. There was no window, no sunlight, no exit. They were kept there for almost two years.

Tears streamed down her face as Marnie read this. It almost broke her heart to think of gentle Ray in such inhuman conditions—the man who had risked his life to create a healthier world—to *save* it, in fact. To think that humans could do such horrific things to each other to *prevent* progress, not preserve it. How was it possible for anyone to impose such cruelty, and for anyone to *survive* it? How had Ray tolerated it? Had he lost his mind, in those two years of hell? He sounded sane in his message, but she couldn't imagine what he must have endured.

Orthodox science was experiencing a deep crisis, Ray had said—not only physics, but also evolutionary biology, genetics and others. Although it wasn't really about the *science*, of course. It was about control, profit and power—all supported and enabled by an equally corrupt mainstream media.

It had abandoned the search for truth and instead became a major cog in the gearbox of global mass control. Not surprising, Ray had said, since mind control was relatively easy to maintain if everybody had the same model of reality, regardless of whether the model was valid or not.

This was before CEBS had really taken hold in the US, Ray told her, followed by the other frequencies that had boosted human creativity and innovation, while eroding the corruption that had been taking over the whole planet. He had been lucky.

Lucky? To survive? To hold on to his sanity after such torture? Marnie didn't think she could have survived it… or, if she had, if she could have lived with the memories of what she had been through.

He told her how two female scientists within the organization holding Ray captive didn't like what was happening. They came up with an elaborate plan to free Ray and his companions. By then, one of the four incarcerated scientists had died, from a combination of malnutrition, depression and claustrophobia. But the women had managed to get the other three out of the US and shipped to Europe, where Ray had remained until late 2023.

Sadly, my beautiful gracious Lily didn't make it, Ray had written. Over two years of stress and worry, not knowing where he was, whether he was alive or dead, or how to find out… It had been too much for her and her heart had simply stopped, shortly after he had escaped from prison. They had missed each other by a few weeks, and Ray had gone to a remote Greek island for two months to grieve in solitude.

Marnie hadn't cried this much since her parents died—maybe not even then, given how much more emotionally contained she'd been.

This was worse than *Dr Zhivago*, *The English Patient* and every other tragic love story she'd ever read. How could Ray have gone back to his work after this? How could he still *function*? His determination to bring down the wireless industry and corrupt governments must have kept him going. Maybe he'd also done it for Lily… and her mother? Marnie was convinced he'd been in love with her.

Sometimes she forgot how bad things used to be, when governments were doing such despicable things to their own people. Including Ray. Especially Ray. In the year before CEBS had hit, with governments bringing in draconian measures of control and violating so many civil and human rights, it was like waking up from a really bad, scary dream and then realizing it wasn't a dream at all.

She remembered how frustrated she had been when Ray had ceased contact. She felt petty, now. Humbled. Despite the horrors he'd suffered, he had still written to share his story and let her know he was okay. But was he still in danger? Was that why his message had been encrypted? Things were very different now, with Gravizone solidly in place, but perhaps there were still some who wished him harm for all the good he had done. *How twisted was that?* That was the world they used to live in. She prayed they never would again.

He hadn't been in Russia, he told Marnie. He had stayed in Western Europe for almost a year, working on the gravitational system in collaboration with a team of other enlightened scientists in Switzerland. They had finally launched the network in 2024, and the rest was history.

Marnie thought Ray sounded incredibly… *accepting* of what had happened. She couldn't imagine being even remotely reasonable after being tortured, and then getting right back to working on what had landed him in prison.

What matters now, Marnie, he had said in his message, is that we made it. We found a way through the insanity and we beat the bad guys.

This made her cry all over again. More than anything, she wanted to comfort him. Yet no words, no hugs, no tribute could ever be enough. What Ray had accomplished was as heroic and magnificent as the abuse he had survived was murderous.

People had no *idea* what this man had done for them.

93

"Marn, is it possible for things to get too good?" Lucy was having her weekly zone-in with Marnie.

"Too good in what way?" Marnie was still absorbing Ray's message, and it had taken her a while to switch back into positive new-world mode. She doubted Ray could imagine things getting too good, after all he'd lost.

"Well, you know how everyone used to love drama, shock and gore and horror stories, and people would stop to gawk at accidents on the street. Good news was boring and didn't get half as much airtime."

"You're thinking we'll get tired of all this good stuff when the novelty wears off?"

"Yeah. Won't we? Sometimes I wonder if it's just... too good to be true, you know?"

"Are *you* getting bored with it? Are you tired of Charlie being so smart or your life being so good?"

"No. I love it... mostly. I was just wondering about the way humans are... or *used* to be. I guess I'm afraid some bad guys will come along and decide this isn't the way they want things." Lucy paused, trying to sort out new truth from old fear.

"Luce, you remember we used to say we couldn't believe people could do such awful things to each other. More and more awful stuff was happening and we kept thinking it couldn't get any worse, but it did. And then CEBS..."

"Yeah."

"But all those things happened because of what had been lost along the way."

"And now we're getting that back...?"

"Mostly. We're still working on it but we've regained enough to want to keep going. I don't think we'll ever go back to that old way, and there are enough people now doing amazing things that the good is greater than the dark stuff."

"Things were really going down the tubes before, weren't they, Marn."

"They sure were. Most people couldn't see it, but we couldn't have gone on like that for much longer. The whole tech takeover thing, with governments using scare tactics and viruses to take control over people's lives… we weren't heading in a good direction."

"Thank God for CEBS, then. I don't know where we'd be if that hadn't happened."

Marnie had a pretty good idea, given the way things had been going with the wireless industry, corruption, climate change and all the other seemingly unstoppable scavengers.

"I have a feeling there's something else on your mind, Luce."

Lucy smiled. Marnie knew her so well. "I'm wondering… How good can things get? And how good can we *stand* it?"

"Well, we kept thinking the bad stuff couldn't get any worse, but it did. I think we have the same potential in the other direction."

"We can't imagine things getting any better but they do…"

"Yes, and we're using so much more of our brains, Luce. You know that, and look at Charlie."

"Yeah, I know. He's amazing."

"But we *all* are. That's the thing. We're so much more switched-on now. We're wiser and more connected to everything. And that connection matters more because we feel it more deeply."

Lucy nodded, reassured. "Yeah. And we feel each *other* more deeply, so we'd be much more affected if we treated each other badly now." She still found it amazing how fast things had evolved. Maybe that was part of what scared her, the sheer speed of things.

"We used to be so numbed out that we over-stimulated just to *feel* something, with comfort foods or drugs or social media. But now we really feel things, so that old toxic stuff would feel kind of shocking and awful, wouldn't it?

"It just wouldn't fit any more. There'd be no place for it. Who would want it?"

"Well, bad guys, somewhere…"

"Luce, they're outnumbered now. Stop worrying. I really don't think that will happen. I'm seeing so many really smart, wise kids at school— and parents. Delsie's seeing the same thing with her clients, right? And you're both documenting all this stuff. So you know it's happening everywhere."

"Yeah. I forget sometimes that this is how things are *meant* to be, and that the old way was totally unnatural."

"I know. Imagine six years ago telling people that life would be this way. They'd have laughed at you. They wouldn't have understood it or even wanted it. They were so fixated on their wireless gadgets that they probably couldn't have imagined loving this kind of living. It would have sounded utopian and… just plain unrealistic."

"That's what Delsie says. There was so much emotional crap in the way before CEBS came along. People wouldn't have been able to relate to all this highly evolved stuff."

"Exactly. But so much junk has been cleared off the human slate and we're going in a whole new direction that no one could have envisaged."

"It's almost like going back to childhood, isn't it?" Lucy said. "And kids are leading the way, showing us how much they can grow and learn in the right environment."

"I just *love* that," Marnie said. "I see how open and receptive the kids are when their brain power and creativity are not suppressed or hijacked by all that negative conditioning."

Lucy had recently had a similar conversation with Charlie. She had been thinking about how smart he was and how Delsie's young clients were evolving in similarly spectacular ways—but also facing some challenges because they were still in the minority, and those taking care of them were usually less smart than the kids themselves.

"Maybe kids are getting smart too early in their lives," she had said to Charlie, "before they have a chance to sort of adapt to normal life."

"Normal life?" Charlie scoffed. "Who wants *normal*? When do you think people get smart? When they get older and are told what to think and believe?"

"Mmmm… good point."

"And the answer to that unasked question is *no*," Charlie said.

"What question?"

"*Is it possible to be too smart for your own good.* If you think that, then you're not quite smart enough."

Lucy shared this with Marnie.

"So, according to Charlie, you're not smart enough. Is *that* what you're worried about?"

"Yeah. Maybe."

"Luce, smart kids can be manipulative, without even realizing it.

Their brains are so sharp that they say stuff they may not mean or even fully understand. It just comes out because it's clever. You can't take it on and let it mean something negative about you."

"But how to respond to it, Marn? That's the thing. I don't feel smart enough to deal with him telling me I'm not smart enough."

Marnie laughed. "Yeah. I hear you. But you are. I've seen the way you are with him and you're brilliant. Don't let his smartness intimidate you, okay? Enjoy him but hold on to who you are and enjoy that, too. Otherwise, there's no point to any of it."

"Yeah. Okay. Thanks."

"Remember what you used to tell *me* to do, back in the old days?"

"Lots, probably, given what I bossy brat I was, growing up."

"Yeah, you were a brat, but it fueled your creativity and it kept you rebellious and *unboxable*. You always used to tell me to *lighten up*! That's what you need to do now, Luce. It's an exciting time to be alive, and you can have a lot of fun with Charlie if you don't take him or yourself too seriously."

"Thanks, Marn. I needed that. Grav ya later!"

94

June 2027

Lucy had to laugh—or would, when she calmed down. After all she'd said to Marnie about things being almost too good to be true... She was getting a graphic reminder that there would always be challenges to tone her emotional muscles.

As if the very existence of Charlie weren't challenge enough. Today, he was being about as bratty as a child could be, having one of his rare tantrums, refusing to tidy his room, make his bed or do anything he was told to do.

"It's pointless! I'll be going back to bed in a few hours. This is just one of those stupid rules adults make so they feel in control of things." He had then flung things around his room, yanking clothes out of drawers and throwing them on the floor, demonstrating just how out of control he was.

"Just because you have an amazing brain doesn't mean you can do whatever the hell you want," Lucy said, feeling furiously impotent.

"You're having a hormonal moment."

"Don't you *dare* talk to me as if I'm some hormonal *event*."

He looked at her.

"Even if I am being bitchy."

Charlie made a valiant attempt not to grin.

"Are you turning into a smug, obnoxious brat?"

"No. I think I was born that way. Maybe it runs in the family."

"If it runs in the family, then you've finally met your match, Buster, because I've had a lot more practice than you."

"Duh…"

"Don't get sassy-smart with me, Charlie." She took a breath to clear her head and remind herself who was boss. "Go upstairs. Clean up your room and don't come out until it's done."

"Or what?"

"Or your privileges will be revoked."

"What privileges?"

"Basic stuff. Life on earth, food, shelter—that kind of thing."

He looked at her, deadpan. *What was she going to do, put him out on the street?*

"Listen, kiddo, we give you a lot of leeway because you're so smart. If you abuse that, then I guess we misjudged you, thinking you were decent too… but I guess I sometimes forget you *are* just a kid. And kids sometimes have tantrums."

"*You're* the one having a tantrum," Charlie shouted, glaring at her defiantly. Despite his tender heart, he had a temper like a rabid dog.

Lucy sighed. What *were* the rules, anyway? She'd never even known the old ones before becoming a mother in this whole new world where every convention had been tossed out the window and you just made things up as you went along. That was the beauty and freedom of creativity, but it could sometimes turn parenting into a game of chess where the best players were your own kids. With Charlie, it could feel like checkmate before she even knew it was her turn to make a move.

"Go to your room. Now. And stay out of my head till I say you can come back in."

Fuming, Charlie stomped off, reminding Lucy of the way she had behaved when her parents had had the audacity to die and abandon her, taking all their money and her college fund with them.

Maybe she and Nate had spoiled Charlie by giving him too much freedom before he knew what that really meant. Catering to his intelligence wasn't doing him or them any favours.

She yelled up the stairs after him. "And act your age. You're behaving like a rebellious teenager." She wasn't sure, but she thought that generated a smile.

She discussed it that evening with Nate, who had been out when the meltdown happened.

"How do we discipline him when he's like that and has an answer for everything?"

"Just treat him like the kid he is, Luce. He needs discipline. Maybe he isn't getting enough of it and we need to impose more boundaries."

"I don't like the way I sounded or the way I handled it."

"I'm sure you handled it just fine."

"Maybe he needs more time with his dad," Lucy said, realizing the truth of that as she said it. "He hardly sees you during the day when you're working, and you go very easy on him when you do spend time together. Which means I'm always the bad guy."

"Yeah." Nate sighed. "You're right. I need to take a firmer hand and not leave it all up to you. Why don't I take him camping this weekend?"

"Great idea!" She'd have the whole weekend to herself, which suddenly seemed acutely appealing. "You can teach him to fish, put up the tent, cook on the campfire, paddle a canoe... all physical stuff that will get him out of his head."

"We'll go on Friday afternoon and come back Sunday," Nate said, nodding. "You'll be okay here with Fargo?"

"Of course. You can't take her fishing with you."

In January, they had finally decided to get another dog and had gone to the pound to find one in need of a loving home. As they had walked between the wired enclosures, looking at the chaotic assortment of dejected animals, they'd all stopped when they saw Fargo. Lucy thought she had never seen a more mournful, heart-rending *what-took-you-so-long* look than the one on this beautiful little face.

"That's the one," Charlie said. Lucy felt a twinge of annoyance at him pre-empting her own sense of rightness about this dog, which felt like hers, even before they took her home.

As far as Lucy could see, Fargo was a cross between a Spaniel, a

Collie and a hyena. She seemed to find everything hilariously funny, grinning non-stop. She was also a very handy foot-furnace, plonking herself down on Lucy's feet whenever Lucy sat down or even remained standing in one place for more than a few minutes.

So, no. Fargo would not be going camping with Nate and Charlie.

Lucy saw them off at the door, armed with fishing rods, knapsacks, food rations, water canisters and other survival equipment, the tent and sleeping bags already packed in the back of the Swave. It was the first time Charlie had gone away without her and she couldn't help worrying.

"Have you got thick sweaters and socks in case it gets cold at night?"

"Mum, don't worry," Charlie said. "Nothing will happen to Dad. I'll take really good care of him for you."

Nate grabbed him around the waist and hauled him out to the car, both of them laughing like maniacs.

Lucy watched them from the doorway, piling their gear into the trunk, then Charlie climbing into the passenger seat and slamming the door.

Nate tapped on his window, making a time-out signal with his hands, and bounded back up the path to Lucy.

"I need to tell you something before we go."

"You're not coming back?"

"Of course we're coming back."

"Is it *private*?" Lucy gestured towards the Swave. Charlie was making faces at them through the window.

"Yes. I already told him to stay out till we'd finished talking." Nate put his hands on her shoulders, looking at her intently. "Anyway, listen. You're using him."

"What do you mean, *using him*?!" Lucy was hotly indignant. "My days are *consumed* by him, while you're out taking care of business and doing whatever you want."

"Exactly. All your focus is on him, not you. I know you're also handling orders and keeping track of Tate, but that's not *your* stuff, Lucy. Those are not *your* creations. You need to find something that feeds you and enables you to evolve, rather than giving all your energies and focus to Charlie and using him as a legitimate excuse for not doing something more daring yourself."

"*You're* just working on the business too."

"Yes, but I don't have the same creative drive as you."

"Why did I marry you, then?" Lucy was suddenly feeling childishly petulant. Definitely more practised than Charlie.

"Now you're using *me*." He held up his hand as she started to object, arms tightly folded across her chest, glaring at him. "Don't make this about me or Charlie. This is about you finding your own creative fulfillment. Get back to your writing. You haven't done any for ages."

"I'm tired of writing. I did enough of that in the old business. I don't think I want to be a writer, anyway. I'm not that good."

Nate folded his arms, looking at her pointedly. "When are you going to give that up?

"Give what up?"

"All those put-downs that you trot out when your insecurity is triggered. Where did you get that stuff, anyway? Surely not from your parents."

"No. I probably came up with them myself, given how *creative* I am, maybe based on them not being there for me or making me feel important in their lives." She knew she was being a bitch, and she had promised Charlie she would love herself more, but she couldn't seem to help herself.

"Doesn't matter. Your writing is a doorway. You know how it works. You start flexing one creative muscle and it wakes up the others that have been waiting for you to show up."

"Dad! Let's go!" Charlie was getting impatient.

"Hang on!"

Nate turned back to Lucy. "I'm going to spend more time with Charlie—do this kind of thing more often, so you have time to yourself. Okay? You were right. He needs this and so do you." He kissed her pouty lips. "And so do I." He gave her a bear hug, then turned and jogged down the path before she could say another word.

Shit. Lucy felt blindsided and naked. Angry and resentful. How *dare* he say she was using Charlie… *or* him! What a load of crap. She had never been so creatively challenged with anything, having to deal with a genius 5-year-old every single day, trying to find ways to keep him engaged, stay on top of everything and keep herself sane. Nate had no idea how much energy and ingenuity it took.

She took a grudging breath. Hadn't he just said that? *Exactly*, she could hear him say. She needed to put some of that energy and ingenuity into her own life, rather than investing it all in Charlie.

Another breath, anger still percolating.

She *had* felt a burst of freedom at the prospect of having the whole weekend to herself. But freedom to do what? What did that mean?

Do some writing, he had said. She bristled with resistance. She was documenting Charlie's evolution for Delsie, and they had discussed writing a book together about gifted kids. But that didn't really feel like a project for *her*—just another branch of the massive Charlie tree that had become rooted in her life, demanding constant pruning and cultivation.

She cleaned up the kitchen, banging things around and slamming cupboard doors as an outlet for her frustration. But it was giving her a headache, so she stopped. Why was she so angry? Because Nate was right? Because she felt unfulfilled? Because she resented Charlie for eclipsing her? Was she *jealous?* That was a tough one to acknowledge, but it struck a clanging chord.

She imagined Delsie saying she was beating herself up for not loving herself more, which made her smile.

She wiped down the countertop and looked out the kitchen window. Sun, trees, nature, silence. Writing. A doorway.

She remembered when she had first started writing, shortly before Nate showed up on Marnie's doorstep. It had been fun. Pure nonsense, but certainly creative. That digi radiation stuff she had written about… sounding like Marnie—maybe even *channelling* Marnie. None of that was really *her*, Lucy. Was that something to play around with? Letting the words come to her from the ethers, not thinking about them or researching them the way she used to for those business blogs she wrote?

Okay. She would write. Stream of consciousness stuff. No agenda. She looked around for inspiration but nothing grabbed her. How to get started… Her gaze settled on Gwen, sitting on the countertop. Okay. She would get the latest news and whatever showed up on her screen she would write about. Just as a launching pad. Nothing to do with reality, logic or what was going on in the world, unless that somehow showed up in some creative way.

She needed some paper and a pen—things she rarely used now, with almost everything done in the Gravizone. She ran upstairs, rummaged in the drawers in Nate's office and found an unused writing pad. More rummaging yielded a nice dark pencil and a pen, like items stolen from a museum.

Back downstairs and into the living room, picking Gwen up along the way, with Fargo hot on her heels, curious about this sudden burst of energy.

She sat down at the table, writing pad in front of her and Gwen to one side. She did a few wild squiggles to check that the pen worked. Yes. No more stalling. Fargo settled herself on Lucy's feet and let out a big sigh of contentment. It always made Lucy think of brooding hens, as if her feet with little chickens being protected until they were big enough to go out into the world on their own.

Lucy closed her eyes and beamed a request for the latest news to come up on Gwen. Keeping her eyes closed, she waited for the screen to settle. A tiny *ping!* as some text and images floated up. She opened her eyes and looked.

Pope declares the Vatican is being turned into a university for spiritual enlightenment—like the old mystery schools of Ancient Egypt. Tuition and accommodation free to citizens from all over the world.

Holy shit. That was courageous. Inspiring in itself. The Vatican City… *a uni campus.*

She zoned off and sat back.

What would courageous look like for her? *What did loving herself mean?* What did she want? She'd lost track of her own dreams, subsumed by what Tate was doing. The business no longer gave her a buzz, she realized. Not like before.

She could do with some enlightenment. The Pope had the right idea. Was he still the Pope? Had he stood down or did he now stand for something else? Her mental cogs starting whirring… POPE: *Promotion of Planetary Enlightenment?* That put a new spin on things.

Lucy had no time for religion. People often argued that it did a lot of good in the world. But it was *people* who did the good, not the religion itself, although sometimes even the do-gooders didn't see that. The guy was right. They were better off without it.

She started scribbling.

The world is hopeless till it's popeless. Out with popery and pot pourri. Both smell incensed.

It was silly and irreverent but she had become far too serious, worrying about Charlie and running the business. And what did irreverent *mean,* anyway. What did it matter? It was just thoughts in her head that didn't offend anyone. Offence was just another made-up concept, anyway—a way of controlling things and keeping people in order, telling them they couldn't say or even think certain things.

Where was the freedom in that? How could you have free speech if you didn't have free thought? How could anyone exercise their right to free speech if their minds had already been programmed with someone else's thoughts and beliefs?

Lucy believed religion was the biggest programmer ever—the biggest *scam* ever. And dissolving the Church had caused the biggest *scandal* ever. Ever since the Pope had made his shocking announcement just before Christmas last year, Catholics everywhere had been reacting with every emotion on the human spectrum.

She started scribbling again.

This has opened up a whole new vati-can of worms. And those worms are wriggling all over the place, with bishops, archbishops, priests, nuns and every other rung of the religious ladder running for the hills or pretending they have never been anything but saintly all along, and the Pope has lost his marbles.

But that wasn't going to work. And people's reactions often said more about them than about religion itself. What did hers say about her? That she still had a free-thinking mind?

More random scribbling.

Can we not live licentiously, taking popetic licence? Shame and sin were never in our nature ...until they were papally implanted. Sexercise your rights! They should never have been sexorcised in the first place.

Fuck. That triggered something inside her...

Fargo looked up. *Walk? Did someone say* walk?

"No. I said *fuck!* Not walk."

Fargo grinned, ears perked. *Someone definitely said* walk.

Sexorcised. What was that about? Had she been *sexorised*? Whatever the hell that meant. Something about her rights... This was touching something deep in her core—something that had been covered up when she got married and immediately became a mother.

They were living such different lives now, in this world of infinite possibilities and self-determination, where you could be whatever you wanted to be. Before, there had been pressure to succeed; now, success was defined more in terms of how much *good* you were doing for the world, rather than how *well* you were doing for yourself.

People seemed more inherently driven in a positive direction. She could feel it in herself—the urge to be good, do good *and* do well.

Yet even that had its constraints. In that context of greater goodness, was it still okay to do something… *naughty?*

Malice in wonderland.

Was that even possible in this wondrous new world? It sounded deliciously tantalizing, sending a tingling *frisson* down her spine. But why? Had she lost something along the way?

She loved her life. Right? *Right?*

Fuck.

Fargo raised her eyebrows. "Okay. Walk. Let's go."

Fargo shot like a bullet into the hallway, screeching to a halt at the front door.

Lucy followed more slowly, pulling on a light jacket and taking Fargo's leash from a hook on the wall.

They would walk to the park, then maybe she'd go for lunch somewhere. She couldn't remember the last time she had done that on her own. Had she ever?

Fargo needed no encouragement or direction. She seemed to know exactly where they were going—or she had already decided and it just happened to coincide with where Lucy was going.

Lucy didn't put her on the leash unless there were other dogs around or a lot of traffic. Right now, there was none of either, so Fargo could roam free.

They walked to the park and did the full circuit, Lucy walking fast and Fargo covering twice the mileage with her zigzagging reconnaissance of every bush and park bench.

Still pondering the muddled feelings stirred up by her writing, Lucy wasn't ready to go back home. But she needed to drop Fargo off if she was going to get lunch somewhere. They walked back to the house and Lucy gave Fargo some fresh water and one of her favourite doggie snacks. After wolfing it down, Fargo flopped into her basket, did her usual slow pirouette, then settled down.

Lucy got her pen and notepad from the living room, shoved them into her cream shoulder bag—the one Marnie had given her years ago, now looking battered, the leather cracked in places, but still her favourite—along with her keys, wallet and a bottle of water, and went out, pulling the door firmly closed behind her.

95

She was hungry and decided to go to the Edgy Café, to treat herself to an elaborate lunch. As she walked, she was aware of feeling different, lighter—excited about something *indefinable*. Was it simply that Charlie was not around, intruding into her thoughts, demanding her attention even if it was just because he was there, a powerful presence that was hard to ignore? Or was it the sense of freedom, the fact that she had time to herself and could do whatever she felt like doing, for two whole days?

She had told Charlie that this weekend was *private* time for her and she needed a break, without him beaming at her or trying to pick up on her thoughts. He had promised to stay out, although she was getting good at making those mental boundaries herself, usually able to block intrusions if she wanted quiet headspace.

It was 11.45 and the café was gearing up for the lunch crowd. Lucy chose a table against the wall, facing the window, and settled down with a menu to see what looked good. A zippy young male waiter brought her a glass of water, then stood poised to take her order.

She opted for the homemade curried onion soup, grilled chicken with roasted veggies and… what the hell, a glass of red wine. Pinot Noir, room temperature.

Then she settled back to people-watch as her mind continued sifting through her swirling emotions. She had triggered something important, although she sensed a part of her not wanting to dig any deeper, afraid of what she might find if she allowed herself full access.

The waiter brought her wine and she took a few savouring sips, the alcohol opening up her throat and warming her chest. She was about to pull out her notepad and jot down more thoughts, when she spotted someone who looked vaguely familiar. Standing near the door was a tall guy in jeans and a multi-coloured shirt, with tousled brown hair, quizzical eyebrows and a five-o-clock shadow framing a square jaw and a generous smiling mouth. Something about him…

He was looking around the room—looking for someone or maybe deciding where to sit—when his eyes lit on Lucy. His look hit her like a wallop in the stomach. Holy shit. It was that hunk… Stefan *somebody,* from high school. She couldn't remember his last name, and it had to be eight or nine years since she'd last seen him, but it was definitely him.

He seemed to recognize her, too. After a moment's hesitation, he headed for her table, his long legs delivering the full package in just a few economical strides.

"Lucy Dalton," he said, smiling. "I thought it was you. How the hell are you?"

She smiled back. "Stefan…" Then shrugged an apology. "Sorry, I can't remember your last name."

"Mansfield," he said. He gestured at the vacant chair on the other side of her table. "Are you waiting for someone? May I join you?"

"No. Yes." She laughed. "I'm eating alone, but you're welcome to join me."

The waiter arrived with her soup.

"Same for me, please," Stefan said, pointing at the steaming bowl. He pulled out the chair and sat down, long legs splayed to either side of the table.

"Lucy Dalton and Delsie Roman. I remember you two. And another girl you used to hang out with… What was her name…?"

"Sherry Merickson?"

"Yeah! The infamous trio, always driving the guys wild with your stunning outfits and badass behaviour." He grinned, remembering. "Hey, listen, eat your soup before it gets cold."

"I will. I'm ravenous." She started on her soup. "Funny you should mention Sherry. She moved to Canada straight after high school and we lost touch, till just recently." Lucy paused, wondering how much to say. "She's… making a name for herself in Vancouver." *A new name for herself.* But Lucy didn't feel like sharing *shermer,* right now. "She was in Vancouver when CEBS hit, and she's not the girl you remember. She's done some pretty radical stuff."

Lucy spooned down more soup. "Delsie got CEBSed too, in

Washington. She and I have stayed in regular contact." She took another few mouthfuls, enjoying the spicy warmth, glad of the distraction. "Tell me about you. What have you been up to in the past eight years?"

"I'm a sculptor," he said, looking quite proud of himself. "I have a small studio here in Cranston."

"What kind of sculptor? Stone, wood... um, metal?" Lucy wasn't sure what other things were *sculptable*.

Stefan explained that he worked with all kinds of media, sculpting stone and wood, as well as creating things out of *papier mâché*, glass, metal, acrylic and fabrics.

"I'm more of a 3D artist," he said, "using whatever materials I can find that present possibilities for something creative and powerful to come out of them."

He seemed to look at her very pointedly when he said that, and Lucy felt things stirring that should not have been stirring... apart from her soupspoon. Stefan was a seriously good-looking guy, although she remembered him being very full of himself in high school, fully expecting girls to swoon over him, which they did.

But it was *normal* to respond to beauty and sexiness, wasn't it? And unhealthy to suppress it, surely.

Did she still respond to Nate this way? Yes, of course she did.

She went back to her soup, Stefan explaining about his studio and a show he was having at the end of the summer.

"Come and take a look," he said. "When we've finished eating, I'll take you down there and show you some of my work, if you've got time." He cocked his head invitingly, as if this was an offer no one would refuse.

Was that the only issue—whether she had *time*? What about what she *wanted*? And what would happen if she said *yes*?

Her body seemed to have some creative ideas about what could happen, and it probably involved a bit more than looking at his *work*. She was pretty sure that this was *not* what Nate had in mind when he encouraged her to find her own source of creative fulfillment. Not that she needed his permission...

Time slowed for this pivotal moment, the world a freeze-frame around her. She should say *no*. But why? And what would she be saying no *to*, beyond the invitation itself? What had she been saying no to that had taken her to this point, where even talking to an old high-school friend set her whole body thrumming with expectant delight and a yearning for some kind of freedom or release?

She had a sudden stunning realization. It wasn't Charlie she resented. It was Nate. He didn't behave like Charlie's dad and he had treated her differently since Charlie was born. But why? Was that her fault or his? Was it just the powerful existence of Charlie between them?

Sexorcize your rights… why had that struck her so deeply? They were her words but she wasn't sure what she had meant by them.

Stefan was saying something, looking at her quizzically. "Lucy? Are you okay?"

She put down her spoon and looked him in the eye. "Stefan, what do you see when you look at me? I'm not talking about my looks. I mean *me*. What do you see? Be honest. No flattery."

He sat up straighter, taken aback by this deep question and the seriousness behind it. Yet he seemed to expand as he considered his response, aware that this was not a woman fishing for compliments.

"I see a woman on the cusp of self-ownership—beautiful, creative and powerful, but not fully allowing herself to decide what *she* really wants," he said, seeming surprised to hear such words escaping his own mouth. "A few moments ago, I thought this woman would accept my invitation to see my work and maybe more…" He grinned sheepishly, admitting his agenda now that it was so clearly unacceptable.

He leaned in for closer scrutiny. "I see a woman grappling with some inner conflict—something certain unscrupulous men could take advantage of—but she's already on the right side of that choice, without even realizing it."

He sounds like a fortune-teller, Lucy thought, with a wry smile of surprise. *A pretty good one.*

He leaned back, pleased with himself. "How did I do?"

Good old Stefan, always making it about himself even if it was about someone else.

"You nailed it," she said. "Thank you. I needed to hear that."

"I'm not sure you did, but maybe I needed to hear myself say it." He grimaced. "I'm sorry, Lucy. I insulted you, proposing such a thing, and I should know better, since I make a living from looking at things up close. When I really looked at you, I could see exactly who you are, and that alone is enough to put a man in his place." He shrugged gamely. "Forgiven?"

"Yes." The high-school jock bearing enlightenment, no sex required. Who'd have thunk it?

The zippy young waiter appeared with Stefan's soup and her main course.

"I need to go," she told the waiter. "Would you mind boxing that up for me to take home?"

"No problem," said zippy. "I'll leave it at the front desk for you. Pick it up when you pay."

This was one of the things she liked about The Edgy. They kept things personal. She could have paid via Gravizone, from her table, but the management liked to get direct feedback from their patrons so they could right any culinary wrongs before people left.

Stefan looked disappointed. *He'll get over it,* Lucy mused, her brain suddenly on fire with ideas, for the book—*her* book, the book she needed to write for herself, *about* herself. *Ownership.* Yes. She got it now.

96

January 2028

Newswordz book editor Gloria Winston interviews Lucy Dalton, author of the bestselling *A Gifted Presence,* awarded Gravi Book of the Year: for books that jump out and Grav you. Now available via Gravizone and all the usual outlets.

GW: Your book is about parenting gifted children, yet it seems to have struck a chord with many adult readers, parents and non-parents alike. Why do you think that is?

LD: Our world has evolved so much, so fast, that many adults need self-parenting to deal with all the shifts. And parenting our offspring is not just about raising a child. It's about raising our own awareness of what it means to be human and what becomes possible when we embrace greater potentials—our own and our child's. A gifted child—and *every* child is gifted—is a living, pulsing, demanding reminder of our own giftedness and of the need to treat ourselves and our children as the miracles we all are. The more we do that, the more our gifts flourish, in tandem with anyone else who shares our journey.

GW: What does it mean to be *gifted*? Since 2020, following CEBS and the other transformative frequencies, many of us have evolved emotionally, spiritually and in other ways. But what is the purpose of expanded awareness or any kind of spiritual/psychic capacity?

LD: Human evolution is the push towards cosmic consciousness, which might sound other-worldly, but is really the quest for the highest expression of love, which is ultimately union—joining with others in the experience of self-reflection and the non-self of oneness, the unifield. We are *all* in the midst of this cosmic comeback. Treating a child as especially gifted separates us, setting him or her on a pedestal of exceptionality that divides rather than uniting that which is trying to come together on a higher plane of co-creation and understanding.

GW: So gifted children are as much about the parents as the children themselves…

LD: Yes, and sometimes it is *more* about the parents, who may have needed that child to come into their lives to wake them up to their own dormant or neglected capacities.

GW: You talk in the book about parents' insecurities and some of the challenges they face.

LD: One of the biggest challenges is the insecurities that often surface for parents, relative to their child. But this is a distortion of a deeper truth. It is not about them at all, yet it is entirely about them, but not in the way they might think.

The insecurities are an expression of a duality seeking to expose itself so it can be dissolved. But if parents focus on the child, while denying their own insecurities, the gift of that child will be only partially unwrapped. It will never be fully shared, enjoyed or used to its fullest measure. It may instead become a burden borne by parents who suppress their own yearnings in favour of their child's, thereby losing sight of what the gift represents, while also having an increasingly difficult time dealing with that thwarted gift, as the child's energies get diverted.

The insecurities are therefore a projection, with parents potentially seeing themselves as *less than* their offspring. In reality, it is a rejection of both parties—child and parent—with the duality polarizing them, pushing them away from each other, rather than serving as a magnet that draws them into union, their two parts making a greater whole that could not otherwise have come into being.

GW: So the child *is* the gift. I think most parents would agree with this anyway.

LD: The child is the gift parents give themselves to take them to a higher place—a kind of higher self-parenting that occurs in parallel with the parenting of their child. So it's not just about cultivating that giftedness and helping that child be all that he/she can be. It's about going on that journey with them and understanding that the brilliance has come from somewhere deep within *themselves* and is now seeking a more direct outward expression through the pure channel of a child without filters, blocks or blinders limiting or inhibiting their perception.

In the simplest sense, our children enable us to know and love ourselves enough to activate and engage all our faculties. If we don't do that and live fully, we may project onto them the things we were not brave enough to do ourselves, distorting their path just as our own was distorted—by ourselves or someone else.

GW: That's not a new concept—projecting our failed dreams onto our children.

LD: No, it's not. What may be a little more illuminating is the concept of using them to keep ourselves stuck, then blaming them if they fail to live up to our expectations, rejecting them for seemingly rejecting our 'support', and then resenting the whole world later in life when we feel unfulfilled. In reality, rejecting our own giftedness is ultimately a rejection of our child, and vice versa. The real tragedy is that we tell children what they are, what they can or can't do and how the world works, based on our own limited experience, which is *always* far less than our true potential.

GW: Why do we use other people to keep ourselves small?

LD: Because someone else diminished us before we became aware of our own genius, and we believed their distorted version of things. As a result, many of us subconsciously fear our greatness, and never get to see what that might look like. But this new generation of children represents our way back to self. We are living in a time when the heart is resuming its primacy over the head, which is where it has always been physically, but not existentially. And there are few things as powerful or wonderful as children for bringing us back into our hearts.

Evolution and personal growth can seem like serious stuff, whereas children bring playful curiosity to every fresh experience of the world. This is what parents (and all adults) can most benefit from—allowing themselves to return to a child-like innocence with their children.

Being responsible for that little person's well-being, safety and development can feel daunting, so it's easy to forget to have fun, to wonder, to dive deeply into our imagination. Yet that is precisely what we need to cultivate in our children and in ourselves, because that is where all creation begins.

Children are catalysts for collective change, not a project to be worked on. They are greater than the sum of their two parents—the best of both parties and a reminder of what we originally fell in love with, in our partner, in life and in ourselves.

GW: So parenting is for everyone, not just parents.

LD: Yes. Parenting is another word for leadership, and all children—our own, someone else's or the child inside us—are beacons shining into our dark scary corners. We can dump our fears and insecurities onto them, projecting our inadequacies and pulling them down into our discomfort zone, or we can see their precious innocence as an invitation to co-creatorship. Our role is not to contain them, but to act as cosmic condiments, drawing out their essential flavour so they become the exquisite, fully realized beings that they can be, far beyond our own imaginings.

Self-parenting should continue till the day we die, because we never want to lose that inner child. Innocence is what keeps us hungrily human, seeking the next new wonder, the deeper layer of inner treasure waiting to be unearthed. That is the gift we give ourselves, and only then can we give it to others.

GW: The gifted presence…

LD: Yes, *our* gifted presence, enriching our world, then everyone else's—the pay-it-forward, play-it-forward, never-ending snowballing of self-love.

PART 4

97

The day reached her slowly as Lucy woke, stretching languidly and wondering for a moment where she was… and when. Then a happy dawning smile claimed her face, spreading to her eyes and reminding her brain. It was Saturday, their special weekend, celebrating Charlie's seventh birthday tomorrow, with family and close friends coming from all over.

Steve, Marnie and Mella were coming up from Jacksonville. Matt, Celle, Migué and Suri were flying up from Mexico—Matt's first time back in the States since he left in late 2019. He'd see some changes.

Delsie was driving down from Washington, DC tomorrow. And Sherry! Flying down from Vancouver. Lucy hadn't seen her since their high-school graduation. Nine years ago. A lifetime. What a blast it would be for the three of them to be together again, after all this time. They'd all changed so much, in a world that had completely transformed. Lucy barely recognized *herself.*

Marnie had also invited her friend DeeDee, who she was hoping would come without the family so they could catch up on their own.

After some time apart, Troy and Annamae were once again a solid couple and would be coming with the twins, Chess and Susie, for the main event on Sunday.

Tate was attending a design conference in Stockholm but would be visiting when he got back next week. And Nate's parents, Nancy and Brandon, were in Europe for a month—a trip planned a year ago.

If everyone else showed up, there were be… Lucy kept losing count. Close to 20, which was about all they could comfortably handle, although everyone would chip in to help.

She opened her eyes, lists unfolding in her mind. Nate was lying on his side facing her, smiling at her whirring thoughts.

"It's going to be a hectic two days," he said. "Stay for a few peaceful minutes."

She moved into his arms, her head on his shoulder, and sighed.

Heady happs, Charlie beamed at her from his bedroom. *Yes, sweetie. This is your special weekend. Starting shortly.* He beamed back his grin.

PRIVATE she whispered in her mind.

Yeah, Mum. I'll go get started on breakfast.

She sent him a virtual kiss, then leaned in to Nate for a real one. Since that very first kiss in the kitchen of Nate's Boston townhouse, as he prepared his famous *achiote* chicken, Lucy had felt an electrical connection. It was still there but now there was something deeper—a full-body fusion that went right down through her core. She felt possessed and adored by him, yet also fully possessed of herself and loving how that felt.

Nate ran his hand up her spine and through her hair, cupping her head and pulling her closer, his body still as lean and muscled and gorgeous as ever. Lucy wrapped her arms around his neck, hooking a leg over his thighs and feeling his hardness against her as his heart hammered against her own. There was nothing else, nowhere else, no one else but him, here, now.

After breakfast, as she stood sipping her tea at the kitchen window, watching Nate and Charlie preparing the BBQ in the backyard, she felt a searing love. She still had moments of resenting her own parents for what they did and for not giving her *this*. But mostly she just loved loving her new family. How could she *think* of ever leaving them, as her parents had done? And then it hit her, just how much they must have loved them to do what they did. *Why* they did it, she would never know. But they must have had a hellishly good reason.

She sometimes had darts of piercing sadness at all the landmarks of her life they had missed, but those were rare. Her life now was forward-focused. Her meaningful past began nine years ago, when she met Nate. The rest was ancient history.

She heard the familiar chime of the Gravibot as it floated by, pausing fractionally at their front gate. A soft swish as something eased through the slot and landed on the doormat. She put down her mug and went to see what had arrived.

On the mat was... an old-fashioned letter in an envelope. Lucy hadn't seen one of those since high school. She leaned down to pick it up—a strange object from another era. Almost all communication happened through Gravizone now, although they sometimes zoned in a special item or received a gift from one of her friends or siblings.

Nate and Charlie were still out in the backyard, so she took the letter into the den, flopping down on her favourite sömasit—one of the coolest inventions ever, Lucy thought. Shaped like an S curve, it was a recliner made from spongy material that moulded to her form, but not like the old memory foam. This was made from a blend of textured bamboo, hemp and polymers that were 100% healthy for the bod and the environment. It was burnt orange, soft as cotton wool, and she loved it, relaxing into it every chance she got, usually just to dream and let ideas find her.

She turned the envelope over, trying to figure out who had sent it and where it had come from. There was no payment mark, no indication of the origin, just her name on the front. She felt a tingle of trepidation, a sense that this was no ordinary letter, beyond the fact that letters were just plain non-existent, these days.

She slipped a finger under the flap and opened the envelope. Folded inside were about ten sheets of off-white paper—weighty stock that felt significant in her hands. The letter was typed, but the greeting was hand-written, and the familiar handwriting sent a chilly shiver down her spine.

She flattened out the pages and began to read.

My dearest Lucy Sedona:

Please sit down, darling girl. This is the hardest thing I have ever had to write, and I know it will be very hard for you to read, but I hope you will be able to forgive us for what we did. We loved you, Matt and Marnie more than you can imagine, and we were faced with an impossible choice: lose all three of you, or intervene and make things right.

Now that you are a mother yourself, I hope you will understand why we did what we did, and might even do the same if you were faced with the same heart-breaking dilemma. But we had some exceptional information, abilities and glimpses into the future that put us in the most extraordinary position—one that I would not wish on my worst enemy or best friend.

I know you were the hardest hit by us leaving, but I also knew you'd bounce back the fastest. I am so happy that you now have a wonderful family of your own, and I know how much you cherish your little boy Charlie. He reminds me very much of your grandfather, who died before you were born.

Wait, wait, stop! Lucy wasn't sure who she was telling to stop—her brain, the world or this time-bending madness—while she tried to make sense of this. Her mother writing to her from the past, reaching her in the future, talking about Lucy's present.

It was just plain impossible. But she could not stop reading.

I will try to explain what happened and why we had to abandon you the way we did. It's complicated, so please bear with me—and I will leave it to you to explain to Matt and Marnie, once you've had a chance to absorb this seemingly impossible situation yourself.

Back in 2019 and long before, our world was evolving in a very unhealthy direction. There was a lot going on behind the scenes to control and commoditize humanity and to reduce the global population. Wireless telecom systems were the infrastructure being used. They were the backbone for a worldwide takeover, but only a small minority were aware of what was really going on.

There were all kinds of smoke screens and whitewashing campaigns. The industry had become very good at creating confusion and doubt about wireless technologies, and governments played their part by fear-mongering and causing the public to fear for their safety if they didn't get vaccinated and tagged for *security purposes*, or didn't have wireless coverage every second of their lives.

The mainstream media had been bought out long ago and rarely reported the truth. Many independent scientists were persecuted, threatened and/or silenced—some of them permanently. We had to keep our work secret, although we worked with one other scientist who helped us get things rolling. You heard about him in the news, Dr Raynor Spence. He took a lot of flak when things went haywire with our plan, and he ended up being arrested and imprisoned, but I'll explain this shortly.

Your father and I could see the way things were going, and we knew the three of you would be affected and would probably not survive. Certainly, you would not have the life you have now. You would not have Charlie, and your relationship with Nate would be… well, purely mechanical, if you had one at all.

Lucy could not wrap her brain around this. *How did she know this?* As if reading her mind, her mother explained.

After decades of research and experiments, I discovered how to travel to the future, and I was able to witness what would have unfolded by 2025 if we hadn't intervened.

Lucy, it would horrify you to see what happened. It was devastating. People had turned into zombies and were being wirelessly controlled—emotionally and physically—every minute of their lives. There was no joy, no love, no music, no passion. Nature had been destroyed, everything was parched, all the trees and wildlife were dead, and the climate was just one big electrical storm after another. It could not have gone on for much longer. Had I still been alive, I would not have wanted to live that life, and we certainly didn't want that for the three of you.

I was a wreck when I got back from that trip and it took me several weeks to recover. I fell into a kind of depression, knowing what lay ahead for you and not knowing for sure, at that point, that we could fix things. Your father saved me, reminding me of what was at stake and that we could—*would*—find a way.

I don't know how many meals I botched as my mind was grappling with how to make this work. I'm not a bad cook, really. If you can do the kind of intricate calculations we were doing in the computer lab, you can cook an omelette!

But we neglected you, there's no denying that. We were consumed with trying to find a way to protect you, and we couldn't just do nothing, knowing what we knew.

It took us years to figure out a way to change things for the better, without causing some other calamity or dysfunctional evolution as a result of having hacked into the future. And I had to figure out how to get back home again, at the right time and in the right place. I almost didn't make it a few times, and that would have been a tough one for your dad to explain—to you and the authorities.

What the fuck…? Had her mother been watching her, monitoring her? Why hadn't she come to her, talked to her, told her what was going on, explained things and spent time with them?

Once, early on, when we were still tweaking the cosmic numbers and portals for getting me back from the future, we didn't get it quite right and I arrived in Walmart naked. (It was only later that we figured out how I could keep my clothes on while time-travelling. Before that, my clothes always disappeared into the ethers, which made things a little chilly and a lot more challenging at the other end.) You can imagine the chaos *that* caused in Walmart. Not that you didn't normally see some very strange bodies in that store, but they were mostly clothed. I was caught shoplifting and had to do some very smooth talking to get myself out of that one.

Lucy barked a grim laugh, and closed her eyes, holding the letter to her chest. This was like reading the most riveting book ever, and not wanting it to end because there was no chance of ever finding another book by the same author.

Anyway, we eventually figured out a way to use the wireless networks to transmit some different frequencies—what you called CEBS—to gradually get people back on track and slowly reduce the dependence and appeal of wireless devices.

We developed some pretty sophisticated stuff. I think you would have been impressed, if we'd been able to tell you about it. But we had to keep everything secret. That was tough. Some days, it was hard to contain myself, the possibilities were so mind-boggling.

But we couldn't risk the information getting out, and we had to take some drastic measures that I'm not proud of. I take full responsibility for them as your dad was *not* in favour, but I felt we had no choice. When our plan was about to be exposed by Matt's computer friend, I had to prevent that from happening. That wasn't pretty and it wasn't supposed to go the way it did, but you can't always control this kind of thing. Ultimately, it was him or you—and a few billion others.

Her mother had *killed* someone? Or she had Jed killed by some hit man...? Lucy closed her eyes again. Could *she* have made that kind of decision? Did she have that kind of single-minded ruthlessness within her—to remove someone who could potentially ruin the plan to save humanity? How the hell had her mum and dad managed to *sleep* at night, with all this going on, while trying to raise three children? She couldn't imagine it.

Despite all our security measures, our first attempt to roll out the system got hijacked by US government agents, and we had to urgently find a way to override their system and prevent any other future access.

In the meantime, you were all growing up and we were barely able to spend time with you. Handing you over to housekeepers or sending you over to Maisie and Doug felt like an impossible compromise. We were missing out on so much of your childhood. But if we didn't do what we were doing, you wouldn't have had a life as an adult.

The letter was getting damp from Lucy's tears. She thought back to all the times her mother had seemed distracted, never giving Lucy her full attention or spending quality time with her. Nothing Lucy did seemed to matter, and now she understood why. She knew her parents' work was important. She'd been told often enough. But she had no idea that what they were doing was for *them*.

The Gravizone system that Ray helped develop and roll out began with our Gengineering technology. We could generate specific frequencies and then program them into a device we called the Franwave. From there, we were able to create an interface with the human energy field, and then broadcast those frequencies, riding on the wireless-internet frequency waves.

The initial frequencies were designed to trigger emotional healing and integration of all the stuff people had failed to process. Even by 2019, wireless radiation had disconnected many people from themselves, affecting their thinking, awareness and health—and, of course, the environment. Our 'hitch-hiking' frequencies caused people to start associating cellphones with pain, while processing their grief. Once their negative emotions had been cleared out and greater awareness took their place, people would no longer want to connect virtually, the way they did before.

A second wave was designed to bring in restorative and creative frequencies, while progressively deactivating the cellphones themselves. The final wave was to promote the development of higher faculties—telepathy, intuition, accessing cosmic intelligence, and what you call *beaming*. These were designed to be transmitted through Gravizone, after we had gone, and Ray deserves all the credit for handling that.

Early on in our research, we discovered that viruses and bacteria could travel via wireless radiation and interface with the human biofield. This opened the door to global genocide and internet bio-terrorism, so it was no surprise that our system got hacked, despite all our measures to protect it.

When the government hijacked the program and started to implement its own plan, which would have overridden ours, we knew our original strategy would no longer work and we had to find another way. So we got Ray to abort the planned rollout and to pretend he had been about to release a deadly virus via the internet, so people would realize it was actually possible and maybe even already happening. That big virus scare in early 2020 fed people's fears and helped him drive home that connection.

So *that's* what all that had been about, Lucy realized.

We Gengineered a more advanced version of our program for the progressive dissolution of the harmful frequencies, while new ones were imprinted. Cellphones would gradually stop working, but humans would start to operate on a much higher level that would inspire and fulfill them like never before. As you know, darling girl, this is what happened, and I cannot tell you how overjoyed we both were to know that you all benefitted and evolved in such extraordinary ways.

We wanted things to evolve in a more natural way, without the need for even more crises to force change. That has always been the dysfunctional way any kind of change has happened, and it was the *result* of dysfunction. Given how far things had already gone, though, that wasn't going to work. This way, it would be through inspiration and a deep collective desire for conscious evolution, due to the uplifting frequencies we managed to introduce.

None of this made any sense to Lucy. If her parents had figured out how to travel to the future, why hadn't they travelled forward in time and stayed here, so they could be here with them now? Why did they have to kill themselves? And why had they sold everything and left nothing behind? What about all their money? The questions were pouring out, fanning some of her old anger and making her dizzy.

Lucy heard Nate and Charlie coming into the hallway. She beamed them a message. *I'm in the den. Need some quiet time. See you in an hour.* Beaming came in very handy at a time like this. Not that she had ever imagined such an unimaginable time.

Remember how you used to hate ironing? You were really into fashion, even at 11 years of age, and you used to wear the wildest outfits. Dad used to tell you to tone it down, but that was never your style. Still isn't, I'm glad to see. Marnie took you clothes shopping a few times and she always came back looking apologetic. *Sorry, Mum*, she'd say to me, when you came home with another crazy pair of pants or funky jacket. *Lucy made a big scene in the store when I said she couldn't buy this. I was so embarrassed.*

You always wanted your clothes to look nice, and maybe you needed that to create your own strong identity, since we gave you so little healthy role modelling. Thank God for Marnie. I certainly didn't have the ironing gene. You used to say that Marnie had something wrong with her because she loved ironing. She even used to iron socks, and you told her she was sick in the head and needed to see a doctor.

I think she just liked creating order in the chaos of our lives back then, when everything was upside down and the whole world seemed to be losing touch with what mattered. I can see the irony of that, of course, since we lost touch with you in the process of trying to preserve those things that mattered, *for* you.

Marnie was the mother I never was to you, which meant she never really had a childhood at all. I think she's finding some of that with her little girl Mella, who is softening her heart and bringing out some of her wonderful wry humour.

What you see around you now—Charlie's exceptional brain, your own expanded awareness, the resurgence in spiritual and psychic abilities, people loving life again and creating all kinds of good things for humanity and the planet—none of that would have happened if we hadn't managed to stop the technological takeover. I'm not saying that to boast, but to explain why we took such extreme measures to preserve life on Earth, especially yours.

I know you're wondering why we left the way we did, getting rid of all our assets and belongings, and leaving you nothing.

Wondering was putting it mildly, Lucy thought, leaning forward in anticipation of an explanation, finally, after all this time.

I cried many nights over that one, trying to figure out a way to leave you something—*everything*. It's another tough one to explain. Lucy, we explored every possible way to do it differently, but that was the only way we could make things work.

In our research, we developed a program called EM-SIG that could identify, map and track everyone's unique electromagnetic signature. We only ever planned to use it as a way to transmit CEBS to certain populations, to create particular effects that would have the maximum positive global outcome. But then the government got hold of it and had a very different idea about how it could be used.

With EM-SIG, you could actually track people's emotions, as well as their location, so when the government eventually had the whole population registered in the system, they could target anyone who was transmitting potentially *dissident* thoughts. Can you imagine? Everyone would be terrified to have a creative or rebellious thought, knowing they would get grabbed by government agents and silenced. Total control. I know from what I saw later that they used this in the other direction, too— transmitting submissive frequencies to subdue people and dumb them down so they stopped thinking for themselves. Not that *that* hadn't already happened long before, due to all the crappy food and brain-scrambling radiation. But this would have left no room for individuality or free thought.

When I travelled to 2025, everyone in the US had been tagged using our program, and they were all being controlled via their electromagnetic fields. There was no escaping it. The government started registering people's signatures into the system in early 2018, using EM-SIG. If my electromagnetic signature had been registered back then, I would not have been able to travel to the future and then come back and change the course of history. If I had gone to 2025 after being registered, I would have been immediately flagged and subsumed by the system, and that would have been the end of me. I would not have been able to travel back home to do any of the things I did. You and Dad would never have known what happened to me, and I would not be writing this letter to you, my beautiful daughter, now living in a world transformed, having never experienced the hell that 2025 would otherwise have been.

So Dad and I had to remove our signatures from the biosphere before 2020, and the only way we could do that was by ending our lives. We also had to remove all energetic and emotional attachments. We couldn't get rid of *you*, of course, which would have defeated the whole point of what we were doing, but we had to eliminate any connection that you would have had to us—if you owned Westfield, for example, if you had some of our belongings, or if you even had our money. All these things have their own frequency or energetic field, and we couldn't risk you being associated with us in any way by telling you what we had done. If we had done that, the new digital regime would have been able to tap into that information, through your emotional connection, and would have found a way to stop it unfolding in 2020 and beyond.

We did manage to set up a shell company for the three of you, and you will be hearing about this shortly from a lawyer. Westfield is still yours, along with a substantial inheritance, although we had to put it all in another name until our plan had been fully implemented and we knew it was working.

I wrote this letter years ago—before we died, obviously—and asked that same lawyer to get it delivered to you at this time. (Not Mr Williams, our old lawyer, who passed away some years ago, as you may know.) Attached is the contact info for the firm handling the estate, and you can get in touch when you're ready, after digesting this and sharing it with Marnie and Matt.

You have turned into a beautiful young woman, my darling Lucy. And I'm not just saying that because you look like me. You're very much your own person, with more wisdom and humour than I ever had. I hope it helps to finally have some understanding of what we did and why.

Fuck, yes. Fuck, no. Lucy didn't know what to think.

We knew you would hate us, Lucy, but we loved you so much we had to accept that. It was the price we paid for giving you a life. I have seen your future and I know that all our sacrifices were worthwhile.

It's not that you—the three of you—destroyed our lives. Please don't ever think that. It was either leave you as we did, to grow your extraordinary selves, or stay with you and descend into hell together, with no future and nothing to look forward to, not even the *capacity* to look forward, to dream, to love or to create anything. Ask any parent—ask yourself: which would you choose?

We hope you will be able to forgive us. Even as I write this, I am still trying to find a way—something else we can do—to help make up for all we were unable to do for our beautiful children back then.

We love you so much and it breaks our hearts to have to leave without even saying goodbye. No parents ever loved their children more or ever had more extra-ordinary offspring for whom they gladly yet sadly gave up their lives. Be happy, my darling Lucy, and enjoy the wonderful life you have created and so deserve. As your abilities expand, perhaps we will be in touch out there in the ethers.

Love always,
Mum & Dad
XXXX

They had got it so terribly wrong. Their parents hadn't abandoned them. They had done something incredible, something unimaginable that required tremendous love and personal sacrifice, and Lucy could barely contain her grief. The three of them had cursed, blamed and resented their parents for doing what they did.

But the truth, Lucy now realized, was that no one had ever, *ever*... she felt the tears surging again... had such fabulous parents.

98

It was going to be one hell of a party—celebrating Charlie's birthday, the success of Lucy's book, which had sold over 300,000 copies since it hit the zone nine months ago, and the first time the whole extended family had gathered together in one place, along with some very special friends.

Lucy had hardly slept a heartbeat the night before, and she had spent most of Saturday preparing the backyard, stringing up lights, arranging tables and chairs under the trees and coordinating the food, which Nate would cook on the BBQ, with contributions from Marnie and Troy. She needed to stay busy to distract herself, her mind still whirling with the shocking revelations from her mother. She had hidden the letter in her bedroom, like a secret lover, needing time to assimilate it before she shared it with her siblings or Nate.

Marnie, Steve and Mella had arrived mid-morning, laden with food and gifts. Troy, Annamae and the twins, equally laden, arrived shortly afterwards. They looked relaxed and happy together, having long ago resolved their conflict and found a new balance in their marriage. Annamae had resumed her studies and was now actively engaged in weather programs, land-reclamation initiatives and a book she was writing about how humans and the planet could consciously co-evolve. Troy took care of the twins three days a week, which had clearly changed him as well as the boys. Marnie liked to think that the chorlies and sunbean oil had helped heal their fractured hearts, although she and Steve had also had long conversations with each of them about the freedom they needed, supporting them in staying committed to their love.

"What changed things between you?" Marnie had asked Annamae.

"I told him he was insecure and felt deeply inadequate, which made him moody and temperamental, liable to fly off the handle if he got triggered or challenged in some way."

"What did he say to that?"

"He flew off the handle." Annamae laughed. "But then he sort of got it."

"But why is he like that? Steve is so solid and confident. The other Romero brothers seem that way too."

"Maybe because he's the youngest and feels he has to prove himself. He's done that with the business but he hasn't really done it emotionally, which is strange with CEBS being around for so long now."

"Well, some people evolve creatively and then do the heart work, although it's usually the other way around." Marnie reflected on how she had evolved, but she'd been working on her adulthood since she was 6. In her case, the challenge had been to allow someone else to support and love her.

"So where did that leave you?" she asked Annamae.

"Listening to myself and realizing it all applied to me, too."

"But how were you insecure? Did you feel inadequate?" Marnie couldn't quite see it.

"Well, I allowed myself to surrender to smotherhood without taking a stand for me and retaining my identity doing what I loved to do. Having one child is already a challenge, but having two at the same time is overwhelming. Don't get me wrong. The twins are amazing and I love them to bits. But there is no time, energy or anything else for you. There is no *you* left."

"I get it." Marnie wondered if DeeDee was having similar challenges… or just not admitting to them. It always made Marnie smile to think of DeeDee having twins. With her double-D name and her huge personality, she gave the impression of being such a superhuman force that the universe probably thought she was two people rolled into one, with more than enough love and energy for two new souls. Which so far seemed to be the case, unless DeeDee just wasn't saying…

But Annamae wasn't quite finished. "Then I got resentful and blamed Troy, when I was really avoiding stepping up and going to the next level, and using him and the kids to not take that big step."

Marnie knew how people used others to keep themselves safe—back in the old world, anyway, when all that fear corroded people's dreams. "Good for you, Annamae," she said.

And it was. The two were now in a good place, loving themselves and their life together, rather than trying to serve the other and giving up on self. Never a good formula, Marnie knew.

The rift had brought them all much closer, and Annamae was now a feisty spirit with an open heart and an easy laugh that everyone loved.

Everyone was out in the backyard, arriving via the side gate. Next came Matt, Celle, Migué and Suri—a family basking in its own aura of blissful togetherness. Marnie had never seen Matt look so peacefully contented, a man who had truly found his core and was no longer afraid of it. She remembered the tortured young guy he had been when their parents died, and how profoundly his move to Mexico had transformed him. She thought of how some people could be *beside themselves*, out of their bodies with stress and fear. He was definitely *inside* himself, fully behind his eyes, with all of him looking out, grounded and at home in his body—in a way that few, pre-CEBS, had managed to be. Back then, Marnie had seen many vacant people, their souls like satellites orbiting their physical form, disconnected from their pain and discomfort rather than fully owning and loving their presence.

At noon, DeeDee had swept in like a blast of exotic sunshine—a high-pressure weather front that instantly lifted the mood. Even if it rained, which was looking blessedly unlikely, DeeDee would always add sunshine. She had decided to come on her own.

"We need quality time together, girlfriend," she told Marnie, "without being distracted by my hunk of a husband or the whirlwind twins." Marnie was secretly relieved, already feeling overwhelmed by having so many loved ones around her. She and DeeDee would spend Monday together, after the party. Millie hoped to join them but wasn't sure she could make it, due to a sprained ankle from a surfing accident.

Delsie had arrived shortly after noon, as Nate was starting up the BBQ, planning to eat at around 1pm. She too had decided to come alone so she and Lucy could catch up, one on one.

Sherry arrived shortly after that, looking luminous, her platinum-blond hair framing a fearless face that had taken on the world… and won. A far cry from the goth girl Lucy remembered. From gothess to goddess. Not a bad turnaround. They hugged fiercely—Lucy, Delsie and Sherry—then stood back to take each other in… all the changes, things shared and sheltered, loves embraced, fears conquered, hearts healed, the inner journeys that had taken them to this point of unimagined existence, loving themselves and their lives.

"Look at you, Lucy Sedona Dalton Cordalis, best-selling author," Sherry said. "Pity I never got the chance to *shermer* you. I still could, of course—publicly expose you for taking so long to get your formidable ass in gear. Never mind that you produced a child prodigy and created a company making world-famous designer shirts."

Lucy laughed. "You never needed an excuse to be outrageous in your art, Sherry. Did she, Delsie?"

"Not the girl I knew," Delsie said, loving all their evolutions.

"Look who's talking," Sherry said. "Famous Washington psychotherapist, untangling the twisted minds of government, getting everyone back on track and causing the whole DC legal system to crash for want of litigants."

They had several lifetimes to catch up on, and would spend tomorrow together, just the three of them. But... maybe not reminiscing. Why give any airtime to that cranky old world, when the present moment was so much more thrilling. *Could things get any better?* Lucy wondered.

She felt an unshakable core of contentment. Lucy used to think a good life—a *perfect* life—couldn't possibly last—or, if it did, it would be terminally boring, with people serenely wafting around in hemp robes, or walking proudly naked on the street, barefoot and smelling earthy, all Zen and smiling dreamily, unfazed by life, wishing everyone peace and happy hedge-eating.

The reality was anything *but*. Amazing things came out of that solid core—inventions, innovation, lateral thinking, spiritual expansiveness, scientific breakthroughs, cosmic consciousness (which was like having your own private movie screen), and all kinds of dynamic creations. The more humans expanded, the more they could do and the more they *wanted* to do.

She used to worry that life would become intellectually unstimulating, with no drama to spice things up. Everyone had been so addicted to drama and over-stimulation, but this kind of stimulation was different. It wasn't the hyped-up, adrenal-burnout, heart-attack kind. It gave you endless energy and time, and made your heart sing. People were not only happier—deeply happy—but healthier and more vibrant than she could have imagined. True beauty came from health, she could now see—sparkling eyes, clear skin, full red lips, all six senses attuned. There was no greater aphrodisiac than a toned super-healthy body, a fertile mind, and a spirit connected to your own cosmic core.

The earth itself had calmed and was breathing gently again. Extreme weather patterns had ceased, cosmi-crops were thriving and soils were regaining their richness. Oceans were pristine, teeming with fish and other marine life, and the rivers ran clear. The pure air was almost heady in its potency, clearing the mind and igniting the brain with just a few deep breaths.

Lucy had never experienced any of the neurological diseases, cancers or degenerative conditions proliferating in the former wireless world, but she had seen plenty of them in others and it wasn't pretty. It boggled the mind now that such rampant sickness had become so accepted and *expected*, back then—normalized sickness, sickeningly inevitable.

Not any more. All that sickness had been replaced with something a lot more seductive. All this beauty. Yawn. *So boring… Obviously.* She smiled to herself—the old cynical Lucy still lingering feistily in there somewhere. There was no way she'd swap all this deliciousness for the drama and dysfunction she'd wallowed in for so long.

She brought herself back to the present—the gifted presence of loved ones gathered, sharing their creations, which were all about sharing… and celebration. The air hummed and pinged with promise, sparkling photons dancing in delight. Some days, like today, Lucy could actually see them.

Maybe dogs could, too. Fargo was ecstatic with so many humans milling around her, grinning her hyena grin, chasing butterflies and dandelion fluff to burn off her manic energy.

Now that everyone was here, Lucy wanted to eat. She was so ravenous from all the excitement and activity that she could have eaten the tablecloth. And all that pure oxygen could really go to your head. She was arranging plates and cutlery on the food table as Marnie brought out the last of the food platters.

The side gate creaked open again and Marnie turned to see who it was. Ray! Her heart leapt and she almost dropped her plate. *How on earth…?*

Putting the plate on the table, she rushed to greet him, overcome to see him after so long and after all he had been through. He looked thinner and far older than he should have, but his imprisonment had obviously taken a deep toll.

"Ray," she said, her eyes filling up as she reached out to embrace him, to give him all the love in the world.

"Marnie." He returned the hug warmly, although he felt fragile in her arms. "Thank you for inviting me."

She looked at him, puzzled. "I didn't—" Steve appeared beside her, hand extended towards Ray. "You must be the infamous Raynor

Spence," he said, shaking heartily. "Truly honoured to meet you, Sir." He gestured towards the rest of the family. "So glad you could join us. Please, make yourself at home and let me get you a drink."

"Ray, I'll be right back," Marnie said, taking his jacket as Steve led him towards the drinks table, introducing him to Nate, who was stoking the massive BBQ and getting ready to cook the food.

Going inside to hang up Ray's jacket, Marnie marvelled at Ray's sudden appearance. But without Lily, of course, whose death still weighed heavily on her heart. Had she, Marnie, led the authorities to Ray? Was it her fault he had been imprisoned and that Lily had died of a broken heart? She would sit down with him as soon as she finished bringing out the food.

The backyard was filling up with family, laughter and the sounds of life being loved. Like a real Romero feast, Marnie thought, smiling to herself. She could never have imagined this, back when she'd been enveloped—almost subsumed—by the thronging Romero clan. Now, she was at the hub of her own.

Coming back outside with a platter of fried chorlies, nuts and other snacks, she paused to observe Lucy: her forever baby sister now an accomplished author, mother, wife and wise woman who had truly found her centre. Arranging things on the food table, Lucy looked beautiful, Marnie thought, so like their mother, with her dark hair falling over her shoulders, piercing green eyes that still danced with mischief but no longer shot angry daggers at the world.

And Matt, a peaceful warrior whose hard edges had been replaced with a loving self-acceptance—a wise presence that touched and soothed everyone he met. He was holding Suri in his arms, smiling at his son as Migué tried to keep a GraviTass suspended in the air, with patient coaching from Charlie.

And Mella, her sweet little 2-year-old… It was almost too much perfection for Marnie to bear. She would have to pace herself, she thought, going back inside for the last plate of food.

When Marnie came back out, Lucy was tapping the table with a knife to get everyone's attention.

"A toast," she said, lifting her glass. "To Charlie, the most extraordinary gift any parent could ever wish for."

"Thanks, Mum," Charlie said, grinning. "You're both coming along nicely, too."

Everyone laughed.

"To my amazing, gracious, handsome husband," she turned to Nate, "who never stopped believing in me, who is still trying to teach me how to cook, and who never ceases to surprise me with his insights and terrible jokes." She looked at him fondly, her heart full of love for this man who had saved her from herself.

"I wish my parents could be here to share this with us." She paused, taking a deep breath, thinking of her mother's shocking letter. She hadn't mentioned it to anyone, not even Nate. She needed to process the enormity of it and digest it herself first.

"This is a momentous day. Not just because it's Charlie's birthday but because, on this day, nine years ago, my parents…" she looked at Matt and Marnie "*our* parents… passed away, and it turned our world upside down." They nodded, remembering who they all had been.

"Not a day goes by that I don't think of them, sometimes longing for them, sometimes still a little angry at them for leaving us. But they gave me something very precious, apart from life itself. I had to find *me*, on my own terms, instead of continuing to be the self-centred little brat I was, back then, who felt entitled to have it all because they had given me so much."

She paused to drink some water, her hand shaking as she put the glass back down on the table.

"Anyway, I just wanted to say how blessed I am to have such a precious family and close friends who also feel like family. I could not have got here without Marnie and Matt, and everyone here has been a part of our journey. Now that I'm a parent myself, I can love my parents a lot more, even if I don't understand what they did… and I wish I could tell them that." She cleared her throat, wiping her cheek. "I will always miss them."

Lucy raised her glass again for a final toast.

The side gate creaked as it opened and Lucy turned to see who it was. *Who still had to arrive?* She'd lost track again. Maybe Marnie's friend Millie had made it after all…

An older couple stood at the entrance, looking uncertain, lost—the man holding the gatepost and the woman holding on to him, both visibly shaking with emotion.

Her heart froze and her glass fell to the ground, bouncing soundlessly on the grass.

Nate looked at Lucy, concerned. "It's okay, sweetie. Probably just some friendly gate-crashers. Or maybe they're lost and need directions. I'll go see—"

Lucy grabbed his arm and held him back, her nails biting into his skin. Nate looked at her and looked again at the woman... an older version of his beautiful wife. *Some relatives Lucy hadn't mentioned?*

All eyes turned towards the visitors and a hush fell over the group, like a freeze-frame in a movie. Even the birds stopped singing to mark the moment.

Nobody moved, except Fargo, who dashed towards them... to chase them off, it seemed... but no. She plonked herself down on the woman's feet. Never a guard dog, Fargo was a grounding force that pinned you to the earth and helped you stay there.

Lucy could hardly breathe. Her whole body felt frozen. She barely noticed Nate's arm squeezing her shoulders.

Mella ran to Marnie, spooked by the sudden silence. "Mummy," she said, clutching her leg. "Who?"

Marnie's throat was desert-dry and she couldn't speak. Steve reached down and scooped Mella up onto his hip, putting his other arm around Marnie to steady her. "I think they're your grammaw and grandaddy," Steve whispered into Mella's ear.

Her voice cracking, the woman finally spoke. "My babies... I cannot tell you how sorry I am," she said, tears streaming down her face.

"On the other hand," said the man, cheeks glistening as he gestured at them all with a shaky arm, "this is the phenomenal result, the reason for it all."

The woman looked close to collapsing, her hand on her heart, holding tightly to the man as she struggled to stay upright, knees buckling and words no longer possible.

As one, the Dalton siblings moved towards them—Marnie, Matt and Lucy converging and clinging to each other as they stumbled towards the gateway. They fell upon their parents, sobbing, incoherent with grief, wonder and unspeakable joy.

Behind them, Charlie jumped up and down in unbounded delight, pumping the air with his arm. "Grannie! You did it! I knew you'd figure it out."

Ray leaned against the large oak tree, sobbing quietly. *Frannie... you came back.*

"It's her," Celle whispered to herself. *The woman from the beach... and the market.*

"*La mujer del espíritu...*" Migué smiled, reaching for Celle's hand.

"My God," DeeDee thought. Millie was right. Doc Dalton *was* alive...

Sherry watched in grateful wonder. This was a stellar moment—the mother of all cosmic comebacks.

Nate and Steve stood together, awed by the miracle unfolding before them, paying silent homage to their women being gifted finally with parents, life coming full circle, the natural order restoring itself, hearts bursting with love, gratitude and pride.

No longer needed as a foot soldier, Fargo went back to chasing butterflies.

And the birds resumed their singing.

ACKNOWLEDGEMENTS

My heartfelt, massive thanks to Dee Rowland for her stellar contribution—to this story, as a sounding board, eagled-eyed super-sleuth, champion of ideas, supporter of risks and creative inspiration; and to my life, as a friend who has shared and enriched a journey like no other.

I would really like to thank my agent, but I don't have one, so I will instead thank my husband, Lewis Evans, who has been the greatest agent of change in my life.

I am also deeply grateful to Chloë, for her relentlessly fabulous sisterhood, and to the other friends and family members who lent their personality and/or names to the lifeforce of the characters, sharing the journey with me, within these pages and beyond.

ABOUT THE AUTHOR

Olga Sheean is an editor, disruptive thinker, compulsive wordsmith, relationship therapist and mastery mentor specializing in human dynamics, creative potential and conscious evolution. Dedicated to exploring and exposing the true nature of reality, she writes widely on the underlying drivers of global crises, how to reclaim our personal autonomy, and how to fulfill our quantum potential. Using her own unique framework for self-mastery, she helps people transform the negative subconscious programs that drive their circumstances, relationships, self-worth and success.

Olga has worked as a photojournalist for the WWF International in Switzerland and as an editor for the United Nations in Geneva. A former magazine editor and health columnist, she is a prolific writer who has published over 300 articles in various magazines and writes her three blogs: The O Zone—a place of positive e-missions; Beyond Belief—exposing the deeper truth; and EMF off!

In her downtime, Olga does kundalini yoga, loves walking on beaches and biking along country roads, plays 'silly Scrabble' (inventing new words), enjoys reckless, rule-free table tennis, and reads voraciously.

For more info or to contact Olga, please see her empowerment website (https://olgasheean.com), where you can read about relationships and empowered, holistic living, access her blogs, purchase her books and recorded affirmations, and sign up for her newsletter.

You can download her free documents on electromagnetic radiation from her EMF website, which has further details about *EMF off!—a call to consciousness in our misguidedly microwaved world*, additional resources and information about electromagnetic radiation: https://emfoff.com.

Other books by Olga Sheean

Available at https://olgasheean.com/books

Find your self and your perfect mate
by Olga Sheean

Fit for Love—find your self and your perfect mate

ISBN: 0-9738222-1-X

This fully illustrated guide to healthy relationship may be the most rewarding emotional fitness program you ever undertake—one that will generate more breakthroughs and miracles than you could ever have thought possible. Filled with wisdom, exercises, practical techniques, catchy full-colour illustrations and inspiringcase histories, *Fit for Love* takes you on a journey of self-discovery, healing and empowerment, showing you how to access and transform the negative subconscious programming that has prevented you from fully knowing or expressing your true self. Through this book, you will gain an understanding of your powerful ability to create what you want, to enjoy lasting, healthy relationships, and to upgrade all aspects of your life.

A practical and insightful book that reveals how our relationships are powerful pathways to self-realization and personal fulfillment.

—John Kehoe, author of *Mind Power into the 21st Century*

The Alphabet of Powerful Existence—an A–Z guide to well-being, wisdom and worthiness

ISBN: 978-0-9879291-2-9

This is a practical guide to self-empowerment, featuring 52 themes (one for every week of the year) and offering simple, transformative steps for resolving conflict, positively reprogramming your mind, making powerful choices, and creating more love, money, ease, success and fulfillment in your life. Upgrade your relationships, finances and business; fill in your 'missing pieces'; activate your creativity; and enhance your self-worth and personal magnetism.

Olga Sheean brilliantly inspires us in practical ways to live a dynamic, healthy, fulfilling life on our terms. This book will enable you to change your circumstances, heal, and discover yourself. An enjoyable, easy read. I couldn't put it down!

—Bev Ogilvie, author of
ConnectZone.org—building connectedness in schools

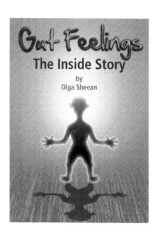

Gut Feelings—the inside story

ISBN: 978-0-9738222-3-6

A body odyssey with guts, attitude and a bellyful of laughs—a quirky off-the-wall story about the internal shenanigans of the body and the external dynamics of modern-day relationships. Nowhere else will you learn about lymphomaniacs, the real purpose of your appendix, or the spiritual significance of chocolate cake. This book is a madcap marathon through fact and fiction, adventure and enlightenment, mix-ups and makeovers, inside and out. With the growing worldwide trend towards greater self-responsibility, this is the perfect gift for someone you love—or someone who just doesn't get out much.

This book is a masterpiece—a humorous, all-encompassing, richly informative study of human beings that enlightens and educates the reader in a very digestible way. I recommend it for everyone over the age of 12. I also see it as a tool for teachers who are educating young adults on the challenging topics of health, self-responsibility and emotional well-being— topics that this book makes very accessible and fun.

—Aviva Roseman, MA (Young Adult Literature)

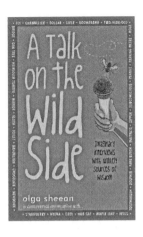

A Talk on the Wild Side—imaginary interviews with unlikely sources of wisdom

ISBN: 978-0-9879291-3-6

Ever shared laughs with a hyena, chatted up a strawberry, or had a chinwag with a boomerang? Forget about all those gurus out there, telling you how to live your life. Wisdom is all around you, available in the most unlikely places—from dinosaurs to dandelions, bridges to boomerangs, peanuts to parking metres, toothbrushes to toilets, and plenty of other wiseguys you've never talked to before. A Talk on the Wild Side is a collection of outrageous conversations, filled with irreverent insights, off-the-wall humour, and a surprising number of salient truths. Life will never be the same again—and you'll find yourself talking to the strangest things. (Just don't let anyone see you doing it.)

A fantastic, thought-provoking read. You'll learn more about yourself from a park bench, a maple leaf and a newborn baby than you could possibly have imagined.

—Mike Tse, filmmaker/animator

Tell Me the Truth—a code for freedom

ISBN: 978-1-928103-13-4

This book is your antidote to the tsunami of commercial spin, social stimuli and bad news clogging our news channels and our consciousness. It challenges you to remember who you are and to change direction in favour of humanity and life. See the spin for what it is; let go of over-stimulation so you can reconnect with the real you; and trade the bad news for the good news and the truth about you and your world. Bad news and commercial spin promote fear and distort the truth, causing us to forget who we are. They misrepresent our quantum reality and disregard our creative capacity for change. The deeper truth is something else altogether. When we embody it, we find freedom.

Be inspired to live your life out loud! This book is an uplifting meditation on life, written with extraordinary wisdom and insight. Not limited to any age, but a 'must' read for young people who stand at the crossroads of their lives, seeking answers, direction and fulfilment. I wish I'd had this in my formative years but I'm very grateful to have it now.

—Elize Potgieter, lecturer, Informatics and Design
Cape Peninsula University of Technology, Cape Town

EMF off! A call to consciousness in our misguidedly microwaved world

ISBN: 978-1-9281033-10-3

A unique blend of wisdom, humour, personal experience, hard-hitting science and quantum physics, this book presents a compelling case for a complete rethink of how we live. Backed by solid scientific evidence and an in-depth understanding of human dynamics and spiritual connectedness, it explores the biological, psychological, neurological, emotional and environmental impacts of our insatiable hunger for wireless connectivity.

Only by consciously engaging our sorely neglected hearts and souls can we truly understand what is driving us and how we can become the game-changers of our own reality. This book provides practical steps for doing this, explaining how to activate our spiritual faculties and take ownership of our own lives.

Olga Sheean takes us on an intimate personal journey. Along the way, she challenges us to cultivate our deeper truth, reconnect and choose love. Our relationship with technology is like nothing our society has ever faced, and only we can cure our own addiction. I'm so thankful for this book.

—Theodora Scarato, MSW, Executive Director
Environmental Health Trust (https://ehtrust.org/)

Made in the USA
Middletown, DE
12 February 2021